To Cyndie,

HAYMAKER

Adam Schuitema

Thanks so much!

SWITCHGRASS BOOKS NORTHERN ILLINOIS UNIVERSITY PRESS DeKalb

Published by Switchgrass Books, an imprint of Northern Illinois University Press
Northern Illinois University Press, DeKalb 60115

Printed in the United States of America
24 23 22 21 20 19 18 17 16 15   1 2 3 4 5
978-0-87580-719-5 (paper)
978-1-60909-173-6 (ebook)

Book and cover design by Shaun Allshouse

Library of Congress Cataloging-in-Publication Data
Schuitema, Adam.
Haymaker / by Adam Schuitema.
pages; cm
ISBN 978-0-87580-719-5 (pbk.: alk. paper)
-- ISBN 978-1-60909-173-6 (ebook)
I. Title.
PS3619.C4693H39 2015
813'.6--dc23
2015003646

This book is a work of fiction. All names, places, events, and characters are products of the author's imagination or are used fictitiously. Any resemblance to actual persons, events, or locales is coincidental.

We were only 15 miles from the Pictured Rocks on Lake Superior.
Gad that is great country.

—Ernest Hemingway,
in a letter to Howell Jenkins

"All the same, London's creeping."
She pointed over the meadow—over eight or nine meadows,
but at the end of them was a red rust.

—E. M. Forster,
Howards End

For my parents

Prologue

The county highway climbs an upland just south of town, and for a minute or two—there, above the tree line—you witness God's view of this place people call God's Country. A cloud bank approaches from the west, but most of the sky remains startlingly blue. It's July and—for up here—hot.

A rich shade of green cloaks the land below. Summer's brief in the north, but here it is, and there are leaves. The green stretches in all directions, but to the north it ends at a distant white ribbon that runs, unspooled, along its edge. This is the shore, the sand reflecting the sun. It marks the start of that other blue—the lake—which reaches north to meet and become the horizon and then drown it.

The road descends, pushing northward. The forest stubbornly gives way to a rigid geometry, the skeleton of almost all American towns: a grid of paved roads and, on the outskirts, a few that are still dirt.

After the skeleton comes the skin: houses and businesses where early settlers carved space from woods with blades fresh from the whetstone. Cars and trucks roll through its streets. People saunter down its sidewalks. On the main street—and there's always one, the spine of these American towns—is a man with a camera taking pictures. On the opposite sidewalk, a girl pushes a stroller and spies on him.

Take this town and suspend it in time. Hold it with laced fingers, like the worker holds the trapped sparrow he's found in the fireplace. Then store the memory away.

This town's about to change.

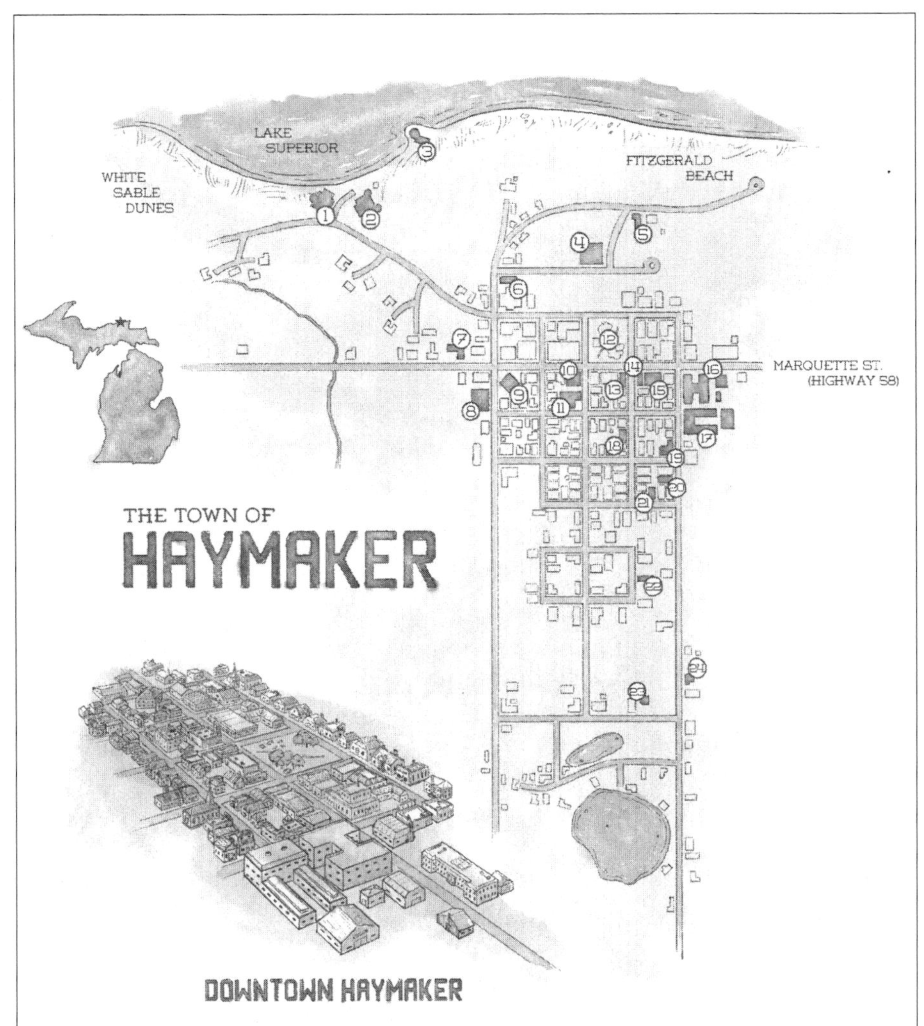

1. BLY HOUSE
2. TATE HOUSE
3. FITZGERALD POINT LIGHTHOUSE
4. PULPWOOD MILL
5. SHIPWRECK CAFÉ
6. KUSTY'S
7. SARVER TOWING AND REPAIR
8. FARMER FRESH FOOD
9. CIVIC CENTER
10. FRESHWATER COMMUNITY CHURCH
11. LAROCK MEDICAL
12. PARSON PARK
13. THE VENISON
14. RITA'S FLORAL AND GIFT
15. STAR-PICAYUNE
16. HAYMAKER HIGH SCHOOL
17. HAYMAKER MIDDLE SCHOOL
18. HAYMAKER HERO SHOP
19. WILLOW STREET SCHOOL
20. CAPAGROSSA HOUSE
21. HOLLINGSHEAD HOUSE
22. NOVAK HOUSE
23. MARX IDITAROD TOURS
24. DEBOER HOUSE

RISEN FROM SAWDUST AND SWEAT

YEAR ONE

Chapter 1

Friday, July 11

Unless worn on battlefields or hunting grounds, camouflage can draw attention more than it conceals. Some don't wear it well, even here in the north country. Especially when it's burnt orange in color and the first gunshot of deer season is still months away. Ash Capagrossa noticed the man in the orange camouflage pants the moment she turned onto Marquette Street. He was armed with a camera.

Ash knew hunters. Half the men and many of the women here in Haymaker trekked through the surrounding forests every fall to climb into tree stands and fire on bucks. But this man trekked down Marquette Street in the middle of summer, carrying a sleek silver camera with a telephoto zoom lens protruding toward its targets: Parson Park, North Country Real Estate, the offices of the *Star-Picayune.* He walked quickly, his head lowered except when aiming at businesses, landmarks, and the occasional unsuspecting pedestrian. As he approached Schoolcraft Avenue—the end of the downtown strip—the man in the orange camouflage paused in front of the Civic Centre. He spent several minutes photographing the two sky-blue police cruisers parked outside, as well as the front entrance and the people who came and went through its doors.

From the other side of Marquette Street, Ash pushed her baby brother, Patrick John, in his stroller, and she watched the man. She had a camera, too—a digital Kodak her mom had loaned her that morning. It had been a summer of boredom and babysitting; she looked for something worth shooting.

As the man in the orange camouflage focused his lens, Ash brought the stroller to a stop, grabbed her own camera, and centered him in its rectangular viewfinder.

Denise Capagrossa had stood that morning in the bathroom, wearing a robe and a wrapped towel around her head. She was only thirty-two—she'd had Ash at eighteen—and Ash would study her on these mornings as she got ready for work. Denise was slim and muscular without exercising. Muscles showed through her arms and stomach, tough and tired—more sinew than softness. It was nothing like Ash's own body.

They'd stood in front of a cluttered counter—half-rolled toothpaste tubes, cotton balls, blonde hair dye that Denise had once used and which Ash had just started applying to her cornrows. Ash stood with Patrick John slung on her right hip, towering over her mom as she watched her in the mirror. She was five ten and fourteen years old. Her shoulders seemed twice as broad as a year ago, and her breasts continued growing, getting in the way of her jump shots.

"You two go out and get some fresh air today," said Denise.

"I've pushed P.J. down every sidewalk about a hundred times. I counted all of the stop signs between here and the beach. Guess how many."

"Call him Patrick John." Denise pinched her own belly skin and shook her head. "You shouldn't be anywhere near the beach. He's only eight months old." She bent her head to the side, inserting an earring. "Keep him out of the sun."

Ash touched her own right ear. It was pierced in four places. "There's nothing to do. We need money."

"Yes, *we* do," said Denise. "For mortgage and groceries and diapers. That's why I work all day. That's why you babysit him all summer. Day care costs fortunes." And then she said what Ash didn't want to hear. "Tell your dad to pay his child support. Maybe we'd both get some days off."

Ash kissed Patrick John on the cheek. "I don't care about watching him, except it's every day."

"Not the weekends."

"Yes, too! Sunday mornings."

Denise attended Freshwater Community Church. She'd started two months ago, after signing the divorce papers. After Albert Capagrossa had moved to Sault Ste. Marie to work at the casino and live with a woman named Caroline.

Denise gave Ash the option of coming along to church or staying home with the baby. "Well, that's your choice."

"We're bored," said Ash.

And that's when Denise abruptly bent down, rummaged through the diaper bag on the floor, and handed her the camera, which had been there for months, although Ash never saw her take cute little baby photos anymore. "Here, go take some pictures. Of people, places, and things."

Ash grabbed it with her free hand, stared at it for a moment, and then, with only the faintest of hesitations, aimed it at her mom and clicked the shutter button. Denise's eyes went wide, and she clutched her robe at her chest. "What?" said Ash. "You're a person."

"You little shit. Right now I'm a *thing*." Then Denise walked past her, across the hall to the bedroom, and shut the door.

A half hour later Ash left the small blue house, pushing the stroller along Cooper toward downtown. Patrick John lounged in his seat, playing with a set of oversized plastic keys. He wore sunscreen, a baby baseball cap, and blue sunglasses to prevent the sunburn Denise always warned about. They'd spent the early mornings of the summer like this, crisscrossing the streets of the small Michigan town, looking for distractions during those long hours while Denise worked the register at The 12 Months of Christmas. Later Ash would bring him home to feed him his bottle, rice cereal, and pureed fruit. Lullabies at ten, followed by a nap, during which she'd vacuum the floors and scrub the countertops and feel like she'd hardly made a dent. Cereal bowls with congealed, three-day-old milk filled the sink. A white trash bag, swollen with dirty diapers, slumped in the back hallway. Laundry lay everywhere, covered in cat fur.

Yesterday Patrick John's teething had sent him into a screaming fit even Anbesol couldn't cure. When pacifiers and swaddling failed, Ash put him in his crib, ran to her room, and cranked up some music to drown out the screams. Minutes later she returned, nearly crying herself, and kissed the wet streaks on his red face. "I'm sorry, buddy. I'm so sorry." And when he calmed in her arms, Ash wondered if his first word would be "Mama," and if, when he said it, he'd be looking at her instead of Denise. Ash didn't know which would be better, which would be worse.

She glanced now over her shoulder, checking for traffic, and then steered to the opposite side of the road. She took a deep breath and sighed. Even with the morning's warm sun Ash felt the usual exhaustion—a soft trembling in her brain between her eyes, like a struck tuning fork. The new school year would actually seem like a finish line.

The stroller rolled luxuriously over a stretch of new sidewalk and was maybe the nicest thing their family owned: swiveling front wheel, ergonomic backrest, and even some type of disc brake system. Her uncle Donnie had called it "a goddamned plastic boondoggle," but that was just because of who'd given them this gift. Denise's coworkers had thrown her a baby shower at the dimly lit brewpub called The Venison, and at some point old Roosevelt Bly—The Man in White himself—had struggled through the door with a huge box topped with a gold bow. "Just showing off his riches," Uncle Donnie said.

As Ash and Patrick John now approached Marquette, they passed the high school and the old basketball courts with their rusty chain nets. More than school—more than anything—Ash looked forward to the start of her freshman season of basketball. She could only squeeze in an hour of play late in the evenings, so she pushed herself till the rubber grip of the ball split her dry fingertips and they bled. Sometimes she'd play imaginary games of one-on-one, against a player from another school, against her mom or her dad.

They turned left onto Marquette Street, and from a distance—for the first time—Ash spotted the man in the orange camouflage pants. His camera reflected the sunlight in little white bursts. Summertime tourists traveling between Pictured Rocks and Whitefish Point often stopped for a spell in Haymaker, and they'd snap some photos of the shoreline or of their kids licking waffle cones. But this man was alone. He was thin with glasses, a dark mustache, and a V-neck T-shirt displaying a picture of a buck in silhouette. He walked slowly, with his head turning in all directions, and didn't aim his telephoto lens at objects of normal tourist interest.

Ash strolled along Marquette Street, past the Haymaker Professional Building, staring at the man with every step. She slowed to a stop and bent down to peek at Patrick John. The keys rested in his slackened grip. He turned his head toward the sounds of children in the nearby park.

"You want to take some pictures, P.J.?" Ash grabbed the camera from a stroller pocket, crouched down, and held it in front of him. He dropped the keys and reached for it. "Yeah, you like to take pictures."

They strolled on, past the charming worn-brick structures across the street, most built in the 1920s and now housing places like The Venison, The 12 Months of Christmas, and Rita's Floral and Gift, where Ash's uncle Donnie lived in an apartment upstairs. The man in orange camouflage had crossed to that side of Marquette and now stood in front of the old Neptune Theater.

He craned his neck to look up at the marquee, which jutted out into the street with one side facing eastbound traffic and the other facing westbound. Over the years it had advertised *Gone with the Wind*, *Some Like It Hot*, *The Sound of Music*, and *Star Wars*. Then, for two decades, it advertised nothing, the letters slowly falling from the sign until only a letter K remained, and no one could remember what word it had once helped spell. But in May—after renting out the high school auditorium every Sunday for the past three years—the booming Freshwater Community Church bought the Neptune and made it holy. Today, one side of the marquee read:

"LOVE THY NEIGHBOR?"
SERMON BY REV. BERNARD ZUBER
SUNDAY—9 AM

The other:

BEAT THE HEAT: TRY OUR SUNDAYS

The man shuffled back and forth beneath it, reading both sides more than once, before glancing up and down the street, raising his camera, and taking a picture.

Ash and Patrick John continued forward, approaching Parson Park and the statue of Frederick Parson, the seventeen-year-old veteran of World War I who was the first citizen of the town ever killed in combat. The boy's body lunged forward, bayoneted rifle pointed toward danger. His determined face also looked serene and beautiful—both too young and too old for him. He looked a little like Dominick Murphy, the power forward on the boys' varsity basketball team whom Ash often thought of just before sleep.

On a bench beside the statue sat that old sentinel, Earl Henneman. Though legally blind, he was known to walk from his house to the VFW or to this same spot, doing his best to gargoyle away any kids who tried to climb onto the statue's shoulders or hang by its gun. He could hear rubber-soled shoes squeaking up the bronze.

Today, however, he politely nodded as the stroller crossed a patch of gravel near the sidewalk. "Hello," said Ash, surprised he'd noticed her. Then she looked for something that was photo-worthy. A blue jay perched on a dogwood nearby. She reached for the camera, raised it to her eye, and pushed the shutter button. Then she knelt beside Patrick John. "Birds," she said, shaking her head. "This is for shit, little man."

The man in the orange camouflage had moved on from the Neptune. Ash was closer now and could see his high forehead, dark-framed glasses, and thin mustache. He looked to be under thirty. His T-shirt was a size too big, the sleeves ending past his elbows. He kept tugging his pants back up over his hips like some kid at Halloween dressed in his dad's oversized gear.

"Who's taking pictures?"

Ash turned and looked back over her shoulder at Earl. "What?"

"Who's taking pictures?" he asked.

Other than shouting apologies years ago when he'd yelled her down from the statue, Ash had never spoken a word to him. "Oh, me."

"No," he said. He aimed his milky eyes in the direction of the Neptune. "Somebody else. I heard their camera across the street. Is it Cecil Grove?"

Ash shook her head. "Who?"

"Cecil Grove. That fella who takes pictures for the paper."

Ash wondered if Earl could even see the photos in the *Star-Picayune*. "No, I don't think so," she said. "But I don't know who this guy is."

Earl wiped his lips with his hand. "Then find out who he is and what he wants."

"Why?" she asked.

And he replied with the same suspicious tone of her uncle Donnie. "I just don't think he's from around here."

Ash nodded, and as the man continued west down Marquette Street, his camera pressed to his chest, she and Patrick John trailed him, slightly behind, from the opposite sidewalk. It felt, finally, like summer vacation—a glimmer of freedom and risk.

As the man's pace quickened, so did Ash's, evolving into a near jog before she hit a buckled section of sidewalk where an old oak had shrugged its roots up to the surface. Patrick John's head snapped forward. The handlebar dug into Ash's belly. He began crying, and she leapt to the front of the stroller.

"Oh, I'm so sorry, P.J. I'm sorry. You're okay. You're okay." She pushed his sunglasses back onto his small nose. "You're happy, ain't you, little bud?" The man was a block ahead of them now, but he'd stopped in front of the Civic Centre, a gleaming new building made of blue glass, shaped like a diamond, and divided into four parts: firehouse, courthouse, town offices, and police station. Ash got behind the stroller once more. "Let's go, buddy. Let's gather some intelligence."

One of Haymaker's three powder-blue police cruisers pulled into the Civic Centre parking lot. Behind the wheel was Sergeant Brenda DeBoer, whom Ash knew from her periodic visits to the school, when she warned about the dangers of drugs, alcohol, and firearms. After passing the man, Sergeant DeBoer flashed her brake lights, parked askew, and stepped outside. She wore sunglasses. "Good morning, sir."

The man pulled the camera away from his face long enough to steal a glance at her before snapping a few more shots of the building.

"May I help you, sir?" asked Sergeant DeBoer, taking a few steps toward him.

The man walked sideways, over the curb and a few steps into the street, taking pictures the whole time.

Sergeant DeBoer stopped, her hands on her hips. "Excuse me."

"What?" The man's voice was high-pitched. "What am I doing wrong?"

"Nothing. I just wondered if I could help you with anything."

"I'm good." He took another picture.

Ash raised her own camera to her eye and took a series of shots.

Sergeant DeBoer stepped closer to him. "Are you with the newspaper?"

"Nope. I'm just a free man in a free country." He walked backward now, farther into the street.

Sergeant DeBoer strode to the sidewalk and then stopped again. "Are you a photographer?"

The man raised his eyebrows, pointed at the camera, and then twirled his finger at his temple in a sign of stupidity. "You a detective?"

Ash took another shot. She took another.

"I think it's best if you leave the premises."

The man pointed at the Civic Centre, jabbing his finger forward. "Look. I'm past it. I'm *off* the premises."

"That's fine."

"You overtax the citizens to build this place and then act like they can't set foot on its holy ground."

"Are you a citizen here, sir?"

"I'm gone." The camera was at his chest but pointed at her, and he continued to take photographs. He was smiling now. "You work for the people of this town." He waved his right hand in a huge arc, gesturing toward the whole block, toward Ash on the far curb. "I'm gone."

And then he turned and reached Ash's side of the street. She fumbled with her camera before stuffing it in her back pocket. But the man never even looked at her. He hit the intersection and headed north on Schoolcraft, toward the lake and the beach, pausing for only seconds to photograph the post office on the corner. Sergeant DeBoer watched him leave, her hands once more on her hips.

Ash crouched down next to Patrick John. His sunglasses had fallen off, and he was sticking one of the lenses in his mouth. "You're not going to tell Mom, are you, little man?"

He held the glasses out in front of him and stared at them, cross-eyed.

Ash stood up, thinking about Sergeant DeBoer and Uncle Donnie and blind old Earl Henneman—people who didn't or wouldn't trust this man in orange camouflage. And she wondered what he was really doing photographing the Civic Centre. Maybe he had a friend in the building's one jail cell and wanted to study the pictures later, to plan an escape. Maybe he was just interested in the modern architecture. Maybe he was crazy.

She followed him in the direction of Lake Superior, defying her mom. But it was July and there were no dirty diapers right now and up ahead was a man who, for all she knew, might be a suspect in some future crime. Sergeant DeBoer might request help and ask if any member of the public had information that could lead to his arrest. And Ash would step forward with image after image of evidence.

Ash and Patrick John kept twenty or thirty yards behind the man. She thought once or twice that he slowed and peered subtly over his right shoulder, but then he stopped, pulling what appeared to be a map out of his back pocket and studying it. Ash stopped, too, pretending to wipe Patrick John's nose as an alibi. A few clouds had moved in; a few raindrops dotted the ground. When the man continued—at a slightly slower pace—Ash once again followed.

And when he spun around to face her, she was so shocked that she merely froze and stared at him: the slightly bent frames of his glasses, the thin mustache that failed to reach his upper lip.

"Say cheese," he said, smiling.

Minutes later, headed home under a graying sky, Ash shook her head and scolded herself. She'd caved to reflex. She'd uttered "Cheese" right before he'd snapped her photograph and continued on his way.

Chapter 2

Friday, July 11

Rusty's advertised itself as the only tavern in the Upper Peninsula that still had a dirt floor. People usually dressed accordingly, wearing their oldest work boots and paint-speckled pants. It had begun to rain tonight, and everyone had come prepared for the indoor mud except for Roosevelt Bly, who'd just walked in, and a man he soon noticed sitting in a corner booth. This other man was a stranger. He kept his head down, drank little, and scribbled away in a black-and-white composition book.

Seventy-nine-year-old Roosevelt Bly was a regular, and as far as not dressing for the mud, others would say he should have had more sense. But Roosevelt was not one for old work boots. Known throughout Haymaker as The Gold-Plated Cowboy or The Man in White, his entrances—to Rusty's or anywhere else—were symbolic and choreographed. He wore his customary western-style white sport coat with matching white belt, white boots, and white beaver felt Stetson. A slim black bolo tie trickled down his chest. Everything else was gold.

He wore a gold watch on one wrist and a gold shackle bracelet on the other. On his left hand, every finger except the thumb wore a gold ring. On his right, there was only an old wedding band, duller than the rest.

During most of the summer the floor at Rusty's was hard and dry, and Roosevelt needed only to dust his boots with a fine cloth when he returned home. In the winter it simply froze, and a man might find his boot print from months earlier, cold and preserved in front of the urinal. But in the spring, autumn, and during midsummer rains like tonight's, Rusty Leach, the owner of the place, would set a path of cardboard squares across the ground from the front door to the bar. After entering, Roosevelt bound gingerly from square to square while tipping his hat to the few men who nodded at him.

The interiors of some bars and restaurants in the U.P. are decorated to look like lumberjacks had frequented the place a hundred years prior. Rusty's looked like such a haunt because it was born as such. The only phony thing in the place was Rusty's hair, a red-brown toupee that—by the end of a busy night—dipped low on his brow like Roosevelt Bly's hat. The walls of the tavern were constructed of logs cut by the men who were the first to drink here, when the place didn't have a name and the original proprietor had simply painted the word BAR on the outside. In honor of that history, Rusty displayed no other name. The only sign out front read SNOWMOBILE PARKING IN THE REAR.

Curled and yellowed photographs hung on the walls, many of them nailed to the wood with no frame. They showed mustachioed shanty boys working at gang saws and breaking up jams on some northern river. Beside these pictures, Rusty displayed cant hooks, peaveys, boom dogs, crosscut saws, and other tools of the trade that were left decades ago, by men who'd come straight from work and gotten so drunk that—forget the tools—they could not remember their own names or the names of their women.

And Rusty's was dimly lit, creating the anonymity that most of the rogues in the place appreciated. This was not by design but from neglect. Lightbulbs had burnt out across the room, and neither Rusty nor his old-maid sister, Bep—whose white hair had yellowed from bar smoke and who served drinks and wiped spills of all sorts—rarely bothered to replace them. Every once in awhile another burnt out, and the place slipped a little closer to total darkness.

Roosevelt sank down on a stool beside Donnie Sarver, a man in his mid-thirties whom most people in town characterized, in a word, as mean. His hair was black and a bit oily but always fell over his brow in a way many women found handsome. He had narrow eyes and an angular jaw, which focused one's attention on his intense stare. Like most in the bar, Donnie sat and drank by himself. He also lived like most here at Rusty's: working hard during the day, smoking and drinking at night. His body was lean and tough, veins showing through the undersides of his arms. Both of those arms were covered in sleeves of tattoos, and a man couldn't individually make out the designs unless he sat right next to Donnie and could see that, yes, that's an anarchy symbol; sure, that looks like a wolf. At his famed annual "Welcome Wagon Shit-Kickin'," Donnie would remove his shirt before fighting, revealing a torso also covered in ink and the name JANE, in unadorned black letters, across his throat.

Roosevelt nodded at Donnie and then smiled at Rusty across the bar.

"Presbyterian?" asked Rusty.

"It's as if we've met in a previous life." Roosevelt looked up at the mirror that faced patrons seated at the bar and made eye contact with Donnie. "So, Mr. Sarver, how are things at Sarver Towing and Repair?" He smiled as he spoke—a habit people said they could hear in his voice. Blind Earl Henneman had once remarked on it.

Donnie looked off to the side and snuffed out his cigarette. "Put a transmission in an old Mustang today."

"That so?"

"It is."

Rusty placed the Presbyterian—bourbon, club soda, Vernors ginger ale—in front of Roosevelt, who sipped it slowly and then returned it to the cocktail napkin. "And is that a minor surgery, like a gallbladder removal, or more along the lines of a coronary bypass?"

Donnie pulled his beer slightly from his mouth and met Roosevelt's eyes in the mirror again, smirking slightly. "I don't know a whole lot about medicine," he said, "but I think it's fair to say that I'm a fucking surgeon beneath the hood."

Roosevelt removed a cheap cigarillo from his breast pocket and smiled. Most men feared Donnie—his eyes and his reputation and his winning streak—but at seventy-nine, Roosevelt was untouchable. "The same way you're a surgeon with your fists?"

Donnie belched softly. "I'll let you jerk that chain. I don't need to."

"Touché."

"That's right."

Roosevelt sipped and smoked and did so, still, with that smile. "I'm glad business is good."

"Well, I ain't perched atop a heap of gold like you. I don't go home and dive into a pool of jewels and swim around and shit. But I'm okay."

"Is that what I do?"

"When you ain't reading or queering or doing whatever you do in that big house of yours."

Rusty laughed with his back to them as he washed glass mugs in murky water. "Don't be fooled, Donnie. He's a dandy, but he loves the ladies, and I hear the feeling's mutual." He turned and nodded at Roosevelt. "Stephanie Noles? That waitress over at The Venison?"

"Fuck," said Donnie, "she's like twenty-two years old."

Roosevelt shook his head. "She's a lovely girl and I enjoy her company and I did cook her dinner a few weeks back. But she treats me as she should, like an old uncle or something." He tapped ashes into a tray. "We talked about the men she's dated. And how she wants to be an actress. I told her to fear not and get up and leave home. Like I did."

"But she'll land in Hollywood, and you landed here," said Donnie. "Explain that shit."

An old Loretta Lynn song played on the jukebox. Roosevelt smiled and shrugged and smoked his cigarillo. He turned slightly on his stool, away from them. Usually at Rusty's it was the lovers or small parties who caught the eye; men drinking alone were the norm. But those men usually stared into space or into their drinks, or perhaps spoke quietly and sporadically to men at other tables. They certainly did not sit and write, unless it was an IOU or a woman's phone number.

Roosevelt leaned toward Donnie and nodded at the dark booth in the corner where a mustachioed man with glasses sat writing. "Who's our friend?"

Donnie followed his eyes. "I can count my friends on my right hand, and he sure as shit ain't one of them."

"Think he's from out of town?"

"If he is, he definitely ain't counted on my right hand."

"You say anything to him?"

Donnie, for the first time, looked Roosevelt in the eye, without the benefit of the mirror's reflection. "And say what?"

"Hello."

"Hello. Let me tell you something, old man. If I say anything to that guy, it's gonna involve the words 'get,' 'out,' and 'son of a bitch.'"

Roosevelt tipped his hat. "Touché."

Donnie went back to his beer while Roosevelt stared a little longer. The man hadn't stopped scribbling since he'd first noticed him.

"I'm going to order that young man a drink." Roosevelt raised his index finger to get Rusty's attention.

"You do that," said Donnie. "You be a gentleman." He looked in the opposite direction, up at a news program on an old TV.

"Rusty, serve the man in the corner another of what he's drinking, and let me foot the bill."

Rusty pulled a Budweiser out of the refrigerator. "You don't know him?"

"No, sir. It's a small town, but I'm still meeting new people."

Rusty set the beer atop a cocktail napkin on the bar. "Bly, if it wasn't for this job, I wouldn't talk to nobody. And gladly so. I wouldn't talk to you." He looked over at Donnie. "I sure as hell wouldn't talk to *him.*"

"Right back at you, wigwam."

Rusty nodded at Roosevelt. "Talking and socializing. That's why people think you're a queer."

"That and the getup." Donnie fluttered his arms.

Roosevelt removed his white hat, smoothed down the silver hair underneath, and carefully replaced the hat on his head. "I am of another place and another age."

"Stone Age," mumbled Donnie.

Bep picked up the beer and limped it across the room to the stranger. When she set it down on his table, the man finally looked up from his work and shook his head. She nodded and then pointed toward the bar. The man stared at them, squinting through his glasses. Then he nodded at her slightly, pulled the beer closer to him, and began to write again. He did not acknowledge Roosevelt.

"Rather rude, is he not?" he said, snuffing out his cigarillo.

"Then maybe he *is* a friend of mine," said Donnie. "A bastard half brother or something."

Roosevelt stood up with his drink, adjusted his gold belt buckle, and walked in the direction of the man. He realized people tended to watch him when he crossed a room—it was the slow deliberateness of his stride and the blinding white—though today it was also the curiosity of two strange men—one known and one unknown—coming into contact.

Roosevelt stood in front of the man and waited until he looked up. Then, with the brim pinched between two fingers, he made the slightest of tips with his hat. "Hello, sir. I don't believe we've met. I'm Roosevelt Bly."

"Good to meet you," the man mumbled. He dropped his eyes and then meekly raised them again. "Thanks for the drink."

"My pleasure. And what do folks call you?"

"Lee," he said.

"Ah, like the general."

"It's my first name," said the man.

"Like the assassin then."

The man was reading over something he'd just written. Roosevelt examined him from up close. He had narrow eyes and a small mouth. His left ear was pierced, though he wore no ring or stud. Along with the orange camouflage pants he wore a shirt with a picture of a buck standing in front of a full moon.

"May I sit?"

The man's eyes widened, and he looked toward Rusty and Donnie and Bep, as if someone at the bar would sympathize with his discomfort. Then he looked at Roosevelt. "I'm going to be leaving soon."

"You got a full bottle of beer there."

"I'm probably done drinking."

Roosevelt noticed the camera on the seat next to Lee. It was out of its case. "That," he said, picking it up, "is a beaut."

"Hey," said Lee, reaching for it. But Roosevelt was already sitting in the seat across from him, turning the camera in his hands.

"This is no tool for a tourist shutterbug. Do you work for a newspaper or magazine?" He removed the lens cover. "We had a journalist from some New York men's magazine here a couple years back. He was doing an article on kayaking or fly-fishing or something of the sort. He came during Boomtown Days, which is when Donnie—that's him there, the gentleman I was sitting next to—does this strange little ritual where he takes on all comers." Roosevelt raised the camera to his eye and aimed the lens at Donnie. "Literally. Fights them tooth and nail. Fights someone who's new to the town. The man ended up spending his whole article on Donnie Sarver." He lowered the camera and handed it back to Lee, who quickly returned it to its leather case, zipped it shut, and set it in a backpack beside him.

A silence fell between them. More shadows owned this end of the bar; more lightbulbs had burned out in this corner. Obligation set in. Lee lifted his beer to his mouth and sipped. Roosevelt did the same with his own drink. "Cheers." He swallowed and set his glass down. "So, are you from out of town?"

Lee smirked and shook his head. "You ain't the first to ask me that today."

Roosevelt nodded. "Oh, that surprises me not one bit. But there are different reasons for asking it." He cocked his head toward the bar. "Men like Donnie ask by way of threat. They want this place to be like it was a hundred years ago—railroads and whorehouses and trees falling to the saw. The tourists, artists, and weekend warriors who come up here leave the taste of excrement in their mouths." He took another sip. "Others, like me, ask by way of conversation. Meet people. Learn their names. Learn their stories." He shrugged. "But I'm an outsider, too, so maybe that's it."

Lee leveled his eyes on him for the first time, nodding slightly. "I appreciate that. And I believe you, sir. Though I'm not real big on revealing my story to strangers."

"That's not a problem," said Roosevelt, "because I am. And with over half a drink left, you'll be lucky enough to hear the start."

Lee smiled. He pulled the composition book close to him. "Actually, I'd love to hear it." He found a blank page and uncapped his pen. "So you're an outsider, too. Been here a short time?"

"I have, by Haymaker standards." Roosevelt rattled the ice in his glass. "Twenty-nine years. Thirty in October."

Chapter 3

Saturday, July 19

A green sign along the highway announced the forty-fifth parallel: halfway between the equator and the North Pole. And an instant later Josef Novak had crossed it, inching closer to the pole and to the U.P.

Traffic grew heavier as he headed farther north—the flatland tourists charging into the weekend with mountain bikes and kayaks strapped to their RVs. But Josef was no tourist. He traveled to the north woods for research: to immerse himself in a town and its people, to establish an outpost, and eventually to sell others on the idea that this place was indeed the promised land.

Just a week ago he'd been sipping cold coffee in a brick office building in Michigan City, Indiana. There, in the shadow of a power plant cooling tower and just blocks from the outlet mall and the casino, he'd planned a future—for both himself and others.

Privately, Josef called their office the War Room. Were it to be made public, he'd refer to it as Freedom Community Headquarters. He served as Director of Communications and Public Relations for their cause. Everything now had two or three names, depending on the audience.

Empty coffee cups lay scattered throughout the room, and if Josef kept his eyelids closed for just a couple of seconds, his eyes smoldered and began to burn. Gorman Tate—the leader of this cause—had once dubbed him The Perpetual Motion Machine. Josef stared at the whiteboard on the far wall and ran his fingers through his hair. He was thirty-nine and had started to gray slightly, but his hair was still thick, and he ran his fingers through it so much during the day that by evening it puffed out in all directions.

He approached the whiteboard, picked up a marker, but then just stood there, forgetting what he was going to write. He set the marker back on the tray and surveyed the empty War Room. In certain ways it resembled a high school civics classroom. Two flags hung from the drop ceiling: the Stars and Stripes, along with the yellow Gadsden flag with the rattlesnake and the warning DON'T TREAD ON ME. A framed portrait of Thomas Jefferson hung on the wall by the door, and a smaller one, of Thomas Paine, hung below it. There were also maps.

But in other ways it resembled the modern work space of some software company or advertising agency. In one corner were three cubicles with computers, phones, and filing cabinets. In the center of the room were oval-shaped tables and state-of-the-art office chairs. The furniture was clustered around an easel-like whiteboard from the latest meeting of the Freedom Congress. Josef had led the meeting, and his small, neat handwriting covered the board, including a list from the brainstorming session: RATTLESNAKES, WOLVES, COYOTES, PORCUPINES, EAGLES, CACTI, BEARS, GRIZZLY BEARS, BLACK BEARS. Scribbled in a tight space in the upper corner were the words VOTE NEXT MONTH ON NAME.

And yet there was much about the space strikingly different from a classroom or business. The books stacked throughout the room—and there were many of them—included *Atlas Shrugged*, *Capitalism and Freedom*, *The Road to Serfdom*, and one called *Selling the Dream: A Public Relations Strategy for Libertarians* by Josef A. Novak—by him. Dozens of bumper stickers decorated the walls and cabinets: I'M PRO-CHOICE ABOUT EVERYTHING . . . I FEAR GOVERNMENT MORE THAN TERRORISM . . . LIBERTARIANS DO IT BY THEMSELVES.

Dominating the room was a map of the United States—ten feet long by six feet tall—that covered most of one wall. Somewhere on this map was the town where Josef, his wife Jeanie, and their two daughters would soon live. Which town, however, depended on Gorman Tate.

Internally, they called it the PIZ map, or Possible Immigration Zones map. Carl Farmer—as good-natured as anyone working in the War Room—found this as funny as a child breaking wind and would say things like, "I'll be right back, I have to take a PIZ" while he grinned and headed for the bathroom. That said, he knew what the map meant and understood its importance. Colored thumbtacks dotted the nation, scattered throughout most of the fifty states but concentrated on a few key regions. Most of the tacks were red and appeared far away from major population centers. A number were stuck in the

West—Montana, Idaho, Alaska. Some were east of the Mississippi, in northern areas of Wisconsin and Michigan. A few others stuck out of New England. Mixed in with all the red tacks were a few yellow, and only in New Hampshire was there a single green. That was about to change.

Josef walked to a light switch by the door and dimmed the room. The blinds on the windows were closed tight, and only a few ambient lamps shone. He liked darkness while he worked, whether during the daytime or after the sun set. He looked up at the PIZ map—at all the colored tacks of futures and opportunities—and took a deep breath.

A few computer monitors glowed blue in the dimness. On one of them was an image of a beach with gunmetal waves breaking against a pier. Josef rolled an office chair across the room, in front of the PIZ map, and stepped up onto it. He wore the type of clothes that he'd once worn every day at Crow & Associates: gray slacks, a dark tie, white shirtsleeves rolled to the elbow, and starched collars. He called it his uniform, what a person wears when conquering the world, or liberating it. As he stood on the chair, boyishly balancing and removing a green tack from his pocket, he felt a quick surge of the optimism he used to feel in those early years at the PR firm, looking out his office window toward the sweeping Chicago skyline.

Someone rapped on the door three times and then entered. Carl Farmer held a white pizza box in one hand and a large fountain drink in the other. Backlit by the bright hall, he stood in silhouette, filling the doorway. He'd played high school baseball with Josef—each at bat, it seemed, a home run or a strikeout—though football was his calling. His freshman year he'd started as defensive tackle at a community college but blew out his knee in the third game. When Josef had just moved back to Michigan City, Carl was the only old friend he'd run into. At a diner off the highway, the two of them had talked about everything from high school to sports and especially politics, on which the two were of like minds. That was when Josef introduced Carl to the ideas he'd been grappling with, the ones in his own book and the books of others. By the end of the night, they were teammates all over again.

"Wow, you're smiling," said Carl. "You either got some good news or you're drunk."

Josef held up the green tack. "Know what this is?"

"Another tack. Another town." He set his drink on a bookshelf.

"Look closer."

Carl squinted. "Is it green?"

"You got it."

"As of when?"

"As of an hour ago," said Josef. "Gorman reviewed the zoning info sent from Denny last night, and after seeing some new pictures decided to give it the go sign. It's a finalist." He leaned forward on the chair, resting one palm against the wall for support. Then he reached up toward the top of the map, to a yellow tack stuck in Michigan's Upper Peninsula, where land met wave on the Lake Superior coast. It was one of the northernmost zones marked on the map. Josef plucked out the yellow tack and replaced it with the green.

"So you talked to Gorman?" asked Carl. "What'd he say?"

"He said, 'This is the place.'"

"He did not."

"He did. He's quoting zealots now."

Carl sat down with the pizza box on his lap and reached for a slice. "Better than becoming one."

Josef shrugged. "There's good zealots and bad zealots." He stepped down from the chair. "Someone's got to set things in motion sometimes. Or help grind them to a halt when they jump the rails."

"So are we setting things in motion," asked Carl, "or grinding them to a halt?"

"Both." Josef ran his fingers through his hair and grabbed a slice of pizza. "Gorman's going to send me up there next week to research. If this really *is* the place, then I'll have to start drafting the recruitment pieces, along with PR aimed at the locals. That part might be tricky. Hopefully not."

Carl squinted in the direction of the computer monitor, where a wave crashed into a pier. "Is that from the probe?" He grinned and shuffled his feet, wheeling himself over in the chair. He'd been shopping for diamond rings and was ready to move. Marissa said she'd only marry him when they were certain of the future—of the new town for their new life.

Carl moved and clicked the mouse, and a long series of images flashed by. A main street in a small town. Several two-story, century-old buildings. A theater. A park. A girl with blonde cornrows, pushing a baby in a stroller. Several shots of a stern-looking police officer.

"Uh-oh," said Carl. "Our first brush with the law. Which probe is this?"

"Lee Mooneyham," said Josef.

Carl shook his head. "Idiot." He continued to click. "Oh well. Screw the law."

"No," said Josef, "just limit it. Make it protect our liberties."

Carl shook his head slowly and smiled. "Yeah, I know. But it's too late in the day for that shit. You need a drink. Recline and unwind." He leaned toward the image on the monitor, squinting to read the words on the side of a police cruiser while taking another bite of pizza. "Haymaker," he said with his mouth full. Then he stood up. "I need to get home." He walked across the room and opened the door. A triangle of light swelled over the carpet. "Fight the good fight. See you tomorrow."

Then it was dark again, and though the sunlight stretched on through the evenings of these summer nights, the dark—for now, when Josef was alone—could bring on those surges of optimism. He stared at the floor for a few more seconds before looking up at the PIZ map, and then he approached one of the whiteboards, finding a slim edge along the marker tray that was free of writing. He picked up a marker and began writing the name, over and over, in the tender, fantasizing way of a schoolgirl attaching her first name to the last name of her sixth-grade crush.

Haymaker.

Haymaker, Michigan.

Haymaker, Michigan: A Freedom Community.

That was last week, and now he drove on, approaching the actual place. After slicing through the flat farmlands of southern Michigan he now felt the shift, here above the forty-fifth parallel, to something truly northern. He sipped coffee from a thermos and happily sang along to classic rock stations. Billboards aimed at tourists had sprung up: The Mystery Spot, Ryba's Fudge, the world's largest crucifix.

He thought of how he'd kissed his daughters good-bye while they'd slept—Olivia, who was four, and Grace, who was two. Then he'd walked to his bedroom and leaned over Jeanie while she lay in their dark, predawn bed. She opened her eyes as he brushed her cheek and stared at him for a few moments. "It's almost happening," she said, smiling faintly as she closed her eyes once more.

Two towers emerged over the highway, sprouting and then looming over the tallest evergreens: the Mackinac Bridge. The road rose as Josef neared the straits, and then the ground fell away, his little Honda arcing over the bridge and the water. With the sudden elevation came a sudden view. The earth split into two stunningly blue swaths of water: Lake Michigan to the left and Huron to the right. Also to his right were three green islands, two without any appearance of civilization and the other dotted with bright white buildings. This was Mackinac, where cars were not allowed, only bicycles and horses. His parents had gone there for their fiftieth wedding anniversary and still talked about it. His mother, who was Czech and one of the few who pronounced the "J" in his name as a "Y," had said, "You must go sometime, Yosef. You must." And now after seeing it—even from this distance—he decided that it would be their first family vacation, once he and Jeanie and the girls were settled in Haymaker. Once the north felt like home.

Josef passed beneath the second tower, and the road edged downward, toward the trees and limestone cliffs beyond the far side of the bridge. This was the Upper Peninsula. This was the place—and these were the emotions—he would have to express to others.

He would not express his paranoia. Before leaving, he'd filled the car with a set of duffel bags. The first was packed with clothes—all casual. He was done with the starched shirts and ties. His northern uniform was T-shirt and jeans. The second bag held a laptop, books, and writing materials. And the third was one he'd hidden even from Jeanie when he'd hauled the bags into the garage last night. It contained a flashlight, a few flannel blankets, a couple of roadside flares, a pair of sturdy hiking boots, a box of granola bars, and a gut-hook hunting knife he'd bought earlier that week at an army-navy surplus store.

Josef had never journeyed to this part of the world before. He'd never traveled farther north than Fond du Lac, Wisconsin. And all of the reading he'd done this week on the U.P. had created an impression of a place not so much lawless as it was ruled by the laws of nature. So he'd packed these survival tools in case his car broke down, in the middle of the woods, in the middle of the night.

The knife served one purpose: a weapon against bears. Some people feared sharks or snakes, but for Josef it had always been bears. A few times a year he had nightmares about them. Although he knew the fear was irrational—this was not the Yukon, and he had a cell phone, and he lived in twenty-first-century America—he'd packed this third bag and felt better because of it.

Josef's heart quickened as he drove a few more miles, past the limestone outcroppings, and exited the interstate. There were no four-lane highways beyond this point. Forests closed in on him, the green flecked with white birch bark. He thought for a moment about his third duffel bag.

For nearly ninety minutes he pressed on through an infinity of trees that was broken only briefly by Newberry and a few smaller towns. Though he shared the road with some RVs and minivans, traffic was mostly light. Logging trucks hauling huge stacked loads sometimes passed him going in the other direction, flashing by with such a rush and force that the wind blew his car slightly onto the opposite shoulder.

Adrenaline and a day's worth of coffee drinking began working against his bladder, but he was now on county highway H-37—the homestretch. At one point the road climbed above the tree line, and Josef could see the distant town and, beyond it—like a darker strip of the sky—Lake Superior. He wouldn't stop. Finally the trees began to thin, and he saw, standing alongside the road, an orange sign with black letters.

HAYMAKER: RISEN FROM SAWDUST AND SWEAT

Just beyond this was a yellow deer-crossing sign, the bounding image of the deer peppered with silver bursts. Bullet holes.

Although he wanted to explore right away, the urge to piss made him head straight to the Duneview Motel. On the way he saw a few signs with arrows pointing visitors to places like canoe rentals, the Ophelia B&B, and The 12 Months of Christmas. Josef let himself smile. The town happily welcomed outsiders.

The parking lot was nearly full of tourists' vans and SUVs. He parked and jogged past all of them—the pressure in his bladder now more of a throbbing pain—and entered through the screen door of the motel office. A woman sat behind the counter, circled by cigarette smoke and watching a bass-fishing show on a small TV.

"Help you?" she asked, still seated.

"Hi. I have a reservation for three nights. Josef Novak." A quick flash of fear struck him as he said his name. For a moment he wondered if he should be sneaking into town in some way—using an alias and paying in cash. As if the town would see him and the Freedom Community as some kind of conspiracy. Something they'd try to stop.

She stood and opened a manila folder. "Novak." She flipped through a few pages. "Spell that? Wait—right here. Josef. With an 'F.' Three nights."

He slid his credit card over to her, and she took it and wrote down his information. "Do you have any special rates for long-term stays?" he asked. "I might be back quite a bit in the future. For a few weeks at a time." He took a deep breath, worried that he'd said too much.

She shook her head while handing him his card and receipt. "Nope. The rate is the rate. One night or a hundred."

He nodded, signed his name, and thanked her. Then Josef stepped outside and began jogging toward his room. Maybe the woman was watching him go, wondering why he was running. Wondering why he had an Indiana address. But he had to piss so badly now that even the paranoia hardly mattered.

Only after squeezing into the small bathroom and relieving himself did Josef take a moment to examine the room. The décor was brown, all of it. And the smell of the place reminded him of a childhood friend's cottage near the Indiana Dunes—a mixture of wet towels, old carpet, and sand. The furniture was worn, the shade of the bedside lamp permanently crooked. But the room was clean, and the bed, which he fell onto while rubbing his eyes, was comfortable. He stretched and yawned. There was no phone, which didn't matter; he had his cell. Someone had, however, taken the time to screw a Budweiser bottle opener into the wall beside the towel rack. And there was, at least, a TV, the remote screwed onto the end table. He closed his eyes, felt them burn from fatigue, and then hit the power button on the remote.

He found WGN out of Chicago and watched a half inning of the White Sox, but at a commercial he began flipping, landing on channel 29. The only image on the screen was a modest tree-lined stretch of road, a green park, and a statue. Josef sat up and peered closer. He recognized this from Lee's photographs. It was Parson Park, here in town. The camera panned left, revealing a portion of—he realized now—Marquette Street, some of its businesses, and a few sidewalk pedestrians. Then it panned right, displaying more of the same on the other end of the street. And this was all it did. Left to right to left, like a pendulum of sight. Garbled classic rock played at a low volume. Nothing remarkable appeared on the screen, but Josef reclined again and watched this for a few more minutes, the voyeurism of it too compelling to abandon just yet. There was, with every pan of the camera, a hope that something remarkable lay just offscreen.

He awoke two hours later, confused by the strange room and the quick, unexpected passage of time. The channel 29 street view still illuminated the TV. He stood, turned it off, and then staggered to the bathroom to splash water on his face. His stomach felt hollow from not having eaten since a McDonald's in Gaylord, but he wasn't ready to step into some local restaurant just yet. Though he hadn't even left his room, he'd felt strangely conspicuous since arriving. He grabbed his keys and returned to his car, deciding to hit a grocery store and see this town—in the flesh—along the way.

He started by heading toward the shore, first passing a ramshackle bar with no sign and then the abandoned Pulpwood Paper Mill. This grim jungle of pipes and smokestacks had put nearly two hundred locals out of work when it had closed in the late eighties. Over the past week, Josef had read whatever town history he could find in books and online. The local economy was still reeling.

A narrow, tree-lined road gave way to an enormity of space. Before him stretched the beach and Lake Superior, though it might as well have been the edge of the flat earth. The universe grew huge. Land and sky and freshwater sea all melded into a borderless blue. It made him think of what they'd been planning all these years, the great migration that would finally take place, and he felt it again: the thrill of being part of something big.

He braked along the stony sands of Fitzgerald Beach. Somewhere not far offshore, black waves rolled over the carcass of the SS *Albertus Cummings*, a Cleveland-bound freighter sunk in 1965 by forty-knot winds. Eighteen men and twenty thousand tons of iron ore lay now on the murky underbelly of the lake. He'd been researching the area's history, both the proud and the tragic.

Josef looped back into town, looking for life. He found it on Marquette Street, where people of all ages wandered down the sidewalks in the late-day sun. Children ate ice cream as their parents happily squinted while tilting their faces toward the sky. On the corner of Dawson, teenagers idly slouched and laughed outside of T's Pizza and Elysium Coffee, standing in puddles of shade. Josef shook his head slightly and smiled, remembering these same kind of teenage summer nights, when he and his friends would smuggle booze and cigarettes to a bonfire or darkened school playground. He'd only just arrived here, but he'd started to recognize this town.

He slowed as he passed Parson Park, peering through the passenger's-side window and up toward the roofs of the buildings, looking for the channel 29 camera that filmed this block. He didn't see it and slowed some more. A car behind him honked before arcing around him. On its back bumper was a faded sticker reading SAVE THE MILL and another that said MAKE SUPERIOR THE 51ST STATE. Josef looked up and spotted the camera. It was attached to the marquee of the Neptune Theater—Freshwater Community Church—turning its head from side to side, a red light atop it glowing in the shade. He passed beneath the marquee, reading, on one side:

"THE GIFT OF SIGHT"
SERMON BY REV. BERNARD ZUBER
SUNDAY—9 AM

On the other:

OUR CHURCH IS PRAYER CONDITIONED

Continuing forward, Josef saw a dull blue-and-white sign with flaking paint announcing the offices of the Haymaker *Star-Picayune.* He'd pick up the latest copy when he got to the grocery store. He wanted to know if this was a real paper, with editorial teeth, where people spouted grievances on an op-ed page. Or if it served up fluff: fifth-grade plays about old French fur traders, or the fishing conditions at the Two Hearted River.

Josef cut one block over and drove back in the direction from which he'd come. Farmer Fresh Foods—the 3-F—stood on the corner, a modern-looking supermarket that filled him with relief. He'd been to small towns where the grocery stores sold live bait near the checkout. Anything like this—any modern amenity—would be critical when it came to convincing outsiders they'd feel comfortable here.

Before stopping to pick up some bread and lunch meat and beer to bring back to his room, he made one final detour. From the glove compartment he pulled a scrap of paper on which Lee Mooneyham had drawn a crude map and then headed south on Schoolcraft. A minute later he pulled off onto the shoulder, his front-right tire dipping into a gully, and parked beside a field full of stumps and scrub. He stepped out of the car and stared at the wasteland.

The stump field was larger than he'd imagined, and yet he'd passed it earlier on the way into town without ever noticing it. The landowner was a guy named Jimmy Bruce who ran a baseball card shop out of his home's basement and had supposedly obtained the property last year after his parents died in a car crash. He was looking to sell.

Pine stumps dotted the landscape—the remains of trees felled over a hundred years ago and soon after baked by intense brush fires. Only a few shrubs, wildflowers, and blueberry bushes grew here now. Lee had discovered this patch of earth, and Josef had researched it well. Here—right here—could be their home.

He could not yet say if this was the Promised Land, but if so, it was an ugly one—a swath of old burnscape that looked like rows of gravestones. It would take a massive amount of work to remove all those stumps. And yet he smiled, imagining where the main drive might run and what the terrain would look like after landscapers had sculpted it with flowering trees and gardens. He imagined American flags.

Chapter 4

Friday, August 1

Clara Hollingshead stared at the light-blue gel coating her now glossy mound of a stomach. It looked like some moon with an unmarked surface, foreign and flawless. She adjusted the towel draped over her hips to cover a few dark pubic hairs peeking out and then glanced at her husband, Gary, who smiled back weakly and dropped his eyes. Clara finally willed herself to look at the monitor.

The ultrasound technician, a young woman named Tiana Ray, sat on a stool beside her. "Well, Mayor, let's say hello to the little one."

Ten months earlier, in this same room, the monitor had remained dark, and other than the soft crackle of the ultrasound, the womb had remained silent. A blighted ovum, they'd called it. There was an amniotic sac, but nothing else had begun to grow. She thought about that moment every day—Gary stricken dumb, creasing his brow and shaking his head, while she tumbled into a strange realm of mourning, missing something that she'd never known, that had never really existed. But it had.

Today, a pulse—like an echo picked up from a distant satellite—grew louder, and familiar forms quickly took shape.

"Hi there, baby," said Tiana.

Tears welled in Clara's eyes. "Hi," she said. She was forty-one and had no children. Except now she did—there, on the monitor. She inhaled and ran her fingers through her sandy blonde hair before finally exhaling.

"That's it?" asked Gary. "It's still there? It's okay?" His hands nervously stroked his beard.

"It's there, and I think it's fine," said Tiana.

The fetus was three months along, but this was already their third ultrasound. Clara had started bleeding at eight weeks. She and Gary approached each visit to LaRock Medical—which had only just recently obtained the equipment, thanks to a grant Clara herself had sought—with more fear than excitement, more longing than expectation.

"Look, honey." Gary rose from his chair and pointed at the screen. "You can see its head."

The round skull curved down and out again, revealing a full profile.

"My God, that face," said Clara, smiling and crying. "The poor thing has its mother's nose and chin. They're protruding." Gary bent toward her and kissed her on that nose and that chin.

They were all smiling there in the dimly lit room. But in a moment Clara willed the smile away. "Does everything look all right, though?"

Tiana moved the wand over the glossy belly and pointed at the screen. "You can see the spine here. And the hands. And there's the heart."

It looked like a pair of lips, opening and closing, mouthing the sound of that celestial pulse. "Hi," said Clara again.

"Here," said Tiana, pointing at a dark mass on the monitor, "is the subchorionic hematoma."

"God, it's still there."

"But it's smaller."

Clara looked to Gary again, but he wouldn't meet her eyes. He stared at the monitor.

"Yeah," she said, "it does look smaller."

"She won't have to go back on bed rest, will she?" asked Gary.

Clara rolled her eyes. "That was the longest month of my life. The café about fell apart while I was gone."

"That's up to Dr. Tracy," said Tiana. "But I'd say that, considering its reduction, you'll have just a little longer before it's business as usual."

"Don't get me wrong. I will if I have to. As long as the baby's born fine." She looked at Gary. "You could roll me onto my side every half hour so I don't get bedsores." They both smiled. Hope flared up in Clara, but she tried to ignore it. This was already their third pregnancy. Anything could happen yet. In her mind, the baby was a fragile thing, and when she walked, she did so on the front of her feet, as if carrying around something made of china and glass.

"Can you tell if it's a boy or a girl?" asked Gary.

Tiana moved the wand again. "No. Too early for that."

"I wouldn't want to know anyway," he said. He turned to Clara and mouthed the words, "I love you," and she whispered, "Me, too." Gary was a large man, and he might have looked overweight if he weren't six foot six. His hair had receded to the halfway point of his head, though the beard gave balance to his face. He was utterly masculine, capable of great power, yet he almost always spoke gently and softly, smiling sheepishly whenever they kissed or embraced. They'd been married ten years.

Their eyes lingered over each other's, and something else flared up in Clara, something that always seemed to come along with hope or joy or any brightness of days. She remembered Gary's affair—which he'd confessed almost three years ago now, and which they'd seemingly put so far behind them. There had been counseling and meetings with their priest and even a private renewal of their vows. But that time had also stoked the symptoms of Gary's mental illness, which he'd mostly managed over his adult life through therapy and medication. His guilt over the affair had cracked a dam in his mind, and his psychosis—though brief—sent him to a Marquette hospital after he'd convinced himself that he'd be arrested for his infidelity. That the FBI had files and photographs. That any sirens in the distance meant they were coming for him, to punish him for his sins. He returned home and slipped into a prolonged depression of drinking, sobbing, and nightlong readings of Scripture. And because of all of Gary's own chaos during that time, Clara had never had a chance to fully grieve the broken marriage. She'd never fully poured out her rage at him.

This—this pregnancy, the great summit of their long married existence—was finally within reach. Yet there were these dark memories of their past, with her always, like the large grease burn on her left forearm. A caution and reminder of pain.

"Well," said Tiana, "in the weeks ahead, when I'm able to tell the sex, I'll be sure to keep my lips sealed, to you or anyone." "Good," said Clara. "I govern this town. I serve coffee to this town. People here act like they're not social, but believe me, this town can't keep secrets."

She governed Haymaker. She served coffee to Haymaker. Clara was once the longtime waitress at a tiny diner on Schoolcraft called The Spoon, but six years ago she'd left to start her own place, The Shipwreck Café, a slightly larger restaurant up on Superior Drive, right on the beach and with a view of the lake. Many Haymakes had grumbled that the place didn't need a second breakfast haunt, and that the Shipwreck—because of its location and nautical décor—would only attract tourists. But in time Clara had won over locals with her pasties and omelets.

Then two and a half years ago, Reginald McPhee, the town's eighty-something mayor, died of pneumonia. He'd been ice fishing at Little Deep Lake during a March thaw. How his old hands clawed him from the water back to solid ground remains a local legend. He died two days later.

Between her tours of duty at the two popular eateries, Clara had become one of the most well-known and well-liked people in all of Haymaker. It was Greta McPhee, Reginald's widow, who'd urged her to run for the vacant post. Clara, excited by the prospects and still wanting to punish Gary—if only through her own success—did run, against "Slim" Jim Johnstone, the high school football coach. Unfortunately for him, Johnstone's team went 3–6 that year. Things may had been different had Reginald died one year earlier, when the Huskies had won the conference championship. But Clara came out ahead with 59 percent of the vote. A landslide.

It wasn't long before the part-time job seeped into the other hours of the day, into the already long days at the Shipwreck. When the bleeding began a month ago—when this third pregnancy seemed to slip away like the others—Clara had to immediately cut back on her work at the diner. Cut back on filling mugs, on making change at the register, and especially on meeting and greeting the early risers at six in the morning.

The mayoral workload eventually lightened, with the busiest nights spent once a month at the Civic Centre, overseeing city council meetings and the ten to fifteen Haymakes who actually attended. Most were regulars. Most were over sixty-five.

"I'll let you get dressed," said Tiana. "Dr. Tracy will be in to talk about what we see on-screen. But I think it's looking better."

Clara stood up and pulled on her maternity underwear and her blue jeans with the thick elastic waist.

"How are you feeling?" asked Gary.

"Fine. I don't want to think about it because I'll jinx it. But I can't *not* think about it. If I could work, I could take my mind off everything. But when I lie on my back and watch soaps and courtroom shows all afternoon, I go crazy."

"I know."

She sat back down and tied her shoes. "Do you want to get a bite after this?"

"Gee," he said, "let me check my schedule." Gary, like many in town, made a living through a menagerie of jobs. He repaired lawn mowers and snowblowers in the garage, and in between he fashioned wood carvings of old lumber schooners that he sold at Ingrained, the craft shop and gallery downtown. In the winter he also helped his buddy, Jeremy Marx, with his dogsled tours, grooming and working the dogs, leading some of the trips into the forest. "I think I can squeeze you in between one and one ten."

"I just don't want to go home. I'm sick of it. I miss the sun."

Now fully dressed, reclined slightly in the chair, she let out a long sigh. The room was white and silver, antiseptic and angular, and they sat there waiting for the doctor to translate the ultrasound, the hieroglyphs of life.

They searched for distraction and found it. The plan had been to lounge at Big Deep Lake for a little while before getting lunch, but when they headed south to the outskirts of Haymaker, they spotted the Michigan Midway.

"I forgot it was in town," said Clara.

Gary looked at her. "Do you want to stop?"

"Yeah. I could go for an elephant ear."

For one week every summer the lights, machines, and tinny music materialized overnight in an abandoned lot that had once housed an old Buick dealership. They parked the car and walked across gravel toward the midway's entrance. "Two more weeks in bed," said Clara. "Keep me away from razor blades and shoelaces."

"Don't talk like that. You don't have to be in bed the entire time, just off your feet. We'll make it fun. We'll have picnics in the yard."

"Oh, I'd give cash money to see you setting up a picnic next to your workshop, by that stack of old tires." They passed through the gates, into that world of sugar and sound. Kids ran in packs from the Hall of Mirrors to the Paratrooper to the Scrambler. Their parents stood in separate packs sipping Pepsi through straws and checking their watches. Clara and Gary sat on a bench in front of the massive Octopus, whose tentacles rose and dove while spinning the screaming riders. Clara had to nearly yell to be heard over the multiple calliopes. She nodded at the ride. "That would be good for the baby. Go buy us some tickets."

Gary stood. "How about I get us some food." He turned and headed through the crowd to a vendor.

Clara shut her eyes for a long stretch of time, sensing the sunlight through her closed lids. When she opened them, she saw the Tilt-a-Whirl in the distance with its bulbous red cars slowly and gently turning before, unexpectedly, catching some sudden momentum, the cars whipping once, twice, from the terrible inertia.

Gary returned with two Polish dogs, two elephant ears, and two Pepsis.

"I can't drink caffeine," said Clara.

"Damn, that's right. I'll go get you a lemonade or something."

"No, I'm not thirsty." She set her hand on his knee. "Just stay and eat."

They ate and didn't speak for several minutes. Gary studied her face for a while before finally saying, "Hey, this is all good news. The hematoma's shrinking. The baby's fine. In a couple weeks you'll be back on the job."

"Jobs, plural."

A pounding sound awoke them from their relative daze. To their left, a mammoth ride called the Zipper had come to a stop. Shadowy riders high in the air peered through the cramped cages that would loop like a Ferris wheel while at the same time rotating them forward and back. There was a problem with the cage nearest the ground. A man in bibbed overalls hit the door with a mallet, trying to get it to stay shut. Two boys sat inside, waiting for him to finish.

"Uh, as mayor, maybe you shouldn't witness this," said Gary.

"Uh, as a soon-to-be mother, maybe I shouldn't witness this." She scanned the area, a sly yet weary grin on her face. "Look at this stuff. Look at the people responsible for the rides. I wouldn't trust my child to go on any of them. I probably wouldn't let my child eat the food they serve here."

She lifted her shoes off the pavement, where they stuck slightly from gum and spilled drinks. The man with the mallet nodded at a young man in a Packers cap who then pushed a button, starting the ride again. Joyous screams poured out of the cages.

Clara touched her belly, looked at Gary, and without meaning to—without wanting to—thought of Joanna Blue. She was the manager of the meat department at the 3-F, the woman with whom Gary had had the affair. It had lasted, on and off, for two years before he'd finally broken down, confessed, and begged Clara to stay with him.

He smiled now, watching the Zipper. Then he turned to her, still smiling, though he must have seen something on her face. His expression changed. "You must be thirsty. You need something to drink. I'm getting that lemonade." He stood up and jogged away from her.

Gary tried so hard to be good now, and to have her notice that goodness. Clara lost sight of him in the crowd. Kids continued to sprint frantically from ride to ride, taking in as much pleasure as possible. It was only the first of August, but they seemed to sense the end of summer bearing down on all of them.

Chapter 5

Saturday, August 2

Brenda DeBoer eased her black pickup into the cramped garage, knowing just how far to pull in so that the closing automatic door would miss the back bumper and the car badge that read FRATERNAL ORDER OF POLICE. She shut off the engine and sat in silence for a moment, listening to the ticking under the hood while rubbing her eyes with the palms of her hands. She'd taken a warm shower at the station, had changed into jeans and a T-shirt, and her comfort now begged to become sleep. For a Friday night in summer the twelve-hour shift had been a quiet one. The highlight had come early on, walking through the midway, shaking hands with people and bending down on one knee to speak with children. After ten years in Haymaker these connections had become easier, but just barely.

The rest of the night included pulling a couple of people over for speeding. Around midnight she'd responded to a malicious destruction of property call at the home of Wally Kingman. Someone had smashed the driver's-side window of his truck and taken a couple cases of cigarettes that had been sitting on the seat.

Brenda had patrolled the late-night streets, especially around the local bars, looking for swerving vehicles and cars with no headlights. A little after closing time she stopped by Rusty's because Pete Wozniak, a retired barber who lived in a trailer off Oshkosh Drive, had refused to leave. At the first sight of her he smiled and bowed and peacefully left through the back door for the short walk home.

She answered the call from Penny Frey, who, at two thirty, reported that her teenage daughter, Kendra, hadn't come home and wasn't answering her phone. Ten minutes later Brenda got the call saying Kendra had fallen asleep at her friend's house watching a movie and was now back beneath Penny's roof.

Around three o'clock there'd been a domestic dispute at the home of Leon and Cynthia Savage. Leon claimed she'd thrown a blueberry pie at him followed by a few closed fists. Cynthia said he'd threatened her and then begun punching the walls. They both seemed right. The kitchen wall now included two deep holes in the Sheetrock beside a long purple smear of pie filling.

Besides property destruction, these domestic disputes took up most of her time, and so Brenda could almost smile when friends and family would ask her how a thirty-four-year-old woman like herself with a live-in boyfriend could go without any talk of marriage.

She stepped out of the truck, her near-sleep making the garage seem to sway. Then she stepped over all the sporting equipment lining the walls: golf clubs, tennis rackets, snowshoes, frame packs, Coleman camping stove, sleeping bags, a dome tent, a couple of kayaks. Brenda was strong and fit—a former all-state softball player—and even on her days off had little patience for books or TV.

She stepped into her house, removed her shoes without untying them, and shambled into the living room. Her boyfriend, Brian Beckett, sat cross-legged on the sofa in a T-shirt and boxer shorts, watching cartoons and eating cereal. He immediately flashed a smile. "Hey, babe. Have a seat. I got plenty of *Looney Toons* and Froot Loops for the both of us."

Brian was a Haymake, born and raised, and he never felt her sense of claustrophobia. In the winter, he worked as a Snow Soldier—part of the small band of civic employees who kept the roads as clear of snow and ice as possible during the long, dense winters. In the summer, he did various custodial and maintenance work at Blue Spruce Park and the beach. During the long stretches of downtime he could lounge in the house for days without ever leaving. But he happily ventured into the outdoors with Brenda on her days off, to hike or bike or fish. He was twenty-nine with pale blond hair and a smooth, boyish face that Brenda had always loved. She called him Blond Boy. Brian didn't act protective or ask too many questions about her day. Unlike every other man she'd dated since moving here ten years ago, he was completely comfortable loving a cop.

Jesse and Owen, her two rescued greyhounds, rushed into the room in a flurry of tongues and tails. They lived for two things: their open expanse of backyard and Brenda's return.

She squinted as she sat in the bright living room, the sun streaming in through the windows onto the white furniture and light beige carpet. The furniture still felt new after several years—needing to be broken in—and she'd grown sick of the glut of throw pillows always in her way. But somehow Brian, there on the firm cushions, managed to look comfortable in any room, on any furniture, in any situation.

"You're like an eight-year-old," she said and smiled. The dogs licked her hands.

He grinned back. "What?"

"Saturday morning. Cartoons and sugar cereal. You going outside when you're done to play G.I. Joe with your friends?"

"Maybe. Or just ride our dirt bikes. Make some jumps and ramps."

"A little kid on summer vacation," she said, shaking her head. "There's nothing sweeter. You should have seen them all at the midway."

"Oh, we should go."

"See," she said, smiling again. "You're one of them."

"Hell, yeah. I admit it. It's good to escape the crap of the grown-up world."

Brenda leaned back and sighed, hunting for comfort. "Sounds familiar." She arched her back. "The crap of the grown-up world."

Brian's cereal bowl was almost empty. He cupped it in both hands and lifted it to his mouth, drinking the last of the pink milk. Then he set it on the coffee table and wiped his mouth with his forearm. "What about when you have to deal with kids? Some brats chucking stones at cars or something."

"That's just the adult in them trying to break through."

He went serious now, looking not at her or the TV but at the carpet. "What about the older kids who try to hurt themselves?"

Brenda didn't flinch—she hardly ever flinched. "I don't know. Maybe they're stuck not wanting to be kids *or* adults."

Brian stood up, scratching the back of his head with one hand and picking up the empty cereal bowl with the other. He turned and walked toward the kitchen. "Remind me to never complain about my jobs."

"Don't *you* start," said Brenda.

He was around the corner of the kitchen wall now, out of her sight, clanging silverware in the sink. "Start what?"

"Talking about my job like it's on some different plane than anyone else's." She stood up. "I hate that shit." She walked down the hall toward the bedroom. "I'm a zombie. Good night."

"Good morning," said Brian. "Sleep tight. Tennis this afternoon?"

"Talk to me in five or six hours."

She closed the door behind her. The bed was remarkably unmade, the comforter, sheet, and both pillows on the floor. The fitted sheet had slipped from the corner, exposing bare mattress. Brenda covered it and made the entire bed, tucking everything into a perfect crispness. And then, with the pillows situated, with the comforter just right, she gently peeled the layers of the bed at one corner and slipped beneath them. Once there, she began to undress, dropping her socks, pants, shirt, and underwear on the carpet beside her nightstand.

The sun seeped through the miniblinds. Seven thirty passed. Then eight. It wasn't from the light; Brenda could usually crash through anything to get to sleep. Her brain kept settling on a call she'd received months ago, in January.

She stood up and walked naked across the room to turn on the old window air conditioner. The nights were rarely so warm that they needed it, but Brenda had always slept best in a cold room. It rattled and hissed, but soon the cool air came pouring out. She returned to the still-crisp bedsheets and pulled the covers up tight to her chin.

Little rivers of thought filled her mind. She imagined them as red and blue—arteries and veins. Counting backward from a hundred didn't help, and soon Brenda thought about her old home in Grand Haven, in the Lower Peninsula. She thought about Kim Witt, her best friend from high school who was now raising three kids. She thought about her parents, especially her mother, who—like Kim—could not end a phone call without saying something about being safe, taking care of herself on the job. All of which led her mind to Brian—Blond Boy—drinking cereal milk from the bowl, never cautioning her about her work, about drunkards' gunfire or ex-con rapists. This was not a small thing. Her thoughts tumbled onto marriage.

And then, as usual, they tumbled onto kids and the fact that every female officer she'd ever worked with eventually became a mother and stopped moving up through the ranks. They needed regular hours—off the streets and out of cruisers. Some couldn't face down danger anymore. Some thought it was selfish.

But Brenda had climbed upward, becoming sergeant, but also becoming a member of the regional CNT—Crisis Negotiation Team—handling hostage, suicide, and barricade situations. The team was made up of individuals throughout the eastern U.P., and she sometimes had to travel great distances. She'd earned the role through her steadiness and focus, completing training two years ago. FBI agents had drilled her on all of the different scenarios and how to keep callers on the line until she could calmly diffuse the entire conflict, like a bomb.

In her first six months she'd received two calls for suicide attempts and one for a hostage situation. Both of the suicide calls had come from teenagers—a boy trembling and cradling a hunting rifle and a girl in Grand Marais who'd stood at the edge of the pier during a windstorm, threatening to let the waves take her. But Brenda had talked them both back from the brink.

The one hostage had been an eight-year-old girl, a pawn in a custody dispute. Brenda spoke to the father for three hours, asking him why he was angry, asking him about his feelings for his daughter, and then convincing him that he was hungry. She arranged for a pizza delivery. No tricks. No games. And a half hour later the man left his shotgun in the living room and walked outside, arms raised, before the SWAT team pinned him to the ground and cuffed him.

This was clean and neat and nothing like the call she'd received in January. A forty-eight-year-old man in St. Ignace—who suffered from PTSD and seasonal affective disorder—had just lost his wife to ovarian cancer. His teenage son had called 911. On this night a blizzard had blown in from Canada, and despite the sirens and flashing lights—despite the illusion of speed—Brenda could only drive thirty miles per hour, fighting the icy roads, squinting through the whiteout fields, and arcing around a dozen spun-out cars in ditches. She finally arrived at the man's house at two a.m. As she fishtailed into the driveway, a sheriff's deputy emerged from the blizzard dark, motioning her to stop. He opened her car door and told her that the man had hung up on them ten minutes ago and pulled the trigger.

"I got to go find his son," he shouted over the wind. "Kid took off running into the storm. No idea where he is."

Brenda struggled up the driveway ice and entered the house. Then she crept up the stairs and stepped into a small, bright bathroom. Another deputy stood inside already, looking down at the dead man who lay in the tub, fully clothed, his legs hanging out over the edge. Hair and bits of flesh plastered the white porcelain. The blood ran neatly down the drain.

Brenda raised her head, fluffed the pillow, and lay down again, though the next memory patiently waited: her first found suicide, during her first year in Haymaker, just months after college and the academy and her move up north. This call had come after the fact. A teenager had threatened his parents, said that he'd kill himself, and minutes later a shot thundered down from the attic. The parents wouldn't go up there, couldn't bear to be the ones to find him. And so Brenda, twenty-four years old, rose up the creaking steps, the couple clutching each other at the foot of the stairs with the woman screaming, "Bring him back to me! Bring my baby right back here!"

In a terrible way, the screams made it easier for Brenda to enter the attic. What could have been worse than finding the boy—a huge hole in his throat—in utter silence?

She stood up quickly, swinging her legs over the edge of the bed and losing her balance in a flash of dizziness. Then she turned off the air conditioner and reached for her scattered clothes to dress again. Brian was gone, running some errand, when she walked back into the living room. The box of Froot Loops stood on the coffee table. She sat on the couch with her legs tucked beneath her the way she'd once sat as a girl, Jesse and Owen clambering for position beside her, and began flipping through the Saturday morning cartoons. She didn't recognize any of the new shows or characters. But finally she found *Looney Toons* and stopped. Tweety Bird—her favorite. Brenda leaned forward and scooped a handful of dry Froot Loops out of the box.

Chapter 6

Thursday, August 7

Josef pressed the red tack into the wall, an act resembling the rituals of the PIZ map, though this was very different. He stepped back and examined the large American flag to be sure he'd hung it straight and then turned and did the same to the yellow Gadsden flag on the opposite wall. The two managed to breathe some small amount of life into the empty apartment the Freedom Community had just rented here on Marquette Street, above The 12 Months of Christmas.

Josef sighed and ran his fingers through his hair again, making it feather and puff out. Scratches from a former tenant's dog, as well as some other larger gouges, peppered the hardwood floors. The walls wore a single shade of paint throughout, an off-white approaching yellow, that flaked off onto the windowsills, atop various dead flies.

Today was his first time back in town since his initial visit in July, when he'd found this room and the FOR RENT sign in the window. The fact that Gorman had so quickly mailed a check to the building's owner, and that he'd sent Josef back here already, were proof that Haymaker was becoming the favorite of all the possible towns. Gorman had asked him to make this apartment a kind of outpost—War Room North, he called it—and Josef would stay for a week at a time, getting the lay of the land—both physically and politically—as they planned for the potential large-scale migration. Josef's job was to reach these potential people—people who, like him and the rest of the leadership—felt passionately about smaller government and personal liberties. His job was to inspire them—not simply to vote or protest or do something small, but to leave their homes, jobs, and friends to start anew someplace essentially unknown.

The members of the Freedom Congress planned on driving up in a few days, to see Haymaker themselves in time for the monthly conference call. As always, Gorman would attend the meeting from his house in Florida.

Josef picked up a crate of books and set it against one of the off-white walls, beside the air mattress where he'd sleep. Other than some ancient appliances, the rest of the place was empty save for a fan, his duffel bags, an old office chair, a cheap desk that he'd assembled out of a box this morning, and his laptop. Sun streaked through windows, lighting up dust flecks in the air and warming the room with its late-summer heat. And yet, if he stayed silent and approached one of the floor vents, he could hear Christmas carols rising up from the shop below.

Nearly all of the books in the crate concerned the topic of Michigan's Upper Peninsula. He picked several up and carried them over to the desk. A book on the lumber history of the region. Another on hiking and backpacking the densely wooded trails. An almanac with maps and charts and facts on everything from casinos to waterfalls to record snow totals. And there—in its red, white, and blue dust jacket—lay his own book, *Selling the Dream.* Josef ran his fingers along the edges of the pages. He nearly always carried a copy with him, not to brag or to share with others, but as a reminder to himself of what he believed and what he'd pledged.

But it often reminded him, as it did now, of his father, who'd died from a stroke last year at age seventy-three. Arnošt Novak—the brilliant Czechoslovakian-turned-American nuclear engineer—had embraced the promise of the United States like few others. After his defection to the West, he'd bought an old '64 Lincoln Continental convertible—baby blue, with the suicide doors—like the one Lyndon Johnson used to drive around his ranch. "America on four wheels," Arnošt would say when showing it off to new friends.

As a young man he'd risen through the ranks of the Communist Party, had earned the trust of comrades, and had been considered not merely a brilliant nuclear engineer, but a loyal one. In time, the Communists let their guard down.

A specialist in the technology of nuclear power plant cooling towers, his talent made him invaluable to the Party. So prized was Arnošt that they feared—if kept on a short leash—he would resist, pull back, and flee to the West like some of his colleagues. Instead, they granted him unprecedented freedoms. He spoke at international conferences in Helsinki, Brussels, and Tokyo. Never had he done anything to alarm the Party, never had he done anything but present ideas so virtuoso that they made up for his lack of charisma. The Communists in Prague were so charmed by his intellect that in 1964—as a way to flaunt the scientific superiority of the East—they sent him to a nuclear energy conference in Ottawa. To thank him and further earn his loyalty, the Party even allowed him to take his wife and two young children—Josef's older sisters—along as a sort of holiday. By the time his superiors realized he was missing from the conference—absent from his own lecture on feedwater pump technology—the Novaks were at the other end of the Canadian capital, requesting political asylum, and passing through the gates of the American embassy, accompanied by United States MPs.

A few years later they emigrated again, to Chicago. And a few years after that, the family relocated a short ways east, to Michigan City, where Josef was born and where Arnošt served as consultant during refurbishment of the NIPSCO power plant.

All of this—all of it—to secure the American dream. And yet, late in life, when his only son became engaged in politics, wrote a libertarian treatise, and helped form a group that would literally bring freedom-loving people together as a collective force, Arnošt said almost nothing at all.

"The man fled Communism so his family could have freedom, and yet when I start working on liberty in its purest form, he acts like I'm part of a cult."

Josef had confided in his mother, Miroslava, a few months before Arnošt's death. She'd shrugged. "I think it is the idea of living all together in the one place," she'd said. "He sees that like a commune."

Josef threw his hands over his head. "Unbelievable! We're searching for the same thing he was. A fresh start. A more perfect liberty."

"Now, I know he is wrong about all that," said Miroslava, "but anything that reminds him about the Communism drives him crazy. It still does. I tell you, he hates the color red. He will only eat green apples."

"That's a lie."

"No, Yosef. A joke." She patted him on the cheek. "You must lighten yourself."

Josef turned from the desk and surveyed the walls. He needed a level; the American flag clearly dipped to the left. After removing three of the red tacks, he inched the flag upward and pinned it back in place. He stepped away once more. It looked precise now, in its proper place. He could return to his work.

Chapter 7

Saturday, August 9

Donnie leaned over his bathroom sink, his face just inches from the vanity mirror. His pores appeared huge and dark. Creases emerged under his eyes. He raised the silver tweezers to his left nostril, pinched a dark hair, and pulled so slowly that he watched the sinus skin tug out a ways before the hair came free.

"God!" He winced and shook his head before raising the tweezers and looking closely at the hair and its large white follicle. "God!" He began sneezing.

Somebody knocked on his door. It was only ten o'clock, early for a Saturday when everyone knew he drank till closing on Fridays and didn't work at the shop on summer weekends.

He wore only a pair of white briefs; nothing over his tan skin nor the dark ink that covered his trunk and arms. Still sneezing, he set the tweezers down and walked across his apartment. He lived on the second floor of the old Union Trust building, above Rita's Floral and Gift. Next door stood The 12 Months of Christmas, and on the other side the offices of the *Star-Picayune*. His front windows looked out across the street to Parson Park. It was a location, Donnie was fond of saying, just perfect for sniper fire. "You could take out anyone on this street from my northwest window. Bam. One. Bam. Two. Like hunting ducks in a puddle."

Donnie stepped over the debris of his days and paused in front of the door before opening it. "If you're the police, go away. If you're a whore, come back later. If you're neither, you better hope you're armed to bother me on this morning."

"What if I'm family?" asked the voice on the other side. "You gonna shoot me then?"

"Jesus, Ash." He walked to the couch, dug through a pile of old clothes, and then slipped on a pair of smoke-smelling jeans before opening the door. His niece, Ash, stood outside, slouched like any good teen, wearing cutoffs and a Detroit Pistons jersey. "To what do I owe the pleasure?" he asked.

She stepped inside.

"Oh, please come in."

"I will."

Ash shook her head at the sight of the balled-up clothes, half-empty beer bottles, and all the rest in the stark room: girlie magazines on the coffee table, binoculars on the windowsill, various greasy car parts on the shelves, and a pair of nunchucks sticking out of the couch cushions.

"Doesn't meet your high standards, eh?" asked Donnie. "You prefer your own shit show?"

"We have a baby in the house. What's your excuse?"

"That baby the one forgetting to do laundry? That baby the one leaving all those greasy pots and pans in the kitchen sink?" He leaned against the wall, beside a poster of a woman in a pink bikini.

"You crying?" asked Ash.

"What?" He touched his face.

"Your eyes are all red and watery. You're sniffing snot."

"Been sneezing."

"You sick?"

"No."

"Allergies?"

"No, been pulling nose hairs. When you gonna pull yours?"

"Gross." She reached into her pocket. "Mom asked me to bring this check over. For the work on her car." She held the check out to him.

Donnie leaned forward to read the written amount. "No," he said, "that ain't right."

"Two hundred?"

"I told your mom one hundred."

"She said someone at work had the same thing done and it cost them two hundred."

"At my shop?"

"In Newberry."

"Well, there you go," he said, leaning against the wall again. "Tell her to send you back over here with a check for half as much."

"I'm not walking there and back again." She set the check down on the coffee table, amid the mess, and backed away.

He stared at her for a moment. This kid was just like her mom, his sister Denise. Along with that old, crazy cowboy in the white suit, they were the only people in town who could look him in the eye.

"Since you're here," he said, "you want me to make you up a vegetarian omelet? Maybe some English tea or orange juice sprinkled with champagne?"

"Funny," said Ash. She nodded slightly. "Is that a new one?"

"What?" Donnie looked down at the tattoos covering his chest, past the one of a hatchet and the one that read I AM SUPERIOR. "This?" He pointed. "The wolverine?"

"Is that what it is?"

"Yeah."

"Looks like a dog."

"It ain't. It's not new, but it's my newest. Got it a couple months ago."

"It looks like a dog."

"*You* look like a dog, kid."

Ash's eyes dropped, and she gently fingered her cornrows.

Donnie made a half step toward her and then stopped. He'd sharpened his words over the years so that—like old bayonets—they could do more than cut a man. They could rip out the insides. He lowered and shook his head. "Hey, I was just kidding. You gave me shit, so I'm giving you shit. We got that back-and-forth thing going. All fun. Don't think hard about it."

She looked him in the eye again—seconds passing where she didn't flinch—and then her eyes dropped to his throat. Donnie touched the tattoo there that read JANE. She'd been his girlfriend—Jane Bannister—a woman who, ten years earlier, was driving to her parents' place in Brimley when she tried to pass an RV on a sharp curve and collided with a logging truck.

"Hey," he said, "your mom say anything about someone moving into that place above her shop?"

"I have no idea what you're talking about."

"Some guy." Donnie bent over to pick a crumpled plaid shirt up off the floor. "I saw him the other day carrying boxes and shit up to that empty apartment."

"No. It's not like we talk about stuff like that."

"The fucker had Indiana license plates and was hauling stuff up the stairs like he was moving in. I only saw him for a second."

Ash crossed her arms and leaned against the wall. "Why don't you spy on him? You like that kind of stuff."

"I don't have a window facing that way." He picked up an old pair of socks. "Or I would."

Ash smiled and said, almost under her breath, "Did he have a camera?"

Donnie looked up. "What'd you say?"

She shook her head. "Nothing. There was that guy, like a month ago, walking around town taking pictures of everything." Ash curled her thumbs through the belt loops of her shorts and began sauntering around the room. "I thought you'd be all over that one. He was doing something, but I don't know what. He got in a fight with Sergeant DeBoer."

"A fight?" Donnie approached her.

"Not like a fistfight. Just an argument. But it was right there on the street in front of everyone. I took pictures."

"Go get them."

Ash made a face. "No. Why?"

"What'd this guy look like?"

"I don't know. Skinny." She shrugged. "Glasses and mustache. Orange pants."

"Camouflage?"

"Yeah."

"No fucking way."

"You really shouldn't swear in front of minors."

Donnie furiously scratched the back of his head. "He was at Rusty's. Roosevelt Bly bought him a drink and then talked to him like an old friend. Goddamn that senile clown. When he came back to the bar, I asked him what that was all about, and he said he wouldn't tell me because it'd just get under my skin and I got enough under there already. God*damn*."

"I'm going," said Ash. She walked slowly toward the door.

"Wait. You took pictures of him when *he* was taking pictures?"

"Yep."

"E-mail them to me."

"We had to stop paying for Internet."

"Jesus Christ. Twenty-first century. Go get the camera and bring it back here." Donnie reached into his pocket, swore quietly, and then walked into the bedroom. There was no bed inside, just another couch where he slept. He lifted up one of the cushions and returned holding a money clip full of crisp twenty-dollar bills.

"Whoa," said Ash, "what's that for?"

"Emergencies." He handed her a bill. "Get the camera, get me a Mountain Dew, and you can keep ten bucks."

"Really?"

"Yeah. But I want it in"—he looked at his watch—"thirty minutes, max."

"What kind of emergencies are you worried about?"

"Twenty-nine minutes. Go."

◆ ◆ ◆

Ash returned a few minutes late, but Donnie didn't complain. He'd used the extra time to clean himself and his apartment. He didn't like the way Ash had turned her head slowly, inspecting everything. He put on a plain black T-shirt and his steel-toed boots. He scrubbed his face and combed his hair.

As for the apartment, dishes remained dirty, but at least now they were neatly stacked. Sheets and blankets remained on the sofa but tucked and folded in such a way as to resemble a made bed. He ensured no pornography lay about on the coffee table and then considered removing the poster with the pink bikini but didn't. He put the nunchucks in a closet.

Ash opened the door and walked right into his apartment without knocking.

"Make yourself at home," said Donnie.

"Most of them didn't turn out very good." She stared at the display on the back, clicking through the images. "They make the guy look far away, but he was a lot closer than that. Trust me. I followed him right up close."

Donnie took the camera from her and examined each photograph in turn.

"Don't delete the ones of Mom and P.J. and the birds," said Ash.

"You take your ten bucks?" He paused and stared at one of the images—one where the man in the orange pants stood in front of the Civic Centre, arguing with Sergeant DeBoer. Donnie knew her well. She'd arrested him twice—once for DUI and another for punching and shattering the side window of Ricky Wepplo's van. "Put the pop and the change on the coffee table."

"Anything else?"

He looked up from the camera. "You bring me that other check?"

"Mom wouldn't do it. She said it was worth two hundred and paid you two hundred."

"I'm a son of a bitch, kid, but I ain't a crook with family."

"She didn't say that. I didn't say that."

"Yeah, right." He came to some images of Patrick John. "And I'm just kidding. Keep the change. All of it."

Ash stood still, watching him. "We didn't say you were a crook."

Donnie nodded. "Okay. Thanks for the check. Thanks for the camera. I'll upload them and return it tomorrow."

"Anything good there?"

"Maybe. But it's not the guy I saw next door. You get any of a car or anything this other guy was driving?"

"No." Ash touched her blonde cornrows. "I'm gonna go."

"You gotta watch the little shit again?"

She opened the door and shook her head. "Mom's got the day off. I'm gonna practice at those hoops by the high school." She removed the bandage on her right middle finger and pointed the blood-stained tip at him. "If I can."

Donnie nodded. "Guys dig jock girls with scars."

She raised the middle finger at him.

He smiled. "Still playing at those shit hoops? Thought your dad was going to stop by sometime to put one up on your garage."

"Thought so, too." She left and shut the door behind her.

"Keep working on your left-handed layup!" Donnie called. Then he turned toward the kitchen to get a beer, pausing at the coffee table where the two-hundred-dollar check lay. He picked it up and began to tear it down the middle but stopped halfway. Work at the shop had been slow lately. He'd been spending too much at Rusty's. And he'd been wanting to take a long road trip somewhere—out West. Maybe to Vegas.

Donnie walked to the kitchen and stuck the half-torn check to the refrigerator with a magnet that advertised Marx Iditarod Tours. He grabbed a can of Miller Lite and leaned against the kitchen counter taking long sips, staring at the check, thinking about Ash. With the last swallow of the beer he plucked the check from the refrigerator, tore it all the way through, and tossed it in the trash. Then Donnie walked into the living room, picked up his binoculars, and gazed out his northwest window, which was just perfect for sniper fire.

Chapter 8

Tuesday, August 12

Five people sat in metal folding chairs, around a silent conference phone, in the austere confines of War Room North. They spoke little, checked their watches, and nervously bounced their knees like patients in a doctor's waiting room. Gorman would call any moment.

The oscillating fan turned toward Josef, tossing his hair every few seconds. He crossed his legs at the knee and stared at the phone. He facilitated these meetings. The phone faced him.

To his left sat Denny Zellar, a stout and heavily bearded Chicago lawyer who specialized in zoning laws. Next to Denny was Susan Abram, a thirty-nine-year-old CFO for an ad agency out of Indianapolis. She had four kids under ten years old and an aversion to maternity leave, having gone into labor at the office each time, and each time returning after one week off. She handled all things financial for the Community.

Across from Josef sat Calvin Matchinski, the twenty-three-year-old wunderkind with a background in digital media and Newtonian physics. Josef had met him at a drug-legalization rally. When Calvin was a kid, his father had spent five years behind bars for repeatedly selling marijuana to HIV-infected customers. Now this kid was responsible for social media and interactive design, and was the developer and webmaster of freedomcommunitynow.com.

Large, stoop-shouldered Carl Farmer rounded out the group. Besides Josef, he was the only member currently employed full-time by Gorman, a project coordinator who simply did what needed to be done: managing the production of print pieces; overseeing mailings; running to the store for more red, yellow, and green tacks. He'd been nearly giddy when he'd arrived in town with the others yesterday. "This place is gorgeous, man! It's fucking unspoiled!" But he'd remained quiet this morning, and Josef now sensed in Carl a kind of brooding.

These five individuals, together with Gorman himself, formed the Freedom Congress. Another twenty-five or so individuals made up a second ring of Freedom Community support—staunch Midwestern libertarians who pitched in whenever Josef needed additional hands or feet or voices. Some had spent weekends and even vacation days serving as probes, investigating all of the towns beneath those yellow tacks on the PIZ map. For this special northern meeting, one additional chair stood in the circle, vacant and waiting for the late arrival. One of the probes would join them today.

"What time is it?" asked Susan.

Josef glanced at his watch. "Five after." Then his eyes shot to the door before his gaze resettled on the phone.

Gorman attended the monthly meeting via phone call, dialing in from his home in St. Petersburg, Florida. Though a member of the Congress, he possessed veto power like some Security Council member of the U.N. But nobody here ever—ever—compared themselves to the U.N.

Gorman was the momentum-maker—the libertarian philosopher, long-range forecaster, and financial backer. He'd built the War Room. He'd spearheaded the nationwide search for the flagship town. And he'd mapped the overarching strategy: to concentrate a large number of libertarians into one small town—making an immediate impact that would snowball to the county, state, and even federal levels of power.

But everyone in the Congress knew that the ideas meant nothing without the money. After graduating from an Albuquerque high school with a 1.6 GPA, Gorman had inherited a few thousand dollars from a dead great-aunt and, together with a boyhood friend, bought up a gas station/car wash. Over time it became a local chain and later spread to Texas, Arizona, and Nevada. Gorman grew bored, sold his share at the age of thirty, and bought a six-bedroom house in Las Vegas, where he became a self-taught, subpar poker player. With his savings dwindling, and after selling his house, he began his second business venture, which Josef always worried could come back to haunt their current efforts.

Gorman invested in—and eventually managed—a number of legalized brothels in the mostly deserted corners of Nevada. Not only did his wealth return during this five-year stretch, but he further refined his libertarian theories, especially concerning victimless crimes. He began to push back against the law, opening escort services in Reno and Las Vegas, where prostitution was illegal. And then the law pushed back when detectives found a few of the girls had supplied false identification and that Gorman had hired sixteen- and seventeen-year-olds. He'd avoided charges and forever avoided the business and Nevada altogether.

"Vegas is a lie," Gorman had confided to Josef during one of their early meetings. "It markets itself as an anything-goes utopia of sin, but the fact is that those casinos want the city to squeak with clean like Orlando. They can make more money now off shopping and family fun parks than they can off gaming. They're worse than the feds when it comes to power and control."

He'd spoken then as he spoke always: calmly, with a half smile and a shine in his eyes, often smoothing down his mustache with his left hand. His voice boomed without effort from his tall but thin frame and was the fountainhead of his indefinable charisma. The rest came from his physical distance, preferring e-mails and phone calls to meeting in person. He'd become a guru with a disembodied voice. Gorman played this mystery better than any hand of poker—holding it close to his chest, bluffing and betting and raising the stakes with that same half smile. It made some people nervous. Susan hated the term "guru."

"It makes him sound like the head of a cult," she'd once said to Josef. "Enough people think we're crazy for trying this. Don't make it any easier for them."

And Denny—who distrusted leaders as a rule—had nodded in agreement. Only a month ago, Denny had approached Josef in the War Room after the rest of the Congress had left. "Gorman's the voice of God," he said. "You're the voice of reason. You know eventually you need to take charge."

Josef shook his head and stared at the floor, half believing that Gorman could hear them a thousand miles away. "Come on. Don't say that. Gorman's our man."

He wished that Gorman would visit them more often. The rest of the Congress needed to look him in the eyes—those eyes that always shone like a person with a secret, a person who knew something or *felt* something others didn't. Josef believed in the foresight of those eyes. Others dwelled on the risk of the plan—leaving homes and jobs and friends to move to some near wilderness. It was Josef's job to get people to fasten their hopes to this man in Florida and just let go—roll with the inertia of his glinting eyes.

Josef knew the risks. He and Jeanie would lie in bed and mumble thoughts about uprooting the girls and moving to an American no-man's-land. Most who knew the plan believed it would fail, including the greater libertarian community. Yes, they met the logistics of the plan with skepticism. But many also considered Gorman's views—on things like bigamy, incest, and organ trafficking—as extreme.

"Libertarian Lite," Gorman had said. "They're just believers in Libertarian *Lite.*"

Others online warned of the plan's dangers—of "invading" an entire town just as Gorman sought to "liberate" it through a wave of reforms. "We've seen this in the Middle East," wrote one critic. "It's a god complex. The furthest thing from a democratic ideal."

Josef didn't always know what to believe, but he believed this: Gorman was doing something. Other libertarians either wasted time talking or diluted their efforts, trying to change the whole country at once. But Gorman was no idiot. He believed in steady increments of change. And with each new rumor and concern, his charisma merely grew.

The outside door rattled on its hinges as someone outside knocked. Carl stood up to let the person in. The rest of them continued to wait silently for Gorman, their eyes glazed over, except for Susan, who was studying a sheet of paper in her hand with the various nicknames written upon it.

"I still like Eagles. It's quintessentially American. Emblematic of freedom."

Josef glanced at the flag on the wall. "It's cliché," he said.

Denny stared at the floor. "What's their high school mascot?" he asked.

"What?" said Josef. "Who?"

"Haymaker High School."

Carl unlocked and opened the door, and thin, mustachioed Lee Mooneyham stepped inside. He'd traded his orange camouflage pants for a pair of cutoff jeans.

Josef spoke up. "Everyone, this is Lee Mooneyham from Decatur. A couple of you, I think, have met him before. The rest have probably heard of him. He's one of our most dedicated volunteers." Lee grinned hugely at this. "Gorman wanted him to be here today because, other than myself, he's the only person who's spent much time in Haymaker."

"I have seen the light," said Lee.

"What's the mascot of Haymaker High School?" Susan asked him.

He had a strange grin on his face, not realizing she was talking to him at first, and then responded, "Haymaker?"

"Yes. What's their mascot?"

"The Huskies."

"Haymaker Huskies," said Carl, sitting heavily into his chair. "Nice ring to it."

"The complete opposite of what we're going for," said Josef. He looked around the circle—Lee in the final chair, completing it. Josef leaned forward;

he felt a charge of adrenaline. "A husky is a pack animal. It's leashed, it's harnessed. It goes where it's told against its own will. It's beaten down doing work for someone else. That, I'm afraid, is quintessentially American these days. We need a mascot that's the total opposite. Like eagles, which are strong and independent, only something more original. Something that isn't lofty and looking down on everyone. We'll see what Gorman thinks."

The others slowly nodded.

"I hope he thinks this is where we're moving," said Lee.

"It better be," said Carl. "I'm ready." He chewed on the inside of his cheek. "Jesus Christ, let's go."

The phone rang and Josef lunged at it. "Gorman?" He smiled. "Good evening. Let me put you on the speaker." He pressed a button, and the circle expressed a collective, jumbled greeting.

"How are the nation's freedom-loving people on this day?" asked Gorman.

Josef and the others melted like children receiving praise. This voice on the other end sounded—as usual—slow, precise, and assured. But today the voice also sounded tinged with an excitement Josef hadn't heard since their earliest conversations almost two years ago, when they'd sat along the third-base line at Wrigley Field. Josef was a Sox fan, but Wrigley impressed out-of-town guests in a way the South Side park did not, so they'd sat shaded from the hot sun by the upper deck, enjoying a breeze that circled through their section, both of them mildly and happily drunk as they made plans for a libertarian revolution. Gorman talked about how they'd make one of these communities succeed, and then he'd start a franchise of them and work as a consultant for other libertarians dedicated to such a dream. This was when Josef had first noticed that glint of bottomless perception in Gorman's eyes.

"How's that Florida weather?" asked Josef.

"Ungodly," Gorman answered. "Damn this humidity. You know, I'm sitting right now in a condo overlooking the bay in a living room that has a leather couch and a TV and that's about it. I've lived here for a couple years now, and I've never unpacked. I'm surrounded by cardboard boxes. And do you know why? Because I've known all along this was temporary, that I was bound for a new home—and soon. Real soon. By God, I think that we've finally caught up to the horizon. We've been looking at it from such a distance, but I think we've finally reached the point. The point of decision. The point of destiny."

Josef's neck and back felt stiff. He sat rigidly, barely breathing, tense in the most wonderful way.

Gorman continued. "If rumors have leaked up there, as I imagine they have, all of you likely know the heart of this conversation already. I've had extensive discussions with all of you in your various areas of expertise, and I am officially stating that—after poring over all of my notes and materials and gazing at all parts of the map until my eyes were about to bleed—my gut and my soul are steering me toward one place, and that place is Haymaker. In Michigan."

The eyes of those in the room—which had all been staring at the phone, as if gazing at Gorman himself—rose and met the eyes of each other, some with joy and excitement, others with clear worry and doubt.

"Hello?"

"We're here, Gorman," said Josef. "That's great. We're all here just smiling to ourselves and to each other."

"Well, no doubt some of you are, but I know from those earlier discussions that some of you have your doubts and concerns. I'd like to air those here and now, so everyone can chime in and we can debate this. We are a congress, after all."

"But in the end," said Susan, "it's *your* money, Gorman. Donations aside. You reserve the right to make decisions unilaterally."

"Thank you, Susan. I appreciate that. But I have a sense that donations are about to pick up, and thus, the voice of many will help guide us. I have a sense that once our main man Josef starts spreading the gospel all around, and people north, south, east, and west realize that we're for real now—we've got a town, we'll soon have property, and we're moving up there with or without them—they'll hop on our bandwagon like it's headed to heaven. And maybe it is."

Now they did smile, all of them.

"Let me lay out the pros," said Gorman, "and others can lay out the cons. Our plan, from the start, has been to bring a relatively small number of libertarians together in a place of low population in order to influence the local vote, and from that point steadily work our way upward, to the county, the state, and eventually the nation as a whole. It sounds like a heady idea, but you will be amazed at how quickly dominoes fall. I've seen it in my own business dealings."

Out of the corner of his eye, Josef saw Susan lift her head and look at him, but he didn't return her gaze.

"So we've studied a lot of geographical areas around the country," said Gorman, "and, again, areas of very low population density were favored. Most were out West. Others were in the Northeast. Yet there is this one place in the Upper Peninsula of Michigan—where you all are sitting right now. It's a place that, quite frankly, I'd never given much thought to. But one of my longtime friends—my only longtime friend; he's dead now—was a guy named Hugh Jenkins who used to spend his childhood summers up at his grandparents' in the U.P., and he described how these old-timers were die-hard about their liberty. A few even talked about secession—making the place its own state. He gave me a real sense of the populace up there, and I got to tell you all, these Yoopers, as they're called, may not realize they're libertarians, but God in heaven, they are. It's our job to show them the light."

Lee looked around the circle, smiling and raising his eyebrows. No one acknowledged him.

"And so we started looking at this part of the country as well, and like all of the other places, the key was to then find a locale with liberal zoning laws, because God knows some local government might get the idea to use zoning as a way of keeping a large-scale migration of libertarians from happening. We talked to town officials in various places, some without zoning laws, but most of them leaning toward instituting such shackles. So Denny went to work to find us the ideal place, and he found us Haymaker."

"Gorman, this is Denny." He leaned forward, elbows on knees.

"There he is. Hello, Denny."

"Hello. Look, I admit that Haymaker suits us just fine when it comes to zoning. And from the little I've observed since I got here last night, other things look good. But where I—and I know I'm not the only one to raise this concern—where I have a worry is with moving to any town in Michigan. Most of the places we were looking at—Montana, Wyoming, New Hampshire—have low state populations. Though the population of the U.P. itself is very low, the state of Michigan has almost ten million people. It'll take a far longer time to influence an entire state of that size. And isn't that one of our long-term goals? A libertarian governor? A libertarian senator?"

"You speak well, Brother Denny. And I've heard this concern, and I know this concern. It is, quite obviously, a con. It is something to debate."

Susan straightened up. "I have something else to debate."

"Ah, The Velvet Hammer. Hello, Susan."

"Hi. I'm sorry, I might be sounding incredibly selfish or weak or something when I mention these things, but I'll be the one to do it. I just got here last night, too. And it *is* charming and the lake *is* beautiful, but it's also incredibly isolated. There aren't malls or Walmarts or anything like that. You need to go a hundred miles just to see a newly released movie." She smirked and shook her head. "On top of that, we're pretty far north of the equator for my liking. It's a lovely day today. But it's August right now. From what I hear, the winters are brutal."

Gorman softly chuckled on the other end. "Yes. I, too, always imagined Eden as a sunny, tropical place. Don't apologize, Susan. These are the types of concerns that our potential recruits will express as well. Yes, these places are far from 'civilization,' if you will, but that's precisely why they have the independent streaks that they do. The rise of libertarianism will not come out of New York City. It will not come out of Los Angeles. It will arise from the small towns, and those towns will be the ones to eventually influence the metropolises. Now, as far as the weather, you're right, I hear it's not the best up there. But in all honesty, that's one of the reasons the population never grew. You could say the same about deserts or mountain ranges. If these places were meteorological paradises, they'd be overflowing with people by now."

Josef inched his chair closer to the phone. "Gorman, this is Josef. This next issue is one that doesn't affect me personally since I work for this organization, but what about jobs? If we do move here and embrace the isolation, we increase our influence. But if people can't earn a living and support their families, they're never going to stay, and our community's going to be a ghost town before it ever experiences a boom."

Gorman chuckled again. "You all are really peppering me today. But that's good. That's why we're here. No, that's a big concern. I do know that our research shows an incredibly high percentage of our people are self-employed. Many are in the computer or Internet business. Some are antitax and independently wealthy. And there are some—and I would be one of them, if I were someone looking for a job—who would make the sacrifice and drive to bigger towns like Marquette or Sault Ste. Marie. It's not ideal, but it's worth the price of liberty. There are also some opportunities in the local economy, and certainly our mere presence will demand more. For example, I'm hoping to get a lot of libertarian construction workers to help build all the housing that we'll bring to the area. We looked at places closer to some of the larger towns. The problem was that we couldn't find enough land for sale in those areas. And that's where Haymaker comes in. That's where one of the pros—if not the *biggest* pro—comes into play. There's a tremendous amount of acreage available in Haymaker, some of it scattered throughout the town, in areas along the lake, but a huge section of it is on the southwestern edge of town, butting up against the state forest. This would be the place of our initial large-scale migration. Josef, do you want to talk a little about that?"

"Sure," said Josef. He opened a manila folder and removed a packet of paper. "Obviously many of us, when moving to our Freedom Community, will be looking to find a house with a small yard and a place to raise a family, et cetera. But there aren't enough houses for sale in Haymaker to support all the people who—we hope—will be moving in. So what Gorman and Denny and I have discussed at length is the idea of creating a community within our community, a concentrated area of condominiums on one section of land that could house hundreds of new arrivals. And some people might choose to stay there, but likely, after living in the condos for a year or two, they would find a new vacant house to move into, or look for a place in town to build their own. They'd then leave and make way for another person or family from the outside looking to join us in Haymaker."

Susan smirked. "Let's remember, there will probably be a sudden rise in empty houses after we gain some momentum. Some people who don't want anything to do with us—and we have to realize they're out there—will pack up themselves and get out of town."

"I want to talk about that in a moment," said Gorman. "But first, is our friend Lee Mooneyham there?"

Lee slapped his hands together. "I'm here, Mr. Tate."

"Welcome, my friend. You been hassling any more coppers of late?"

"No, sir."

"Good man. You met with a realtor while you were scouting out Haymaker for us. Tell us about him."

"Yes, sir. I met with Bud Wilmington from North Country Realty. He sounds fairly sympathetic to some of the things we're aiming for. He and his wife even homeschooled their kids."

"You hear that?" asked Gorman. "They homeschooled their kids. Lee, talk a little more about what you found in Haymaker. Give us a sense of the people and their political ideologies."

"Sure. Well, there are some libertarians in Haymaker, like anywhere else. I don't know exact numbers—"

"I've got them," interrupted Josef. "The population of Haymaker is 1,052. Of those people, 589 are registered voters. In the last presidential election, 430 did vote, and of them 219 voted Republican, 194 voted Democratic, and 17 voted Libertarian."

"That may not sound like much," said Lee, "but percentage-wise, that's huge for us, ain't it, Mr. Tate?"

"Compared to the national average? Massive. Keep talking, Mr. Mooneyham."

Lee reached into his back pocket and removed a square of paper, which he unfolded and began referring to. "Well, I spoke with someone else. I was referred by Bud to Tara Lynn Joseph, an accountant in town who is also friends with Kenneth Kline, who ran for governor of Michigan on the Libertarian ticket last election. Anyway, Tara Lynn and I talked some about the 'atmosphere.' She echoed the views of Bud. People in Haymaker, she said, don't like the government in their face. They don't like bureaucracy, they don't like taxes. And here's something I know is rare but I sure wish other places would adopt. The police chief, a guy named Lenny Boston, is an elected official. So if he overreaches, he's out on his ass."

"As it should be," said Gorman. "Go on."

"And get this. There's this guy here who every year has a public fight with someone. I know it sounds nuts, but he has a fight and lots of people come, and he calls it a Shit-Kickin'. And the cops leave it be because of an old court case that allowed such things to happen. It's a thing of beauty."

"Let me step in here," said Josef. "I hate to bring this up—and I wish I hadn't read it—but this is a huge concern."

"Speak your mind," said Gorman.

Josef winced and rubbed his forehead. "I've done some research on this guy. His name's Donnie Sarver. He made national news with this once. The full name of the event is the Welcome Wagon Shit-Kickin'. In other words, his fights are always between himself and some outsider, somebody new to the town." Josef paused and looked around the circle. "Let me say that again. His fights are always between himself and some outsider. This guy may be an exaggeration of the public sentiment, but it's a sentiment that I think you're going to find in Haymaker and every other red, yellow, and green tack on our PIZ map. The places that are the most individualistic are often the places that are most insular. They don't like outsiders because outsiders, no matter who they are, screw up the status quo, no matter what that is."

There was a moment of pause in the War Room, and for the first time that evening, a pause on the other end of the conference phone. But eventually Gorman spoke again. "Let's have Mr. Mooneyham keep talking. There's more to say, and I think it will serve as an antidote for Mr. Sarver and others like him."

Lee's face went serious. "Yes, sir. Well, I asked Tara Lynn Joseph point-blank. I says, 'What would the people of Haymaker do if a few hundred libertarians moved in? How would they react?' And she says to me, 'I'll tell you how they'd react. With open arms.' She said that. 'With open arms.' And she said there's no planning board. It's a thing of beauty, right, Mr. Tate?"

"It is."

"So I went farther. I says, 'How do you think the people would feel about, say, cutting funding for the local school system to make room for charter schools and a more free-market system?' And she says, 'Some of us have already been talking about it.' She says she once even presented a resolution that would make Haymaker a 'U.N.-Free Zone.' It hasn't passed yet or anything, but the idea's out there. She says it's gaining support."

Silence fell over the room again.

"So there you have it," said Gorman. "A low population. No zoning. No planning board or certificate of occupancy. A base of libertarian support. A larger libertarian sentiment. And lots and lots of land for sale. It is, without a doubt, my first choice for our Freedom Community, and I ask that we vote right now on whether or not Haymaker is the place."

"I second that motion," said Lee.

"No you don't," said Susan, whirling in his direction. "You're not a member of the Congress."

"Sorry. I got caught up."

"Then I second it," said Carl. "Let's do this. Let's vote. We've been sitting and planning for two years. People who used to be behind us have drifted away because they thought we were all talk. I want to do this. I want to get going."

"Then we'll vote," said Gorman. "All those in favor of choosing Haymaker as our flagship Freedom Community, raise your hand. Josef, you count the votes. My hand, by the way, is raised."

Josef looked around the circle. Lee lifted his hand—caught up again, it seemed—before quickly putting it back down and letting the Congress do the voting. Carl's hand was already raised, as was Calvin's. Josef raised his, and he waited because he knew what would happen. Denny and Susan reluctantly raised theirs, though he figured they'd have been less reluctant if Gorman were right there in the room to see.

"Do we have our results?"

"It's unanimous," said Josef. "Liberty begins in Haymaker."

Carl let out a loud whoop, and Lee joined in with a piercing whistle. Susan spoke up to put an end to it. "What about the name?" she asked. "Are we still going to vote on our mascot, or whatever you want to call it?"

"I think we should," said Josef. "Now that it's official I need to draft our communication materials, and Carl and I could really use some sort of visual identity for them."

"That's right," said Gorman. "I have the list in front of me. As I recall, we wanted something that stood first and foremost for independence. And these certainly fit the bill. Rattlesnakes. Wolves."

Josef spoke up again, glancing around the circle as he did. "Getting back to the whole Donnie Sarver idea of people perceiving us as a threat. I think the last thing we want to do is call ourselves something as threatening and dangerous as a rattlesnake or a wolf."

"I agree," said Gorman. "Though I like the idea of something that's peaceful by nature, but that, if threatened, stands up and protects itself and its own. That's what we're all about. Our liberties are being trampled, and we're through putting up with it."

"Some of these get to that idea," said Josef. "Cacti, for example. Though we should make it geographically relevant. There aren't many deserts in the U.P."

"Cacti," said Susan. "That's awful."

"Porcupines might work," said Carl.

"It might," said Gorman.

Calvin spoke up. "Gee, why didn't anyone put 'skunks' on the board?"

"I like the Black Bears," said Josef.

"Personally," said Denny, "I find bears a tad threatening."

Though the gut-hook hunting knife lay sheathed inside his duffel bag in the corner of the room, Josef shrugged off Denny's concern. "Grizzly bears, yes." He removed another sheet of paper from his folder. "They're man-eaters. But I did the littlest bit of research. Black bears eat mostly fruit and things. They're independent and individualistic animals. They roam free through huge portions of land. They're certainly not out to get men, but God help someone who stumbles upon a mama bear with her cubs. Then they protect their own, all right."

There was a stretch of silence.

"Plus," continued Josef, "they're native to the region. Geographically relevant."

"I'm sold," said Gorman. "Not too cutesy. Will make a good logo. All in favor, raise your hand."

The circle spoke; all hands rose.

"It's unanimous on this end," said Josef.

"As it is over here," said Gorman. "We are officially the Freedom Community Black Bears."

"In a fight, who would win," asked Lee, "a husky or a black bear?"

"Definitely the black bear," said Carl.

"Unless there was a whole pack of huskies," said Susan.

Gorman spoke up again. "Let's move to action steps. The first thing is for all of you to continue to do your jobs, but to now do them with your aim on Haymaker. Josef, the biggest point of action is with you because our next step, more than anything, is to spread the word like new age apostles. We have our mailing lists. We have our e-mail contacts. Let's tell the libertarian world that we're moving to Haymaker. Our job is to start writing and producing marketing pieces for these people. Tell them the reasons why we chose this place—the reasons we've discussed today. Create a pamphlet or brochure or some such thing and share the story. And then—and this is the important second half of your mission—really get a sense of the public sentiment up there, because your prediction is probably correct. There will be people who are set in their ways and resistant to change, even a liberating one. So get a sense of how you can communicate our message to the Haymakes as well. I don't want to call it crisis management, but there, I guess I just did."

Lee raised his hand to speak. "I thought of someone you should talk to," he said. "This guy seems to know both sides of the fence—the insiders and the outsiders. I'll give you his contact info. You should see this guy. He's nuts, but he's great."

Josef nodded. Already the words and phrases were forming in his head, already he was imagining this place as home.

"That's all for now," said Gorman. "Class dismissed."

« HAYMAKER AT A GLANCE »

Overview

◆ *Haymaker is a peaceful and charming town in Michigan's Upper Peninsula that time has not forgotten, but rather protected, allowing its ruggedly independent populace to live freely in nature, in a community, and in the privacy of their own homes. Nestled between the towering White Sable Dunes, lush forests, and the picturesque shore of Lake Superior, Haymaker truly is a place of beauty and wonder. But just a short drive from these sandy beaches and dense woodlands runs Marquette Street, which could just as well be named Main Street for the way it harks back to a time of traditional American quaintness. With a population of approximately 1,000, Haymaker is both large enough for fellowship but small enough for those looking to make it a home . . . and to make a difference.*

You've known for years that the Freedom Community has been seeking its flagship town. Well, we've finally found the place where the self-evident truths of personal liberty can take root, growing and prospering to create the America our Founding Fathers intended.

Now we welcome you to learn more about our decision and how you can make history with us.

Chapter 9

Saturday, September 6

Ash could hear the axes biting into the wood from three blocks away. By his flinching and the turning of his head, she knew Patrick John could, too.

She had to babysit him all day—again—despite Uncle Donnie's big fight. Despite her mom's promise that she'd have more time to herself once school began. Ash shifted him from one hip to the other, struggling with the backpack that hung from her shoulders. "You're getting to be a little hoss," she said and then kissed his fat cheek. She rarely carried him around like this anymore, but she didn't want to bother with the mammoth stroller this weekend. Marquette Street was full of people, packed—as Uncle Donnie would say—elbow to asshole.

Orange pylons blocked cars and trucks from entering. For two blocks—and for the entire Boomtown Days weekend—this stretch of downtown was for pedestrians only. There was little concern about disrupting tourists. The celebration was purposely held every year on the first weekend after Labor Day. Most tourists had returned home now, below the bridge, and despite the crucial economic benefits, most Haymakes preferred it this way.

The result was a festival atmosphere, a miniature Bourbon Street. People moved freely between T's Pizza, The Venison, and Parson Park. The town had no open-air drinking ban, and so now, at ten forty-five in the morning, men and women walked under the surprisingly warm sun holding large plastic cups of The Venison's microbrews. And they walked below the marquee of the old Neptune Theater, which read, on one side:

"IN HEAVEN, EVERY DAY IS A BOOM DAY"
SERMON BY REV. BERNARD ZUBER
SUNDAY—9 AM

On the other:

FOR FAST RELIEF, TAKE TWO TABLETS

Patio furniture with bright-orange umbrellas lined a section of the sidewalk, and the people lounging there talked loudly and hooted with laughter. A man with a bald head and shaggy black beard slouched before a microphone with an amp and guitar, singing old Waylon Jennings songs. Behind him, lining both sides of the street, stood tall, half-finished log sculptures—bears and eagles and owls emerging from the wood—as chain saw artists demonstrated their talents all weekend.

Ash walked past the singer and through a throng of partiers. Patrick John twisted and turned in her arms, taking it all in. "You want to see the lumberjacks?" she asked him. "Look at you, with these chubby arms. You want to chop some wood yourself?"

They crossed the street and broke free from the claustrophobia, pausing at a stretch of grass beside the statue of Frederick Parson. Earl Henneman wasn't sitting at his usual bench, guarding his post. Two little boys climbed over Frederick's bronze back and shoulders. The crowd thickened again as Ash and Patrick John walked on toward the concession stands, bleachers, and the white band shell where a man Ash could not yet see barked to a cheering audience. *"Ladies and gentlemen, lads and lasses, shantyboys, barons, and all the creatures of the forest, the stage is set, the axes are sharpened, and we are about to begin the second round—the final four—of the Jack and Jill crosscut competition!"*

A man and a woman with numbers pinned to their shirts grabbed hold of opposite ends of a huge saw. They approached a log set up horizontally at hip level. Someone sounded an air horn, and the couple began fluidly slicing through the wood in quick strokes. The crowd's cheers seemed to spill out of the park as the couple sawed through and the end of the log fell to the stage. *"Twenty-eight point two-three seconds for Mr. Ron Gladden and Ms.—I'm sorry, Mrs.—Irene Mumphrey."*

Ash cheered, though she preferred the climbing competitions, when men with spurred climbers and steel-core climbing ropes ascended sixty-foot cedar poles erected beside the stage. The axe-throwing wasn't bad either.

She looked at her watch. "Oh crap, P.J., we have to go see Mom." It was almost eleven. At noon—high noon—Ash had to be at the gravel pits. She switched him to her other hip and slowly pressed back through the park and the people, across the closed-off section of road, and through the front doors of The 12 Months of Christmas. "Don't touch anything," she said to Patrick John, who was playing with a strand of blonde hair that had come free from her cornrows.

Betty Mead, in a white sweater and red turtleneck, balanced on a stepladder, hanging mistletoe above the cash register. Denise stepped quickly out from behind the counter when she saw them approaching. "Hey. What's up?" She cupped Ash's elbow in her hand and moved her to a far corner. "Betty's in a mood," Denise whispered. "She's stroking out because of all the drunks wandering in this morning. She mentioned maybe closing early today, which would mean less pay, which means I don't want her bad mood any worse."

"We won't stay. It's just that I don't know what to do."

"About what?"

"I promised Uncle Donnie."

Creases surfaced on Denise's brow. "Promised what? About the fight?"

"I promised him I'd go." She had to lie now. "I don't want to."

"And you shouldn't," said Denise. "It's bloody and barbaric."

"Blood doesn't bother me," said Ash. "Neither does Uncle Donnie looking like a fool and acting all crazy." She paused before speaking again. "But he said if I came to the fight, he'd give us free oil changes for a year."

Denise cocked her head. "He said that?"

Ash nodded. He *had* said that, though Ash hadn't planned on mentioning it. It was charity, and it was a bribe. She didn't like people in a family bribing each other. Plus, he'd gone to all of her junior high basketball games. It was her turn to cheer for him.

Patrick John grew heavy in her arms. The straps of the backpack dug into her skin. "Can you take him for a minute?"

"No," said Denise. She looked over her shoulder. "Take him back outside with you."

"I will. But I need someone to take care of him so I can go to the fight. It's at the gravel pits."

"The gravel pits?" Denise shook her head, looked at the floor, and mumbled, "Idiot."

Neither spoke for a stretch. Carols flowed through the speakers overhead. "Do you know anyone who can watch him?" asked Ash. "It's just for, like, an hour. I have to go home and get my bike and ride over there."

"Look, Linda's in the stockroom taking inventory. She takes her lunch at twelve and always goes gaga over Patrick John. I'm sure she'd watch him for an hour."

"But I need to leave before that. The fights don't last long."

"Then find someone who can watch him for those fifteen or twenty minutes until Linda can."

Ash shook her head, walked across the room, and opened the door to the outside.

"And put some sunscreen on him," said Denise.

Country music poured in from the street, mingling with the in-store rendition of "Silver Bells." "Good-bye now!" called Betty from the ladder.

"Merry Christmas," said Ash as the door closed behind her. She crossed back to the park with Patrick John squirming and fussing in her arms. Then she sat on Earl's empty bench. The little boys were gone. She sat Patrick John down on the soft grass at her feet. The sun shone right into his eyes, and he began to cry. Ash slid a few inches down the bench, her shadow draping over his face and calming him as he blinked away the last tears. After slipping the backpack off her shoulders, she removed a baby-bottle cooler, unzipped it, and pulled out a cold bottle of formula.

"You thirsty, hoss?" She scooped him out of the grass and cradled him against her left arm so that he was still shaded from the sun. He grabbed the bottle and plunged it into his mouth. As he drank, Ash squirted sunscreen on her palm and applied it to his face and limbs. Then she glanced at her watch and shook her head. It was quarter past eleven. She'd never make it. She thought about when Uncle Donnie had invited her, the look on his face, how it was happy and sad all at once.

Out of the edge of her eye Ash noticed a tall, thin, and strikingly white figure sit down on the neighboring bench. Roosevelt Bly looked over, smiled, then gave a little wink to Patrick John with an accompanying "bang-bang" pistol hand gesture. Like everyone in Haymaker, Ash knew some things about the man, but not a whole lot. Her mom had once worked for him, and though Ash didn't believe them, she'd heard those same rumors about his wealth, his dead wife, and the young women he was known to court. She felt nervous with him nearby. He was sort of a local celebrity, like Mayor Hollingshead or Dominick Murphy, the basketball star.

"Good afternoon," he said.

"Good morning," she replied.

"So it is. I'd forgotten, what with the music and the revelry and all."

Ash nodded, looked down at Patrick John, and then over at Roosevelt again. "It's too busy today for the stroller."

Roosevelt sat with his legs crossed at the knees. Most men, she'd noticed, crossed at the ankle. He creased his brow. "What's that?"

"I usually take him out in the stroller you bought us," said Ash, "but the crowd's too big, so I'm just holding him today."

The confusion slowly left his face, and he smiled and nodded slightly. "I don't blame you one bit. And no worries. I've seen you using it plenty of times."

"You have?"

"Sure. All summer long. Pushing him around town. And down by the beach."

"I'm not supposed to take him all the way to the beach," she said. "Even though he likes it. He likes the feel of the sand on his bare feet."

Roosevelt nodded again. "I know I do."

Ash glanced at his shiny white cowboy boots with their pointed tips. She couldn't imagine the sight of his feet but figured they were as white as the boots themselves.

"Been watching the lumberjack show?" he asked.

She shrugged. "Just a little. I'm supposed to be at the gravel pits soon, but I don't think I'll make it." She picked at the little cuts on her fingertips that were still healing from the summer months of outdoor basketball.

"What's at the gravel pits? Oh, wait. The brouhaha?"

"The what?" she asked.

"Donnie Sarver's fight?"

"Yeah. I told him I'd come." She hesitated before continuing. "He's my uncle."

"That's right," said Roosevelt, "he *is* your uncle. Oh, that Donnie's a character and a half. I often drink with him at Rusty's, though it would be a stretch to say that there's a social contract of any sort. He doesn't seem to like people."

Ash's eyes narrowed. "He likes certain people."

"I considered watching it one year," said Roosevelt, "but it's not my style. I'm pretty nonviolent, you could say. Wasn't drafted during the Korean War because of the rheumatic fever I'd had growing up. In all my years, I've never been in a single fistfight." He uncrossed his legs and leaned toward her. "And I'll be eighty years old on Thanksgiving. Forget the turkey. I'll be the old bird at that table setting."

She smiled and subtly looked at her watch. It was eleven thirty.

"So you won't get to see your uncle draw blood," said Roosevelt. "That's a real shame. Your mom won't let you see it?"

"She will. But there's no one to watch my brother from now until noon."

"Oh no?" He smiled broadly and squinted out at the crowd. "Maybe I could help."

Ash stiffened and said nothing.

"I miss little ones," said Roosevelt. "I myself have two daughters. Getting to be pretty old themselves. I don't get to see my grandchildren much, though. One family lives in Boise and the other in Denver. I have two granddaughters, one grandson, and one great-grandson, who's two." He shook his head slightly. "I've never met him."

Ash relaxed, waiting for him to continue, though he didn't. Finally she spoke. "That sucks."

"It does suck." He looked at her and smiled once more. "Did you know your mother once worked for me?"

She nodded. "But I don't know what kind of work."

"When she was about twenty or twenty-one years old. She answered an ad I'd put in the *Star-Picayune* for an assistant. For some reason I felt like I needed someone to help me with my mail and my bills and to manage the people who were coming over all the time to renovate my house—my place on the lake. It was a silly idea. There wasn't enough for her to do, and eventually I had to let her go. No complaints about her work ethic, though." He gave a little nod toward the street. "She still have her job at the Christmas store there?"

"Yeah."

"That must be strange, working there on a warm, sunny day. Or even in February, for that matter. I only set foot in there in December. The rest of the year the mere sight of the place makes me sad. I can't explain it."

Ash had never considered this, that adults—even old men—could be saddened by such things, the way she got sad at the sight of bent basketball rims with no nets, or little kids on recess playgrounds, standing off by themselves.

"Will you do me a favor?" asked Roosevelt.

Ash nodded. Now that he'd said this, about his sadness, she knew that she would.

"Will you ask your mother if I can look after the little boy for a half hour? I'll be right here on the bench with him. She can watch me through the window if she likes."

Ash nodded again. It was eleven thirty-five. At eleven forty, her mom relented while looking out the window at Roosevelt sitting there alone on the bench. By eleven forty-three Patrick John rested in the old man's arms—it was barely a fifteen-minute babysitting job by this point. And by eleven fifty Ash was pushing her bike out of her garage, hopping onto the seat, and pedaling furiously down Cooper Avenue, toward the dirt roads and gravel pits.

« HAYMAKER AT A GLANCE »
Its History

◆ *Don't be confused by the name. The land in and around Haymaker has never made much in the way of hay—or other agriculture, for that matter—though its original settlers had hoped otherwise.*

Ezekiel Harrison, a third-generation farmer from northern Ohio, received a large inheritance from a distant East Coast uncle and purchased ten thousand acres from the Schoolcraft Land and Lumber Company—sight unseen—in 1871. The company had assured Mr. Harrison that over half of the land was without forest, and they were true to their word. Much was swamp. The rest was sand. And the length of the crop-growing season paled in comparison to the long winters.

But redemption came in the form of that same Schoolcraft Lumber Company when, in 1877, it built a mill on the banks of Oslo Creek. Soon lumberjacks poured into Haymaker, erecting shantytowns, working long hours, and drinking away their money and their nights. But, over the years, many of these wild men settled down, built permanent houses, and started families. They lived close to the land and respected the rights of their neighbors. Lumber became king of the local economy, and Haymaker trees helped build new cities throughout the Midwest and rebuild Chicago after the Great Fire.

The lumber industry fell on hard times in the mid-1900s, but the resourceful Haymakes (as residents call themselves) soon transformed the town into a mecca for tourists and outdoor enthusiasts.

Haymaker continues to evolve, its history a series of stories bringing us to the present day. And now a new breed of freedom-loving people aim to not only make this place their home, but to make their own history.

Chapter 10

Saturday, September 6

Josef, again, had done his research.

In 1941, a commercial fisherman named Pete Czolgosz—grandson of Leon Czolgosz, the northern Michigan native and anarchist who'd assassinated President McKinley—had lunged into an argument. His foe had been a young Civilian Conservation Corps worker named Harry "Ham Hock" O'Donnell who was a member of the outfit in Seney assigned to plant aquatic foliage for a wildlife refuge. The argument centered on the inaccurate retelling of the day's Tigers-Yankees game, which had played over the radio. Both men were drunk and seated around the bar at the place that would one day be called Rusty's. Czolgosz threw a beer bottle and missed. Ham Hock grabbed a peavey handle off the wall and began swinging it like a bat, though he missed as well. The two shoved each other and grabbed fistfuls of each other's shirt collars before stumbling outside to continue the fight. Czolgosz had a pair of extremely long thumbnails, which he used to slice up Ham Hock's face. The young CCC worker returned the favor by landing one wild but powerful fist to Czolgosz's temple, knocking him unconscious. By the time his blurred vision improved, Czolgosz was in the county jail, looking through a set of bars to where Ham Hock sat in the adjacent cell.

Had all this happened a generation or two earlier, the fight would have led to no more than a blurb in the local papers. But the wild lumber days of Seney, Newberry, and Haymaker were relics by then, as were the gamblers, prostitutes, and miscellaneous roughnecks who'd lived through them. The Luce County sheriff in 1941, Frank Huggler, decided to make an example of the two to ensure no return to the rowdy past. But during the trial Ham Hock's lawyer, a recent Ann Arbor graduate named Lou Smith, unearthed an old law on the Haymaker books that allowed for "the physical defense of an individual and the defense of his family, property, or honor." Witnesses in the bar testified that each man had felt slighted by the remarks of the other and that the fight was begun "in unison." It was, Smith argued, "a noble sort of duel, though far less violent than what men in France had engaged in a century prior." The vagueness of the term "honor" led to the successful acquittal of both men, as well as a handful of others over the ensuing decades.

A few years ago, a writer from a men's magazine made mention of the law. The article was supposed to describe fishing in the Two Hearted River, but instead it focused on a local who'd begun exploiting that law, creating an annual town spectacle in the process. That local was Donnie Sarver.

Josef had researched this, too. And now he'd come to witness it. From the Freedom Community's point of view, Donnie was a double-edged sword. He literally fought to keep outsiders like them from settling in the town. But Josef would admit that, despite the potential trouble a man like Donnie could cause for them, this law had gone a long way toward pushing Haymaker to green-tack status on the PIZ map. It allowed consenting adults to settle their disputes in an agreed-upon—albeit violent—fashion. The town's history of gambling, prostitution, and other victimless crimes hadn't hurt either.

From his research Josef also learned that the "Welcome Wagon Shit-Kickin'," as it was known, was held every year—at high noon, of course—during the Saturday of Boomtown Days. The location, however, always changed. It seemed Donnie continually sought new backdrops for the event, to add to the drama. Last year it had taken place on a rocky path along Oslo Falls. The year before near the abandoned paper mill. Once Donnie had held it in Rusty's parking lot, as a sort of homage to the Czolgosz-O'Donnell brawl that had made all this possible. But Josef's favorite detail was this: the Haymaker police actually oversaw the spectacle.

When Mayor Hollingshead came into office, she'd put an end to any Shit-Kickin' promotional materials affixed to public property, so it had taken Josef two days to discover the location for this year's fight. Luckily, he overheard a group of men discussing it at the 3-F, because it wasn't the type of thing he wanted to go around asking about. That could call attention to oneself—to the fact that one was an outsider. The kind of person asking for his shit to be kicked.

◆ ◆ ◆

Donnie had begun the whole thing seven years ago, as a response to the influx of newcomers moving into town. Many were wealthy retirees building huge summer homes on a small stretch of beach. Donnie referred to them as "illegal aliens" and "flatlanders," a term he used for anyone from the Lower Peninsula. He'd posted bright orange signs on lampposts and telephone poles throughout the town:

ATTENTION FLATLANDERS, ALIENS, APPLE-KNOCKERS,
LOPERS, AND TROLLS:

ANY AND ALL PERSONS NOW
LIVING IN OR OWNING PROPERTY
IN HAYMAKER WHO HAVE MOVED
HERE IN THE PAST YEAR AND
WERE NOT BORN IN THE U.P., HEAR THIS.

YOU ARE NOT WELCOME!!!

DONNIE SARVER
HEREBY ISSUES A CHALLENGE.
ANY OUTSIDER WHO WISHES TO
END THIS AND ALL FUTURE AND
INEVITABLE CHALLENGES,
MEET HIM SATURDAY AT HIGH NOON
IN THE PARKING LOT OF GASSY CHARLIE'S.

THE WINNER WILL BE THE ONE STILL STANDING.

* NO WEAPONS OF ANY KIND, NOR PADS, HELMETS, ETC. *

Donnie hadn't expected anyone to show, especially since the retirees were mostly over sixty-five. But a Wisconsin man in his late thirties named T.J. Ferguson, who'd purchased a hunting cabin on the edge of town, got drunk that Friday night at Rusty's and assured everyone in the bar he'd be there, "without pads, helmet, or fear."

Ferguson outweighed Donnie by close to fifty pounds, but he threw such slow punches that even the old men in attendance could telegraph his attacks. Donnie, on the other hand, had twenty-three black hash marks—like the tallies of a world-war flying ace—tattooed on the skin over his ribs: one for every fight he'd ever won. And he'd never lost. In combat as in conversation, he was quick and mean. He snapped three jabs with his left fist, dropping Ferguson to one knee. The final right hook was more for show, merely hastening Ferguson's fall. In terms of both might and showmanship, the punch was a success, and a similar face-off occurred every year afterward between Donnie and some fresh meat.

Josef arrived at the fight a little before noon, rattling along a dirt road before passing the orange sign of the gravel pits. The entrance gate was shut and locked with a chain, but just to the side were faint tire tracks running through a dry brown field. Josef followed them, entering a kind of lunar landscape: craters and dust and huge piles of rock and sand. One pile towered over a group of maybe twenty-five people, who stood in a half circle, waiting. A number were the kind of rough-looking men Josef had expected—bearded and broad-shouldered and grim—though a few looked like they could be headed for a round of golf. A couple of women and boys were sprinkled in, too, as well as one girl with blonde cornrows who was sweating and trying to catch her breath. She looked familiar.

Though he'd never even seen a picture of him, Josef spotted Donnie right away. He stood about thirty yards in the distance, his back to the crowd, his shirt off, and his tattoos giving his flesh the appearance of snakeskin. Another man—obviously the opponent—jogged and hopped in place like a boxer still wearing his robe. He looked to be over six feet tall, with a slight paunch but wide shoulders and a thick chest. He wore dusty jeans and a red sleeveless T-shirt that was darkened with sweat.

Josef parked and walked toward the crowd. Then he stepped discreetly beside a boy in his early teens who was chewing sunflower seeds and excitedly spitting out the husks. Josef spoke in a low voice "Do you know anything about his opponent?"

The boy shrugged. "He's just some guy. A snowmobiler who moved up here for the trails." He laughed to himself.

"What's so funny?"

The boy spat another husk. "Donnie hates guys like this. Snowmobilers can visit in the winter and spend money at his shop on parts and oil and crap—that's all cool. But he hates the dopes who decide to come up here for good. This guy's toast."

Donnie squinted up at the sun and then turned and walked toward the crowd. "Mr. Ray Valentine," he called out, "what is the time?"

A stocky, bearded man pulled free from the crowd. He wore a short-sleeve work shirt from Sarver Towing and Repair, with RAY embroidered over his heart. He smiled as he addressed them all. "I believe it's high noon! Time for a Shit-Kickin'!"

And with that, the crowd—which had stood in reverence as if in a chapel —roared its approval. One man let out a high-pitched whistle that made the blonde girl plug her ears.

"Well, then," said Donnie, smiling and hamming it up in a way Josef would've never expected from him, "let me haul out the old Welcome Wagon. You, sir," he said, pointing to his opponent, who continued to shadowbox, "state your name, where you live, and most importantly, where you're originally from."

The man stood still momentarily before taking a large, defiant step toward Donnie. "I'm Erik Schwartz, you rancid fuck. You know that, 'cause in January I beat your ass in the snowmobile race. I'm from Toledo, but now I live in Germfask. I could have lived in Haymaker, but I'd have needed too many vaccinations, you disease-ridden sack of shit."

Most everyone let out an extended, "Ooh," though a few men cheered and shouted things like, "That's right, baby!" They were friends of the opponent.

"You heard right, ladies and gentlemen," said Donnie. "I'm sad to say that, for the first time ever, nobody from our quaint little town took up my offer, so I had to extend the reach of the Welcome Wagon this year to include anyone from the surrounding counties."

"Shut your nut-sucking mouth," said Schwartz. "Let's go."

Donnie surveyed the area. "Fuck," he muttered, "where is she?"

"Late," said Ray. "So I'll state the rules before she arrives." Ray's smile dissipated as he surveyed the audience. "This is a duel of one-on-one fisticuffs. It is, in this framework, completely legal within the town limits of Haymaker. It becomes immediately illegal, however, if any foreign object is used. That means the obvious, like guns and knives, but it also means these rocks, or even a handful of dirt in the eye. Second, it becomes illegal if anyone—anyone—steps into the melee to help either party. Don't even step between them to break it up. You think someone's getting seriously injured, that's what Doc Brewer is here for." Dr. Brewer, a handsome elderly man with sharply parted silver hair, held a white towel and waved to everyone. "He can call the match, though I know we'd all prefer he didn't unless absolutely necessary. And last but not least, no wagering. It'd be a fool's bet anyways."

A tension pain rose up through Josef's back and neck. He'd never been in a fight himself and had only witnessed two in his life, both while in college—frat boys at bars sloppily tugging, rolling, and missing punches.

Gravel crunched beneath the tires of an approaching powder-blue police cruiser. The officer parked and got out, and a jolt of adrenaline struck Josef's chest. He recognized her from Lee's photographs.

"Donnie!" she yelled as she approached. "You told me you had permission to hold the fight here!"

"I do."

"Why's the gate closed?"

"Wanted to give it that underground feel, Sergeant DeBoer. It's bad enough I got the endorsement of the local authorities."

"You don't have our endorsement," she said, coming to a stop beside Dr. Brewer. "You know what you can do and what you can't." She looked at the crowd. "So does everyone else. If you do what you can't, you go to jail."

Donnie smiled. "Well now, I think we're finally ready." He raised his fists, flexed his upper body, and stared at his opponent. "You ready, mud hen?"

Schwartz spat. "Ready to make you cemetery-dead."

"You hear that, Officer? We're a-ready to go."

Josef and the rest of the crowd took a few steps forward, slightly closing in on the two men. Ray stepped between the fighters with his right hand raised. Everyone fell silent. He glanced at Donnie, then at Schwartz. "Commence!" he yelled and dropped his arm.

Schwartz charged Donnie and grabbed his head, pushing it down with two fistfuls of hair. He was faster than he looked. Then, with his right hand, he pounded down on the back of Donnie's neck. Donnie fell to his right knee, seemingly dazed, but he was actually stooping toward Schwartz's midsection, wrapping his arms around his waist in order to lift him up off his feet and tackle him onto his back. Dust clouded out from beneath their two bodies.

This was not what Josef had imagined. The punches were not clean. They did not snap when they connected. It reminded him of the frat boys.

Donnie managed to pull his head free from Schwartz's grip, a bright bald spot now on his head, a dark tuft of hair in Schwartz's hand. Schwartz rolled over in the dirt and began to stand. And then Donnie took command of the fight, grasping Schwartz's head and shoving it downward. Schwartz threw a series of punches into Donnie's tattooed ribs and kidneys, but they were only glancing blows. Donnie planted his left knee in the dirt for balance and then unleashed a series of strikes with his right knee, clean shots right to Schwartz's head and face. They came one after another, knee after knee, until someone in the crowd—maybe Dr. Brewer—shouted, "He's limp!" and Donnie quickly released his hold, withdrawing into a crouched position. Erik Schwartz, the snowmobiler from Toledo, slumped forward, his eyes glazed and his head rolling into the dirt.

Ray leapt into the arena. "Your winner and still Welcome Wagon Shit-Kickin' champion of Haymaker, Donnie Sarver!"

People cheered, a few approaching Donnie to see if he was okay. But he was already smiling and raising his arms in victory. Schwartz's friends, along with Dr. Brewer and Sergeant DeBoer, checked to ensure that the defeated was all right. His left eye had already swelled shut, and a knot on his forehead protruded so high it looked sickly, like something out of a cartoon. Donnie joined the group in assisting Schwartz to his feet before patting him on the back and saying loud enough for most everyone to hear, "Welcome to da U.P.!" Then he looked at Schwartz's friends. "Next year ain't booked yet if any of you are interested."

Josef stared, absorbing all of this, fascinated by the swelling on Schwartz's face, fascinated by the smile on Donnie's. He didn't realize that the crowd around him had already dissipated, and he stood a little off on his own.

Donnie thanked Dr. Brewer and tipped an imaginary hat to Sergeant DeBoer. Then he walked off by himself, gently rubbing his right side, which looked red and ready to bruise. Josef didn't realize he was staring until Donnie shot him a look in return, smiling and nodding before saying, "Thanks for coming. Hope to see you here again." Then Donnie approached his Silverado and grabbed a can of beer from a cooler in the back.

Afterward, while driving to the apartment above The 12 Months of Christmas, Josef tried to remember his own reaction at that moment. What was the expression on his face? What was his body language? How tight were the fists of his own two hands?

« HAYMAKER AT A GLANCE »

Its People

◆ *Perhaps more than any other reason, we've chosen Haymaker, Michigan, as the site for our first Freedom Community because of its people.*

Haymakes enjoy their elbow room, and they enjoy the right to live how they see fit. But they do this without slipping into reclusiveness. They respect their neighbor, their neighbor's choices, and their neighbor's property. Yet they still reach out to lend a hand, greet a handshake, or to join forces to defend their mutual inalienable rights.

These are not a soft people. As you drive into town you'll see a sign that reads HAYMAKER: RISEN FROM SAWDUST AND SWEAT. They come from hardy stock: lumberjacks, sailors, fishermen, and miners. They put the "rugged" in "rugged individualism."

Yet they're also friendly, helpful, and (most importantly for us) welcoming—a populace steeped in libertarianism even if it doesn't fully know it. We believe we will blend in with the existing community, and we believe they will blend in with our Freedom Community.

Chapter 11

Saturday, September 6

Ross Road twisted and climbed through trees before dead-ending on the top of a hill where the sky opened up. Josef steered slowly, his nerves still a bit rattled from the fight at the gravel pits. He'd recently bought a cheap bed and TV for his place, and he'd spent the rest of the afternoon lying around with his shirt off watching college football. The afternoon had grown unseasonably warm and humid, and War Room North was low on luxuries like air-conditioning.

At the top of the hill stood two houses unlike anything else in the town: spectacular Victorian mansions gracing the vista with arches and turrets and intricate paint designs that included about a dozen colors: dark greens and reds and yellows, black and brown and violet. The sight of them, after emerging from the shade-filled forest, made Josef think of make-believe. He felt especially far from home.

The two houses were fraternal twins, not identical. The first was a bit larger but boxier and simpler. Its grass had succumbed to weeds. A FOR SALE sign stood in the front lawn. The second house, about fifty yards farther down the road, was full of life. The colors in its stained glass were mimicked below by mums, dahlias, and sunflowers. Josef parked in the drive, behind a white Lincoln Town Car and beside a lovely barn that had been designed to reflect the Victorian look of the house. He stepped out and approached the front door. The air had cooled, and he took a deep breath. Lee Mooneyham had told him this man was nothing to worry about.

As Josef stepped onto the front porch, he could further appreciate the place. The steps and railings displayed little carved images of trees and animal faces. The front entrance was adorned with carved triangular patterns and a window shaped like a setting sun over waves, the rays tinted orange and reaching to the ends of the door.

It opened before he could knock. Though the light that framed him was dim, the man standing before Josef shone in white and gold like that same setting sun. A white hat crowned his head. "You must be Novak of the Indiana Novaks," said Roosevelt, smiling brilliantly and extending his hand for a shake. "Welcome to my home, good sir."

"Thank you for having me," said Josef, shaking hands and smiling back. Lee's description of the man had seemed so over the top—so cartoonish—that Josef had believed it was more tall tale than truth. But in this first instance—with this first handshake—he was put instantly at ease by a man who was so clearly at ease himself.

"Why don't you come inside and take a load off," said Roosevelt with a wink and a "bang-bang" pistol hand gesture. He closed the door and led Josef into the foyer. "Give your eyes a moment to adjust from the light. The place might seem like a catacomb at first."

It did. But when his eyes adjusted, Josef realized that the house's exterior was almost drab by comparison. The stained glass caught the waning sun, spilling red, green, and blue over the floor like watercolors. The ceilings were hand-painted at the edges, where baby-blue patterns snaked from corner to corner in pretty vines. But most fascinating was the wood—archways and mantels and handrails—all alive with carved animals, some of them tame little woodland creatures, but others spawned from magic: dragons and mermaids.

"My God, Mr. Bly. You should charge admission."

"First, call me Roosevelt. Second, you are very kind, but charging friends would be less than hospitable." He moseyed down the hallway, and Josef followed, his head oscillating. "And speaking of being inhospitable," said Roosevelt, "I have absolutely failed you in terms of dinner. All of a sudden an hour ago I look up from the book I'm reading and see the clock and realize that any chance of making something worthwhile had passed me by."

"It's okay," said Josef, "I've already eaten," by which he meant a bag of tortilla chips and two cans of light beer.

They entered a wood-paneled room at the back of the house lined with bookshelves except for the north wall, which was mostly glass, the view opening up to dune and beach and then Superior, which went on forever.

"I can't believe that houses like this actually exist."

"Have a seat," said Roosevelt. "Let me make us some drinks. I have a bar here in the corner. Imagine if all libraries had this. Imagine the renewed love of books." He began to make himself a cocktail at a fully stocked bar cart. "What are you drinking?"

Josef was barely listening. He was looking at the lake and, to the west, the glimmering White Sable Dunes. "Any whiskey is fine. A little ice."

He sat in one of the two leather chairs that faced the lake. An end table stood between them. Roosevelt handed him his drink, sat down beside him, and crossed his legs at the knees. "Cheers," he said, raising his glass a few inches.

"Cheers." Josef sipped, still looking out at the lake. "You must have fun up here on the hill."

"Every day," said Roosevelt.

The two looked silently out on the lake for a few moments before Josef said, "I didn't realize how different it was compared to Lake Michigan. I can't tell what it is, though."

"Neither can I, but I know what you mean. Whether it's because it's colder or cleaner or deeper, I don't know, but it does look more alive than the other four."

The two of them sat silently again, in a comfortable silence Josef usually only experienced with Jeanie. He had never met Roosevelt until now and had only spoken to him once on the phone—briefly, a few weeks earlier. He loved the sound of the man's voice. "What's the history of this place, Roosevelt? And the place next door?"

Roosevelt reached into his breast pocket. "Mind if I smoke?"

Josef shook his head, and Roosevelt removed the cellophane from a cigarillo.

"That a Cuban?" asked Josef with a smile.

Roosevelt smiled, too, the cigarillo tucked into the corner of his mouth. "Got it at the 3-F this morning. At the counter where they sell the lottery tickets. I am a connoisseur of many things, but sadly, tobacco is not one of them. But I enjoy their peculiar taste." He lit it and began to slowly puff. "But to answer your question, this place is called the Schoolcraft House, as it was originally built by David S. Hopkins of Grand Rapids for a Mr. Thaddeus J. Schoolcraft between 1887 and 1889."

"You've got this down."

"I do." Roosevelt reclined and blew smoke toward the ceiling. "Schoolcraft was one of your old-time lumber barons. No doubt a smoker of truly fine cigars. He'd founded the Huron Land and Logging Company and made this his summer dwelling. The place next door was the house of his partner, Henry Pullman Smith. And this here place became the home of Roosevelt Ulysses Bly thirty years ago, though I didn't get serious about fixing up the place until much later."

"Well, it's amazing now."

"The one next door's available," said Roosevelt. "We could be neighbors."

"Little rich for my blood."

Roosevelt smiled. "It's not much of a seller's market up here in Haymaker when it comes to lumber baron homes designed in the Queen Anne style."

"How long's it been vacant?"

"Seems like as long as I've lived here."

"And that's been thirty years, you said?"

"I did. Thirty years. Blink of an eye."

Josef turned to scan the bookshelves to his left. He nodded at a picture frame. "That your family?"

Roosevelt continued looking out at the lake. "It is. My daughters and their families."

"Do you see them much?"

Roosevelt sipped his cocktail, frowning through the glass and shaking his head. "No," he said as he set it down, "but I do get phone calls. On the first of every month. One calls me at about six o'clock and the other at eight." He leaned toward Josef. "Why, it's the most remarkable thing, Mr. Novak. It's as if they have it written on their calendars, something to check on a to-do list. But that surely couldn't be the case now, could it?"

Josef shrugged, not knowing what to say.

"Please forgive me," said Roosevelt, reclining again. "I sort of broke the fourth wall there."

Josef swirled the ice cubes of his now-empty tumbler.

"Let me freshen that up for you." Roosevelt took it from him and headed for the bar.

"I'm sorry. I don't normally drink so fast."

"I don't normally drink so slowly," said Roosevelt, returning with more whiskey. "I need to stop gabbing so much. I just enjoy company so." He settled back in his chair. "Now, where were we again?"

"Thirty years."

"My God, so it's been."

"Where are you from originally?"

"Wyoming," said Roosevelt.

"There's a state with some federal lands."

"Lived most of my life carrying on the family trade of raising livestock."

"How was that?" asked Josef.

Roosevelt pinched both of the lapels on his white suit and ran his fingers up and down the fabric. "Does it look like that was my cup of tea?"

"No, sir."

"Right you are. And my wife, Eileen, she didn't want me involved in that rough-and-tumble work. I opened a five-and-dime for a while but was just as poor of a shopkeeper as a cowboy. Yet I ended up back in ranching out of necessity."

Josef took several deep sips. Orange light reflected off the water from the west, out of view. "So how did you end up here?"

Roosevelt exhaled his smoke with a sigh. He was seventy-nine years old, but this was the first moment when Josef thought he looked his age. "I first came to the U.P. as a boy to visit my older brother, who was a member of the Civilian Conservation Corps. He loved the area and stayed. Lived most of his life in the west part of the peninsula. Iron Mountain."

"So what brought you back here for good?"

"My Eileen died." Roosevelt didn't flinch as he said it. "Thirty-one years ago. Pancreatic cancer. We got married when we were eighteen, and she and Wyoming had been my life for so long. But when she died, I couldn't stand looking at the place. Mountains reminded me of her. I wore nothing but black for one year. Then I switched to white and got out when I had the chance."

"What was the chance?"

The smile returned to Roosevelt's face, breaking the surface like a spring-thaw lake. "A man aiming to build a ski resort. Hotels and restaurants. Even an indoor water park. He offered me an ungodly amount of money for my land."

Josef smiled, too. "So that explains this?" He motioned with his glass at the room and the view.

"It does." Roosevelt laughed. "And there'd be fewer rumors about me in this town if people would take the time to have a drink with me like you're doing now. Learn my real story. I love this place and its people, but some of them are insane sometimes. There are a plethora of false stories about me."

"Like what?"

"That I'm a mobster. That I once robbed banks. That I'm a homosexual. That I'm a womanizer. That I'm the head of a cult. That I think I'm Jesus Christ."

Josef finished his drink and let out a laugh.

"Some stories are extreme," said Roosevelt, "and maybe only children's fairy tales, but they've all made their way to my ears at some point. Most started because of my money and my house, and my appearance of course. But mostly I think it's because I'm from the West. I'm from somewhere else. And they want to know why. Why did I come all this way to settle on their doorstep?"

Josef could feel Roosevelt's eyes on him, but he looked out at the lake. He wasn't ready yet for the full reveal. He stood up to make another drink and began talking a little about Jeanie and the girls.

Eventually, Roosevelt sat up in his chair and cleared his throat. "I'm aware that the two of us have been engaged in a bit of a dance thus far, and that perhaps I've been leading." Their eyes locked—serious, but not threatening. "I've told you how I ended up here, Mr. Novak. Now maybe you'll return the favor. If you're not interested in buying the old Smith house next door, is it fair to say that you're interested in buying some other home here in Haymaker?"

"It is," said Josef.

"And is it fair to say you won't be the only one?"

"How much did Lee tell you?"

"Very little. Why don't you tell me some more."

Like Lee Mooneyham before him, Josef couldn't tell exactly why he felt comfortable revealing plans about the Freedom Community to this man, but he did, and he began to talk. They needed allies in the town to help during the migration, and they especially needed ones with perspective and keen eyes. When Josef finished giving Roosevelt the big picture of the Community's plan, he settled back in his chair and waited for his reaction. The sun had set; the lake had gone dim.

"Well that—" said Roosevelt, grinning, "that is a plan, all right. That certainly qualifies as a bold and ambitious plan."

"You think it'll fail."

Roosevelt had unwrapped a second cigarillo and spoke with a matchstick cupped toward his mouth. "I didn't say that. I have no idea what will happen, exactly. I think it'll be quite interesting to sit on this hill and witness it all. Like a giant ant farm."

Josef shook his head. "You think we're a joke."

The tip of Roosevelt's cigarillo bloomed orange. He pulled it away from his mouth. There was no hint of a smile. "Oh no. I don't think that at all. And don't jump to conclusions about me like everyone else in this town. I'm just not sure you realize what you're in for. Some of the people you'll be dealing with here."

"Tell me," said Josef. "That's the main reason I'm here. I need an insider's perspective."

"But I'm not an insider."

"You're the perfect insider, Roosevelt, because you've been on both sides and you understand both sides—the locals and the newcomers."

"There are people here you should be more than a little worried about."

"Donnie Sarver? I know about him. I saw his fight today."

Roosevelt raised his eyebrows. "You did?" He chuckled. "And you're still going through with this? You all are more committed than I thought."

"We are."

Roosevelt stood and began making two more drinks. "Well, yes, Donnie Sarver for certain. But there are others. They just don't shout their xenophobia from the rooftops like he does." He handed Josef another whiskey, then turned, grabbed the bottle, and handed him that, too.

"What are your politics, Roosevelt?"

He shook his head and waved the question away. "Oh no you don't. This isn't about politics."

"That's exactly what it's about."

"On your end, not mine. And not on the end of most Haymakes." He sighed. "Why not just ask me if I believe in God? Why not ask me how my wife was in bed? Politics are a private affair for me."

"They're not for me," said Josef.

"So then tell me how you got involved in all of this. You said on the phone you used to be in PR but then you wrote a book but then you something. I forget. How did you get caught up in all this?"

Josef was ready for this question. He was always ready for this question, and so when responding, the only challenge was to make it sound natural, like it was the first time he'd ever organized these thoughts into words. He told Roosevelt about his father and his family's defection. "The search for freedom's in my blood."

Roosevelt nodded. He may or may not have rolled his eyes.

"But I have to admit," said Josef, "I didn't realize it until later in life. I was never that interested in politics. Sometimes I'd vote Republican, but then they'd piss me off. And then I'd vote Democratic, and they'd piss me off. Completely skewed logic on both sides. The package deals—all or nothing. I hated that. Certain things on each side made sense, and certain things didn't. But there was no alternative."

He reached for the bottle and poured some more. His hands were shaking.

"And then my best friend from college, a guy named Dale Presley, he was married—*is* married—to a sweet girl named Julie. I was the best man in their wedding. She gets multiple sclerosis at thirty."

"Damn," said Roosevelt.

"And Dale starts helping her research all of these alternative treatments. One of them is marijuana, which really seems to help her. So then Dale starts attending pro-legalization meetings and rallies around Illinois and the whole Midwest, and at some point I'm with him and I get dragged to a meeting where there are a bunch of libertarians. And they're talking about the legalization of marijuana. Keep in mind, I've never done drugs in my life and have never had any interest, but I found myself saying, 'Yeah, what right does the government have to make this illegal for people like Julie? Or for anyone? Fuck them.' And after these people are done talking about legalizing drugs, they start talking about other things."

Roosevelt slowly nodded along.

"And my God, it made sense," said Josef, waving his arm and spilling some of his drink. "All of those gaps I had in my brain left there by the two major political parties were filled in with libertarianism—the things I believed from both ends. Issues of individual freedom. Fuck taxes, yes. But also fuck legalized morality. I'm sorry; I don't normally talk like this. But see what I'm saying? I'm with Dale another time, and after we leave a bar we drive through a seedy part of town to get the drugs for Julie, and I'm thinking, 'How dare they? How dare they make us do this in a civilized nation.' And I'm thinking about how we could get arrested or something. Even though we'd just left a place full of legalized highs. And I find myself thinking, 'Go ahead. Arrest us.' I didn't care. I was so angry."

"And you still are," said Roosevelt.

Josef nodded. "Yes, I am. I'm sorry. I don't show it much. I don't even realize it much. But you see how it started. I did more reading, and I got to thinking more about my parents and what they had to live through under Communism and all of it. And here I am. And my father never understood what I was attempting, which is ironic and fucked-up and a whole different story."

Roosevelt sighed again and snuffed out his cigarillo.

Josef was afraid he'd scared him away. He had to lighten the mood. "So you see, this is a big step. Coming here and having drinks with a guy named Roosevelt. Who could be more terrifying to a guy like me than FDR?" He smiled and made sure Roosevelt saw him.

"I was named for Teddy," he said. "My mother loved the Rough Rider and gave me his name. Then a few years later Franklin Delano takes office, and she about goes crazy. She wanted to change my name to Theodore. She hated FDR. Believed he knew all about Pearl Harbor in advance but didn't do anything because he wanted us to go to war. And when they put his face on the dime in 1946, she never spent one again. She'd use two nickels instead."

Josef was laughing. "Hey, two Jeffersons. You can't beat that."

Roosevelt removed his hat, set it on his lap, and smoothed his silver hair down with his left hand. "So here's where I stand. I sympathize with much of your cause. Much more than you might think. But I'm the type of independent who doesn't like anyone telling me what to think or do, even if it's to 'live free.' You need to make sure you and yours don't slip into the realm of preaching and self-righteousness and all-knowingness. And you need to realize that other people here feel the same way. I may not have a lot in common with them on the surface, but it's here where we share a bond. A guy from Detroit developed some land on the lake a couple years ago and tried to fence off the beach. He may as well have declared war, because in the eyes of these people, he had."

"But it was his property," said Josef.

"Few years back the state supreme court ruled the shoreline is everyone's property. Up to the high-water mark. You better start to realize this. These people love freedom, but it's a particular strain of freedom. I guess what I'm saying is, tread lightly. There's a minefield to navigate."

"You think they'll resist."

"I think they'll revolt."

Josef paused, staring at him. "Will you?"

"I don't know yet."

The sky was dark. The lake was dark. "I need your help," said Josef. "It's my job to communicate our stance to the locals, and I need you to do what you're doing right now—anticipate their reactions."

Roosevelt returned his hat to his head. "Listen," he said, "I'm not your enemy. Not in the least. You and your family are welcome here anytime, both before and after you make this place your home. But I say these things because I like it here, and I don't want to live in a town full of anger and mistrust and incessant political yapping. Life's too damn short. Mine is, anyway."

Josef almost kept his mouth shut. He took one long, final swallow of his drink. Then he stood. He should have shaken Roosevelt's hand right then—thanked him for his advice and hospitality and been on his way. He realized all this the next morning. But he'd drunk too much, so as they shook hands he asked, flat out, "Are you with us or against us?"

Roosevelt smiled and cupped their handshake with his left hand. "You of all people know the danger of package deals."

Josef turned, headed toward the hallway, and stumbled over a rug. And Roosevelt—lunging quickly in a way that defied his age—caught Josef by the arm and held him upright.

« HAYMAKER AT A GLANCE »
Natural Splendor

◆ *The state motto of Michigan is* Si quaeris peninsulam amoenam, circumspice, *which means, "If you seek a pleasant peninsula, look about you." Certainly this is true of the Haymaker region, where natural splendor extends in every direction.*

Any description of Haymaker's beauty must begin at the lake. The town resides on the shores of Lake Superior, the largest of the Great Lakes and certainly worthy of its name. Those of you from the East and West Coasts, take note: this isn't a "lake" of the kind you're probably used to. From its beaches you'll look out at whitecaps and distant ships—no other land in sight—and believe you're standing before the world's fifth ocean.

The beaches themselves are a wonder. If you drive through downtown Haymaker on a lovely summer day and wonder where everyone has gone, you might want to check Fitzgerald Beach, a place to lie in the sun, play in the sand, or hunt for the beautiful translucent stones called agates. And farther down the beach, reaching hundreds of feet above the water, stand the awe-inspiring and hauntingly beautiful White Sable Dunes.

When the weather cools and autumn comes, the foliage throughout Haymaker explodes in magnificent color. Visitors come from far and wide to catch a glimpse of this annual spectacle. Of course, others flock to the area each autumn for another reason. The forests and marshes—brimming with whitetails, geese, and even bears—are a hunter's paradise. Protectors of the Second Amendment, take heart. Michigan has more registered hunters than any other state in the Union.

Certainly at this latitude, winter plays a huge role in town life. But the people here don't hunker down and pray for spring. In fact, with the abundance of groomed trails throughout Haymaker forests, local businesses report that the winter tourist season is every bit as lucrative as the summer. And why not? Haymaker truly is a winter wonderland.

When it comes to the region's spectacular outdoor attractions, all of this is just the start. There are also trout streams, dogsled tours, and natural wonders like Tahquamenon Falls and Pictured Rocks only a short drive away. If you seek the kind of untouched liberty that our forefathers intended, we invite you to seek it in a place that's equally untouched, as pristine as it was in 1776.

Chapter 12

Sunday, September 7

Josef had slept in a state of half-dreams and delirium as if racked with fever. The apartment remained warm and humid from the night before, and when he woke, the sheets were mildly damp and bunched at the foot of his bed. He took a long, cool shower, his head pounding and filled with regret over some of the things he'd said the night before. He dressed and shaved and took a few aspirin. Then he turned the TV to the Marquette morning news. The forecast called for more unseasonable heat with highs in the upper eighties and humidity. Josef had always worried about convincing people to move to a place with brutal winters. Maybe that was just more of his paranoia.

A half hour later he was out in the sun, lugging his bags, wearing denim shorts, an old braided leather belt from his college days, and an oversized tank top that he usually only donned at the YMCA. He was heading home this morning, but before he left he planned on getting a closer view of the White Sable Dunes.

Despite Boomtown Days, Marquette Street was open to cars for the Sabbath as worshipers filed through the doors of Freshwater Community Church. He'd heard that some drove as far as fifty miles each way to attend. Later the orange cones would block it off again. The finals of the Lumberjack Games would take place, and Mrs. Boomtown—reserved for a lucky married woman over thirty—would be crowned.

He stopped at the Fuel-N-Food just down the road and filled up his tank. Then he went inside to pay, a series of tattered SAVE THE MILL stickers plastered to the glass door. "Some heat," said the woman behind the counter as she handed him his change.

"I didn't think it got this warm here in September."

"Didn't. Shouldn't," she said. "Global warming's out to kill the snow machine season."

"Are the winters getting milder?" asked Josef.

"Where you from?"

"Indiana."

"They wouldn't seem mild to *you*," she said.

He nodded and returned to his car, already breaking out in an early sweat.

Minutes later he passed Ross Road, where he'd lit himself up last night, and now followed Juneau Street until it turned to gravel, plunged into the forest, and twisted through the hardwoods. Josef squinted in a sudden shade that felt like nightfall. He never saw any hikers or bikers or other cars. A couple of deer ate at the roadside, bounding into the trees as he passed.

A small orange sign—tucked amid brush—announced White Sable Dunes County Park. Josef slowly turned onto the narrow, rut-filled road, climbing steeply before ending in a teardrop-shaped parking area. There were no cars, only a purple mountain bike with a child seat on the back, leaning against a tree.

He parked and stepped out into an early heat like something he could swim through. No birds chirped or sang. Overhead, the treetops rustled, kissing each other in some breeze he couldn't feel from the ground. A sign at a trailhead said the dunes were a half mile ahead through the woods. Josef thought again about bears. He walked to the back of the car, opened his third duffel bag, grabbed the hunting knife, and attached the leather sheath to his belt. Then he lurched through the soft sand of the trail, remembering how he'd stumbled, drunk, at Roosevelt's last night, and how aggressive he'd become at the end, and how Roosevelt didn't want him to drive, though he did anyway. He'd call Roosevelt later to apologize.

Along the trail, signs explained the formation of the dunes, as well as how the lumbermen had used them to get felled trees out to the wider world. The dunes rose to three hundred feet at a thirty-five-degree angle of repose, and here the men pushed the logs over the edge of the earth, where they slid down to the beach and the waiting schooners.

The forest gave way to ghost trees choked by sand and then to open sky. Next came a kind of desert—stark and surreal. A wall of white sand stretched for miles in each direction, running along the lakeshore. It reminded Josef of standing atop Hoover Dam as a child, but instead of holding back a river, the sand seemed to hold back an entire peninsula. The glare of the sun off the white sand made him squint. There were no trees below, no grasses, and—at first glance—no people. There were only footsteps left behind by visitors who'd made the exhilarating fall and excruciating climb.

He had the same impulse: to plunge, to spill over the edge. He smiled and sat down to take it all in. Despite Donnie's fight, despite Roosevelt's warnings, Josef felt emboldened by the sheer realness of the place. Haymaker was no longer an idea, no longer a tack on a map. All of the time and effort had led to this—a spectacular vista. He wanted to describe it to the world and was already composing certain lines in his head for future promotional materials. *A world unto itself. The edge of the nation. Capturing the horizon.* And then, from the corner of his eye, he spotted a dark speck of movement far below.

Someone was climbing the dunes, though they hadn't made it even halfway up. Josef stood and realized it was a woman or girl, climbing with just her left arm, lunging and slipping. Then he made out the form of a small child squirming in her right arm. Over the sounds of the distant waves and the rustling leaves came the screams. From the child—screams of pain. From the woman—screams for help.

Josef gave himself to the fall almost immediately, his legs churning, his arms flailing. He had no control over his own body. He closed in on the woman and child faster than he'd expected, and for a moment a surge of panic shot through him: he was going to careen right into them. And so he let go of his legs, let them fold up beneath his body. He collapsed in an explosion of sand that knocked the wind out of him and then rolled over once, twice, more. He stopped maybe fifteen or twenty feet farther down the dune from the woman—the girl; he could see that now. She was tall, with blonde cornrows—the girl from the day before, at the fight. And as he clambered toward her and saw her with the baby, he recognized her as the girl from one of Lee's pictures. It was Ash with Patrick John, though he didn't know their names yet. All he knew now was the severity of a thirty-five-degree angle of repose. He looked up at his thin, spiraling trail of footprints. An enormous white wall loomed over him—hundreds of feet of sand.

Josef climbed on all fours, grabbing at the sand and squeezing it between his fingers for grip until he reached them. The baby's skin was bright red; tears streamed down the girl's face. "I can't carry him up!"

"Give him to me," said Josef.

She handed him over. Patrick John flailed, eyes pressed shut, his hair wet and pressed to his scalp. "He has to get out of the sun," said Ash. "He burns real easy, and I didn't bring his hat or sunscreen. It's so hot and bright here!"

Josef pressed the back of his hand up against Patrick John's forehead. The child's skin radiated heat and was a stunningly deep red. "My car's at the top. Just get yourself up."

Ash grimaced, spat a few stray hairs out of her mouth, and began to slowly ascend, slipping backward a little with every bit of gained ground. "Oh God, we're not supposed to be here. We were just going to go down a little, but we couldn't stop."

Josef clutched Patrick John under his right arm, pumping his legs, using his left hand for leverage like a lineman in a three-point stance. But it was too steep; he needed both hands. "Don't talk! Just climb!" he called to Ash. Then he gently lay the screaming red child on the steep sand and pulled off his own oversized tank top. The hunting knife glinted when he slipped it from its sheath and cut the shirt down the middle to make one wide piece of fabric. He pulled it over his shoulder and tied a couple of knots, making a crude sort of sling. Patrick John never stopped flailing, but Josef managed to scoop him up and set him into it. Then, like a marsupial, child pressed to his heart, Josef dug both hands into the dune and climbed.

Patrick John spread tears and spit over Josef's skin and grabbed tiny fistfuls of his chest hair. But Josef continued on, finding the grooves of sand left by earlier footprints. He looked up and saw that Ash had made it to the top and was yelling at him to hurry. When Josef had nearly reached the summit, she took a few steps downward and tried to pull Patrick John free from the sling.

"Just leave him!" yelled Josef, crouched on all fours.

"But he's really red!" She mashed her hand against her sweat-drenched forehead. "Oh my God, what if he's really hurt? What if he's really burned?" Ash climbed alongside Josef until all three were to the top of the dune and then reached out to gently touch Patrick John's face. "Oh God, P.J., I'm so sorry. I'm so sorry. I love you so much. Oh, you're so red." Her eyes shot to Josef. "He's so red!"

"Here." Josef reached into his pocket and tossed his car keys toward her; they fell at her feet in the sand. A long string of spit hung from his mouth and touched the ground. "My car's at the trailhead. Crank the air-conditioning. And my phone's in the glove box. We'll be right behind you." Then he coughed and retched. Nothing came up.

Ash picked up the keys and ran. She was fast and strong for her age—an athlete.

Josef stood almost immediately after she was out of sight. The child never stopped screaming, but Josef felt better as they slipped into the cool shade of the forest.

Maybe five minutes later Ash came sprinting back toward them. "The car's running," she said, handing him his phone. "There's no signal out here." Then she pulled Patrick John free from the sling. "Give him to me," she said and then turned and ran with the child. Josef stumbled forward, trying to keep up.

When he reached the car, Ash sat in the passenger's seat with Patrick John on her lap, pulling the seat belt over both of them. The purple mountain bike was shoved awkwardly in the backseat. Josef got behind the wheel. The car was cool, but the child continued to scream. They bounced over ruts while roaring down the dirt road, out of the park.

"Where do you live?" asked Josef.

"Drive fast but safe."

"I will. Where do you live?"

Ash was kissing Patrick John on the top of his sweaty head. The car ride and cool air had started to soothe him. His body shuddered as his crying settled into a soft, feathery breathing. "No one's home," she said. "My mom's at church."

"Which one?"

"Freshwater. It's on—"

"I know where it is."

They roared down Juneau toward town, and in the new calm and silence she quietly thanked Josef and they learned each other's names. At one point he noticed her looking at the knife on his hip. "Do you live around here?" asked Ash.

"No. Indiana."

"Are you just sightseeing or something?"

He fixed his stare on the road. "I'm thinking of moving up here."

Ash relaxed a little and shook her head slowly. "Why?" She looked out the side window. "I'd rather live on Mars," she said, stroking Patrick John's head. "Don't let my uncle Donnie find you out."

"Sarver? Yeah, I know his story," said Josef. He was on Schoolcraft now, turning onto Marquette.

Patrick John's eyes fluttered in near-sleep. His sweat had dried and his color looked better. "He doesn't look as red anymore," said Ash. "I think the crying made it look worse."

"It'll be okay," said Josef as he pulled alongside a fire hydrant in front of the church.

Ash stepped out of the car with Patrick John's eyes now wide and alert due to the sudden movement. "Thanks," she said. "I don't know what I'd have done. I'd still be climbing."

Josef got out of the car and pulled the bike from the backseat. "I'll go in, too. Make sure she's here." He noticed Ash staring at his bare torso, the sliced-up shirt hanging from it, and the knife. "I have more shirts," he said.

She turned and looked at the front door of the church, the front door of the old Neptune Theater. "God, she's going to murder me," she said and then went inside.

Josef rummaged through his luggage and found a wrinkled blue T-shirt he'd worn earlier in the trip. He slipped it over his head, left the knife behind, and, as he headed toward the door, glanced up for a second to see the channel 29 camera slowly panning over him.

From the moment he opened the door, the music rushed over him like a wind. This was not a choir. This was not an organ. It was heavy and electric, shaking the floor of the lobby, a lobby that hadn't changed much since it was built for cinema decades ago. Deep red carpet spread out in all directions, toward thick curtains over the doorways that led to the theater. Art deco designs ran up the walls. An old glass-encased ticket booth stood in the center, showcasing a cross made of two birch branches. And the old concession stand stood along the back wall, still displaying candy like Goobers and Jujyfruits, but alongside were stacks of literature: prayer books and daily devotionals and pamphlets on everything from Vacation Bible School to music ministry to a Senior Citizen Prayer-a-Thon.

Josef smelled butter. A vintage popcorn machine remained in the corner. A sign above it read JOIN US FOR POPCORN, COFFEE, AND FELLOWSHIP AFTER WORSHIP.

He stepped now toward the music, crouching below a velvet rope to get to the door, which he slowly pushed open to peer inside. On the stage—amid potted ferns and fig trees—stood a six-piece band blasting its way through "Shout to the Lord": drums and horns, guitar and bass, and cymbals crashing like glass. Toward the back of the stage a teenage boy played mandolin. People raised their hands above their heads and swayed while they sang. Their eyes were closed, their heads tilted upward. Above the band remained the old movie screen, upon which the lyrics to the hymn were projected over a green mountain valley backdrop.

And walking slowly down the center aisle, amid the worshipers and the thundering sound, was Ash, holding pink-skinned Patrick John on her hip and waving at someone down one of the rows. Seconds later, a woman stumbled over other worshipers to reach the aisle and her children. People craned their necks.

The family marched toward the doorway where Josef stood, the mother's face cycling through fear, anger, and bewilderment. She paused and looked at him as they passed, confused as her eyes scanned him from head to foot. Ash only stared at the floor. Then they pushed past, and in the relative quiet of the lobby behind him Josef could hear the mother chanting, "What have you done? What have you done?" Then they were gone.

Josef returned his focus to the worship. The final notes of the hymn hovered in the air, and several people toward the back had turned to stare at the man standing in the doorway in his denim shorts and wrinkled T-shirt. He stepped backward and closed the door.

The buttery air in the lobby made Josef aware of the thirst digging at his throat. He found the bathroom and stuck his mouth under the running water of the sink and then splashed it over his face and the top of his head. There were speakers in the ceiling above the urinals, and as he dried off with a paper towel, Josef stood still and caught his breath, listening for a few minutes to Pastor Zuber's sermon.

"This town, which celebrates its Boomtown Days, looks to the past, a past that was built on the felling of trees, trees that went on to build not only this town but towns throughout the state and even Chicago after the Great Fire."

He chuckled into his microphone.

"The Great Fire. That sounds like the kind of phrase a preacher would enjoy lingering over in a sermon, am I right?"

Laughter from the congregation. Josef walked slowly to the stall, stepped inside, and closed the door behind him. He sat down on the toilet, just to rest, to use it as a chair.

"But in all seriousness, I want to focus on this image of the fallen tree, the tree that is cut down and made by man into houses and ships and furniture. Fashioned by man into art. Into churches."

A long pause.

"Fashioned, too, by man into clubs. Into weapons. Into instruments of death."

A shorter pause.

"Fashioned by man into a cross."

He let it sink in.

"During our Boomtown Days we celebrate the fact that a tree that is felled goes on to be raised again, to build something as great as this town and other towns—the foundations of our tangible world. And in this same way, those trees which were chopped down and made into the cross that held the nails that held our Lord suspended between heaven and earth in those hours of agony—those trees, that cross, built something as great as our faith and the foundations of our spiritual world."

Josef leaned forward on the toilet and ran his fingers through his hair. He thought about the libertarian idea of charities and churches helping people after government stepped aside, out of their lives. It could work here, with this kind of energy.

He stood and walked out of the bathroom, then out of the church. He got in his car, made a U-turn on Marquette, and finally steered south, toward Indiana. And as he thought some more about the church, he remembered glimpsing onstage—next to a cross and just behind the mandolin player—a slender pole with an American flag.

« HAYMAKER AT A GLANCE »

Why Haymaker?

◆ *Yes, Haymaker is picturesque. Yes, it has a quaint and thriving downtown. Yes, its people value their personal liberty. But you could say this about many places across the country. What made us decide that Haymaker would be the ideal choice for our first—our flagship—Community?*

In a word: Freedom.

The zoning laws of the town have changed little since its founding in the 1870s. What this means is that people's property is theirs and the government cannot step in and force them to have a deck inspected, or force them to participate in curbside recycling, or force them to remove an old Ford chassis from their backyard. In Haymaker, your property is your own domain—a seemingly simple concept that is fighting against extinction in this day and age.

There is also room to grow—available land—and with the liberal zoning laws, we're free to build. Nobody can step in and tell us not to build the Freedom Community on property that we own.

And because Haymaker is small in size, it won't take long for new libertarian voters to make an impact and begin to loosen even more restrictions on personal freedoms.

There are also, of course, plenty of intangibles that make the town desirable. Walk the streets and you'll sense an America you'd feared no longer existed—Americana as untainted as virgin forests.

Chapter 13

Monday, September 15

Dirty rainwater speckled her sweatpants as Ash dribbled across the concrete court. The gray dusk was wringing out the last of its light as she practiced at the old hoops beside the high school. She squared up and took a high-arced jump shot, the ball clanging against the backboard and the loose rim before chiming through the rusty chain net. Her blonde hair—which was free of cornrows now and pulled into a tight knot at the back of her head—collected the drizzle in tiny beads. She flipped up the hood of her green Michigan State warm-up and jogged toward the ball.

A white Silverado roared into the adjacent parking lot, its tires peeling water from the pavement like a long vapor trail, its brakes alighting the gloaming in a red mist. Uncle Donnie swung open the door.

Ash turned back toward the perimeter, juked an imaginary player—some small forward from Newberry or Munising—and took another shot. The ball rattled against the rim and bounced back to her.

Donnie approached in a march, slipping through the narrow opening of a chain-link fence and onto the court. "What the fuck?" he said.

Ash cradled the wet ball against her hip and said nothing. She had no idea why he was there.

"I just got off the phone with your mom." He stood before her with his arms crossed over his chest, flecks of rain like pinpricks darkening his gray shirt.

"So?"

"So we were talking about her piece-of-shit car, and your brother—the little rug rat—starts crying in the background. And that leads to her telling me how last weekend some guy pulled you and your brother's asses up off the dune and drove you over to her at the church."

Ash could feel the blush, the hot flare of her cheeks. She dropped her gaze and dribbled toward the hoop for a layup.

"You going to say anything?" asked Donnie.

She retrieved the ball and threaded it through her legs. "What's it to you?"

"That guy," he said, jabbing his index finger in her direction, "that guy is the same guy who's living above the Christmas shop."

"How do you know?"

"Your mom recognized him. She'd seen him before. And I think I saw him at my fight, too."

Ash shrugged and continued dribbling. The Band-Aids on two of her fingertips had soddened, exposing the little cuts from the ball's grip. Trickles of blood leaked from them. She wiped them on the thighs of her pants. "So why are you all upset at me for?"

"You *knew* I was looking for shit on this guy. You should have called me that night. Just like with them pictures you took. Why are you keeping this stuff from me?"

She rolled her eyes. "It's not like I think, 'Hmm, this is something Uncle Donnie would want to know, but I'm not going to tell him about it because I like to see him freak.'"

"It looks that way."

"To a crazy person." She straightened her posture and stepped toward him. "You're like Aunt Nola sometimes. You think everyone's out to do bad stuff to you."

"Smarten up, kid." He clutched the ball and tugged it from her grip. She noticed the bald spot from where Erik Schwartz had taken a handful of his hair.

"Give me my ball."

Donnie held it above his head, just out of her reach. They were nearly the same height. "First—questions. What's his name?"

"Josef. And I don't know his last name, so don't ask."

"Where's he from?" Donnie began dribbling with his right hand, keeping her blocked out with his left hip.

"You already know he's from Indiana." With just a single step and half an effort, Ash lunged toward him and stole the ball. She continued full speed down the court, laying it in at the opposite hoop.

"Reach," he said. "That's a reach-in."

"That was clean." She wiped more blood onto her pants.

Donnie's black hair lay wet and flat atop his head, his bangs falling into his eyes. "Why was he at the dunes?"

"God, I *don't know.*"

"Listen," he said, lowering his voice and gesturing with his hand for Ash to calm down. "What *do* you know? Did you learn anything about him?"

She shrugged, set the ball down by her feet, and pulled her hood low over her eyes. "Just that he might be moving up here. But I don't know what that means since you just said he's already living above the shop."

"Okay, look," said Donnie. "Roosevelt Bly told Rusty Leach that this Josef guy came over to his house. They hung out and shit. And I want to know why. I want to know what they talked about and what the fuck the cowboy has to do with this."

"So go ask him."

"He won't talk to me. He'll just grin and play with his goddamned hat." Donnie removed his wallet from his back pocket. "So I'm going to give you fifty bucks." He pulled out three bills and held them before her. "Go talk to him. Find out some information. Just don't tell him I sent you."

Ash stared at the money but didn't take it. "You're acting like it's a movie. Like I'm your spy. I hardly know Mr. Bly. He lives on the other side of town. I can't just show up and knock on his door."

"Tell him it's for school." The money turned limp in the rain and clung to the outsides of Donnie's fingers. "You got to talk to old people for your history class. Shit like that." He shook his hand with the money. "Find out something good and I'll give you twenty more."

Ash huffed through her nose and took the money, her eyes still downcast. The toe box of her high-tops pinched, the toes tight and on the verge of blisters. She outgrew shoes too fast—outgrew everything too fast. Now she could save for another pair.

The rain had stopped, but a true autumn wind blew outside the darkened library window as Roosevelt Bly fingered the spines of the books on his shelves, pausing over the titles of Mark Twain, mulling over which to reread. A Presbyterian and a cigarillo lay on the end table beside the leather chairs. The doorbell rang.

"I'm coming!" he called as he left the library, and then again as he crossed the living room. "I'm coming!" Once more, in the foyer: "I'm still coming!"

He opened the door and at first didn't recognize Ash in the early nightfall. Her cornrows were gone, and she slouched in a way that hid her height. "Hello, Mr. Bly."

"Well, hello there, Ms. Capagrossa. To what do I owe the pleasure?" He glanced over her shoulder at the purple mountain bike lying in the dune grass. "Did you bike here? It's after eight o'clock, and rain's still dripping from the trees."

Ash stared at her feet. "It's no big deal."

Roosevelt smiled and waited. The silhouetted trees beyond Ash shook in the rising wind.

"You know the other day, when you watched P.J. for a little while?" she asked.

"I remember it like it was yesterday."

"I think it was a couple Saturdays ago."

"So it was," he said.

Ash looked up now, but not into his eyes. "Well, we're missing one of his toys. A bunch of big plastic keys. They're all different colors. Do you know where they might be?"

He shook his head and frowned. "I'm afraid I do not."

"I didn't know if maybe you saw him drop them somewhere, or if you accidentally put them in your pocket or something and accidentally took them home with you."

"I'm afraid I haven't had any baby toys in my household for about fifty years."

Ash nodded and looked down again.

Roosevelt twisted a gold ring back and forth on his middle finger. "Did your mom ask you to come here?"

"No," she said. "We haven't talked much the past week. She's still mad at me."

"Oh? Why's that?"

"I screwed up huge. I took P.J. to the dunes and he got sunburned really bad."

Roosevelt's forehead creased. "I'm sorry to hear that. Is he all right?"

"Yeah. Dr. Snell gave us some stuff to rub on his skin every day. He's fine."

"That's good. That's a relief." He watched her there in the doorway, giving her the time he sensed she needed for something. "Do you want to come inside? I have some apple cider in the refrigerator. It's a long bike ride back to your side of town."

She seemed to be thinking about it, but then said, "No, that's okay."

"You sure?"

She looked at the ground. "Yeah." She looked up. "Wait. Okay."

"Okay?"

"I'll come inside for something to drink." Then she finally looked him in the eye, still without a smile.

"Good thinking," said Roosevelt. "Autumn without cider is like winter without cocoa or summer without lemonade. It's a rule. You must drink it." He stepped aside and motioned with one hand for her to enter. "Ladies first, old men last." While Roosevelt walked into the kitchen and removed the jug from the refrigerator, Ash stood in the foyer, gazing at the stained glass, at the painted vines along the ceiling. She approached the stairway and slowly ran her hand along the carved image of a mermaid on the banister.

Roosevelt poured their drinks. "Look at that cider," he said. "It could make a fish thirsty."

She joined him in the kitchen, and the two stood quietly and sipped. He pointed at the bloodstains on her leg. "What happened?"

Ash shrugged and held up her left hand, which was spotted with the stains of blood—dried and brown like fallen leaves. "Basketball."

"Ah, right. I've heard you're quite a prospect."

"From who?"

"Your uncle brags about you at the bar."

"He does?"

Ash followed Roosevelt as he wandered into the next room and sat in a wooden rocking chair beside his huge stone fireplace. "What brings you here, Ms. Capagrossa? Besides toy keys." He motioned toward the couch. "Have a seat, my dear."

She slowly settled into its cushions, staring at the glass of cider cupped in her hands. "Uncle Donnie asked me to come here."

Roosevelt laughed. "Well, speak of the devil. By the way, how did his fisticuffs turn out the other day? Did you make it in time?"

"Yeah."

"Is his unbeaten streak still intact?"

She nodded. "He won."

Roosevelt pumped his fist in the air. "Good for him. Good for all of us. The town is safe for another year. So what was it he was sending you for?" he asked before taking another sip.

"Is it?"

He lowered the glass from his lips. "What's that?"

"He wants to know if the town's safe. I think he's crazy, but he thinks something's going on."

"In terms of what?"

"People from out of town."

Roosevelt leaned forward in his chair. "I guess what I'm wondering," he said, "is first, what's Donnie talking about, and second, why didn't he come over and talk to me himself? Wait—and third, why's he think I know anything?"

"Because he visited you." Ash stared at him now. "Josef."

Roosevelt closed his eyes and nodded slowly, knowingly. "Aha. I see."

Ash shifted in her chair and reached into her back pocket. "And this guy, too. Do you know who this man is?" She held a photo out toward him.

Roosevelt chuckled. "This sounds like a police interrogation. You're a regular Brenda DeBoer." He took the photo from her and squinted at it. It was a picture of a man in orange camouflage pants standing in front of the Neptune Theater with a camera raised to his eye. "I do, just barely. I met him a couple months ago at Rusty's. His name's Lee. He told me his last name, too, but I can't remember it now. Started with an M. Where'd you get this?"

"I took it." There was a confidence in her voice he hadn't heard since she'd arrived. "Uncle Donnie wants to know what you two talked about." She dropped her gaze and shook her head. "I know it's stupid."

Roosevelt continued to smile. "I don't see how a private conversation between two people is any of his business. Not that I have anything to hide. God knows I'm an open book." He handed the picture back to her. "I talk to just about every new person who sets foot in Rusty's, or in Haymaker, for that matter."

"Like Josef."

Roosevelt cocked his head. "Do you know him?"

Ash stared at him again. "He helped me and P.J. at the dunes."

"My head's spinning on its axis," he said. "Quick question for you, Ms. Capagrossa. Why are you doing this for your uncle? Coming here instead of him?"

She hesitated. "A favor. He's always fixing our car. He gives us deals." She turned and looked out the dark window, toward the lake she couldn't see. "He's always come to my games."

Roosevelt stood and sauntered to the refrigerator for more cider. "I don't believe he'd set foot in my home. Thinks I'm too good for some people. Because of how I dress, and because I live out here on the dunes."

"He doesn't think you'd tell him anything."

Roosevelt faced her, holding the handle to the refrigerator door. "And you're probably maybe just about right." He stepped away from the refrigerator, laid his palms on the countertop, and looked straight at her. "I'm not about to tell the tales of one man to another man without there being good reason. If your uncle wants to know some details, he can ask me face-to-face. I'll be at Rusty's tonight, and no doubt so will he. But to quench your own curiosity—I'm sure you have some by now—yes, the two men—Josef Novak and the man with the camera—know each other. Josef came to see me last weekend, and we talked about this town. These men are looking to move to Haymaker, and they're looking to bring some friends."

Ash stared at the floor again, wincing a little. "But why do they want to come to Haymaker? Why would anyone live here if they didn't have to?"

Roosevelt took a few steps in her direction and crouched down beside her. "I'm originally from a thousand miles away, yet here I am. You're young, and I understand that right now you probably want to get out of Dodge and head to bigger cities and such. And you might just do that. But someday you might find yourself coming back here, and you'll be happy about it." He patted her knee. "There are going to be some changes around here, and some people will be unhappy." He stood up and walked to the refrigerator again. "There is no perfect place," he said, his back to her. "Not on this earth."

« HAYMAKER AT A GLANCE »

Our Community within the Community

◆ *We realize that the very word "community" might seem at odds with individuality, and some might balk at the idea. We're very aware of this delicate balance and hope that, in a short amount of time, there won't be a need for a libertarian community within the larger community. We hope it will all be one.*

But in the short term, our newly purchased land will be the site of condominiums available to those of you making the move. Construction of the development—called Freedom Springs—will begin early next year. Many of the contractors and workers are libertarians who have already committed to the move. Quality will be high because crews will be building their own homes, as well as yours.

Phase One of construction will feature 100 units—enough to house everyone making the move as part of the first wave of migration. Of course, many will choose to find or build their own houses right away. Others will use Freedom Springs as temporary housing before moving to a more permanent home—thus freeing up condos for the next group of new arrivals. And some will choose to stay in Freedom Springs for years to come.

The choice is yours. And isn't that really the point of all this?

It's time to live where you choose, with whom you choose, and how you choose.

It's time to move to Haymaker.

Chapter 14

Monday, September 29

In the 1920s, little Haymaker, Michigan, laid claim to two newspapers: the *Star* and the *Picayune*. Mr. Abraham P. Lemon founded the *Star* in 1919, and in 1921, after he was thrown from his prized horse, Citrus, and killed, his twin sons, Franklin and Orville, became the paper's proprietors. Franklin, a Detroit lawyer who'd left Haymaker in his teens, returned only after his father's death. Conservative in his politics and eyeing elected office, he saw the *Star* as a useful conduit for his voice and ideas.

Orville—a poet, painter, and avowed Marxist—lived in Boston at the time. He, too, had left Haymaker at a young age, and when he returned to the town to claim his inheritance, he returned with plans similar to—and yet very different from—his brother's.

The two hadn't spoken in years and corresponded by mail only at Christmastime. Now they found themselves sharing an editorial office, though little else. The collaboration lasted two weeks, at which time Orville sold his share to Franklin, purchased an office on the other side of Marquette Street, and established the left-leaning *Picayune.*

The publications differed in everything except their mismanagement. Not only did the brothers lack any journalistic experience, but neither had any connections to their hometown anymore. The readers of Haymaker took them for outsiders.

In 1922, Mr. Otis M. Skinner, a businessman who owned eight other newspapers throughout Michigan, bailed out both brothers and immediately merged the *Star* and the *Picayune* into the periodical that still exists in the town today, its office located next door to Rita's Floral and Gift and the apartment of Donnie Sarver.

Donnie walked out onto the landing of his second-story apartment. Wooden steps led down to the flower shop parking lot. It was seven thirty in the morning and he was heading off to work. He sat down, sipped a bottle of Mountain Dew, and laced up his boots, which were caked in dirt from a night at Rusty's.

Merv Grubb exited the *Star-Picayune* building and locked the door behind him. The paper was now a weekly, distributed on Wednesdays county-wide, with a circulation of about fifteen hundred. Merv was head writer and editor for the five-person staff. Now in his sixties, he'd returned to his hometown in a state of partial retirement after years of working at the *Lansing State Journal.* He had the type of eyes that existed in a perpetual squint—little slits that never revealed the whites—and his mouth always curled into the expression of a man just about to tell you something you don't know but want to. Donnie liked to shoot the shit with him. They often joked about their complete mistrust of each other.

He called down to Merv now. "What you doing here on a Monday morning? Thought your hard-hitting news organization only worked three days a week?"

Merv looked up, smiled, and ambled over toward the steps. "Most of the time. Unless we got one of them 'extra, extras.' I was here most of the night."

"You got an 'extra, extra,' huh?" Donnie took another sip of his pop.

"Well," said Merv, his mouth making that curl, "we're not talking V-J Day here, but it's noteworthy for a town like ours."

Donnie lowered the bottle and swallowed hard and fast so he could talk. "Noteworthy how?"

"You know that old stump field over on Schoolcraft? It's been purchased."

"Didn't know it was for sale."

"It was. And the seller, Jimmy Bruce, made a handsome profit."

Donnie stood and descended the steps. "Who's he?"

"Guy who owns the baseball card store down on Parson."

"I know the store," said Donnie, "not the man." He squinted and rubbed his throat with the back of his hand, over the tattoo that said JANE. "How long's he lived here?"

"Thirty-some years. His whole life."

"His whole life?" The fact that a lifelong Haymake could go unknown to Donnie startled him. "And he's about my age? Who bought it?" He didn't like how Merv toyed with information.

"Well, that's where we come in," said Merv. "When there's news, we report it. And this, most definitely, is news." He reached into his back pocket and removed a folded-up sheet of red, white, and blue paper. He handed it to Donnie. "Read it," he said, "and weep."

Clara was five months pregnant and supposed to stay off her feet and behind the register as much as possible. But a bus of senior citizens from Kalamazoo had arrived at The Shipwreck Café this morning, on their way from Pictured Rocks to Tahquamenon for a fall color tour. Half of them ordered the special, a whitefish omelet. Nobody ever ordered the whitefish omelet.

With the place packed, Clara took orders, bussed tables, and boxed leftovers. In the midst of all this, Merv entered the café, settling into the only empty seat—at the counter near the register. He ordered a cup of coffee and browsed the menu.

Clara squeezed her way behind the counter to make change for a customer. "I don't have time to talk this morning, Merv."

"Not a problem, Mayor. I'll wait out the storm. Can work on my article while I dine."

She counted out bills, not listening to him.

"There's a big story I'm working on."

"My God, Merv," said Clara, "you sound straight out of the 1940s. The whole room just went black and white."

"I'm giving you a heads-up. Your job might get a bit more complicated soon."

She moved her lips while counting dollar bills, never looking up at him. "Is another bus on the way? Tell them we're out of whitefish."

"Not this job," said Merv. "Your position as head of our humble town."

She looked up now. "Christ, just be out with it."

"You know the old stump field on Schoolcraft?"

"Of course." She closed the register drawer with her hip and faced him, supporting her aching lower back with both hands.

"It seems it's been sold. Going to be developed."

"Stuff like that never crosses my desk. Someone wants to build houses, build shops, then great. Good for the economy."

"Oh, maybe." He reached into his back pocket. "But on the record, I would appreciate your official response to this." He handed her the red, white, and blue sheet of paper.

Clara was a slow reader, which Gary often teased her about. Her brow creased as she worked through it once and then again. She shook her head. "Where'd you get this?"

"Mailed to the newspaper by this group. The Freedom Community."

She handed it back. "I can't comment now. These people need their food."

"We're printing this story later in the day, Mayor."

She rang up an order at the register. “Then I have no comment.”

“You have to say something. If I run the piece right now, I’d have to say, ‘When questioned, the mayor had no comment.’ That looks bad. Especially to people like Donnie Sarver, who, I might add, just read this himself.”

“What did he say?”

“Things I shall not utter in your presence, ma’am.”

She shook her head again. “I can’t think about this right now.”

“So it’s still ‘no comment’?” said Merv, frowning.

“Give me five minutes.” She turned and grabbed the regular coffeepot with her left hand and the decaf with her right before heading toward the booths. After filling mugs, she slipped away into her office and began scribbling in the margin of an old paper menu. Then she returned to the counter and handed it to Merv. “Say this.”

It read: *When questioned, the mayor, hard at work at The Shipwreck Café, located at 352 Superior Drive—featuring daily lunch specials and bottomless cups of coffee—stated, “If it’s true that these people are planning on moving to Haymaker, they can expect a few open arms, a few clenched fists, and a whole lot of people with questions.”*

Roosevelt entered Rusty’s and headed for a table. He had a newspaper folded under his arm.

Another lightbulb had gone out this week, another lightbulb Rusty and Bep had failed to change. Roosevelt chose a table in the corner, in the dimmest pocket of the place. It was Monday night and quiet, and he wanted to be alone while he read.

He sat and spread open the paper, which was only a single-fold job—four pages, devoted to just the one story. A couple of editorials covered page two, and page three featured a “Word on the Street” section with photographs of random Haymakes and their thoughts on the “libertarian issue.” He’d save that for last, after he’d made up his own mind on all this.

Bep approached. “What are you sitting over here for?”

“Wanted some quiet. Going to read.”

She looked at the paper. “Oh, that.” She waved her hand. “That’s all talk. It’ll never happen.”

“It might.”

“It won’t. The usual?”

“The usual.”

She left him alone in the dim corner. He removed his hat, smoothed down his hair, and thought about the voice mail he’d received a few hours ago.

"Hello, Roosevelt. It's Josef Novak. Hey, by now you probably know why I'm calling. I'm trying to gauge public reaction. We'd sent an outline of our plan to the paper, and they said they were going to print something today. We've got a probe up there right now who's gathering information, but I also value your opinion as much as anyone's. So, when you get a chance, give me a call. I'm excited to hear where things stand. Hope you're well."

Everything was unfolding faster than Roosevelt had ever imagined it could. He began to regard all of Josef's claims as truly possible. They would start arriving this year. There would be hundreds of them in two years' time. Everything he'd said about the group's organization and resources—its leader, Tate—seemed true.

Roosevelt wouldn't return the call right now. He was angry. There was something seedy about the tactics—sending people called probes, who were really spies. And now trying to tap him, make him some kind of informant. Then there was Donnie on the other side, sniffing around, sending his niece over to do his dirty work.

Bep set a cocktail napkin down on the table, followed by his drink. "It's on the house," said Bep. "I think Rusty's worried about that look on your face. You never look like this."

"Thank you, dear," he said as kindly as he could manage. Then he took a sip and began to read the paper's front page.

LIBERTARIAN GROUP PLANNING HUGE MIGRATION TO HAYMAKER
TOWN MAY NEVER BE THE SAME
WHO ARE THEY AND WHY ARE THEY COMING HERE?

From seemingly out of the blue, a libertarian organization calling itself the Freedom Community has planned a large-scale migration of its members to Haymaker, beginning as early as this fall. In a communiqué sent exclusively to the Star-Picayune, *the group announced its intent and outlined its beliefs and plan of action.*

The Freedom Community—based in Michigan City, Indiana—has recently purchased land on the west side of Schoolcraft Avenue near the Juneberry Street junction. Public records indicate the site was previously owned by James Bruce of Haymaker.

The group plans to move upwards of several hundred members into town within a two-year period with the intention, they state, of "expanding basic personal freedoms through peaceful, political means."

Dr. Rich Yeager, professor of political science at Northern Michigan University, interprets the community's plan as just the first phase of a larger strategy.

"It seems they want to make Haymaker a 'home base,' a place to get a political and philosophical foothold before spreading their reach to county and maybe even state levels."

Mayor Clara Hollingshead, when informed of the news, stated, "If it's true that these people are planning on moving to Haymaker, they can expect a few open arms, a few clenched fists, and a whole lot of people with questions."

For those with questions, there are, thus far, few answers. Josef Novak, spokesman for the community, has announced he will attend next month's city council meeting for an open dialogue with the people of Haymaker. "This is by no means anything to feel threatened by," he stated in the letter. "Just as we are excited about the Freedom Community, we are excited about being members of the larger Haymaker community and believe that our presence will benefit the townspeople economically, socially, and politically."

The meeting will likely be a contentious one, with many residents already expressing confusion, shock, and even anger. Donnie Sarver, owner of Sarver Towing and Repair and founder of the town's most infamous annual brawl, claims, "Anyone who thinks this is all just something innocent is fooling themselves. Of course I'll fight this. But so will hundreds of others like me. That's what these outsiders don't understand."

But Bud Wilmington of North Country Realty, who brokered the land sale, sees it differently.

"I think this is a positive for our town. People in Haymaker have always been incredibly independent, even by Yooper standards. The move will only enhance this. And enhance the economy. This is a win-win."

Next month's city council meeting will take place Monday, October 13, at 7:00 p.m. in the Civic Centre. The public is welcome and encouraged to attend.

« HAYMAKER AT A GLANCE »

How to Make History in Haymaker

◆ *We're calling ourselves the Black Bears, and this is our flag and this is our seal. Black bears roam the Upper Peninsula . . . and soon, so shall we. Like these animals, we think for ourselves, we need lots of personal space to survive, and we're generally peaceful, content to be left alone. But like these bears, we'll fight back if our lives, our homes—our freedoms—are threatened.*

So if this sounds like you, and if Haymaker sounds like the place for you, we invite you to join us. Be a part of a movement. A revolution.

Be a part of history.

Read through the supplemental materials included here. Check out freedomcommunitynow.com. And call up those people listed on the site who've already made the decision.

Then get in your car and drive.

Load the U-Haul. Gather the kids. Call the dog. Then head north. We need you, because everyone has something unique to offer the Freedom Community, and each freedom lover is one more person who has said ENOUGH to the status quo and YES to a brighter future for this now-troubled nation.

You're not too young: we need your energy and drive.

You're not too old: we need your wisdom and experience.

Enough talk. Enough theory. It's time to show up or shut up.

We'll see you in Haymaker.

Chapter 15

Monday, October 13

Two hundred metal folding chairs stood like soldiers in sharp, neat rows, surrounded by hoses and helmets and extinguishers. Clara had ordered that the meeting be moved to the other end of the Civic Centre—to the firehouse garage bay—knowing the all-purpose room where they normally held city council meetings was inadequate for tonight. Haymaker's lone fire truck sat parked along the curb out front. A few children gathered around it as if there were going to be a parade.

The start time was seven o'clock, but Haymakes began arriving around six. The few elderly residents who faithfully attended every council meeting arrived bewildered and angry when they discovered the only remaining seats were in the back. A buzz of talk coursed through the firehouse. Clara peeked at the crowd through a doorway, then closed it and performed the sign of the cross.

She'd seen it all coming. The *Star-Picayune* had started publishing two issues per week, and at the Shipwreck she'd been working two jobs at once, dispelling rumors while filling coffee mugs. At home, she lay in bed slowly rubbing her large, smooth belly and refusing to answer the phone. Gary had told everyone—even her own mother—that she couldn't talk, she needed her rest. And he was right.

Clara opened the door about an inch, peeking again at the panorama of townspeople and trying to snag some conversations. Reverend Zuber sat beside Walt Finley, the history teacher, and spoke about the future of the public schools. Earl Henneman sat in the front row and loudly asked Greta

McPhee, widow of the old mayor, if all these people under one roof were a fire hazard.

"Can you have a fire hazard in a firehouse?" she asked.

Snow Soldier Brian Beckett questioned Coach "Slim" Jim Johnstone about whether the libertarians might privatize plowing services. And a few others toyed with the rumors that the libertarians had already infiltrated the city council.

In the back of the room stood Merv with pen and notepad, and his partner, Cecil Grove, outfitted with a camera. Over by the entrance, Brenda DeBoer, in uniform, stood beside Chief Lenny Boston, while the department's third officer, Travis James, watched from the back. They were eyeing everyone, but especially Donnie, who'd reportedly made a threatening phone call to Jimmy Bruce, the recluse who'd sold the stump field.

Donnie sat restlessly amid his newly formed crew, including his best friend and convicted auto thief, Russ Gillickson. Apparently Donnie had been spending a lot of time with a small group of men at Rusty's, holding court at a long table in the back of the tavern, speaking in a low voice like a man over a hundred years ago planning to assassinate President McKinley.

Ash slouched near the back of the room. She'd dragged along Victoria Plunk, a friend and teammate, so that she could more easily avoid small talk with Roosevelt or Uncle Donnie or God forbid Josef, the man who'd saved Patrick John at the dunes. The two girls wore winter jackets, long shorts, and high-tops. They'd come straight from a coed pickup game at the high school gym.

Mayor Hollingshead and the six council members entered through a side door and settled down at a long cafeteria-style table up front. Microphones were set up in front of each chair. Beside the table was a plain wooden podium. And in the center aisle that bisected the audience stood a lone microphone stand where residents could voice their questions and concerns.

A rush of applause greeted the council members when they entered, as if they were the town's defenders from invasion or, at the very least, the home team stepping onto the court. Ash kept quiet, her hands in her jacket pockets.

Mayor Hollingshead immediately spoke into her microphone. "Order, people. This isn't a pep rally, it's a civic gathering. Let's also make it a *civil* gathering." The eyes of the council members flanking her darted back and forth, scanning the crowd.

The meeting began like any other. Ash had attended last month's—a requirement for her social studies class. They covered the previous meeting's minutes and then turned to various issues of small-town governance.

Installing a flashing stoplight at Marquette and Schoolcraft. Pruning tree limbs along Juneau that were interfering with power lines. The crowd would have none of this, and a rising dissent bubbled up as they mumbled and shook their heads.

Councilwoman Rita Gumpert, owner of Rita's Floral and Gift, spoke up. "Mayor, I move we proceed right to the debate regarding the Freedom Community."

Cheers and applause thundered throughout the crammed firehouse.

"I second," said Ernest Mears.

Clara turned her head. "All in favor?"

Everyone agreed.

"The ayes have it." She rested her open hands on her belly and sighed loudly into the microphone. "Let's begin."

Josef opened the side door with a loud metallic snap. He strode into the garage with Carl behind him, toward two chairs in the front row marked RESERVED. People craned their necks. A swell of chatter followed. A couple of people booed. And Donnie cupped his hands to his mouth and shouted, "Aliens, go home!"

"People! People!" shouted Mayor Hollingshead. "Citizens!" Josef followed her eyes to the two tense-looking cops at the door, as if she were about to signal something to them. But she only shook her head slightly, and the cops relaxed.

Josef sat down, a remarkable calm having settled over him. This was his job—what he'd worked and prepared for. And he was ready. He wore a sharp gray suit and smoothed his blue tie over his chest.

Carl sat upright, his fists clenched and jaw rigid. Two weeks earlier he'd proposed to his girlfriend, Marissa. Haymaker was going to be their home, where they'd start a family. He stared straight ahead at the council, refusing to acknowledge the crowd behind him.

"This council will now address the issue of the Freedom Community," said Mayor Hollingshead. "I suppose that's why most of you are here. Please forgive us for the overcrowding. Consider it a wonderful exercise in civic participation."

The firehouse fell silent, anxious for the debate.

"I'd like to welcome Mr. Josef Novak and Mr. Carl Farmer, representatives of—" a few people booed, "of—citizens!—representatives of the Freedom Community, who will hopefully provide us with more specifics regarding their potential move to Haymaker. I expect a lively democratic experience tonight—plenty of discussion and a fair amount of disagreement. But here's something we must all agree on, right now." The mayor leaned forward, removing her hands from her belly and pressing them down on the table. "All opinions will be respected, and all will be heard through the *proper procedures.* Any more outbursts, anything like that, and you're gone." She nodded toward the police presence near the door while still looking at the crowd. "You're gone."

Josef took a deep breath and slowly exhaled.

"Let me now recognize the group's communications director, Josef Novak."

Josef stood, nodded in appreciation at the mayor, and then stepped forward to the podium. Carl approached the front as well, setting up a shaky wooden easel and several large panels of foam core before returning to his seat.

Josef nodded again, this time at the townspeople. "To go along with what Mayor Hollingshead said, let me thank all of you for the incredible turnout tonight. One of the reasons our organization chose to make Haymaker our home—out of all the towns in the United States—is its undeniable spirit of democracy. Voter turnout is remarkable here. There's nothing worse than a politically apathetic community, and Haymaker is certainly not that."

He smiled generously, aware that, in his suit, he must look like a politician himself.

"That's just one of many reasons why we chose this place." He held up a copy of the *Haymaker at a Glance* brochure. "This is something that I've written for libertarians interested in making the move. It describes this town as I've come to see it, with fresh eyes. And I think you'll find it a very pleasing and complimentary portrait. In my short amount of time spent here, I've fallen in love with this town."

A skeptical murmur rippled throughout the crowd.

"Carl here will leave a stack of these brochures after the meeting, and we encourage everyone to read what we have to say about this place. I think it'll help lessen any fears you might have that we're somehow out to 'invade' Haymaker or dramatically change it in any way. The fact is, we already like most of it as it is."

"What do you mean *most* of it!" a woman shouted.

"Order," said the mayor. "Citizens!"

"Let's hear him out!" yelled Bud Wilmington. Many turned in his direction.

Josef glanced at Roosevelt, who was in the third row and easily noticeable in his customary white. The Gold-Plated Cowboy wore a tense expression and shook his head ever so slightly. Josef remembered their conversation weeks earlier, Roosevelt's warning about sounding preachy and self-righteous. "I apologize. That came out wrong. What I mean is that every town—even the most picturesque ones like Haymaker—have things that could be improved.

Just like people, no town is perfect. In addition to the aforementioned brochure, Carl will also have some literature that describes libertarian ideas in general and our Freedom Community goals more specifically. These ideas might be new to some of you, but others, I suspect, already know quite a bit. In fact, I know some of you already consider yourselves libertarians. Some of you voted Libertarian in both the presidential and midterm elections. And though some of you may never have considered yourselves as such, you'll likely find that your core beliefs about limited government and individual rights match up with ours."

The earlier ripple of skepticism now grew into a wave of discord. People turned to those next to them. "I'm not a libertarian. Are you a libertarian? I'm not."

Josef shook his head, angry at himself.

"So what are you saying here?" Ray Valentine stood up. Josef remembered him from the Shit-Kickin'. "Are you saying you're here to *liberate* us?"

Josef recognized the trap, the implied language of war. He wouldn't take the bait.

And then Carl shot up, his face red, his hands still clenched. He turned and stared at Ray—at the whole town—and said, "Yes! That's exactly what we're saying!"

Josef took a step back and covered his chest with one hand like his mother used to do when shocked. Carl sat down again, his arms crossed. He looked at Josef and smiled. A foaming uproar surged through the crowd like breaking waves.

"That's enough!" shouted the mayor.

Josef leaned again toward the podium. "Think of the economic boom!" he yelled. A hush slowly descended over the townspeople. He sensed them listening now and remembered the faded SAVE THE MILL signs around town. He made sure to mention businesses by name. "More shoppers at the 3-F. More diners at The Venison. More patrons at the mayor's own Shipwreck Café."

Someone broke the crowd's silence. "You're a shipwreck!" It was a woman in her seventies who couldn't have been over four foot ten. "And you're gonna take this whole town down with you!"

"Ma'am, that's both untrue and unfair."

"To hell with fairness," said a large, bearded man in the second row. "You put people's backs to the wall, then act surprised when they bite and claw you away."

The mayor stood up, stunned. "Gary!"

He shrugged his shoulders at her and sat down.

"Let me move quickly to specifics," said Josef, "and then you can take turns asking me questions." He stepped to the easel, shuffled through the panels, and then spoke quickly, aware of a rising heat under his skin, sweat trickling down his back. There were pie charts, demographics, bullet points, and facts that left his mouth and died on his lips. It wasn't until he revealed the artist's rendering that people perked up and strained their necks to see. This was it: the Freedom Community as it would look when all of the stumps were ground to dust and all of the libertarians began to arrive. Rows of white condominiums. Green yards and hanging flower baskets. American flags flying from every porch. "When we speak of a Freedom Community, we're referring to two distinct things. First, this: an actual neighborhood, a community within the larger community of Haymaker."

"You're creating a compound," said an old man in the front row whom Josef believed was blind. "A commune." He turned to the old woman next to him and mumbled, "I know his type without seeing him."

Clara spoke politely. "Earl, please. We can't have interruptions."

"I assure you, it's no commune," said Josef. "It's a place for people to get settled, to get grounded. A way station. Then they'll buy or build their own houses. Of course, some will move into a house right away. My family will. Because Freedom Community, in the second sense, refers to Haymaker as a whole. Those of us who settle here have no interest in being fenced off from the rest of the town. We want to integrate into it. Truly be your neighbors."

"What if we want to fence you in ourselves!" yelled Ray Valentine with a huge grin. "What if we want to put bars around you and poke at you with sticks like a bunch of animals!"

"Get him out of here!" said the mayor. The chief nodded toward the back of the firehouse, and a young blond officer, who had gone all but unnoticed along the back wall, made his way through the chairs, grabbed Ray by his arm, and escorted him through a door to another part of the Civic Centre.

The place erupted, and for the first time all night a hairline fracture—the slightest of schisms—crept through the Haymakes. Many cheered for Ray. Others booed, happy to see him go. And the rest seemed to press their collective hands against their collective ears, like panicky children whose parents were fighting.

Then Donnie stood up. The woman in uniform, whom Josef also recognized from Donnie's fight, took a step forward but then stopped with her thumbs hooked in her gun belt and simply watched him like everyone else. He smiled and slowly inched through his row until he reached the center aisle and the microphone stand. "Is it question time yet?" he asked.

"No—" said the mayor.

"Yes," said Josef. "It's fine." He returned Donnie's smile, suddenly emboldened, and nodded toward him. "Shoot."

"Oh, I will."

The mayor spoke again. "Donnie, you know the rules, you know the consequences. And you know how much is on the line right now."

"More than anyone," he said. He turned toward the two cops by the door and gave a little wave. "Evening, officers." He looked around the room. "Good friends of mine. We go way back. Much history." His smile then eroded like a dune—imperceptibly, grain by grain. "I know a lot of you people here think I'm a joke, though you'd never say it to my face. I'm all inked up and I curse a lot and I like to fight, so you think you probably have me all figured out. But believe me—and I'm saying this now," he shook his index finger in the air, "I'm saying this—you have never really seen me fight. Don't ask me why I feel the way I do about all this. About people coming up here and changing things to fit their likes and needs—just don't ask. But believe me, I feel it."

Donnie took a deep breath, smiled once more, and stared at Josef. "Did you know this guy's daddy was a Communist?" He nodded. "Yeah, he's not the only one smart enough to do research."

"Do you have an actual question, Donnie?" asked Clara.

Josef stayed silent and returned Donnie's stare.

"Yes, Mayor. But not for him. For everyone else." He removed the microphone from the stand and turned around, surveying his fellow Haymakes. "A soldier going off to war knows he might get shot or blown up, but if he's brave he still goes. Our friend here says he knows some of you are libertarians and that you're on his side, whether you'll admit it out loud or not. Well, I know that deep down a lot of you feel more like *me* than you'd like to admit. You're angry to the point of bad things. So my question is, are you going to fight back?" He swung around toward Josef. "You're here trying to recruit, eh? Fine. Here's your competition. You bring your army, I'll bring mine."

Cheers, boos, and whistles rained down on the meeting. The mayor shouted for order, but now people stood and yelled amongst themselves. Roosevelt Bly—a month shy of his eightieth birthday, bedecked in white from head to toe—stood up on his chair, waving his arms. "This is quite enough!" he shouted. "Find your seats and plant your asses! This is a town hall meeting, not a goddamned jailbreak!"

The storm ebbed under the sight of this man who shone like a full moon.

"We are good, civil people in this town," he said, lowering his voice. And as the room fell silent, that voice took the tone of a lullaby. "That's right. We're all back now. Back from the brink. This is communication. This is civilization." He stretched his open hands out around him. "We're free to agree or disagree with these visitors and their ideas, but to act like savages is to act like Haymaker is not really a town at all, not a bastion of humanity amid the forest. We might as well be deer. Might as well be bears."

Donnie broke the spell cast by Roosevelt, his voice booming into the microphone once more. "Who the fuck are you to talk, old man? You're not even from here. Of course you don't care about outsiders coming in—you're one of them."

Roosevelt didn't flinch. He remained standing on the chair. "I care very much about any significant changes to a place that I—"

"No! Because I know about you, too! I know that you've been talking to these trolls. You think you're so smart and so above all of this. I know more than you'd ever think. And I'm sick of looking at you and your fake cowboy getup—"

Roosevelt stepped down and strode in Donnie's direction, stepping over people's legs in the crowded row. "You want to fight me, Donnie? Go on, make a spectacle. Make an impressive showing."

About a dozen people stood up and corralled Roosevelt in the other direction. The police chief jogged to the podium, shouldering Josef out of the way. "Ladies and gentlemen, this meeting is adjourned. The time is now eight thirty and the fire department needs its space back."

Josef looked at his watch. It was five to eight.

"Consider this a cooling-off period," said the mayor into her microphone before leaning back, hands on belly, and closing her eyes.

The chief waved the other cop over. Then he looked at Josef and Carl. "You two are going with Sergeant DeBoer." She finally pushed through the crowd to meet up with them. "Help these guys get out of here," he said to her. "They're gonna need it."

People began to shuffle out the doors, but Donnie's crew lingered. One of them lifted his steel folding chair up over his head and began thrusting it in the air to punctuate his words. "Hay-mak-er! Hay-mak-er!" His buddies chimed in, lifting their own chairs.

"I got this," said the chief, burrowing toward the noise.

Sergeant DeBoer turned to Josef. "Where are you parked?" "In the back."

"Nope. We're not taking you there. People are leaving that way."

Josef and Carl followed her through the side door, down a long white corridor, through security clearances that required her key card, and out one more door to the dark night and her cruiser. "Where are you staying?"

"I'm at the North Gateway Inn," said Carl. "On the outskirts of town."

"That's good. There's a bit of buffer between here and there."

"I'm right down the road," said Josef.

She shook her head. "I'm going to take you both to the motel. It'll be safer."

Carl sat in the front seat beside Sergeant DeBoer. He was a big guy and needed the extra leg room to stretch the knee he'd blown out in his football days. Josef sat in the back, in the cage, like a criminal.

Nobody said anything as they turned onto Schoolcraft and headed south. The silhouettes of pines stood against a charcoal sky. But after a few moments Josef leaned forward to the plexiglass, near Carl's ear. "We're here to liberate them, huh?"

"I was pissed off, Josef."

"You're saying you're here to liberate us? Yes! That's exactly what we're saying!"

"I wasn't going to keep my mouth shut anymore. After all this—all these years of planning and meeting and bullshit—and Marissa and I are going to move here, to this? *Fuck* them."

"Fuck *you*!" screamed Josef. "The most important moment in the history of our movement and the history of our planning and you piss all over everything because your *feelings* are hurt? Your job was to set up the easel, pass out some brochures, and then just sit the fuck down with your mouth shut. It's *my* job to communicate! It's *my* job to put out fires, and you end up being the one who stands up with a flamethrower and torches the place!"

He took several deep breaths and then turned to Sergeant DeBoer. "I'm sorry for raising my voice. I'm sorry for what happened tonight. And I'm sorry for any hassle our presence creates for you."

She shook her head slightly. "It's my job. I'm actually an outsider myself." She grinned. "I'm from under the bridge. A troll."

"So how'd you manage to fit in?" asked Josef.

She squinted from the headlights of a passing truck. "I carry a gun, so it's a little easier."

Josef sighed, sat back, and rubbed his temples. "Let's put that in the brochure, Carl. Maybe tie it to Second Amendment issues. *Carrying a gun makes things a little easier.*"

They arrived at the dimly lit, twelve-room motel. "Take care of yourselves," said Sergeant DeBoer. "Call the station in the morning, and we'll arrange to pick you up and take you back to your car." She gave them her business card. "When are you guys going to start moving here, by the way? Are we talking six months? A year?"

"It'll be in waves," said Josef. He stepped out into the cold parking lot. "But a few of us will arrive real soon." He hesitated. "The end of the month."

She nodded, wished them well, and drove off, her taillights like cinders in the dark northern night.

◆ ◆ ◆

On the narrow road, under the invisible sky, Brenda thought about the changes that would come to her job—to her life. She knew Lenny would want to prepare thoroughly for this first wave. There'd be late meetings with the mayor, a darkened house when she returned home to Brian every night.

She arrived at the Civic Centre, the unlit windows and abandoned lot like the midway after it left town each summer without a trace. She circled the building to be sure nobody was lingering and then pulled up toward Josef's car. In the back lot, near a Dumpster, slumped a red Honda, its back window smashed in and all four tires slashed. She slowed to a stop and stared at the Indiana license plate. "A goddamned giveaway," she muttered. Asphalt glass reflected a streetlamp like the lake reflecting stars.

Chapter 16

Friday, October 31

A nine-year-old wizard and a half-pint ninja stood side by side beneath a huge oak tree—one of the last with leaves—with their arms stretched above their heads. Another leaf fluttered down to them, amid a few scattered snowflakes.

"I got it!" yelled the wizard. He caught it between his fingers just before it hit the ground.

"One, two," said the ninja as he clapped leaves between his palms. "That's five. I got five points."

"Boys!" called Mrs. Teunis, the fourth-grade teacher at Willow Street School. She wore a black cloak and hat, green makeup, and a nose with a giant rubber wart. "Get back in line. We're about to leave."

Brenda stood at the corner of Willow and Cooper. The light bar atop her cruiser cast blue and red hues over her face and uniform. Under cold, gray clouds the entire student body of the elementary school had lined up behind her. From one end to the other they represented a horrible display of either evolution or devolution. A gaggle of kindergartners led the pack as they did every year, dancing and hopping in place, dressed as happy clowns and princesses and superheroes. But as the line snaked back toward the school, the children grew in size—first grade, second grade, on up to sixth—and the clowns and princesses disappeared. By the middle of the line those wizards and ninjas emerged, along with soldiers, pirates, and witches. With the archery season well underway and the firearm season ahead, many of the boys wore the camouflage of deer hunters.

At the tail end of the line stood Mr. Lindquist's sixth graders—the blood-and-guts crew. Died purple hair. Fake blood splashed over white shirts. A plastic axe sticking out of a skull. They slouched and shoved and laughed, just happy to be free from their desks.

Mike Rozycki, the school principal, was the only person besides Brenda not in costume. He was an ex-military man, and he strode alongside the students, nodding sharply and punctuating his words with quick claps. "Are we ready? Are we set?"

The teachers tiredly nodded. Even the kindergartners had begun to shove.

"Wait. Where's the dog?" he asked. Young Ms. Hughes, the kindergarten teacher dressed as Dorothy from *The Wizard of Oz*, shrugged her shoulders.

"Forget him," said Mike. "We don't have time. Let's go." He flashed a hand signal to Brenda, who walked around the cruiser to the driver's-side door. The treats had been passed out. The apple-bobbing and song-singing had ended. And now the final leg of the school's Halloween party had come: the annual Monster March up Cooper Avenue into downtown.

Brenda idled out into the lane, past the orange cones set up to block the road from other traffic. She rolled down her window and watched the parade in her rearview mirror. The long snake of students uncoiled, the little kids up front overwhelmed by the freedom of being allowed to walk in the middle of the street, and the older kids at the back reveling in the liberty that came from being at the end of the line—farthest from Principal Rozycki—where they could toss rocks at street signs and flirt with the opposite sex. Mr. Lindquist was powerless somehow now that they'd breached the walls of the school.

Parents stood in front yards and on sidewalks along Cooper, waiting for a chance to spot their little ones and exchange a wave. They used to toss suckers and Smarties out to the students, but the ensuing wrestling and asphalt-diving had led Principal Rozycki to put an end to it.

As the snake stretched down the road, a rusty brown hatchback passed by going in the opposite direction. "Slow down!" shouted Brenda. She parked and stepped out of the car. The hatchback's tires squealed as it turned into the faculty parking lot at the school, and then they squealed again as it skidded to a stop. The driver instantly emerged from inside—a large gray dog wearing an orange-and-black tank top with matching shorts.

"It's Harry Husky!" yelled a first-grade cowboy. And so it was. Harry Husky, mascot of Haymaker High and perennial grand marshal of the Willow Street School Monster March, had finally arrived, though late, and now sprinted across the school grounds to the front of the parade. Principal Rozycki stopped, hands on hips, to watch him approach. This year, Harry

Husky was played by the tall and gangly Charlie Henke, a painfully shy teenager who, when he donned the costume, became not only extroverted but also wildly gymnastic. With Charlie beneath the fur, Harry Husky could perform backflips and even the splits, though today the main contortion seemed to involve his neck. In his rush, the Husky mask had gone crooked, the eyes and muzzle facing backward before Charlie straightened it again. The sixth graders pointed and screamed in laughter—another wonderful excuse to stumble out of line and celebrate.

"The speed limit on this road is twenty-five during school hours," said Principal Rozycki as Charlie met up with him. "And you're ten minutes late."

"Sorry," came a soft and muffled voice from beneath the fur. "Sorry."

The Monster March continued north. Knights, football players, and Egyptian queens roamed past houses decorated in orange lights with fake tombstones and cobwebs. Residents clapped and cheered. Brenda turned onto Marquette with Harry Husky, the principal, and the kindergartners right behind. Patrons and employees of downtown businesses walked out to the curb to watch the ceremonies and cheer.

Above them all, Donnie sat in the open window of his apartment, straddling the sill as he smoked a cigarette under the gray skies. He'd taken the day off and spent the morning lying on the couch, reading a book about iron ore freighters. He'd lain low since the town meeting, watching for any changes to the stump field—workers or bulldozers—and peering with binoculars through this window.

Donnie had once enjoyed Halloween the way most kids enjoy Christmas. When he was twelve, he and his buddies had managed to trick-or-treat at nearly every house in Haymaker. A couple of years later, he'd gleefully toilet-papered birch trees and smashed pumpkins. Even today, he enjoyed the sight of the Monster March more than he'd admit. When Ash was younger, he used to watch it from street level. In a few more years, when Patrick John entered kindergarten, Donnie would do the same for him. But he'd woken up today not even realizing it was Halloween. The date had lost its significance for him. Though that was about to change.

The rest of Willow Street School twisted around the corner. Eventually the ghoulish sixth graders made it onto Marquette, accompanied by a low but booming thump of bass. Donnie leaned farther out the window, trying to find the source of the music, and then turned around. It was coming from the opposite direction. At first he thought it might be the marching band, but then—on top of the bass—came the scraping sound of electric guitar. He recognized the song but couldn't identify it yet.

A pickup truck approached from the opposite end of Marquette Street. Then another. Then another. The drivers of the trucks stretched their left arms out the windows, brandishing American flags. And from each passenger-side window someone waved another flag that Donnie didn't recognize. Men, women, and children filled the beds of the trucks, dancing and singing and waving flags to the rhythm of the song. It blasted from speakers mounted on the lead truck: Neil Young, "Rockin' in the Free World."

Brenda stopped in the middle of Marquette Street and jumped from the cruiser. People on the street gawked, utterly confused by this other parade headed straight for the Monster March. Principal Rozycki and Ms. Hughes stopped dead, and the kindergartners bumped into them before tripping over one another. Harry Husky danced and skipped on—oblivious—performing cartwheels and waving to the people along the sidewalk.

Brenda jogged toward the motorcade with her right palm pressed out in front of her. "Hey! Stop!" She was as mystified as anyone.

The trucks closed in—ten in all—though only idling now. Behind them rolled a longer string of cars and RVs, all flashing their headlights and honking their horns. The music continued to roar: Twisted Sister now—"We're Not Gonna Take It." People waved the flags to the beat of the song—both the American flags and these others, which were dark blue and red with a white outline of a bear.

And then, to Brenda's shock, another mascot emerged—a furry black bear with a kind of Yankee Doodle hat atop his head. He waved to the crowd and especially to the schoolchildren, who stood there, thunderstruck. Even the sixth graders looked to the teachers for reassurance.

Principal Rozycki ran forward, stood beside Brenda, and shouted at the trucks. "Turn around! Get out of here! This is a parade!"

The people ignored him. They continued waving the flags and screaming "Whoo!" as if at a concert.

Brenda then recognized Carl Farmer standing in the bed of the lead truck. He wore a Chicago Blackhawks jersey and was singing at the top of his lungs, pumping his right fist in the air. A tall, thin man with a gray mustache stepped past Carl and climbed onto the roof of the truck. He was maybe in his early sixties, with a ball cap, a long gray ponytail, and a gold hoop earring. He held an American flag in one hand and the bear flag in the other, and then, looming over the street, crossed the flagpoles above his head in an X. Brenda knew in an instant it was their leader. It was Gorman Tate.

"What are you doing?" she yelled. By now those shop owners and their employees—who had stood and watched the March from the sidewalk—had wandered into the street and clustered in the small no-man's-land between the two parades. Tim Rogers, owner of The Venison, was there. So was Rita Gumpert. Brenda spoke directly to Gorman. "You can't do this. You need permission. You need a license."

"That'll change," he said, smiling down at her.

When people describe something as happening in a blur, they mean something like this: Donnie, sprinting out from behind the flower shop, zeroing in on the lead truck, and Brenda—in a moment of trained reflex—seeing him from the corner of her eye, catching him, and tackling him to the ground. Pain shot through her left arm. Her humerus had snapped.

"Get out of here, Donnie!"

"Free country!" he yelled.

"That's right," said Gorman, smiling from his perch. "Free country. Maybe you should be on our side, brother."

"Go stab yourself!" said Donnie, pulling himself free from Brenda. "Go fuck yourself and stab yourself!"

Brenda climbed to one knee but stopped there. She felt light-headed with pain. When she closed her eyes, everything looked white instead of black.

Some members of the libertarian parade took Donnie's words and made them a chant. "Free country! Free country!"

Principal Rozycki and Tim Rogers held him back now, each grasping one tattooed arm. Donnie kept screaming. "God's mercy on you swine!"

Brenda reached for her portable with her right hand—her left hanging limp at her side—and called for backup. The black bear mascot with the Yankee Doodle hat strode past her and began to playfully shadowbox with Harry Husky. Charlie—from beneath his mask—shoved the bear, sending him sprawling on his back so that the bear's head rolled a few feet down the road. There lay Lee Mooneyham.

"What are you doing?" yelled Lee. He stood up—a man's head with a bear's body—and tackled Harry Husky. A kindergartner dressed as a pumpkin screamed, and soon many younger kids who weren't already in tears began to cry. Townspeople surrounded the lead truck, pointing and shouting. Sirens sounded in the distance, barely audible under music pounding from the speakers. Guns N' Roses now: "Paradise City."

YEAR TWO

Chapter 1

Sunday, January 11

Josef's Honda lurched over ruts and permafrost as he entered the construction site of Freedom Springs. When paved, this main thoroughfare would be called Glory Road. Bulldozers, dump trucks, and excavators rumbled around him. Many of the workers were newcomers—libertarians with cold-weather construction experience. After digging foundations they set frost-free blankets over the exposed earth to keep it from freezing. To support the heavy snow loads that would settle on the condos, they used two-by-sixes instead of two-by-fours for the framing and placed trusses every foot. Each building would include two condos, and the first was now complete, serving as a model that newcomers could tour. The framing for another stood like a skeleton against the gray skies, and workers had already dug the foundations for two more. Chain-link fencing lined the field's perimeter, topped with razor wire.

All of this work had occurred only after the removal of the stumps. It was Roosevelt who'd told Josef what those stumps meant to the locals. "They've been squatting in that field for a century now. Some people are hoping that your construction crews will hit them like a wave against the breakwater and give up by spring. Those stumps are their last hope." But in the end the workers hauled in a three-ton grinder with a cutter wheel so savage that its forty teeth quickly turned all of the stumps into strewn chips and mash.

Josef visited the site each week and met with the general contractor. He communicated the progress in a newsletter he'd started writing called *The Paw*, which was published every Friday and mailed to all residents of

Haymaker—locals as well as the newly arrived. Construction updates were just a part of it. Most articles involved crisis management, countering the concerns raised in that week's *Star-Picayune.* Even in this age of new media, the Haymaker newspaper—which had for years reported on small-town minutiae like the middle school students of the month and the new book arrivals at the public library—had suddenly grown the editorial teeth Josef had both hoped and feared it would. Nearly all feature articles in the *Star-Picayune* now focused on the "libertarian issue." The op-ed section had doubled in size.

No crisis had been greater than the events of Halloween, when two parades had collided head-on in what Merv Grubb had termed "Monster March Mayhem." It was the first time Josef had questioned Gorman's judgment. "It's like telling them we come in peace," he'd told him, "but doing it with guns blazing. Gorman, I couldn't disagree with it more, and I personally won't take part in it."

It had begun with a throwaway statement during a conference call, with Carl saying they needed to create "a spectacle—to show them we're serious." After the city council meeting in October, Carl had sent Gorman a fiery report, and Gorman had of late seemed more aggressive. After years of patience and planning, Josef believed he was turning reckless with the goal now in sight. Gorman himself had planned the entire Halloween extravaganza. Instead of waiting until the summer, when several condos would be built and ready, he'd sent word through newsletters, phone calls, and social media that anyone who could make the move right away should meet in Michigan City before dawn and drive north, in one huge caravan, to Haymaker.

Josef—along with fellow members of the Freedom Congress Susan and Denny—avoided the spectacle altogether, spending that morning gathered in Denny's motel room, drinking Bloody Marys and waiting for news from the front. In the months since that initial fervor, Josef's job had been to walk the line in his writings: calming the fears of locals while simultaneously energizing that first wave of Black Bears, who now lived in motel rooms—many unemployed—under sunless winter skies. All of the charm and natural splendor that he'd written about in *Haymaker at a Glance*? It was buried under two feet of snow.

Josef turned his car around, nearly seasick from potholes, and left the development for the main road. As always, the streets were covered in a tightly packed layer of snow and ice. He'd planned on going home to work, a home paid for in part with a bonus check of $25,000 Gorman handed him a day after "Monster March Mayhem." "To thank you for your hard work," he'd said, "and to ease your worry-filled mind." Bud Wilmington sold Josef and Jeanie a yellow Cape Cod on Parson Avenue that had a detached garage and two birch trees in the front yard. The place was smaller than their home in Indiana, but like everything else, it was temporary. They'd build in a couple of years.

Josef drove slowly through the town with no real purpose, though he told himself it was all for research, to get to know the place better. He passed Little Deep Lake, where ice-fishing shanties dotted the smooth, white surface. A pair of snowmobiles cut across the road a short ways in front of him. They were everywhere, and the buzz of their engines wedged into the space between his skull and his brain. Even at home, watching TV, he could hear them whining through the town.

He looped south, through the winter-numb neighborhoods. Snowdrifts rose up the windward sides. Propane tanks slouched under a heavy layer of white. Enormous woodpiles slowly dwindled. And boats sat outside of garages like summertime ghosts.

Eventually—like almost everything and everyone in Haymaker—Josef made his way to Lake Superior. He pulled up to the public lot at Fitzgerald Beach and parked in front of the chained-off entrance. An orange NO SNOWMOBILES sign stood at either end. He turned off the engine. Canadian gales howled against the windshield. The beach itself stretched long and white into the distance, except for a few spots where the raw winds had sliced over the lake and exposed patches of sand like skinned knees. At the edge of the pier the water remained unfrozen, though the white lighthouse was encased in pale blue ice. The waves curled against the sides of the pier and, like a barber's straight razor, seemed to sharpen as they continually scraped past.

After a few minutes he started the car again and headed home, where packed shipping boxes still lined the basement walls. And when he opened the side door and stepped into the kitchen, his cold lungs filled with warm, sweet air.

Olivia sat on the counter peeling a banana. "Mommy's making pancakes."

Over at the table, Grace anxiously waited for breakfast, a napkin tucked beneath her chin.

Jeanie stood before the stove. "We're going to make funny faces on them with pieces of fruit."

Olivia shrieked with laughter and held the banana up to her mouth like a giant yellow grin. Josef hugged her, smiling himself, and kissed her on the forehead.

◆ ◆ ◆

The Capagrossas approached Freshwater Community Church in their salt-stained Chevy Malibu. The marquee of the old Neptune Theater read, on one side:

"FIELD OF BLOOD"
SERMON BY REV. BERNARD ZUBER
SUNDAY—9 AM

Denise parked along the curb and stepped out of the car. Ash—her hair dyed a dark purple—unbuckled Patrick John from his car seat and slowly followed, passing beneath the marquee.

GOSSIPS GET CAUGHT IN THEIR OWN MOUTHTRAPS

After dropping Patrick John off at the basement nursery, Denise and Ash walked down the church's main aisle, slipped into the fifth row, and settled into their red velvet seats. The band had already begun pounding out "Our God Is an Awesome God," the lyrics visibly shaking on the movie screen from the beat of the bass drum. Ash put her fingers in her ears, and Denise swiftly slapped one of her hands down. She'd required Ash to attend every Sunday since September, since Josef had rescued Patrick John at the White Sable Dunes.

"You can thank God each week that your brother's okay," Denise had said, "and pray to God each week you don't screw up like that again."

So Ash sat here today, the music hurting her ears, fidgeting in the tight seat and wishing the old man beside her would let her have the armrest. Melted snow dripped from her boots. Winter had settled on Haymaker, and it felt, to Ash, like a blanket that calmed and quieted the town. There were two feet of snow on the ground, the temperature hovered in the low to mid twenties, but locals kept saying things like, "Got us a mild winter this year," and, "Shit, it's like spring." They said these things for effect, to intimidate and distance themselves from the newcomers—the "invaders," as some called the Black Bears. But they also seemed to say it for themselves—for reassurance. To remind themselves that they had thick skin, in both senses of the phrase.

The song ended, and in the new quiet Ash took a deep breath and let it out slowly, her palms pressed against her thighs. Every Sunday when she sat here she thought about that day at the dunes. And she thought about the close call she'd had with Patrick John just this week. While scooping him up out of his high chair she'd playfully lifted him too high. His head shattered a wine glass that hung suspended upside down from a ceiling rack. She screamed—glass at her feet, the jagged stem stabbing downward. He began to cry, but it seemed to come only from the loud noise. Ash ran her fingers gently over his head. Not a scratch. Lately, everything seemed fragile. The fresh snow was like a soft pillow.

But all winter long the temperatures cycled between cold and mild, the snow falling hard for a few days before receding to slush soon after. The locals, for all their bluster, were right. It *was* a tame winter. The third one in a row. All of this worried Uncle Donnie. Over the years she'd seen him reading articles on melting ice caps and ebbing glaciers. This Christmas, at Grandma Sarver's house, he'd played poker at the kitchen table, drunk on whiskey, and at one point—from out of nowhere—bellowed, "If I could only have one superpower, I'd shoot ice from my eyes and freeze these fuckers right out of town." Ash couldn't think of any other way to stop them from coming. She wondered if any of the worshipers in this sanctuary were praying to God—right at this moment—that He bring a fiercer winter, that He blast away those who didn't belong.

Maybe some said this prayer for financial reasons. Groomed snowmobile trails threaded this area like spiderwebs, and winter tourism was as important as that of the summer months. In the past, flatlanders arrived pulling their white trailers, checking into the Duneview, the Lumberland Inn, the Black Birch Motel, and the North Gateway Inn. Restaurants filled up after sundown, and in the morning the snowmobilers brought their machines to Uncle Donnie's shop for repair. Their distant buzz filled the skies like some winter insect.

Yet there were less of them this year—partly because of erratic snow and slushy trails, but mainly because the motels in Haymaker were full of Black Bears staying long term while waiting for the construction of their condos in the old stump field—now called Freedom Springs. The motels didn't mind—they stayed continuously full. Neither did The Venison, T's Pizza, The Shipwreck Café, nor The Lucky Lumberjack. But the newcomers sure as hell didn't give any business to Sarver Towing and Repair.

Drums, guitar, and horns returned: the band thundered through the start of "Lord, We Lift Your Name on High." Ash stared at her fingertips, which had begun to heal as she'd moved from the rough-gripped surface of the outdoor ball to indoor play. The JV season had begun, and after seven games she was averaging twelve points and five rebounds a game. Coach LaGrave had begun to call her Rainbow not only because of her ever-changing hair color, but also because of the huge, exaggerated arc of her jumpers and the fact that most "ended in a pot of gold."

She attended the varsity boys' games on Friday nights. They were 6–1, and two nights ago Michigan State head coach and fellow Yooper Tom Izzo had been spotted in the crowd. With less than a month before National Signing Day, he'd come to scout Dominick Murphy. Ash tried to block out the noise of the church with the imagined sounds of the court—high-tops squeaking on hardwood and the blare of the horn during substitutions. Two days ago, Dominick had scored twenty-one points and pulled off two circus-like, behind-the-back assists that had set the crowd off like a bomb. Someone reported seeing Izzo clapping and nodding his head, and Ash imagined a few years from now being scouted by a Big Ten program, being offered a scholarship to East Lansing or Ann Arbor or anyplace remotely south.

A junior named T.R. Schmidt now started at point guard. He was new; his family had moved from Ohio to Haymaker just months ago, as part of the first wave. Ash didn't know if he was a Black Bear, if he shared his parents' beliefs, or if he was like other teenagers, caring for politics as much as gardening or decaf coffee.

Prayers commenced, deacons took the offering, and eventually Pastor Zuber approached the podium. He wore a navy suit and dark red tie. His hair had gone salt-and-pepper in recent years, and Ash thought he looked a tad bigger in the belly than she'd remembered from even a year ago, when her mom had made her come to church during Advent. But his eyes looked strangely younger of late. He clenched the edges of the podium as he spoke. And when he did speak, he didn't shy away from the dominant issue of the town. Last week he'd preached how a tide of libertarianism would carry legalized sin onto their white shores: prostitution, drug use, and all-nude strip clubs "that would have made the girls of the boomtown's brothels—eight in number at the peak of those lumber-mad days—blush a deep red."

Ash had a hard time concentrating during any sermon, but she sat up straight in her seat during the climax of the morning's speech:

"We remember the arrest of Jesus, as told quite vividly in the Gospel of John—the angry mob with torches; Simon Peter cutting off the right ear of Malchus, the high priest's servant; and there, betraying Christ with a kiss, Judas, the archetypal traitor. We hear, in times of war, of traitors, and is there ever a person more despised? In explaining our innate, God-given morality, C.S. Lewis wrote, 'In war, each side may find a traitor on the other side very useful. But though they use him and pay him they regard him as human vermin.' If we see even a Communist spy as human vermin, then what oh what was the man who conspired against the Son of God? We know the story of the betrayal, but we often forget the epilogue, as told in Acts, chapter one, verses eighteen and nineteen. As you'll remember, Judas was paid thirty silver coins by the chief priests. But do you remember what he bought with those thirty silver coins? He bought a field. The passage reads, 'With the reward he got for his wickedness, Judas bought a field; there he fell headlong, his body burst open and all his intestines spilled out. Everyone in Jerusalem heard about this, so they called that field in their language *Akeldama*, that is, Field of Blood.' Ladies and gentlemen, you may be sitting right now wondering where I'm going with this comparison or where I have already gone. You may be wondering if I've really meant to make this point, considering the recent events in our town, or whether or not I've just stumbled here by coincidence. For all of you then, let me now assure you. Just as Jesus sometimes taught in parables, ladies and gentlemen, so do I."

It was now about three weeks until January 31—D-Day, the due date—and Clara lay in bed amid scraps of colored paper, scissors, and stickers. Her eyes slowly closed in fatigue, the baby book she was working on balancing atop the dome of her belly. Nobody had welcomed the winter—and the strange calm it had brought to the libertarian storm—quite as much as she.

Gary entered the bedroom. "Are you sleeping?"

"Almost," she said.

He approached, his heavy snow boots thudding over the hardwood floor, and gently picked up the baby book and laid it next to her on the bed. "Do you want another pillow?"

She shook her head, eyes still closed. "And I'm not hungry. And I'm not thirsty."

"I'll let you rest, then," he said, closing the door—though not clicking it shut tight—and then his heavy bootsteps dissipated down the hall.

He was helpful. He was so terribly helpful. When not mushing or fixing up a few snowblowers in the garage, he was cooking meals, vacuuming the floors, scraping her car windows, shoveling the driveway, and salting the front stoop almost hourly so that neither she nor the baby would be harmed.

Clara understood this final act the most. She'd had the grim thought that, after all this, something would happen to the baby during its final days in the womb. But she also knew that all the other help was more than a husband's obligations or a man's form of nesting. Gary was still atoning for past sins, still silently trying to prove his goodness. She wished he'd stop. Every act of kindness only cast the shadow of Joanna Blue over what was to become her brand-new family. His only slipup had been his outburst at the city council meeting, when he'd stood up and shouted about people's backs being to the wall. And afterward he'd bought her flowers with a note that read, "Mrs. Mayor, I am so sorry. Your husband/citizen." But his depression always surfaced during the dim winter months, and she sometimes spotted him lying catatonic on the sofa with the TV off as if he were napping, although his wide-open eyes stared at the white wall.

Clara opened her own eyes now, reached for the baby book, and turned to the first page, where she'd placed the image of the sonogram. She stared at the strange skeletal form and tried to imagine—three weeks from now—this child made flesh.

Brenda stood in her kitchen making a grilled cheese sandwich, a suddenly simple task now that her arm was healed, out of a sling. Donnie hadn't made any trouble in town since she'd tackled him and broken her arm. In fact, the department had spent most of the past two months dealing only with minor traffic accidents and cars spun out in ditches. There were a lot more of these this year, a lot more drivers not used to this weather.

When Brenda returned home on evenings like this, Brian was almost always gone, plowing and salting the streets with his fellow Snow Soldiers. She'd make herself dinner in the dark kitchen and eat at the table, never turning on music or the TV but instead listening to the sounds of the furnace while slowly chewing her food. The gray clouds this time of year felt so low she could almost stand on her toes and scrape them with her fingernails. She'd always felt heavy and slow in the winters, missing all the hiking and kayaking they did in the summer months. The thought of snowshoeing or cross-country skiing made her cringe. The thought of spending more time under these skies.

She finished making the grilled cheese, grabbed a jar of pickles from the refrigerator, and fixed herself a glass of chocolate milk. Then she sat at the kitchen table and slowly ate, anticipating Brian's return, remembering yesterday when she'd met him at the door and begun undressing him without either of them saying a word. Snow had fallen from his clothes, and with each layer removed she got closer to his cold skin. They stumbled to the bedroom, kissing while tripping over their unbuttoned pants, and she reached down beneath his underwear and held him where he was small and cold and flaccid. She never did this in the summer. But in the winter she felt this desire—not to make him large or hard but to make him warm. And as he grew warm in her hand she used her other hand to find more cold places on his body. And at the same time he looked for the warmth in her, his freezing hands running over her breasts and thighs, lightning bolts on her skin both painful and wonderful. They sweated in a way they didn't even on hot summer nights, as if their dormant bodies—craving their usual activity—had stored up all of this sweat and let it go at once with everything else. The snow melted from Brian along with the smell of the outside cold, changing to the warmth of the house and then the musk of intercourse. Their nerves were raw from driving all day on the bad roads—in the cruiser, in the plow—but by the time every part of his skin was warm she'd forgotten the town—forgotten everything—amid those few seconds of orgasm, a splinter of time as sharp and pure as diamonds. As ice.

Roosevelt sat at the bar in Rusty's, sipping his Presbyterian and glancing occasionally at Donnie and his crew. They sat at a long table in a dark corner. Donnie's knee fluttered up and down as he tapped his heel. He spoke very little. Ray Valentine slouched in a chair to his left. Russ Gillickson sat to his right, wearing a ball cap low over his brow and nodding his head to jukebox music. Roosevelt recognized the other men around the table, but didn't really know any of them. The dirt floor at Rusty's was frozen solid and hard as limestone. To keep their beers cold, the men simply set them down on the ground between sips.

A few of the men glanced over at Roosevelt—at this man who was not a Haymake and not an outsider. Everybody trusted him. Nobody trusted him. He had known before anyone else in the town what was coming and yet, in the pit of his gut, never felt it would happen. There were rumors of a "second wave," though nobody seemed to know just when this might occur. The newcomers were shooting soon for an even hundred, a number that would look good for Novak's PR.

Roosevelt nodded at Rusty, whose toupee was tilted to the right of his brow. "A round of drinks for the gang over there, and two for the ringleader."

Rusty nodded. "You like to be the peacemaker and the peacekeeper, don't you."

"No need to talk peace when there's no talk of war."

Rusty shrugged and looked at Donnie's table. "Maybe that's what they're mulling over." He filled the glasses, and Bep walked over a tray full of beer and whiskey. As she set it on their table she nodded toward Roosevelt, who peeked nonchalantly under the bill of his white beaver felt hat. Donnie mumbled something to his men, and in unison they looked at Roosevelt, raised their drinks in a toast, and poured them onto the cold, hard dirt.

Roosevelt turned to Rusty. "I think I'll pay my bill now."

He paid, walked calmly outside without further acknowledging the men, and drove home. It was only eight o'clock but long past nightfall, and as he approached the dark dead end of Ross Road, he noticed—parked in front of the old Smith house—a gray Lincoln Navigator with its engine running and its headlights shining. Roosevelt pulled up behind it and stopped. A heavyset man in a bulging ski jacket trudged through the snow in the front yard. He held a flashlight, which he shoved in his pocket as he approached the FOR SALE sign, and then he gripped the sign with both hands, rocking it back and forth.

Roosevelt stepped outside and walked around the front of his car. "You finally give up on that one, Bud?"

Bud Wilmington looked up. "You wish, Bly." He pulled the sign free and then slogged toward Roosevelt, plunging groin-deep as he reached the plowed snowbanks at the road's edge. "No, sir. All I had to do was find another person like you. A mild eccentric with lots of money."

"Bought it for yourself, then. Congratulations. Certainly is a golden age for you."

Bud stood panting now in front of the headlights. The breath bloomed from his mouth, and steam rose from his bald head. "Well, you're right about that last part. But nope, I sold it to an out-of-towner. A man who's been living alone for the past few months in the Lovebirds Suite at the Ophelia. A Mr. Gorman T. Tate, Esquire."

Roosevelt nodded slightly. "Well, then," he said, "looks like I'll finally have a neighbor."

Bud smirked and shrugged. "You'll have something, my man." He opened the door to the Navigator and shoved the sign onto the passenger's seat.

Roosevelt said nothing in return. He simply got back in his Town Car and drove to the end of the road, to his own dark mansion.

Chapter 2

Saturday, January 24

Ash and Victoria Plunk sat on the aluminum bleachers, wrapped together in an enormous camouflage blanket that had belonged to Ash's father. Like the other fifty or so people in attendance, they waited for the start of the race.

Before them stretched the frozen surface of Big Deep Lake where eighteen snowmobiles roared in anticipation of the Haymaker 100, an endurance race begun four years earlier by Pete Lundberg, owner of Superior Auto Sales, who was looking to expand his operations into motorsports. The drivers had lined up in two long rows of bright green, red, and blue machines, rumbling atop the ice as they waited, rattling the bleachers. In the second row, on a black Polaris, sat Uncle Donnie. He'd won the race in its inaugural year, but flatlanders had dominated the event for the past two, including last year's victor, Erik Schwartz—the transplant from Germfask Donnie had trounced in last summer's Shit-Kickin'. Donnie wore all black except for a bright orange lightning bolt he'd painted on the side of his helmet.

Ash unfolded the one-page event program and scanned the racer information. Most were Yoopers, including a few other Haymakes, though a couple were from out of state. And one was a Black Bear named Doug Butcher, whose hometown was listed as Haymaker, though Ash knew from Uncle Donnie that he was originally from New Hampshire. "He was one of those sons a bitches on Halloween shaking his fist and waving his flag." The man was dressed in red, white, and blue atop a red Arctic Cat with the words LIVE FREE OR DIE across the sides.

Victoria said something, pulling her right hand out from under the blanket and pointing to the chain-link entrance of the raceway.

"What?" yelled Ash. They both wore orange foam-rubber earplugs.

"I said, 'Oh my God, look at the dogs!'"

Two teams of dogs—huskies, mainly—came to a stop near the makeshift winner's circle, about fifty yards from the starting line. A PA announcer spoke from somewhere.

"Ladies and gentlemen, a warm welcome to Jeremy Marx, Gary Hollingshead, and the hardworking canines of one of our sponsors, Marx Iditarod, who want to remind you that next weekend is the Marquette Mush, a hundred-and-five-mile dogsled race from Marquette to Haymaker. This charitable event will raise money and awareness for the Superior Animal Welfare Shelter. Pledge forms are available at the concession stand. Let's hear it for them."

The dogs paced and fretted from the noise of the racers. A few howled at the gray sky before the drivers got them moving again, turning back the way they'd come.

"Okay," yelled Victoria, "so how far is the course?"

Ash squinted out across the lake. Hay bales, old tires, and orange pylons circled its perimeter. "It's four miles around."

"So how many times do they go around?"

Ash shrugged. "Well." She paused a moment, doing the division. "Like, twenty-five, I guess."

"Oh my God, are you serious? I'm not freezing my ass off for twenty-five laps."

"You can warm up in the car every once in a while."

Victoria was sixteen and drove her dad's old Chevy Tahoe. She yelled louder than usual over the noise. "Oh, I will!"

Ash shrugged and stared at the racers. She'd been thinking a lot about Uncle Donnie these past couple of months, watching him like everyone else, waiting for him to explode in some way. Last week during worm dissections, her biology lab partner, Nolan Reid, had said, "I heard your uncle's on the terrorist watch list. That he wants to blow up the Mackinac Bridge." Ash had merely rolled her eyes. So far, for the most part, she hadn't noticed much of a change in him.

Ash herself still didn't know what to think of these newcomers. She knew the Black Bears were called libertarians, which had the word "liberty" in it, which she'd been taught her whole life—at home and school and everywhere—was a good and American thing. These people waved American flags and said they loved freedom, and she couldn't in any way figure out why that was a problem. T.R. Schmidt, the point guard with Black Bear parents, kept scoring points on the boys' varsity team, and she and the rest of the crowd kept cheering. And then just the other night, while her mom was watching TV and drinking a glass of wine, Ash had asked what she thought of them. "Hey, you know," she'd said between sips, "it's a free country. They want a free country. I like a free country. Who knows? Maybe I'm one of them. Maybe not. Probably not. But maybe I am."

And then Denise had turned away from the TV and leaned toward Ash. "When your uncle was young, he would have loved them. He would have been right on board. Up until Jane died. Then, who the hell knows what happened? Now he's a dog pissing on his territory every few feet so people know it's his."

The voice of the PA announcer returned.

"Ladies and gentlemen, welcome to the fourth annual Haymaker 100."

People applauded with gloved and mittened hands, making little sound.

"As our eighteen racers prepare to begin, please address your attention to the podium at the winner's circle area, where Charlotte Hoover, minister of music at Freshwater Community Church, will now lead us in the singing of our national anthem."

A small American flag whipped furiously in the wind. Everyone in the bleachers stood, hands on hearts. There was debate as to whether men should remove stocking caps.

In the lower section of the bleachers were about a dozen people wearing red, white, and blue; Ash figured they were here to cheer Butcher. One of them—a man with a heavy black beard—unfurled another American flag, one so huge it caught the wind like a sail, cracking in the air above the heads of those near him. The Black Bears held the Stars and Stripes above their heads as most everyone looked in their direction. Victoria leaned and spoke into Ash's ear. "Oh. Shit."

When the anthem ended, the PA announcer once again broke the brittle air.

"Now let us bow our heads as the Reverend Bernard Zuber of Freshwater Church leads us in prayer."

Pastor Zuber stepped to the podium in a bright yellow ski jacket, his cheeks and ears blazing red from cold.

"Holy Father, we ask on this winter morning that you protect these men as they prepare for competition. Keep them safe. Keep them strong. And help them to honor You through their deeds here today. Amen."

Ash opened her eyes and looked again at Victoria. "That was short," she said.

Victoria blinked away the light and raised her head. "Because it's cold as crap."

A man walked gingerly to the middle of the track. The snowmobiles roared in fresh anticipation. So did the fans. The group of Black Bears began chanting Butcher's name. "Make us proud!" someone cried. Then another one of them—a fresh-faced man with red sideburns dipping below his hat—reached down by his feet and lifted up a large cardboard box. He pulled out what appeared to be a fur coat but then threw it awkwardly over his body, zipping it to the neck before stepping into a pair of brown, furry pants. His friends laughed and cheered him on, raising their coffees, cocoas, and Budweisers over their heads.

Finally the man with the box removed a huge bear head and set it over his own. Ash had heard about Liberty Bear and his fight with Charlie Henke on Halloween.

"Why has everyone become a stupid joke?" yelled Victoria. But Ash said nothing, pretending she couldn't hear her over the noise.

Finally the man standing on the course lifted a green flag above his head. Behind him stretched the track of frozen lake, a wide swath of snow cleared all the way around to reveal the cloudy ice. He dropped the flag, and the engines erupted, causing the earth to tremble, causing Ash to cover her already-plugged ears. She half expected the ice to crack open and swallow all the racers. But the ice here went deep, and within seconds the racers stretched across it like a brilliantly colored snake. In a minute they were small on the horizon, rounding the lake, their sound a low rumble of white noise that massaged Ash's head and relaxed her. But as they passed by after the first lap, she tensed up again. Uncle Donnie had already fallen to the middle of the pack.

By the twentieth lap, Ash was experiencing a kind of hypnotism. For the early circuits the machines had stayed grouped together, buzzing by the bleachers and then leaving the crowd in relative silence while they arced off into the distance, shrinking to specks on the far side of the lake. Now they were more spread out, and every few seconds another racer seemed to approach and fly by. Uncle Donnie had climbed back to fifth. Doug Butcher kept switching between second and third.

Victoria had left after lap eighteen, saying she was going to blast the heat in the car and take a nap. But for Ash the numbness had led to something like comfort. She stood to get a hot chocolate from the concessions, but on her way she saw Roosevelt standing a little ways off from the Port-a-Johns. He wore a long white coat that went all the way to his ankles. She was struck by the sight of him in the snow. He was camouflaged.

"Mr. Bly!" she called while approaching.

He turned, looking confused and old, but upon recognition slipped effortlessly back into his gleaming self. "Ms. Capagrossa!"

They bought hot chocolates and sat together in the bleachers. He nodded at the rowdy group of Butcher supporters toward the front. "I see Evel Knievel has some fans."

"Who?"

"The guy decked out as the star-spangled banner. The patriotic-looking fellow."

"I guess." She looked him up and down. "Aren't you cold?" She never saw old people out in this kind of weather unless they were shuffling in the direction of some warmth.

Roosevelt touched his coat. "This oilskin duster is a magical thing." He smiled and nodded toward the race. "So, supporting your uncle again?" he asked.

A wave of heat passed through Ash's body. She remembered Roosevelt at the city council meeting, stepping down from the chair, yelling and approaching Uncle Donnie. She shrugged. "I just like sports and races."

Roosevelt smiled a bit and looked at her out of the corner of his eye.

"What?" she asked.

He shook his head and stared out at the track, but she was left with a strangeness she'd never felt with him. Something she didn't like.

"Is that such a bad thing?" she asked.

He continued to watch the race. She didn't know if he was ignoring her or truly couldn't hear her amid the noise. She didn't ask again. And neither said a word until two laps later when a driver attempted to go wide and pass a cluster of his rivals while coming out of the fourth turn. Instead, he lost control, spun around twice, and slammed into the stacked hay bales in front of the bleachers. An EMT crew approached on snowmobiles. Everyone stood and went silent. Ash stretched her neck to see if he was okay but was secretly exhilarated by the memory of the crash and wanted to see another one just as spectacular. The driver stood up, waved toward the crowd, and then hopped back on to continue the race. The whole thing broke the awkwardness Ash had been feeling.

Roosevelt spoke into her ear. "Your uncle's in real good shape."

As he said this, Donnie squeezed on the inside past the second-place racer until he himself was second only to Butcher's red, white, and blue snowmobile, which led by a margin of mere seconds. With two laps to go, Donnie rode up onto Butcher's shoulder, pressing to pass, but Butcher managed each time to hold off the surge until they reached the next turn. Then Donnie would drop low, looking to pass on the inside. But Butcher would hold him tight and box him in close to the hay bales.

Ash and Roosevelt were so fixated on this back-and-forth that it was only too late that they noticed a third racer come slingshotting around a turn, passing Donnie and settling into second. Donnie became completely boxed in by the two leaders now as they reached the backstretch of the final lap. Everybody stood and screamed. Ash jumped up and down on her seat, rattling the frigid aluminum. Her throat hurt. Roosevelt put his two index fingers to his mouth and let out a shrill whistle. He was cheering for Uncle Donnie, and this mattered to Ash.

The small group of Black Bears bounced in unison while they cheered, their blankets cast off and lying on the ground in heaps. The man with the red sideburns once more pulled out the Liberty Bear costume and struggled into it.

The lead pack emerged from the final turn and roared down the icy homestretch. Butcher flew past the checkered flag in first. The slingshotter—an eighteen-year-old kid from Escanaba named Jordan Daniels—held on for second. Donnie followed just behind, in third.

Ash stood on top of her seat, mouth slightly agape. Roosevelt picked up her blanket, brushed off the snow, and set it over her shoulders. Other snowmobiles crossed the finish line. In the distance, during a gap between racers, Jeremy Marx and his dogs glided across the ice with a large gold trophy, headed toward the winner's circle.

The group of Butcher fans chanted his name and unfurled the huge American flag once more so that it shivered in the wind. And then they unfurled the other: dark blue and red with the white image of a bear.

Roosevelt yelled in her ear. "It's time to go!"

She nodded but remained still. A chain-link fence separated the fans from the track, and Liberty Bear had begun to clumsily ascend it. He plunged over headfirst, landing on his back and then sliding down a snowy embankment, pumping his furry fists the whole time. Soon the rest of his friends were scaling the fence, shimmying down the embankment, and skating their way toward Butcher in the winner's circle. An elderly race official, struggling to balance on the ice, approached them. "Get off the track! This ain't your ice!" But the noise of the engines swallowed his words in midair. The Black Bears surged forward.

Butcher stood now on the seat of his snowmobile. He removed his helmet and the goggles underneath, revealing a beaming middle-aged face with just enough stubble to give it a shadow of handsomeness. Jeremy approached with his dogs and handed him the trophy, which Butcher then used to wave his friends over. A couple of them, including Liberty Bear, lost their footing and fell on their backs, but all eventually made it to the winner's circle, waving their enormous flags.

"It's time to go!" Roosevelt said again.

Ash didn't notice the other snowmobile approaching until the moment had already occurred. Uncle Donnie came ever so slowly from behind, giving Butcher's machine what Roosevelt would later describe as a "love tap." Butcher lost his balance and fell awkwardly to the ice onto his right side. Donnie removed his black helmet with the orange lightning bolt, and Butcher stood to face him. The two began screaming, but Ash couldn't make out the words.

Roosevelt grabbed her by the arm. "Right now!"

Butcher's friends—men and women—descended on Donnie. Liberty Bear reached him first, covering Donnie's face with a huge furry paw and shoving his head backward. Donnie swung a wild fist and missed.

All of the other racers finished the race and, one by one, turned off their engines. But in this quiet, a second commotion filled the wide sky. Jeremy Marx's two lead dogs began growling and barking. They started to pull the sled and the other dogs toward the giant, aggressive bear. Race volunteers and other competitors scrambled into the mix, some reaching for the harnesses, others pulling Donnie away from the fight. The team dogs bared their teeth and barked uncontrollably. One reared back its head and howled.

Chapter 3

Tuesday, February 3

Clara had not expected this: quiet dimness and a soft, glowing calm. Midnight drew near—the birth drew near—as she lay in a room that itself felt like a womb. The epidural was working.

On TV shows the delivery rooms were bright and cold and filled with people. But this—her head floating from fatigue and the needle relief in her spine—was nice. Gary had plugged in a small set of speakers, and now Mozart played softly in the quiet. She'd packed the music with the rest of her things three weeks ago. Music to relax to. Music to enter the world to.

Gary sat in the corner flipping through copies of *Redbook* and *Good Housekeeping*, his knee bobbing to something faster than the music. Clara watched him through half-closed eyelids. He wavered in the dim light like a mirage in his blue-and-black flannel shirt. His beard needed a trimming.

"You look like a lumberjack," she mumbled.

"Try to sleep."

Clara slipped in and out of it, enjoying the effects of the wonderful, wonderful epidural. Time passed more quickly now.

She'd planned on a natural childbirth. She'd read too many books. The delivery room at LaRock Medical was remarkably state-of-the-art with a spacious bathroom and a tub with jets like a whirlpool. Two hours ago—when the pain had swelled to its high tide—Gary had guided her into it. She couldn't lie down but had merely stood under a hot shower, trying to relax as another wave of contractions hit every few minutes. Gary stayed next to her just outside the tub, shifting from one foot to the other. Each time the pain receded, he massaged her wet neck and back.

"My God," she said, "something finally feels good."

Twenty-four hours had already passed. Just before midnight on Monday she'd woken thinking she'd peed herself and staggered to the bathroom with the front of her wet sweatpants bunched up in a fist.

"What's going on?" Gary had asked from the bedroom, his voice coming from that ethereal place of near-sleep, where he was barely aware of his own words.

Clara had walked back out into the hallway, turned the light on overhead, and faced where he lay in the darkness. "I think my water just broke," she said softly.

Gary shot to his feet. His white eyes glowed in the dark bedroom. "What?"

"I think my water just broke. But I'm not having any contractions."

"Does that happen?" He bent to the floor, groping for his jeans. "That's weird, isn't it?" He pulled on his pants and ran past her, down the stairs, to get his phone. He returned with it pressed to his ear, the other hand holding the business card with Dr. Tracy's number.

Clara walked slowly to the dresser and removed dry pairs of sweatpants and underwear. "I don't know if it's worth waking him for this. It's obviously going to be awhile."

"You don't know." Gary tapped his finger on the nightstand, listening to the dial tone. "Fuck that. We're calling."

But Dr. Tracy replied as she'd expected. "If she's not having contractions yet, just stay home. If after twelve hours she's still not experiencing any, then come in anyway. Until then, get some sleep. You're both going to need it."

Clara surprised herself by actually falling asleep, for nearly five hours. Gary stayed up all night. At two o'clock he dusted and vacuumed the house. At three he scrubbed countertops and cleaned out the refrigerator. Around four he locked his rifles and handguns in the new safe he'd bought, a promise made to Clara years ago, if there were ever to be a child in the house. Afterward he stepped outside to shovel and salt the front stoop. Heavy snow fell, blowing hard off the lake. He returned outside just after dawn to shovel again, brush off his truck, and scrape the ice off the windows. Then he started the engine and blasted the heater, certain that the contractions would start at any moment. Around ten in the morning he remembered the truck, ran outside, and found it had stopped, out of gas. He rummaged through the garage for the spare red gas tank he used for the snowblower and poured in two gallons.

Dr. Tracy called around noon. "Still nothing, huh? I guess it's time to head over so we can find out what's up with the little one. See why Baby wants to break the water and then get real comfy again like it's any other day."

Clara donned her red ski jacket—the hood snug against her round, pregnant face—and held Gary's arm over the ice-free walk that he'd created, to the truck. Six inches of fresh snow had fallen overnight. The temperature was ten, the windchill minus five. They joked about spinning out into a ditch, giving birth in the front seat of the truck.

"Let's just pray to the gods of four-wheel drive," Clara said as they backed out into the road. But the short trip was uneventful, the roads plowed and the intersections covered in salt and sand. She smiled. "Remind me to give those Snow Soldiers a raise."

Tiana Ray met them outside LaRock Medical with a wheelchair and rolled Clara inside as Gary stumbled through the sliding doors with two duffel bags slung over his shoulders and an enormous inflatable birthing ball in his arms. Clara planned on sitting and leaning on it during the contractions, like they'd practiced in their weekly class at the hospital in Sault Ste. Marie.

A different nurse hooked Clara up to an external monitor once they were settled in their room. Though Clara didn't feel any, the machine detected some irregular contractions. At two thirty the nurse inserted an IV needle into her arm—the Pitocin meant to induce labor. She stopped by the room every half hour, bumping up the amount until, by four thirty, Clara was standing with the birthing ball trapped between herself and the wall, swaying back and forth as Gary massaged her shoulders. The labor had finally arrived. By evening, waves of pain rolled in every two to four minutes.

"Somebody take this damn monitor off," she said, grabbing the wires that connected her to the machine. "I feel like a robot, and I need a hot shower. Right now."

So she stood in the shower, riding out the nausea that now swooped in with the pain. Dr. Isackson, the anesthesiologist, stopped by with consent forms. "We need your signature in the event that you eventually decide on an epidural."

She shook him off.

"Come on, babe," said Gary as she winced in the shower. "I think it's time."

She reached above her head and clutched the curtain rod. Water dripped from her swollen breasts and dark nipples, onto her massive belly, where it rolled past her navel and curved underneath. "Those blue-haired women at the Shipwreck kept saying I'd change my mind when the pain hit. Damn them."

She signed the papers at six thirty. It was as if someone had stuck a needle in Gary's spine—the relief hit him before it hit her—and he sat back and sighed in the lavender chair in the corner. It took three agonizing tries for Dr. Isackson to finally "find the sweet spot" as he called it, but seconds after he did Clara's eyes grew heavy, her breathing calmed, and she rested. The anesthesia made her hands shake and her teeth chatter. The nurse put two heavy blankets over her, but Clara smiled faintly with closed eyes. "What the hell was I thinking?" she said to Gary. "This is heaven."

There was pressure—severe pressure—but not pain. The room and the hallway outside had fallen dark and quiet by the time a nurse named Katie told Clara she could finally push.

Soon she'd have her baby. Her boy. She and Gary had never found out the sex for sure, but they'd always known somehow it would be a boy. All of the old women at the Shipwreck had proven it with their voodoo. They'd had her pick a key up off a table, and since she'd picked it up by the bow, her child would be a boy. They told her that Clara's salty cravings meant a boy; sweets meant a girl. One woman, "Compass" Rose Patrick, told her to eat a clove of garlic, and if it seeped out her pores, there was a 99 percent chance it was a boy. And all of this confirmed what a palm reader in Jackson Square had told Clara a decade earlier, during a trip to New Orleans. "You'll have one child," the old man had said. "A son. And his name will be royalty."

She and Gary had picked a name even before the conception: James.

"Come look, Dad," said Dr. Tracy.

Gary gingerly peeked around, afraid of what he might see as the head began crowning. "Oh, wow," he said. "He's got really black hair. Look at that."

Dr. Tracy looked at Clara and smiled. "Do you want to see?" Clara nodded, and Dr. Tracy positioned a small rectangular mirror so that Clara could see all that was happening on the other end of her body. Emerging from the darkness of her pubic hair was the slick, dark hair of her child. "This is really, really weird," she said.

After only fifteen minutes of pushing, the child's head came free, and then, like nothing, the rest followed. Clara couldn't see anything except Gary's face. He kept smiling.

"What is it, Dad?" asked Dr. Tracy. He bent forward, his eyes growing larger, the grin remaining. "It's a girl."

"A girl!" said Clara. She could feel her smile through the numbness of her body. The rest she only remembered when, in the days ahead, she and Gary recounted it. Gary cut the cord—which neither thought he'd dare to do—and then she pushed until she'd expelled the placenta.

"I'm glad I won't remember all this," she said.

Dr. Tracy stitched up a second-degree tear while Clara repeated, "I can't believe it's a girl," and "She's so small, she's so small."

After wiping off most of the white, sticky vernix and sucking fluid from the baby's lungs, the nurse swaddled her in a blue-and-white blanket and handed her to Gary, who then brought her over to Clara and laid her on her chest.

"You're no James," said Clara. "You're not going to be king, are you?" She kissed the top of her head. "You're going to be queen." She realized now how much she'd wanted a girl, had always wanted a girl.

Gary rummaged through the pockets of his jacket and found his phone. He dialed Clara's parents first. "Your granddaughter is beautiful."

Clara looked into her daughter's wide, black eyes. "You're beautiful, Mary. You are."

After the phone calls, Dr. Tracy and the nurses left for a few minutes. The new family huddled in the warm darkness, all three of them silent except for Mary's tiny grunts. Snow fell outside, accumulating quietly, like minutes and hours and days.

Chapter 4

Tuesday, February 10

Ash juked her defender with a head-fake before taking one step back—her toes just behind the three-point line—and burying the shot. The basket put the Haymaker Huskies girls' junior varsity team ahead by two over Newberry with little more than three minutes to play. The Huskies wore their white home jerseys with the orange-and-black trim. Ash's shorts came to the bottom of her knees, the way she liked them. On the front of her jersey—above and to the left of her lucky number eight—was a capital C. LaGrave had made her captain after their first game last week, when she'd scored sixteen points and grabbed seven rebounds.

The Huskies jogged to their end of the court, their stances wide and arms stretched in defense. The point guard for Newberry—a sprite of a girl, no more than five one—cut diagonally across the court with surreal quickness, blowing past her defender and squaring up for a jump shot. Ash, playing down low because of her size, lunged toward the girl with her right arm fully extended. Her middle fingertip caught the tread of the ball. The ball ripped off the top half of her nail. Lucy Peabody, Ash's teammate, caught the blocked shot and moved down the court on a fast break, bounce-passing the ball to Victoria Plunk, who awkwardly received it, threw it toward the hoop, and somehow made the basket.

A whistle blew, and a referee jogged to the scorer's table, motioning time-out. Ash's finger had speckled the ball and the court with blood. As a rule, she had to leave the game until the wound clotted and she'd washed up. The finger felt blazing hot, but it wasn't yet the heat of pain. Play resumed while she sat on the bench with Mr. Duncan, the all-sport trainer at Haymaker, kneeling on the floor in front of her with a plastic tackle box full of medical instruments, bandages, and salves.

Ash looked up into the bleachers. Her mom was working tonight at The 12 Months of Christmas, and so she'd had to miss this one. Yet there, eight or nine rows back—sitting far apart from everyone else—was Uncle Donnie, who never missed a game. He nodded at her, flashing a quick smile and pumping his fist slowly in front of his chest.

The game continued. As Mr. Duncan applied something to her finger that stung worse than the original pain, Newberry scored to cut the lead to two. But Ash didn't see that basket, and she paid little attention to the work on her finger. She continued to look back toward the bleachers, beyond Uncle Donnie now, to the double doors near the weight room entrance. Standing with some anonymous upperclassman was Dominick Murphy. He crossed his arms over his lean, muscular chest. His bright orange T-shirt was nearly wet all the way through with sweat, and he held a small white towel that he used to wipe his face. With the game continuing—Haymaker scoring now—Ash watched and waited to see if he'd look her way. She wondered how long he'd been standing there since finishing his workout, if he'd seen her blocked shot.

"You're a bleeder," said Mr. Duncan, taping the gauze tightly over her finger.

She nodded but said nothing, still watching Dominick. And then came the proof that he'd seen her. As he animatedly talked to his friend, motioning with his hands, explaining or illustrating something, he raised one arm—as if blocking an imaginary shot—and then grabbed his middle finger and made a motion to show blood flowing down his hand and wrist. He smiled and nodded. Newberry had taken the lead with little time remaining. Ash could just now feel the pain beating in her finger with each pulse. She smiled.

Chapter 5

Saturday, February 21

Josef and Jeanie stood against the bright white walls of Carl's new condo, eating carrot sticks and sipping Bud Light. Marissa approached them with a wide smile. She was nearly six feet tall—still a few inches shorter than Carl—with a broad nose and long auburn curls.

"It's so great to see you guys!" She wrapped an arm around each one's neck and then stepped back, smiling in a strange, sad way to Josef. "Carl will be so happy you came."

He knew what she meant. Since the move—since the parade especially—they'd spoken only professionally. Back in Michigan City they'd get together every few weeks to watch football or go out for drinks. Now it was only to work on *The Paw* and other communications in the apartment above The 12 Months of Christmas, which had been converted into a fully furnished office known as Freedom Community Headquarters.

Carl and Marissa were the first to move into Freedom Springs—had been the first to put their money down last year—and their housewarming party tonight was as much a celebration for all of them as it was for the engaged couple.

"The place looks lovely," said Jeanie.

Marissa rolled her eyes and waved the compliment away. "Please," she said. "Right now, it's still a mix of my froufrou single-life design and Carl's dorm-room bachelorhood aesthetic. As far as what the builders did, yes. It's a beautiful condo. Everyone moving here is going to be so lucky to have a place like this to call home." She lifted the tablecloth that covered the buffet—chips and dip, vegetables, cold cuts and mayo and rolls—to expose the two card tables pushed together underneath. "In the spring, we'll have some real furniture delivered. For now, we decided to just get through the winter."

Josef nodded. It had become a sort of mantra for everyone who'd made the move. Get through the winter and then construction would accelerate. Get through the winter and then he could meet more of the locals. Get through the winter and more jobs would spring up.

Marissa left them to greet more guests. Standing along the white walls or seated on blue folding chairs, others mingled and snacked. Susan and her husband, Jake, whispered to each other. Calvin Matchinski laughed and joked with Lee. Denny sat alone eating chips and salsa off a paper plate.

Of the dozen or so others squeezed into the living room, Josef knew most only from paperwork and other recruitment materials. Most were men, what Jeanie had come to call "Kodiaks": a more militant member of the Community that—less than four months in—had already grown impatient with the slow pace of change. Carl stood among these men now, shaking hands.

"Should we go over and say hi to him?" asked Jeanie. But seconds later Carl turned around, surveyed the room, and noticed the two of them up against the bright wall. He smiled and approached, holding a bottle of beer, and then wrapped his arms around Jeanie in a warm embrace. "Thanks for coming. Isn't this great!" He didn't mean the condo. He meant the gathering under its roof.

Josef extended his hand. "Congrats. We're so happy for you two." They shook.

"Now," asked Jeanie, "have you picked a date for the wedding yet?"

Carl nodded. "Narrowed it down to next summer. That's all I know. When Marissa tells me the exact date, I'll be sure to tell you."

They smiled. A silence settled over them. "I'm going to make a sandwich," said Jeanie, turning toward the buffet and grabbing a plate.

Carl smiled and shrugged at Josef. "So I guess this can go in *The Paw*, huh? The first residents of the place."

Josef nodded. "Oh yeah. It's a big story. Any positive news that shows progress is great. Takes people's minds off the weather."

They both smiled. Carl pointed toward Josef with his beer bottle. "Hey, did you hear about Greg and Becky Muller? We got some new locals speaking out in support of us. Talking about all the economic growth we're going to bring to the area."

"Yeah, we'll want to interview them. That's important."

Carl lowered his voice, took a small step closer, and pointed over his shoulder with his thumb. "And Dan Kemp back there was talking about how he and some other guys are keeping a tally of any sort of threat or act of intimidation coming our way. Things like phone calls and that note someone slipped under the door at Headquarters. And I guess a couple weeks ago somebody vandalized the house of Jimmy Bruce, the guy who sold us this land. So now you're talking about locals attacking other locals just for engaging in the free market. These are the kinds of stories that need to be told."

Josef looked down at the fresh beige carpet and nodded. "Well, a lot of those things have been touched on in the town paper. I know what you mean—not enough. Clearly. But *The Paw* goes out to all kinds of readers. I want to keep it positive on all sides. Once we play up divisions, the whole earth will crack open under our feet."

Carl took a quick sip of his beer. "Gorman said we should start hyping up the next wave of migration. Get our people charged up. Get the others to realize we ain't gonna stop."

"I'll talk to Gorman about it," said Josef. Before the move up north, Carl would only speak to Gorman during conference calls. Now he spent more personal time at Gorman's new house than Josef did.

A short while later, Josef and Jeanie wandered over to talk with Susan and Jake, to hear how their kids were adjusting to the move. That's when the doorbell rang and the door immediately swung open as Gorman burst over the threshold. "How are the nation's freedom-loving people on this day!" He wore an enormous fur ushanka on his head with the earflaps down, his gray ponytail pouring from the back. In his gloved right hand he held a bottle of champagne. People drifted toward the front door, where Gorman treated them—men and women alike—to a series of enormous embraces. He strode toward Josef. "Let me give you a Black Bear hug, my boy!" Josef's face plunged into Gorman's shoulder. He smelled like pine needles and Stetson cologne.

Gorman stood now in the center of the room, his jacket making him seem like an even larger version of himself. All of the bear hugs had pushed his hat to the top of his head, where it sat like a crown. "Where's the lucky couple?"

Carl and Marissa approached, smiling, their eyes cast downward.

"I say lucky because you, my friends, are like pioneers. You're like the voyageurs who once built outposts on this pure northern shore. For you two are the first to lay claim to what is rightfully yours and plant the flag of the Black Bears in our Freedom Springs. May joy and bounty spring forth for you and all who follow."

The small living room erupted in a roar of cheers and applause. Josef stayed silent, but a childlike grin spread across his face.

Gorman raised the bottle of champagne. "A part of me feels like we should smash this against the wall, like we're christening a ship." He smiled and put his arm around Marissa's shoulders. "Don't worry, my dear! I'm just joking!"

Everyone laughed. He stepped toward Carl and handed him the bottle. "This is a Dom Pérignon 2000. Enjoy it, son. Just don't go mixing it with your orange juice." They all laughed again.

Eventually he removed his hat and coat and settled into the mix. At one point he said, "Don't act differently because I'm here. This is a housewarming party. I am but a guest. Let's play some goddamned charades or something!"

But in time he was standing tall in the far corner of the room with most of the party situated around him. "Jefferson said that the natural course of things is for liberty to yield and government to gain ground. My Christ, that was hundreds of years ago. And look where we are now! Three-quarters of Americans say they want smaller government, but shifting the tide seems too overwhelming for them. Might as well tell Lake Superior to stop crashing onto the shore. They can't turn to Republicans. Republicans want to be your daddy, telling you what to say and do and think under the roof of your own house. And they sure as hell can't turn to the Democrats, who want to be your mommy, walking you to school every day and wiping your ass for you when you get home. The people want fewer taxes. They want property rights. And they want to make their own choices about their businesses, their property, their bodies, their sex lives, their personal expression, and their personal protection." He raised his index finger and shook it slightly. "So they need to know that there's a third way. And it ain't anarchy and it ain't hedonism. It's respect for spontaneous order. Understanding that, given the freedom to do so, humans will—as they have since ancient times—solve problems for the benefit of all, understanding our natural harmony of interests." He took a deep breath and smiled—that smile that inspired more than any words—and spoke softly. "All of us here want change to happen. And we want it to happen right the hell now."

Josef sat across the room, marveling at how Gorman wove the big ideas into the Haymaker landscapes with far less effort than he himself could do in his writings.

"Those White Sable Dunes on the shore." Gorman pointed to the northwest. He knew where he stood and what he faced at all times. "Those were built, grain by grain, over time unimaginable. Now, don't worry—I see the looks on some of your faces—don't worry. I'm not saying liberty will come at that kind of pace." He chuckled, his eyes creased and warm. "But what I *am* saying is that the grains didn't arrive all at once. They built atop each other until—tiny as they are—they towered over the landscape. This town is tiny. This condominium is but a blip on even a local map. But we are—all of us—the first grains." He leaned forward, almost whispering. "We are the first grains." Then Gorman stepped back against the corner of the room, and his voice rode a crescendo that Josef never even saw coming. "And vote by vote, election by election, from our town to the county, the peninsula, the state, and beyond, we will build something great. And the doubters and foes won't notice all of these tiny grains under their noses until it's too late and we've built a great dune that towers over even the mightiest of storms!"

Marissa started crying. Lee jumped up and down like a child. An older man, whom Josef hadn't noticed until now, nodded his head, silently staring at the floor, as if struck dumb by a revelation appearing before his lowly mortal eyes.

Josef stepped outside into the brittle night. Denny stood in the driveway with his back to him. "Getting some fresh air?" Josef asked.

Denny turned around, exhaling smoke and motioning with a cigarette. "The freshest."

Josef walked slowly up to him. "When'd you start that again?"

Denny put the cigarette to his mouth, amid his full beard. "After the move." He inhaled and blew the smoke out his nose. Then he looked straight up at the sky. The stars took up almost as much of the night as the blackness in between. "This is the first time in three months I can remember looking up and not seeing any clouds."

"Don't worry," said Josef. "They'll be back by morning."

Denny lowered his head. "Why are you out here? Too much inspiration for you inside?"

Josef put his hands in his pockets and shrugged. "I don't know."

Denny shook his head and kicked at a stone. He spoke softly. "Pep talks are for recruitment. Once we're here, it's time to fucking talk turkey."

"It's a party," said Josef. "Everyone's been drinking."

"Drinking the Kool-Aid," said Denny. He looked down Glory Road, where three more structures—making up six condominiums—stood in the darkness. The silhouettes of ornate streetlamps, still without power, loomed in intervals. "We need to get people living in these places. And we need to get more built right the fuck away. A person has a mortgage, he's not likely to up and leave at a moment's notice. A person in a motel room, or renting a cabin somewhere? Shit. I can't believe we've held on to everyone so far."

"Everyone so far's a diehard."

"You're right," said Denny. "It's going to get tougher with the next group." He frowned and shook his head. "They'll just stoke more fires. You hear about the dustup at the snowmobile race?"

Josef nodded.

"That shit's only going to get worse. It'll surface in the spring." He flicked his cigarette butt into a snowbank. "Catch-22. We need more people for stability. But when they come, they'll just be fuel to the fire."

"Let's hope Gorman plays it cool this time," said Josef.

Denny chuckled. "You think that. Have you ever seen a guy enjoy stirring the pot like him?"

Josef said nothing.

"And let me ask you this," said Denny, approaching. "If we're all about moving into the neighborhoods with the locals, or at the very least moving into this little gated community right here, why's the guru moving into a big house on the hill, on the edge of town, apart from it all?"

"I don't know, Denny."

"And he was talking about maybe renovating his basement and moving our offices there. We'd be working under his roof. Right under his nose."

"Why are you so angry all of a sudden?" asked Josef, his voice a sharp whisper.

Denny spoke low, almost in a growl. "Don't play it like that. You're just as angry. All of this work, ripping the roots out of our old lives, and now the crazier elements of our brood are getting a foothold? The pragmatists are losing, Josef. I've been talking with Susan, and she agrees. And to be honest, you're the one holding it together. You're still keeper of our voice. You've got to make sure we don't raise it up to a fucking scream."

The door opened. "Josef?" Jeanie's figure stood within a yellow rectangle of light.

"I'm coming," he said. He turned back to Denny. "I get what you're saying. You just need to calm down." He waved him toward the condo. "Come on inside with me."

Josef walked to the door, where Jeanie waited for him. He turned back. Denny lit another cigarette and raised his eyes back toward the sky.

Chapter 6

Friday, March 13

Gary Hollingshead pulled his truck into the parking lot of the 3-F. He'd have rather driven a few more blocks for beers at The Venison, but even this—picking up trash bags, a gallon of milk, and a few frozen pizzas—was a small, welcome break from the sounds and stuffiness of the house. Gary loved the little one. He loved the dark blueness of her irises. He loved that if he put his nose near her mouth, she would suckle it like a nipple. He loved that their names rhymed. Gary and Mary. They would always have that.

But the cold outside air felt exhilarating in his lungs. Back home, Clara continued to struggle with nursing. Mary wouldn't latch on properly; her weight was low. And she'd turned orange with jaundice during her second week, spending a couple of days under the bili lights at LaRock Medical with soft white shields over her tiny eyes.

He parked and stepped out of his truck. The quiet night reminded him of mushing through the twilight woods. The buzz of a late-season snowmobile arose in the distance. It was like the electric wheezing sound of Clara's breast pump. He didn't want to enjoy this solitude and fresh air so much. He lived with enough guilt already. It languished between his skin and his blood and could flow through his entire body with just the right word or sense or memory—flashbacks of Joanna Blue, yes, but also the pull of lust, the desire to flirt that he'd had as a teenager, as a bachelor, and onward as a married man. He loved the rush that came from a new woman's attentions. He and Clara had avoided sex for nearly a year now. Once the bed rest had begun, she seemed to him like a porcelain doll: lovely, innocent, breakable. After the birth she'd given her entire body—her entire self—over to Mary. He would stare sometimes at her nipples: dark and chapped and leaking milk.

When Gary masturbated it was almost workmanlike—a quick means to an end, like the way he drank a hidden pint of rum most nights to fall asleep. Even his fantasies triggered guilt, and he'd begun to consider temporary celibacy, reading the Bible the way he did after losing his virginity at fourteen. *Put to death, therefore, whatever belongs to your earthly nature: sexual immorality, impurity, lust, evil desires . . .*

He realized he should get his meds adjusted soon. Newborns are stressors, ain't they, Doc? And Haymaker in March means the sun hasn't shone in a goddamned eternity, am I right?

The automatic doors slid open, and he stepped inside the store's fluorescence. The place was quiet, the Muzak low. He could hear the hum of the lights overhead. Gary headed for the dairy aisle, which was adjacent to the meat department. For a moment he thought he spotted her—Joanna Blue—there, behind the counter. She'd ducked down to hide from him. She saw him and then she just ducked.

His pulse increased. Sweat broke out on his back and brow. He knew Joanna didn't work there anymore. He'd heard she was dealing blackjack at the Sandpiper Casino outside of town. But he stopped and turned around in the middle of the aisle, stumbling into the cart of an old woman behind him. He apologized and then strode toward the exit. He could buy the things he needed at a gas station. He didn't need to be here. The automatic doors opened with a whooshing sound. The cold air rushed into his lungs, seeming to cool him from the inside. Yet his pulse still beat at the quick, incessant rate of ice melt falling from rooftops when the winter finally surrenders.

Chapter 7

Wednesday, April 1

Brenda slowed for just seconds—checking for traffic—before roaring through the intersection, her tires squealing amid the din of sirens as she veered onto Parson Avenue. A 911 caller said someone was screaming outside his house and trying to force his way in. The address of the house was also the address of the Haymaker Hero Shop. The caller was Jimmy Bruce.

Her cruiser fishtailed into the driveway of the little white ranch. A crude, hand-painted sign—shaped like a baseball—announced the name of the shop from the front yard. Brenda leapt from the car, her hand hovering over her gun as she approached the side door of the house. The upper windowpane was smashed, and the door itself was ajar. Inside, in a distant part of the house, came screams and the shattering of more glass. She stepped over the threshold, pulled the flashlight from her belt with her left hand, and pressed her shoulder against the wall, looking down a dark stairwell. An arrow on the opposite wall pointed downward: CARDS AND COMICS THIS WAY. Another scream rose from the basement. Brenda cautiously descended the stairs, holding the grip of her gun within its holster, and entered a cinder block laundry room where a single lightbulb blazed from the ceiling.

"Police! This is the police!"

A beaded curtain hung from the doorway to her right, and Brenda plunged through it with her gun aimed forward. Collapsed shelves cut across the floor, comic books in plastic sheaths strewn along a green carpet remnant. The air smelled faintly of cedar. On the far wall, beside a table with a cash register, a large case made of glass and polished wood lay on its side, baseball cards in hard plastic cases spilled onto the floor, speckled with blood.

A tension rod holding a white bedsheet marked off another part of the room. On the other side, animal-like grunts and yelps mingled with the sound of bodies scraping over glass. Brenda flung the sheet aside with her left hand. Two men struggled on the floor, utility shelves lying across them. Smashed mason jars covered them with preserves and pulp.

"Police!" Brenda removed the taser from her belt and aimed. "Get off him or I'm going to tase you!"

Jimmy lay on the bottom, covering his bloodied face with his hands. His T-shirt was torn across the front, exposing his soft, white flesh. Beside him lay a wooden baseball bat, streaked with red. The man on top had short black hair and a gray flannel shirt, and she knew without seeing his face it was Donnie's ex-con friend, Russ Gillickson. He'd grabbed Jimmy by the hair and repeatedly slammed his head onto the concrete floor.

Brenda pulled the trigger, the electrodes striking Gillickson in the back. In that instant the whole world seemed to tremor and contract.

Chapter 8

Thursday, April 2

Olivia and Grace were asleep, but the humid, floral air of their nighttime baths lingered throughout the house. Jeanie lay in bed with the comforter pulled up to her chin, and Josef sat up, on top of the covers. The bedroom lamps were off. His face flickered with white light from the TV. Images from Afghanistan cut to the top local story on the Marquette evening news. A gray-haired anchorman nodded slightly at the camera before speaking.

Though we're still a ways away from the dreaded black fly season, many residents in the Luce County town of Haymaker are feeling pestered by a very different sort of swarm. Lisa Suarez has the story.

"Jesus Christ, they compared us to pests," said Josef. "They used the word 'swarm.'"

The screen cut to a series of establishing shots: the sign as one enters the town, a stretch of businesses along Marquette Street, two children climbing the statue of Frederick Parson, and then the brick entrance to the Freedom Community. A woman's voice spoke over the images.

Late last year, members of a libertarian group calling itself the Freedom Community descended upon the sleepy little U.P. town of Haymaker. Citing its loose zoning restrictions, its low population, and its inherent independent culture, the group began its slow but steady march toward its final goal: creating a community within Haymaker that will eventually outnumber the town's original population. At present, over a hundred people from all over the country—and a few from as far away as England and Australia—have made the move.

Josef turned on his bedside lamp, grabbed a pen from the nightstand drawer, and wrote the words DESCENDED UPON and MARCH on the back of his hand.

"There! There!" said Jeanie, pointing at the TV.

On-screen, Josef stood out front of the Freedom Springs entrance with a microphone angled toward him. His name appeared below his image, followed by FREEDOM COMMUNITY COMMUNICATIONS DIRECTOR.

"Our goal is to have a strong enough voting population so that we can elect local officials who represent our liberty-based views on issues ranging from zoning to taxation to education. And it's not just a matter of outnumbering the local populace. We're absolutely certain that, when all of our ideas are expressed, a large number of lifelong Haymakes will see the benefits associated with our ideas and vote the same way we do. They'll recognize the truer sense—the more idealized and realized sense—of American personal freedom that we represent. This is what our forefathers had in mind nearly two hundred and forty years ago."

But many in the local Haymaker population see it differently.

The scene cut to Donnie standing on Marquette Street, in front of The Venison, along with his name and the words ANGRY LOCAL.

"They come in here like they're God's gift. They see a town that has its own life and its own history and decide to make it their own. They say they love freedom and everything America represents, but they march in here like a band of Nazis trying to force us to do what they want."

Josef rubbed his eyes and shook his head. "It's not force, you asshole. It's *elections*. It's *democracy*."

Donnie continued.

"I think if they keep this up, there's gonna be trouble of all sorts on all sides."

The Civic Centre appeared on-screen, the American and state flags waving out front in a stiff breeze.

And that's what has many local officials here worried.

The reporter appeared speaking with Brenda, their words inaudible as the voice-over continued.

Sergeant Brenda DeBoer of the Haymaker Police Department says that, thus far, the brewing conflict between the two sides has remained primarily civil, as pro- and anti-libertarian advocates air their views at town hall meetings and in the pages of the local newspaper. But, just yesterday, James Bruce, a lifelong resident of the town, was assaulted in his own home.

A mug shot of Gillickson: a cut running above his upper lip.

The assailant was Russell Gillickson, a local with a criminal record who was apparently angry at Bruce for having sold the land now owned by the Freedom Community.

A close-up of Brenda followed.

"We have had one violent assault related to the migration. It did not involve any of the newly arrived residents, but of course any assault is a serious matter that will be seriously prosecuted. A few incidents of vandalism have also occurred, and I can assure everyone that those caught defacing any property will be punished fully and swiftly. We have a lot of freedoms here, and people can debate all they want whether there should be more or less of those freedoms. But right now I can tell you that nobody's free to damage another person's property."

"Spoken like she's one of us," said Josef.

And as for the potential for any greater damage, or even more violence?

"We're constantly monitoring any threats to either side. And if anything does occur, it'll be immediately squashed. Anyone seeking to fan any flames, even through talk, should watch themselves."

"Okay," said Josef, "maybe not."

The reporter, Lisa Suarez, now appeared live, standing out front of the darkened Civic Centre.

"And, John, that's just what has so many here worried: that some small argument might spark something much larger. We tried to reach the mayor of Haymaker, Clara Hollingshead, but were denied a request for an interview. We also tried to speak with a man named Gorman Tate, who is said to be the head of this Freedom Community movement, and were told that his communications director speaks for him."

The screen split, showing the reporter on the right and anchorman on the left.

"So, Lisa, what's next for both sides?"

"Well, John, nobody's quite sure. It seems certain that more libertarian residents will arrive, though nobody has a firm grasp as to when. Until then, both sides are seeking support among the townsfolk, even resorting to the 'rah-rah' tactics you might expect of sports fans cheering for their favorite teams. As you can see here—" Lisa Suarez held up a blue T-shirt with the Black Bears logo on it—*"the libertarians are calling themselves the Black Bears."* She set it down and picked up another shirt, orange with black words and logo. *"Meanwhile, the locals have adopted the school's mascot, referring to themselves as the Huskies. So it's the Bears versus the Huskies here in Haymaker. John?"*

"Thank you, Lisa, for that very interesting report." The screen cut to a wide shot of the news desk in Marquette, where the gray-haired anchorman smiled and chuckled softly.

A blonde anchorwoman beside him shook her head as she spoke. *"The Huskies versus the Black Bears, huh? Sounds like the TV6 sports desk will have to cover that rivalry as things heat up. And speaking of which, Dwight Shields joins us now to talk about how things are heating up for the Tigers as their season gets underway."*

Josef turned off the TV and buried his face in his hands.

Jeanie touched his arm. "Josef."

"They were giggling and smirking and patronizing. And look who they get to be the voice of town—that human landfill, Donnie Sarver. *Angry local.* They could have put that next to *my* name. Trust me, it ain't just their side that's angry." Josef stared at the vacant TV before turning it on again and flipping to channel 29.

"It'll all be okay," said Jeanie. "It's the local news. What do you expect? This is going to take a long, long time."

A darkened Marquette Street appeared on the screen. The camera panned. A few cars drove by. Moments later, a few people walked beneath the streetlamps. Just by looking at them, you'd have no idea if they were Black Bears or Huskies.

Roosevelt uncrossed his legs and leaned back into his leather sofa. The sportscaster on the local news talked now about the Tigers, but Roosevelt continued to think about the previous story. Black Bears versus Huskies.

He stood, turned off the TV, and picked up his glass tumbler from the coffee table. A few half-melted ice cubes lay at the bottom, but otherwise it was empty. He walked into the kitchen and was about to gently set it in the sink, when he stopped short and threw it. The glass shattered, the fragments mingling with the ice in the bottom of the sink. Roosevelt turned toward the staircase. He'd deal with it tomorrow.

Chapter 9

Friday, April 3

Who can say where one tragedy ends, another begins, or whether they're all threaded together by something as tough and invisible as spider silk? Brenda drove down Superior Drive along the beach, toward the pier where a woman named Allison Evans had drowned the night before.

When death came to Haymaker, it usually struck the elderly and was therefore no tragedy. When it struck the young, Brenda had to stare at it and study it and piece together its story. She parked the cruiser in the vacant lot of Fitzgerald Beach and looked out across the bleak expanse of steel-colored sky. Along the pier floated the frozen remnants of winter. At its end, the white, skeletal frame of the lighthouse blinked its red eye.

Brenda got out and walked toward the pier. Seventeen people had died here over the decades. Waves had swept over most of them, though in the case of Allison Evans, the twenty-nine-year-old Black Bear who'd arrived on Halloween with her husband and young daughter, it seemed the wind had shoved her off, into the half-frozen waves churning beneath. Her name would be added to the sixteen others listed on a small bronze plaque attached to the lighthouse. Some had been tourists. Some local teenagers. A few suicides. In most cases, the spectacle of whitecaps seemed to have lured them. Then, like tentacles, the waves rose up and snatched them, sometimes slamming them up against the pier before the drowning.

The waves that had killed Allison Evans were subterranean ones, coursing beneath the still-frozen shore but calling to her nonetheless. Her husband didn't know why she'd have been out there. She'd told him she was just going for a drive; she had to get out of their tiny motel room for a while. There were murmurings of suicide but no proof, and Brenda suspected the woman had simply looked for fresh air to clear her mind and had thought this was the perfect place. A coroner had yet to officially declare if she'd died from drowning or hypothermia or something else. Who cared, thought Brenda. She'd died from the lake.

Some in town had thought it less of a tragedy since she was an outsider. Others thought this made it worse—that she'd died on foreign soil. Allison was from North Carolina and had grown up on the Atlantic. Lake Superior was a lonely place for her to perish.

Her death made the headline of the *Star-Picayune*—the first headline in six months not related to the tensions between the newcomers and the locals. A remarkable civility graced the op-ed page for a change, and a piece by Greta McPhee especially struck Brenda.

> *Is it possible that the cold, gray waters of Lake Superior are even colder and more gray to one who is not from this land? Or does the lake treat those from the outside the same as those who were born, raised, and drowned all within these same few miles of Haymaker? Does any of it matter to the lake? Should any of it matter to us? Should it mean more to the locals or to the newcomers that Dwayne Evans, husband of the deceased, has chosen to bury her not in North Carolina, beside her mother and grandparents, but in Lakecrest Cemetery here in town, where she will lie among the ancestors of those who didn't even want her on their land, let alone beneath it?*

Brenda returned to the cruiser, pulled out of the parking lot, and headed toward LaRock Medical—toward the week's other tragedy. Graffiti caught her eye. On a gray cement retaining wall, which ran parallel to the road and held back an eroding dune, someone had scrawled, with bright orange spray paint, GO HUSKIES! BEAT THE BEARS! She clenched her jaw. At first glance it might seem like something a teenager had done, caught up in the frenzy of a homecoming football game. But this was one of several such messages that had mysteriously appeared in recent weeks. On a brick wall near the 3-F someone had written BLACK BEARS ≠ LIBERTY. Another found its way high atop the town's white water tower: FREE HAYMAKER FROM BLACK BEARS. And yesterday morning the police department made the embarrassing discovery of graffiti on the road—right in front of the Civic Centre, on Marquette Street—which said NOBODY IS FREE TO INVADE HAYMAKER. In all cases, the words were painted in orange.

When she'd arrived at the station this morning and checked her voice mail, she'd found this message waiting for her:

"Hello, Sergeant DeBoer, this is Gorman Tate. I'd like to formally introduce myself in person sometime, but this will have to do for now. You know who I am, of course, though you likely don't really know who I am, behind all the myths and rumors, and that's a shame. But I'm calling now in regards to the rash of vandalism popping up around town, all of it with a distinct xenophobic flavor. As you know, the Freedom Community has private security to prevent this and other crimes on our property. And you might also know that we are staunch believers of the First Amendment and are in no way threatened by these or any of the other nasty things being said about us. We have no desire to criminalize such acts outside of their damage to property, which, I might point out, has been mostly public property. However, my fellow sojourners and I are quickly losing confidence in the current public services, and many of us are concerned that perhaps the local law enforcement knows who is committing these crimes—especially when they're done right in front of its own building—and is deliberately turning a blind eye. Were it true, this would obviously not be acceptable, and so I'm simply calling to express this concern. I welcome any future discussion with you, as well as the opportunity for you to set my mind at ease. A good day to you, Officer."

There was no cover-up. There were simply too many suspects, too few leads, and far greater concerns for the police. A woman had drowned. A man had been beaten to near death.

And through it all—to Brenda's amazement—Brian expressed no added concern for her safety. The increase in crimes and anger never led him to a conclusion that would have been all too natural for other men to make. Not even after her broken arm. When she'd leave for her shift, he'd merely grin and kiss her neck and tell her to stay warm.

Camera in hand, Brenda arrived at LaRock Medical, entered its glass doors, and approached the receptionist. "I'm here to speak with Jimmy Bruce."

The woman told her the room number, and Brenda walked down the bright white hall, her shoes squeaking over the floor. The heavy door to his room was ajar, and she rapped her knuckles against it a few times before stepping inside. Jimmy lay in bed, his face swollen as if he'd had wisdom teeth pulled, and the skin was all one deep red bruise—lakes of blood right beneath the surface. In a few days it would turn a sickly yellow.

When she'd restrained Russ Gillickson and her backup, Trevor James, had shoved him into the cruiser, Gillickson had started screaming about treason. "He gave these people the key to the city so they could pour right the fuck in!" And downstairs, paramedics attended to Jimmy among a shattered display case full of rare rookie baseball cards, autographed World Series balls, and a program from 1968 signed by all of the Tigers.

Brenda stepped now toward his hospital bed. "I'm sorry to disturb you, Mr. Bruce, but I have to take a few pictures to document the injuries."

"Okay," he said softly and shifted his weight, trying to sit up higher. His dark hair stuck up like a little boy's. Rolls of belly fat spilled from an opening in his twisted hospital gown. When he spoke, his lips revealed the two missing front teeth, which, while investigating his basement, Brenda later found amid broken glass and bent baseball cards.

She raised the camera to her eye. Jimmy smiled involuntarily—wincing through the flash of reflex—and then dropped his eyes, as if she were some girl approaching him at a bar or a party. Brenda snapped one more picture. "Do you know why he attacked you, Mr. Bruce?"

"No idea."

"What?"

"I have no idea," he said, louder.

"You have no idea why Russ Gillickson smashed his way into your house and did all of this to you?"

Jimmy shrugged and rolled onto his side. His hospital gown went askew again. "Everyone's been wanting to do this to me. He just did it." Then he pulled the gown back in place, smoothed over the fabric with his hand, and closed his eyes tightly—not as if to sleep, but to block out some terrible light.

Before returning to the Civic Centre with the photographs, Brenda made one more stop, at Sarver Towing and Repair. Ray stood out front, leaning against his tow truck with his arms crossed over his chest. "Shit," he said as she approached, "he's been wondering where the hell you been."

Donnie sat in his dim, windowless office, a cigarette clenched between his teeth as he slowly pecked away at his computer's keyboard. "Let me finish these invoices and I'll be right with you, Officer."

"Why don't you finish after I finish." Brenda closed the door behind her and sat across the desk from him in a brown plastic chair. Fake wood paneling lined the walls, hanging loose in some places. The room smelled like burnt plastic.

Donnie looked up, leaned back in his chair, and ran both hands through his black hair. "How's your arm?"

"Been fine for months."

"Good. I'm glad. And I'm sorry for that. You weren't the intended target." He smiled and nodded for a few seconds before saying, "He went rogue."

"What are you talking about, Donnie?"

"You know exactly what I'm talking about. Russ went fucking rogue. He didn't tell anyone he was going to do this. He didn't act like he was about to do this. None of us seen this coming."

"But he's your friend. He's part of your group, right?"

"Group?" Donnie stood and started examining the wall, fingering a faux knot in the faux wood. "Who am I, Mick Jagger? I got a fucking group now?"

Brenda stood up and spoke evenly. "People have seen you and a group of men hanging around Rusty's, sitting in the same corner, talking a lot of politics and town gossip."

"That's a crime now? Talking shit with your friends at the bar? Fuck, lock me up. Maybe these libs got the right idea about too many laws going on."

"I've heard you call yourselves the Bearslayers."

Donnie grinned wide, warm creases spilling from his eyes. "Now where'd you hear that?" he asked quietly.

Brenda didn't mean to, but she smiled as well. "Oh, I've got my sources."

"Oh, I bet you do." Donnie sat back down and put his hands behind his head. "Janey Law. Got her connections. Got her ear to the ground and her finger to the wind."

She dropped her smile. "Are you called the Bearslayers?"

Donnie shrugged and shook his head slightly. "We're hunters. To a man. Got nicknames for ourselves and others. Find a bunch of sportsmen at a bar who don't."

Brenda nodded and held on to her gun belt with both hands. "I'll be in touch, Donnie," she said, turning toward the door.

"Hey, Officer," he said, and she swung around. "Seriously." Donnie lowered his voice. "I didn't sign off on that shit. Something busted in Russ's brain, and now he's going to jail for a long time. I hate that son of a bitch Bruce, but I'm not dumb enough to lay a hand on him unless it's at my Shit-Kickin'."

Brenda nodded. "Know anything about this vandalism all over town? Got any spray paint lying around?"

Donnie raised his palms to her. They were streaked with black grease. "Nothing orange here," he said.

In her cruiser, headed toward the Civic Centre, she approached the Schoolcraft intersection, paused, and then turned south, driving down toward the lake one more time. It wasn't for any kind of investigation. It was—as it likely was with Allison Evans—to clear her head. The sun broke through for a few moments, and in this April half-light she could glimpse the near future, when the leaves would return and the temperature of the lake would warm to the point where she could at least walk through the waves and wade to her hips. And then the sun slipped behind the clouds again. The boundaries between the gray earth and the gray sky dissolved. The horizon was only a myth.

Chapter 10

Thursday, May 21

American flags hung from streetlamps throughout town, and now, with nightfall, the lamplight turned the Stars and Stripes to something like orange and black. Clara drove alongside them, pleased with the patriotism as Memorial Day approached but well aware that the town had never been quite so star-spangled.

"Sort of like an arms race, huh?" Gary had said the night before.

She'd shrugged it off. "The city council gets a request for more flags to honor fallen soldiers, who the hell's going to vote no?"

"I guess. But it's like we got to prove something to those people in the condos."

Clara shook her head. "We want to prove it to ourselves."

She was headed now to those condos—through the gates of Freedom Springs—for the first time. Although the Shipwreck had closed a few hours earlier, she'd stayed late to catch up on her bookkeeping. Eleanor Osborne, one of the waitresses, was babysitting Mary so that Gary could help out Jeremy Marx for a few hours, grooming the dogs and cleaning out kennels.

As mayor, Clara knew she should have visited the development long ago. She'd used the pregnancy and baby excuses with great success, but in reality she'd wanted to pretend—for as long as possible—that the town's evolution would take care of itself. By crossing through its gates—if only to casually drive its streets and see her new citizens' homes up close—she felt she was committing to something. Crossing over to Haymaker's new reality.

Clara unconsciously slowed to a stop as she reached the brick entrance and turned onto Glory Road. Everything looked new and fresh in a way things up here usually never looked. Right out of the box. And for all she knew, she was the first local Haymake to enter this patch of land since the machines had chewed the stumps to shards and dust. She braked at the steel gate that blocked off the entrance. A security guard approached.

"Hello there," she said, smiling beneath the glare of the guard's flashlight, as if performing on a stage. "I'm Clara Hollingshead. I'm the mayor. Someone in my office contacted you or someone else in security to let them know I'd be passing through."

The man checked a clipboard. "ID?"

"Okay," she said, reaching for her wallet. "Sure. If you need it."

"Mr. Tate know you're stopping by?"

She began to speak but then shook her head, confused. "I don't know. Gorman Tate? *Should* he have known?"

The guard handed back her ID, wrote down her license plate number, and then waved her through. "It's fine," he said. "You're good."

As she pulled ahead Clara adjusted her rearview mirror, watching the guard to see if he'd reach for a phone or walkie-talkie, but he didn't. Still, she'd heard the interrogation in his voice, and it made her even more self-conscious. As it was, her decision to come was fairly spontaneous, made late in the day when she knew it would be dark by the time she arrived. In some ways this defeated the purpose—she'd see less of the actual development. But in other ways it served its purpose—any Black Bears would see less of her.

Two full blocks of the development were complete, with the foundations of more condos stretching into the dark, where the streetlamps ended. Clara knew places south of the bridge had subdivisions like this, with developments that went up in a matter of months, places where the big trees were cut down and replaced with flaccid saplings, and the lack of shade and the light vinyl siding everywhere made it impossible to walk the August sidewalks without sunglasses. But none of this fit with Haymaker.

The streets had names like Madison, Jefferson, Paine, and Locke. An American flag hung beside every door, even outside of condos that looked vacant. It might have been for Memorial Day, but she figured it was always like this here. Beside some flew Black Bear flags or yellow rattlesnake Gadsden flags. Each condo looked like every other: neat and angular and beige.

It took only minutes before she'd seen all there was to see, and yet Clara experienced a great relief in finally having done it. She'd always felt better confronting stark realities than dark unknowns.

As she left Freedom Springs the guard gave her a little wave and wrote something on his clipboard. She stopped at the sign, waiting for a pair of headlights to pass before she turned onto Schoolcraft. But the vehicle slowed and turned onto Glory Road—the headlights blinding her momentarily. Red brakes flashed in the night, and when Clara blinked away the light, she noticed the vehicle—a red pickup—had stopped alongside her. A bearded face peered at her from the driver's seat.

"Gary?" They rolled down their windows simultaneously. "What are you doing here?" she asked.

He stared at her, his mouth slackened. "Why?" he asked.

Clara shrugged, confused for a moment. "Because it's weird that we ran into each other here."

He blinked a few times and nodded. "Yeah. No. I meant, why are *you* here?"

"To finally see the place. To get it over with. I'm heading to Eleanor's now to pick up Mary." She stretched her neck, peering out the window as if expecting another truck following him. "Seriously, what are you doing here? Did you finish the work at Jeremy's?"

Gary looked forward, in the direction of the guard and gate, and then shook his head. "No," he said. "One of the dogs got loose. It slipped through a gap in the fence when we were cleaning the kennels and I'm out driving around to find it." He pointed at the guard. "Thought I'd ask this guy if he's seen it. Jeremy's kind of freaking out."

"God, I don't blame him," she said. "Those dogs are his life. If I see it on the way home, I'll call you. So you'll be awhile?"

"I don't know," he said, staring forward again. "Probably not. We should find it soon."

She nodded. "Well, good luck. See you at home. Love you."

"Love you, too," he said, nodding vigorously before a half smile broke across his face.

For those next few miles, driving the dark streets of Haymaker, Clara scanned the roadsides for the dog, feeling like—at any moment—it would form out of the shadows faster than she could react.

Gary idled there after she'd left, his pulse pounding in his chest and neck. He watched his rearview mirror, certain now that Clara could appear from anywhere. She could read minds and see in the dark. She could detect the shrewdest of lies.

Eventually he pulled up to the gate, where the guard—recognizing him—waved him through. He turned onto Jefferson and pulled into a driveway, orange light seeping through the living room's closed curtains. When he rang the doorbell, the little pug began yapping in the foyer.

Julia opened the front door and smiled. She wore the same pink V-neck she'd worn the night Gary had first spotted her at The Venison. She grabbed his hand and pulled him inside. "Get in here," she said, kissing him before the door had fully closed.

"No," he said, pulling away and shaking his head. He stared at the floor. "I can't tonight. I've got to go home."

"Of course you can go home," she said in her slight Texas twang. Her husband was in Boston for business. "Just not yet." She kissed him again.

"Seriously," he said, stepping past her into the living room, which looked the same as the last time he'd been there: white walls and beige carpet and a black leather sofa facing a TV. The rest of the place was bare except for three cardboard boxes stacked in the corner and a single Ansel Adams print hung on the far wall. "I think she might know." He ran his hands through his hair and squeezed his eyes shut. "Oh God, I think everyone knows."

Julia crossed her arms. "You're being paranoid. We're fine."

But minutes later Gary returned to his truck and exited through the Freedom Springs gate, the guard giving him a familiar nod as he left.

Did the guard smirk as he nodded? Even beneath the dim light above his shack there was a glint in the man's eyes.

Gary squeezed his eyes shut again. *He knows he knows he knows. He's spoken to Clara and everyone knows.*

Chapter 11

Thursday, June 4

Ash reclined on the worn cushions of Uncle Donnie's couch. He ran water in the kitchen sink and scrubbed a plate with an old sponge. "You can watch the game," he called to her, "but you're not eating my food."

"I brought my own." With an eye roll of the degree she saved only for him, she grabbed her Coke with one hand and bag of Combos with the other and lifted them over her head.

The NBA Finals had begun tonight, and the picture on the TV at the Capagrossa household had recently begun to flicker. "God," she'd said to her mom, "it's going to give me a fricking seizure."

Denise had glanced at her. "*You're* giving *me* a fricking seizure. Watch the game at a friend's house."

The words had stung in a way not intended. Since the basketball season had ended, Ash had spent little time with friends. Victoria had started dating a junior named Logan Mattlin. They'd hold hands and make out in front of their lockers. Ash would glimpse them through the crowds between classes, horrified. She'd never even kissed a boy.

Donnie walked into the living area, wiping his wet hands on his white T-shirt as he approached the large front windows. Across the street, Parson Park stretched out beneath the nightfall. He opened a window and then patted down his shirt and pants while glancing throughout the room. "Where my cigarettes?"

The pack lay on the coffee table beside Ash's feet. She gave it a nudge in his direction. As Donnie slipped a cigarette between his lips and sparked his lighter, he peeked at the game and shook his head. "LeBron Fucking James."

Among the comforting sounds of high-tops squeaking against hardwood, Ash eased deeper into the embrace of the old couch. From there it was easier to think of Dominick Murphy, to imagine him as one of the players driving the lane and head-faking the opposing center before laying it in. He'd officially committed to Michigan State and in the winter would actually play on TV, surrounded by chanting fans in green and white. And she would watch him.

Something like a flicker arose beneath Ash's skin, a restlessness in her arms and legs. Maybe late tonight, after the game, she'd put in some time at the schoolyard court. Shoot jumpers beneath the pale parking lot lights.

Donnie now sat smoking in the open window with his left leg bent on the sill and his right leg hanging outside. During late-night summer bike rides when she could fly—invisible—down the middle of the street, Ash would often spot him as he was now, smoking in silhouette. "When you get home tonight, tell your mom I need my extension cord back."

Ash stared at the game. "Okay." She was thinking now of T.R. Schmidt, the Haymaker point guard who lived in Freedom Springs. He'd probably be captain next year.

A rapid clacking sound came from outside the open window. Donnie covered his face with his arms. "Goddamn!" Red bursts peppered the sill and the glass and the wall behind him. He fell inside onto the floor, curled and covering his head. Smoke snaked aloft from his fallen cigarette.

Ash screamed and leapt up, spilling her Coke over the coffee table. Then she dove toward the floor, where Donnie was rolling across the room like a man on fire. The clacking continued. More red bursts splattered the wall and parts of the ceiling.

Donnie sat up against a bookshelf and stared down at his chest and stomach. His white shirt was stained red. It covered his hands and forearms.

Ash crawled toward him, still screaming, her eyes shining with tears. "Oh my God!"

He lifted his shirt to study his dark-inked body, fingering the red stains over his tattoos. He shook his head. "The fuck?"

The clacking sound stopped, and the two of them immediately stared at the open window, barely breathing. And then it returned, along with several more colored bursts—not red now, but white and blue. It lasted only seconds before the silence returned for good, leaving a dripping patriotism.

"It's fucking paint," said Donnie. He ran his finger along the red of his shirt and touched it to his tongue.

Ash remained on the floor, crying and hugging her knees to her chest. The game continued on the TV, the sportscasters talking over the squeaking of the players' shoes.

Chapter 12

Saturday, July 4

At the back end of the Freedom Springs property lay a dry stretch of the old stump field that remained relatively untouched by heavy machinery. As Phase One of the development approached its conclusion—the condos now housing over two hundred people—this land had come to represent the next great hope—of growth and momentum. The diehards had answered the call and uprooted their families to settle in Haymaker. But some worried that—barring unmitigated success by the end of its first full year—the Freedom Community's second wave of newcomers would be more like a rivulet trickling into Oslo Creek.

No one worried more than Josef—about population and town tension and the fallout from last month's paintball incident. Lee Mooneyham and two of his buddies, Dan Kemp and Richie Van Dyke, had carried out the shooting on Donnie's apartment and were arrested almost immediately because they couldn't keep themselves from bragging about it on the Community's message boards. Sarver had refused to press charges or even talk to police. Rita Gumpert, who owned the property, filed the official complaint, and Lee and the others were charged only with malicious destruction of property. A misdemeanor.

But then there were moments like this—actual reflections of the dreams he'd had before moving. Josef sat on a lawn chair in that undeveloped stretch of stump field, surrounded by maybe fifty other men, women, and children celebrating the Fourth of July. He and Jeanie wore flip-flops and sunglasses and were sipping beer and laughing with a small group of revelers. Smoke wafted up from grills as men cooked hamburgers and bratwurst. Checkered tablecloths, like the skirts of little girls at play, floated in a soft breeze. The younger children chased and squealed around the newly installed play equipment near the community building. Teenage girls gathered along the shaded, wooded edge of the field, talking and laughing in low voices. Teenage boys crouched in a gravel patch, hovering matches over the wicks of jumping jacks and smoke grenades. One of the few people missing was Gorman Tate, though he planned on arriving toward evening. The grand finale.

Josef's five-year-old, Olivia, ran toward him from the play equipment. She paused for a moment, smiling and clapping as a green-sparked jumping jack spun and hovered over the ground. "Dad!" Then she plunged into his lap so that he spilled a little of his beer. "When are they going to do the big fireworks?"

Jeanie, seated beside him, licked her finger and then wiped a smudge of dirt off Olivia's cheek. "When it's dark," she said.

"When's it going to be dark?"

Josef kissed the top of her head. "Not for a few hours yet."

Her body went limp as if exhausted. "But it's taking forever."

"I guess you'll just have to keep swinging and sliding and having the time of your life until then."

Olivia huffed and trudged back toward the equipment as Josef and Jeanie exchanged smiles.

"There he is!" Carl approached with a beer and a handful of potato chips. "What's up, buddy?" he asked Josef before sitting in an empty chair.

Nothing much had changed over the past several months. Nothing much had changed since the awkwardness at the housewarming party last winter. But they'd both kept working hard at a common cause, and under this sunshine with this generous amount of community goodwill, their friendship seemed, once more, like it had on those days back in Indiana.

"This is a day when we need to take some pictures," said Josef. "This is the kind of weather we need to tell new recruits exists. Even up here."

Carl shook his head and chewed on a chip. "It's gorgeous."

From over by the patch of gravel came a series of zipping sounds. Red and green jumping jacks—twenty or more—spun skyward in all directions. A few of the parents nearby ducked and covered their heads in surprise. One of them—a father of one of the boys who'd lit them—stormed forward. "Don't you *ever* light a whole pack like that! You're *too* damned close and that was *too* damned many!"

"Ah," said Carl, "I can't wait to be a father."

Josef nodded. "Thank God I don't have boys." He turned to Carl. "You two going to wait very long to have kids?"

"Probably not." With a stifled smile he added, "Which is cool. I think I'll dig it."

Jeanie leaned forward, resting her elbows on her knees. "I think you'll be a great dad. A big teddy bear."

From the shade-lined edge of the field, where a cluster of birch bark shone among the pines, two girls began screaming. A few of the adults shot up from their seats. "Oh my God! Get some water!"

Josef removed his sunglasses and stood as well. At first the rising smoke looked no different than the white plumes from the boys' grenades. But it quickly turned black, and a short ways off, among the tall, dry blades of midsummer grass, leapt a few orange tendrils of flame.

A current of panic swept through the crowd, with most of the partiers moving about in the purposeless way of swirling leaves in a chain-linked corner. Two men approached the fire with large Coleman coolers, heaving water and ice through the smoke. Several others were already on their phones, dialing 911. Josef dropped his beer in the grass and began running toward the playground, toward Olivia and Grace.

"Get a hose!" someone shouted, though the fire was too far from the buildings and spigots.

The fire grew laterally, crackling several feet in all directions before slowing as it hit some sandy patches of land. A few people had run to their homes and returned, in full sprint, with small kitchen extinguishers. Olivia stood at the top of a slide, watching it all with huge eyes. Grace was oblivious, peering into a plastic periscope pointed at the distant trees.

"Girls! Get down here!" Josef scrambled toward them, arms extended upward toward the equipment. Jeanie had followed, and the four of them watched the fire spread, though it never reached the trees. Sirens soon followed, and Haymaker's one and only fire truck shrieked into Freedom Springs, gleaming red, and parked at the dead end of Glory Road beside a lonely outpost of a hydrant.

That night, lying in bed, utterly restless, Josef thought little about the blackened earth, or the smell of smolder, or the great relief that had come from watching the flames die out without inflicting any real harm. Instead, he mostly remembered the gawkers at the entrance of the development, standing behind the gate, and especially one old man—a white beard hanging far from his chin—shouting, "Our taxes put out that fire! Our taxes put out that fire!"

Chapter 13

Monday, July 13

Roosevelt Bly entered the stark white all-purpose room at the Civic Centre. City council meetings had returned to the room, the number of attendees having receded from last year's high-water mark—the fiasco at the firehouse—but still much larger than had once been normal. Most in attendance were libertarians.

Merv Grubb stood in the back of the room and waved Roosevelt over. Seventy-five percent of the households in Haymaker now subscribed to his paper—a veritable boom in an era of dying print readership. Roosevelt hated to admit it, but Merv tended to cover the town's tensions with a depth and overall evenhandedness that made his articles must-reads for those on both sides of the debate. The popularity of the paper had—as of last week—led to a startling accomplishment. For the first time in its eighty-seven-year history, the *Star-Picayune* was a daily.

But The Man in White had no interest in such conversation. He ignored Merv, tipped his hat to Sergeant DeBoer in the front row, and then sidestepped to a seat in the third, beside Josef. "Evening, Mr. Novak."

They shook hands. "Good to see you, Roosevelt." Josef turned to three people seated to his right. "I don't know if you've met any other members of our leadership. This is Carl Farmer, Susan Abram, and Denny Zellar."

Roosevelt exchanged pleasantries with the others and then surveyed the room. "Looks like you've got a good turnout among your people."

"How can you tell they're ours?" asked Susan.

Roosevelt shook his head a bit. He wasn't sure. It certainly wasn't fair to say that they all looked alike, or that they necessarily looked different from native Haymakes in physical terms. "Energy, perhaps. The way they're all sitting up so straight. I don't know. I can't explain it. They seem ready to engage, if that makes any sense."

Josef nodded. "We've encouraged active civic participation. Not that anyone needed the prodding once the snow melted. I think we're having our second wind."

"Have you all recovered from the unfortunate events of the Fourth?"

Carl nodded. "No harm, no foul."

"It scared us a bit," said Susan, "but was thankfully put out real quick. Just some black grass. No real damage."

Merv sat down one row behind them. "There are rumors of arson," he said.

Josef rolled his eyes and shook his head. "I was there. It was from kids' fireworks."

"I know that," said Merv. "Any rational person knows that. But I've talked to some folks and browsed a few websites. Rumors spread just like that fire in the brush. Some say it was Sarver. Payback for paint pellets."

Up at the front of the room, the council members whispered among themselves and craned their necks. They seemed to be waiting for something or someone. One member, Waldo Buff, checked his phone. Roosevelt glanced at his watch. It was five past. Meetings rarely started late. The elderly in attendance (of whom Roosevelt did not consider himself a member) insisted on punctuality.

Then he realized the problem. The mayor was not present. Clara Hollingshead was a good-natured woman, a competent leader, and when navigating through the crowds at the Shipwreck commanded real authority. But at city council meetings she could slip in and out of the room at times almost unseen. Roosevelt considered this a virtue. She could have been any of the townspeople in attendance. She was indeed one of them.

Merv leaned forward again. "I think the mayor's late. Might have to mention that in my article."

"You have any kids, Merv?" asked Roosevelt, staring ahead.

"Yes. Grandkids, these days."

"You remember when your kids were babies?"

"Of course."

"You remember getting back from your full-time job, stopping home to nurse your little one, and then rushing off to the town meeting to begin job number two?"

Merv sat silent.

"Cut her some slack," said Roosevelt.

◆ ◆ ◆

An hour earlier, Clara had stood in her basement laundry room wearing a navy skirt and white nursing bra, digging through a pile of dirty laundry to find a relatively clean blouse that she could throw in the dryer with some fabric softener and call good.

Gary was upstairs. He'd just rocked and swaddled Mary and set her in her crib. A sound machine in the nursery drowned out other noise, helping Mary to sleep, and from the basement laundry room Clara could hear the simulated sound of rolling waves through the baby monitor in the adjacent TV room.

The monitor had been a gift from her father. He was a man who'd never given an impractical gift, and he considered tools of safety the most practical of all. The monitor was state of the art. Her father had, as always, put his *Consumer Reports* subscription to good use and purchased the most highly rated monitor reviewed. It had tremendous range and was extremely sensitive. In the winter Clara had heard the whine of snowmobiles through the device, even when her naked ear could not.

The monitor could also pick up voices. Sometimes, if she left the bedroom TV on, she could hear the dialogue from downstairs and actually follow the plot of the show. It could also pick up phone conversations.

Clara finally found a wrinkled white blouse balled up on the floor, and with a plastic water bottle she sprayed it with a fine mist before throwing it in the dryer. Gary's phone rang upstairs. She worried it might wake up Mary and was relieved when he picked it up after one ring. While putting the other scattered laundry back into the hamper her ears began to trace the conversation through the monitor. Gary spoke in a strained whisper.

"No. She's still home. Listen, this is stopping now."

. . .

"I mean it's stopping now. I was going to call you. I fucked up way too much this time."

. . .

"*I* know what's happening. *I* know. And I'm a father now. Jesus Christ, I just put my daughter to sleep. I fucked up so much."

. . .

"No. It doesn't matter. This is it."

. . .

"You ain't listening. I am so fucked in the head now. You can't call me. I can't call you. This is done. Forever. Right now."

. . .

"I don't care. Things were almost good, and now I went and put a bullet in my head."

. . .

"Shut up. It is. Right now. Don't you ever call me again."

The phone beeped as Gary hung up, and Clara stared at the monitor in her hands. She didn't remember picking it up. But she held it—knuckles gone white—and barely remembered later how she'd staggered up the stairs, through the slider to the patio, the monitor pressed to her half-bare chest, crackling with static as it stretched out of range. She barely remembered Gary following her outside, asking her what she was doing as she crossed the backyard, in just her bra and skirt, and fell to her knees in the grass, collapsing in the shade of cedars.

Chapter 14

Monday, August 10

The sun had set, and the dirt floor beneath Roosevelt's white cowboy boots had finally begun to cool. Rusty's was veiled in dim light, dimmer than it had been just days before.

Roosevelt ordered a Presbyterian and then smiled vaguely as he squinted in the dimness. Bep served a pitcher of beer to a table of middle-aged Ojibwe men. At the next table sat a few old-timers—widowers, most of them—who came here on Mondays because the VFW closed at eight. Their lips caved into their toothless mouths, and they poured their cans of Blue Ribbon into small glasses an ounce or two at a time, sipping delicately. Roosevelt still had most of his teeth; a couple of the molars were made of gold.

Donnie and the other Bearslayers were not in attendance tonight, which was a good thing, as Lee and a few of his buddies sat in a corner drinking beer and talking baseball like anyone else.

Roosevelt glanced at his watch and then spoke to Rusty. "Would you mind turning this TV to CNN?" He looked over at Lee's table. "But not the TV on the other side of the bar. Just the one facing us."

Rusty grumbled as he reached for the button. "They'll just make us look like shit. So the viewers feel good about themselves. It's all about showing them a place worse than where they're from."

"Let's postpone judgment," said Roosevelt, though he was without optimism.

Twenty minutes passed before a graphic reading FREEDOM PUT TO THE TEST appeared below two anchormen.

"What's with the two guys?" asked Rusty. "It looks weird with two guys doing the news, with the banter and the chitchat."

"Let's just listen to the story," said Roosevelt.

A woman's voice spoke.

In the tiny town of Haymaker, Michigan, a political storm is brewing.

The screen showed the pier on a rainy day, huge whitecaps crashing over the concrete.

Haymaker, on the northern edge of the country, along Lake Superior, has become the epicenter for a divisive battle pitting neighbor against neighbor, American versus American.

"Jesus Christ," mumbled Roosevelt.

A shot of Marquette Street appeared and then cut to a long shot of Parson Park, followed by a close-up of Frederick Parson's bronze face.

At its core is the very concept of liberty. For it is here—in the heartland—where a growing group of libertarians have established what they call a Freedom Community.

"Since when are we the heartland?" asked Rusty.

Roosevelt shrugged. "We're a little far north to be the heart."

"More like the jugular."

The brick entrance to Freedom Springs stood beneath a low, gray sky.

In the fall of last year, libertarians from all over the country began moving into the town to establish a concentrated area of their members. This community is rapidly growing, and its leaders hope in the very near future to outnumber the other people in the town, allowing for lots of changes in the local government—namely, that there would be a lot less of it.

Josef appeared on-screen.

"We're peaceful Americans, people anyone would love to have for their neighbors. We're hardworking. We're patriots. We love our families. And we want to make this country the type of true democracy that our Founding Fathers originally planned."

"I like him more when he's not on camera," said Roosevelt.

"Why does he spell his name with an 'F'?" asked Rusty. "It looks Russian."

"It's Czech."

"Looks Russian."

The shot switched to the Civic Centre, followed by close-ups of the words TOWN HALL and POLICE.

The migration—or as some locals call it, "invasion"—has met with more than a little resistance. Sergeant Brenda DeBoer of the Haymaker Police says the situation is tense but under control.

Close-up of Brenda.

"It's a debate about civics. People here are debating it civilly. They'll talk about getting a new mayor or getting a new school board. That sort of thing."

A long shot of Marquette Street revealed locals and tourists strolling by.

But that sort of thing is exactly what is fueling such dissent. For many of the libertarian newcomers, it's not about voting in a new school board; it's about abolishing the school board altogether.

Rita Gumpert stood in her shop among floral arrangements.

"They want to privatize everything. They want to privatize the snowplows, for God's sake. Who's going to get up at three in the morning and make sure all that snow is off the roads so people can go to work? So kids can go to school? Are there even going to be schools? It's crazy."

The libertarians see it differently.

Josef returned.

"The world has continually been surprised by the ingenuity of free enterprise. There are lots of things that small communities can't afford to offer all of their citizens. Small schools can't provide all of the resources necessary for today's students. Privatization will go a long way toward innovation, competition, and results."

Lake Superior appeared on-screen, its coastline stretching to the horizon.

Until then, there's plenty of competition within this small Michigan community . . .

Waves rolled onto the beach, foaming around the ankles of a little girl playing in the sand.

. . . and plenty of people wondering who will be winners and who will be losers. Reporting for CNN, this is Gabrielle Park, Haymaker, Michigan.

Rusty still stared at the screen, which had switched to a weather report. A rag and a half-dried beer mug were still clutched in his hand. Roosevelt exhaled deeply and leaned forward, slouching in a way that was foreign to him. He reached into a vest pocket and removed a cigarillo and a box of matches. "Well, that's that," he said. He unwrapped the cellophane from the cigarillo, lit it, and elegantly puffed, regaining his posture. "The world knows our dirty little secret. The media has taken our maidenhead." He chuckled and coughed through the smoke.

"Let's hope that's it," said Rusty. "Let's not give them anything more to report."

Roosevelt set the cigarillo on a glass ashtray and stared into his drink. "I concur. Let's become invisible again. Disappear into the trees."

Although Roosevelt's house stood empty now atop the Ross Road hill, Gorman's lumber baron mansion contained all the members of the Freedom Congress. They sat in plush leather chairs and sofas in the living room. Josef was the only person in Haymaker to have set foot in both Gorman's home and Roosevelt's, and though similar on the outside, it always struck him how different the two men had shaped their homes' interiors. Gorman had retrofitted the place for all the benefits of twenty-first century technology.

The Congress sat facing the sixty-five-inch TV mounted above the fireplace, which Gorman had just turned off. He sipped a scotch and shook his head. He rarely drank. "Well, it's done. Let's see what follows."

Josef nodded. "It could have been worse. It's good that your name didn't come up at all. The danger is that they'll play this off as one man's scheme. The story focused more on a general movement."

"I agree," said Susan. "I mean, we just got our message transmitted all over the country for free. Do you know how many people are going to see that and want to start packing their suitcases?"

Gorman reclined in his seat. "As long as the wider world knows we're serious."

Denny crossed and uncrossed his legs. "Until tonight the wider world didn't know we existed."

Gorman turned to Susan. "How are the coffers?"

She smiled unhappily. "As stated at last month's meeting, we're more than a little in the red right now. But that's condo construction. Those are start-up costs. Everything is as we planned it when we were still back in Indiana."

Gorman turned now to Calvin. "What about hits on the website? More interest? Less interest? How we trending?"

"It's hard to say."

"No it's not. How are we trending?"

"Well, hits are up by about 20 percent, but unique hits are only up by about 5." He paused and looked at Josef, who nodded for him to go ahead. "And most of the traffic is really geared toward the message boards."

Gorman spent little time online. "Keep talking."

"There's a lively debate on the boards. I try to moderate them the best I can, but there are as many if not more Huskies on our site than Black Bears. And they're angry. And they're posting. And someone from California or Texas who's thinking about moving here might read this stuff and decide they want nothing to do with a town where they're so unwelcome."

Gorman stood. "Well, take them down, then." He glared at Josef. "You knew this was happening?"

Denny spoke up. "This was brought up a couple months ago."

Josef remained silent.

"The boards were originally intended for testimonials," said Calvin, "so people who were thinking of coming here and had questions could post them and people in the Community could provide answers."

Gorman pointed at Josef. "Testimonials should be solicited by you, read by you, and edited by you. Questions from prospects should be answered in an FAQ section."

"Those are just never that successful," said Susan. "They come off as in-authentic. People like the message boards. They're raw, but they're real, and people trust them."

"Yeah," said Carl, "they trust the Huskies who say that if you come here, we're going to intimidate the shit out of you."

Gorman reached down for his drink, took another sip, and set it on the fireplace mantel. He cinched the band on his gray ponytail and looked at his reflection in the blackened TV. "I want another huge migration by the end of the year. I want to overwhelm them. I want national exposure. On our terms. I want to show that we're succeeding." He stepped toward a glass bookcase beside the fireplace and plucked a small American flag from a crystal bud vase. He smiled. His crow's-feet turned to sunrays from his eyes. "All right," he said quietly, "let's let freedom ring." He waved the flag back and forth so that the fabric snapped like fingers.

Clara stood in the foyer, holding the front door open with her right hand and dangling Gary's car keys in her left. She held them out to him. "You should have left when I was putting her in bed. I didn't want to see you when I came back out here."

Gary took the keys but made no movement toward the door. "I need to talk for just a couple minutes where it's just the two of us. Not even Mary in the room."

"Afraid she'll understand?"

He looked down. His shoulders began to shake with sobs. "It just breaks my heart holding her and kissing her and then having to leave."

"So don't come over anymore." Clara walked to the kitchen table and picked up a plush ladybug that was still in its plastic box. She shoved it into his chest. "Don't bring her any more gifts."

"Everyone—" He wiped his wet eyes with open palms. "And especially you. Everyone's got it wrong. I'm not living with her. I'm not at some motel with her. I've been staying at Jeremy's place."

"With the dogs, huh?"

He raised his head. "It was a few times, and right after I wanted to die."

Clara stared at him and kept her voice low. "If I hadn't found you out, you'd still be sneaking around with her today. You'd have fucked her plenty by now."

Gary grabbed the collar of his T-shirt and pulled it with both hands, stretching it until it hung limp. "I was ending it that day! You heard it! I swear to God!"

"And you come in here," said Clara, her voice lower still, "and you talk about *your* heart being broken. You talk about *your* heart being broken!" She stepped forward. Gary weighed two hundred and twenty-five pounds. She shoved him, his back slamming against the screen door.

He let his legs go limp and slumped down against it. "I swear to God," he said, his face buried in his knees, his arms wrapped around them in a hug. "I swear to God, I want to kill myself."

"So go kill yourself," said Clara. She reached over him and unlatched the screen door. Gary's limp body slid backward, and as the door fell away, his back and shoulders slowly tumbled onto the front porch. His head rested on the concrete stoop. His long legs stretched over the threshold, the edges of his boot heels still clinging to the foyer rug.

Chapter 15

Saturday, September 12

Ash walked alone down Marquette Street, surrounded by children with painted faces and the music of northern troubadours. Her mom had the day off and was with Patrick John. It was Boomtown Days. Ash had dyed her hair a fiery orange.

She'd had it done last night, to the color of the Huskies, and had it cut much shorter, so that her bangs fell straight and severely to a line just above her dark eyebrows. The rest was pulled into a short ponytail that stuck straight out from her head. The act, she knew, was a symbol, performed in anticipation of Uncle Donnie's fight. A local, familial pride had grown in her all summer, since Lee and his men had shot him up with red paint. In the past, she'd attended his fights with curiosity. But this morning she'd awoken with a kind of bloodlust.

A little girl with a painted pink nose and black whiskers ran past. Couples with red cups of draft beer talked and laughed. The street was closed to cars and packed with people, and in so many ways it felt like any other Boomtown Days celebration in Haymaker. At the park, spectators of the Lumberjack Games gathered before the white band shell, awaiting the start of the standing block chop competition as volunteers onstage set up the aspen logs.

Boomtown Days was busier than ever. Newcomers blended into the crush of people. They ate venison burgers at sidewalk dining tables, their children clutched helium balloons, and many of the men had grown beards and dressed now as lumberjacks. They were adopting histories and absorbing cultures, and though this once might have inspired a soft relief within her, now it simply filled her with disgust.

Ash left the street for the sidewalk and moved down Parson Park's edge. Earl Henneman sat on his bench, guarding the statue, and she wondered if he could tell by sound alone who was a Husky and who was a Black Bear or whether their voices all sounded the same to his trained ear.

Once past the orange pylons, Ash broke free of the crowd. A car passed, and she wished she'd known the person behind the wheel so she could have hitched a ride. She'd just finished driver education, and ever since, she couldn't stand riding a bike. With months before she could drive on her own, she chose to simply walk these days—as she did now, in the direction of this year's Shit-Kickin'.

Uncle Donnie had posted orange flyers all over town, and though Civic Centre employees tore many of them down, they were replaced almost as quickly. He refused to accept blame. "I just set these outside my front door. Who takes them and who decides to post them—that's their business. I'm just providing a service."

Ash was among those doing the posting. They read:

DONNIE SARVER'S
NINTH ANNUAL
WELCOME WAGON
WOULD LIKE TO OFFICIALLY MEET AND GREET
ANY AND ALL MALE MEMBERS (OVER 18)
OF THE FREEDOM COMMUNITY.

SAY HELLO TO DONNIE
AT HIGH NOON THIS SATURDAY
BEHIND THE KENNELS
AT MARX IDITAROD TOURS
ON JUNEBERRY.

COME BE A PART OF THIS ANNUAL SHIT-KICKIN' EXTRAVAGANZA.

FIREWORKS WILL BE PROVIDED.

BE THERE AND BE SCARED.

Ash had spoken to him on the phone last week. "You seem to have had some fun writing it this year."

"I have been inspired by recent events," he'd said. "I have found my muse."

He hadn't seen her orange hair yet, but Ash knew he'd be impressed.

She had a half hour to make the two-mile walk down Cooper to the southern edge of town where there wasn't much of anything besides forest, the two Deep Lakes, and Marx Iditarod. The sidewalks ended after a few blocks, and Ash trudged through tall, sharp grasses and goldenrod. Several cars passed her going south, headed to the fight. A couple of them gave a few short, happy honks, as if to say that they liked her hair. Halfway there, a police cruiser passed as well, off to supervise. And finally came another honk from behind her. Ash turned and shielded her eyes from the sun glaring off the bright white Town Car. The driver's-side window receded as Ash stepped toward it.

"Afternoon, Ms. Capagrossa," said Roosevelt. "I take it you're not headed to Big Deep Lake to fish."

"Nope."

"Headed to yonder Shit-Kickin'?"

She nodded, still uncomfortable in his presence after their past conversations. The way he looked and the way he spoke—he always seemed harmless but confusing, like a person from a foreign land.

"I, too, am headed there, and I can't explain my motivation. If I lived in Spain, I would attend the bullfights, no doubt. Watch them through gapped fingers, as I shall do when Matador Donnie steps into the arena."

Ash looked down at her high-topped feet, waiting for him to say something about her hair.

"Well, come on," he said, "get in. The thing's supposed to start in five minutes, and for some reason I hear they run a remarkably tight ship."

She opened the door and sat inside. The car smelled vaguely of his cigarillos. Classical music played. Roosevelt fluttered his right hand like a conductor. "Mozart's Piano Concerto no. 22 in E-flat."

"Do you know anything about the guy he's fighting?" asked Ash.

Roosevelt nodded. "Well, he lives in Freedom Springs," he said, "but that nearly goes without saying. He works construction. Helped build the development. But otherwise," he shrugged, "I know nothing, my dear."

Ash clenched her jaw. "Uncle Donnie's going to annihilate him."

Roosevelt smiled. "No chance he loses today?"

"No."

They saw the wood-carved sign of a dog howling at the moon and turned onto a two-track that led back to the kennels and the fight. Ash had only come here once, when her dad had taken her on a dogsled ride for her tenth birthday, but she'd never seen the place and the dogs when there was no snow. There were twenty or twenty-five animals in a caged area, each on a short chain with a mat, a food and a water bowl, and a large plastic barrel laid sideways and open at both ends. Some of the dogs lounged inside the barrels while a few others rested on a wooden platform up top. There were a few Alaskan malamutes and even a foxhound, but most of the sled dogs were Siberian huskies. Several paced and strained against their chains while staring at this rare gathering of men on a snowless day.

The parking lot overflowed with cars, and beyond them, on the far side of the kennels, stood a circled crowd waiting for action. It was the biggest turnout in the history of the Shit-Kickin'.

Roosevelt parked on the grass between two maple trees, stepped out of the car, and whistled at the sight of everyone. "Looks like Madison Square Garden here. Where's Joe Frazier? Where's Cassius Clay?" As they walked toward the makeshift arena he began speaking in a Howard Cosell impression that Ash didn't recognize until he explained it to her. "I see Frank Sinatra. And there's Woody Allen. All turning out for the Fight for What's Right. The Breathtaker in Haymaker."

Though Donnie was nowhere in sight, his opponent stood inside the circle, waiting in jeans and no shirt for the fight. For a second Ash thought it *was* her uncle Donnie but with dyed blond hair, because in so many ways he looked the same: his build, his narrow eyes and sharp jaw, the tattoos. But then her gaze lingered on the lean hardness of his chest and stomach—a body that looked angry while the face looked almost serene, and in this way he was a very different man. The presence of her uncle in the same context as this beautiful man sparked panic in her for just a moment, the way it would at times if she recognized that a woman was beautiful and wondered if it meant she was a lesbian. She was almost rooting for this other man.

There were more Black Bears in attendance than she'd expected, including Carl Farmer, and they weren't all gathered in a single cheering section like at the snowmobile race. They stood sprinkled throughout, and Ash was grateful there were no mascots on the scene. Apparently Uncle Donnie and his opponent had agreed to these terms, and both mascots were warned that—if they appeared—they would have to face the winner of the Shit-Kickin' without the protection of their furry, oversized heads.

Those who stood and waited for the fight remained quiet during these final moments before the bell. There wasn't the giddy chatter of a crowd at a boxing match, but rather the quiet reserve of those awaiting a duel. The lights atop Sergeant DeBoer's cruiser flashed red and blue, but in this broad daylight even they appeared subdued.

Ray Valentine checked his watch and then sauntered to the middle of the circle. "Well, folks, let's get this party started, beginning with a few words from our trusted woman in blue."

Sergeant DeBoer took a few strides into the circle, revolving slowly as she spoke so that she could look each attendee in the eye. "If you've been to one of these before, you'll hear nothing new from me." Her eyes met Ash's for a moment before moving on. "This is only legal if it is between these two men and these two men only. Anyone who decides it might be fun to throw a few punches himself—" she looked at Ash again, "—or herself, will be immediately cuffed, processed, and imprisoned. Secondly, this is only legal if it involves the fists of these two men and their fists only. Any weapon, whether it be a rock or a strand of rope, will lead to the immediate arrest of that fighter."

She paused, giving one more long glare at everyone in attendance. "Questions?"

A long pause.

"None," called Roosevelt, startling Ash.

"Okay, then. Ray, the floor is yours."

"Ladies and gentlemen, man and beast, old-timer and newcomer, welcome to the ninth annual Welcome Wagon Shit-Kickin', sponsored in part by Donnie Sarver and all your friends at Sarver Towing and Repair. This afternoon we have a glorious matchup pitting our reigning and undefeated Mr. Sarver versus this man—" he pointed at Ash's beautiful blond, "—Tyson Van Slyke, originally hailing from New Era, Michigan, in a section of the state some of us refer to simply as 'Down There.' Call it the L.P. Call it the Flatlands. Call it some sort of slander, as you will not offend me nor today's sponsors. Please, everyone, a round of applause for our challenger."

The Black Bears in attendance clapped, though not with enthusiasm. Van Slyke seemed neither encouraged nor discouraged by the sound. He continued to look serenely toward the kennels, where some of the dogs had begun whimpering. Ash realized he was going to destroy her uncle.

From behind the main offices of Marx Iditarod came a tinny, muted music.

"And hailing from Haymaker, Michigan—"

Donnie emerged from around the corner of the offices wearing a satin star-spangled robe over his torn and dirty blue jeans. He hopped as he approached, shadowboxing, bobbing and weaving. A mechanic from Sarver Towing—a man named Darryl whom everyone called Fever—walked before Donnie with a boom box over his head that was playing "Gonna Fly Now" from what sounded like an old recording of the *Rocky* soundtrack.

"—defending his Shit-Kickin' crown, His Royal Toughness, His Majesty of Travesty, Protector of the Peninsula, The Czar of the Broken Car, Donnie 'The Bearslayer' Sarver!"

The somber atmosphere broke like a thundercloud. The locals cheered. Ash raised her fists. Roosevelt laughed from deep in his gut. Even the Van Slyke supporters couldn't help but smile from the sheer buffoonery of it all.

Fever pressed the stop button on the boom box, and the final few chuckles from the crowd faded away. Donnie, as always, took center stage.

"Thank you for attending this year's event. As always, there will be a post-Shit-Kickin' celebration at Rusty's, where our forefathers started this all. First round's on me, unless I beat my man here in under a minute. Then you all buy me a drink."

More laughter.

"You'll notice that I'm sharply dressed in red, white, and blue today. This here robe is to show I am a true patriot who hates what has become of our town and the way that these colors have been hijacked by certain newcomers."

An awkward silence.

"So I am taking them back, just as next year I might come draped in a bearskin to take back certain other symbolism, if you catch my meaning." He looked at Van Slyke. "You got some nice tattoos there. That naked chick, especially. In another time and place we probably could've been friends. But this ain't the time, and this sure as hell ain't the place."

A couple of woofs from the crowd. Van Slyke took one step forward, but only one.

"Fellas, fellas," said Ray, stepping between the two men, "let's not start the action till we start the action. How about we all get to opposite ends of this nice ring we've made and then officially have a go at it. How's that?"

They both nodded slightly, but their eyes were completely locked on each other as they stepped backward.

Donnie untied the robe and removed it. "Then let's do this thing."

Ray raised his arm and looked at silver-haired Doc Brewer. "Got your towel, Doc? All right, then." He looked at each fighter and dropped the arm. "Commence!"

They approached slowly, facing each other and slinking in a tight circle for several seconds before either threw a punch. The first came from Donnie—a body blow—that seemed to surprise his opponent, who'd kept his hands up high to protect his face. Van Slyke released a strange, low moan and doubled over slightly. The caged sled dogs began barking. Donnie threw another punch that landed above his ear. Van Slyke returned with a blow of his own, which glanced off Donnie's left cheek. And then Donnie threw a massive right hook that connected with Van Slyke's chin, snapping his head backward. There was a loud clacking sound—teeth snapping together.

He went down and stayed there, stone still. The sled dogs were crazed. Donnie shook his head and spat in the dirt before turning and walking away. He looked disappointed.

"Your winner," said Ray, "and still reigning Sultan of the Shit-Kickin', Donnie Sarver!"

Sergeant DeBoer and Doc Brewer jogged over to Van Slyke, who was already stirring.

Donnie's smile returned. "Anyone time that? Come on, somebody? I know that was under a minute. You all owe me a drink. And there's about fifty of you here, so that's fifty drinks. And I'm thirsty." He looked over at Ash and nodded. "Someone will have to buy an extra one. That can be from my niece. You can do it, Cowboy. You're her wingman."

"I'll buy you three, if you like," said Roosevelt. "You were very impressive today. Both in terms of the fighting and the overall pageantry."

Donnie shook his head. "Cowboy," he said, smiling and looking at Ash. "Cowboy cracks me up." He slipped the red, white, and blue robe on over his sweaty shoulders. "I'll see you all at the bar. And I'm officially taking applications for next year's event. It's a biggie. Tenth anniversary. It'll be a carnival."

Ash barely heard any of this. Van Slyke was slowly rising, his weight resting on one knee while both hands pushed off the other. Most of the sled dogs had fallen silent again. He waved off help from the doctor and others and began to stumble forward. Pebbles and other bits of stone stuck to his back.

She'd never seen this coming. She felt a mix of emotions—disappointment in this beautiful blond man, regard for her uncle, and a mild belief that the worst was over. There was a strong sensation that things really weren't that different. The town would survive. Uncle Donnie would beat the outsiders into submission, one after another. The longtime townspeople who were writing in the paper and debating at the town meetings would win in their ways. Haymaker would quietly slip back under the covers, sleepy again.

Shouts went out, followed immediately by the return of barking dogs. Ash and Roosevelt twisted around to see Fever standing near the corner of the Marx Iditarod offices. He held one of the Black Bear flags in one hand and a Zippo lighter in the other. The fabric had just started to catch fire, and the flames quickly rose up it as Fever began waving it in front of his body. "Victory!" he yelled.

A couple of the Van Slyke supporters lunged toward him, and for a moment it seemed the whole place would become an orgy of shit-kickin'. Sergeant DeBoer ran to put herself between the burning flag and the raging men. Old Doc Brewer even collared one of them and slowed—though didn't stop—him. But in the end it was Carl Farmer who kept the chaos in check. "Leave him alone!" he shouted. "You got to let him do what he wants. This is free speech. This is what we're about." He stood with both palms extended toward his angry compatriots, the flag burning just behind him. "You can hate it like I hate it, but you got to practice what you preach. Free speech never killed anybody. Don't give them the satisfaction."

The place calmed. The dogs quieted once more. Sergeant DeBoer ordered everyone to head home. "I suppose there's nothing left to see," Roosevelt said to Ash. "I'll give you a ride home, and then I'm headed to Rusty's. To the winner go the spoils, and I do owe Donnie a few."

They began walking toward his Town Car. "Don't take me home," said Ash. "Take me back downtown. I want to hang out at the festival a bit."

He nodded. "No problem. Anything in particular you plan to see?"

She shook her head as she got into the car. "Just all of it. Just the music and stuff. Watch the kids."

Roosevelt said nothing more, and they drove down the quiet country road back into town, under a sky that was blue and hard and bright.

Chapter 16

Wednesday, October 21

There's always the running joke and soft shame for a town that has no stoplights. But Haymaker had stop signs—over fifty of them—and last night, someone had vandalized nearly half.

Beneath the word STOP, they'd spray-painted, in black, the word THEM. Every time a driver approached and braked, the signs spoke like a kind of battle cry.

STOP THEM. STOP THEM. STOP THEM.

Halloween was only ten days away, and word was that Gorman Tate planned on marking his one-year anniversary as a resident by leading another wave of newcomers in parade.

Brenda stood at the corner of Hemlock and Cooper, just down from the mayor's house, holding a camera to her eye. It reminded her of the day last year when she'd confronted Lee Mooneyham and his own camera at the Civic Centre. She'd spent this morning driving to junctions and intersections throughout Haymaker, snapping photographs for evidence in a case that would likely go cold. Of all the property damage that had cropped up this year, little was traced back to the offenders. Dustin Jablonski, who hung out only occasionally at Rusty's with the Bearslayers, was caught by security smashing streetlamps with rocks at Freedom Springs. And Brenda arrested three teenagers who were out late drinking bottom-shelf gin and smearing deer blood on Josef Novak's driveway.

Curled, brittle leaves rushed past her feet now, caught in a northern wind. The autumn colors had peaked and gone, and a smell in the air hinted at something arctic. As she returned to her car and started the engine, Brenda looked forward to the return of snow and, for the first time, wished for a harsh winter—to bury this place, quiet and calm it, and then freeze it into at least a temporary surrender. Anything to stop them. Both sides. All of them.

Chapter 17

Saturday, October 31

Brenda stood amid the men and women who lined Marquette Street with their hands in coat pockets and their breath pluming out like smoke from something smoldering. A number of men in full beards wore orange and camouflage, ready for the approaching firearm season, but still ready, right now, for Gorman Tate.

Nobody had found greater relief in this year's calendar than Brenda. Halloween fell on a Saturday, so Willow Street's Monster March had peacefully slogged through the streets yesterday. There would be no collision of parades this year.

The Freedom Community had never formally announced the arrival of more members. They didn't have to. Rumors circulated online, amid blogs and social media, and Merv Grubb synthesized them all in the pages of the *Star-Picayune.* Marquette Street business owners and their employees stepped onto the sidewalk, taking their place among local curiosity seekers, as well as a fair number of Black Bears who'd come to welcome new allies, or were simply curious themselves. Besides Brenda, the other two members of the police force—Lenny Boston and Trevor James—wove through the crowd, glancing at pocketed hands, looking for guns or bombs or even orange spray paint. They scanned the place for Donnie but didn't see him.

Elysium Coffee was normally a refuge for the teenagers of Haymaker, though this morning the whole town seemed to rush inside, looking for warmth before the rumored festivities. Roosevelt squeezed his way outside, a tall covered coffee in his hand, and quite literally bumped into Josef, who was headed in.

"My God, Roosevelt. I'm sorry. Did it spill on your coat?"

Roosevelt looked himself over and brushed imaginary dust from his chest. "I appear to be stain-resistant. Pure as the driven snow." He turned around. "Come on. I'll keep you company while you wait." They stepped to the back of the line, and Roosevelt nodded out the window toward the street. "Why aren't you part of the procession?"

Josef removed his wallet from his back pocket and fingered the green bills inside. "Gorman and I are having creative differences."

"That so?"

Josef nodded, still staring down at his wallet. "It is. He believes in spectacle. I'm more for subtlety." He removed a five, shoved the wallet back into his pocket, and stared up at a chalkboard with the day's specials. "Gorman likes to exaggerate his actions, like he's onstage. Wants to make sure even the cheap seats can see his gestures."

"I get accused of that myself," said Roosevelt.

Josef shook his head. "I just can't tell if it's working or not. And I don't know what he has planned today. He said he doesn't have a plan, but I think he's just keeping it from me."

Roosevelt removed his white beaver felt hat for a moment, smoothed down his silver hair, and covered it again. "What'll happen when he runs for mayor next year?"

Josef shot Roosevelt a look. "Oh, he won't run. Way too polarizing. *Way* too polarizing." He shook his head again. "And the bureaucratic details aren't his thing anyway. He'd go nuts from the meetings and the red tape. He's an idea man. And a money man."

"Well, with Mayor Hollingshead announcing she's not running again, that leaves it wide open for all sorts. Extremes included. And depending on how things play out, people might vote extreme. And not just on your side. Our folks as well."

Josef winced as if he'd stubbed a toe. "'*Our* folks,' huh? That's interesting." He smiled a touch. "I've never heard you take sides before. I always thought you were Switzerland in a big white hat."

Roosevelt nodded toward the barista. "You're up," he said, and after Josef placed his order the two men smiled at each other, waded through a swift and shallow silence, and then began to chat about the World Series.

Clara entered Elysium with a monkey on her hip. Mary the Monkey wore a brown, full-body costume with large ears and a long tail that Clara's sister,

Darlene, had crocheted for her. Clara bought a mocha and made small talk as she passed each table, ambling toward the exit. Roosevelt and Josef sat talking in the corner, and she tried not to reveal her surprise while she raised her cup to them to say hello.

Men and women alike pinched Mary's cheeks and twirled her monkey tail and mentioned how she was looking more like Clara every day. And they were all liars. She didn't look even remotely like Clara. She had dark hair like Gary, and her weight fell within the ninetieth percentile, and their names—as he'd once said—would forever rhyme.

He hadn't visited the house in over a month. Doreen Hayes, a waitress at the Shipwreck, heard from her husband that Gary was living alone at the Black Birch Motel and sometimes seen meandering about the cemetery. Doyle Horner, whom Clara served coffee most every morning, said Gary had been drinking most nights and that some men found him facedown in the weeds outside of the Eagles lodge. And soon afterward Bruce Parrish, who used to bowl with Gary in a league, heard he was attending Frontiers, a men's rehab and counseling group that met in the basement of Freshwater Community Church.

Eventually Clara pulled free from the small talk, slipped outside, and set Mary in the stroller they'd left out front. Her plan was to head down Marquette Street, make sure Lenny had everything under control, and then go straight home. If chaos *did* erupt, she didn't want her daughter anywhere nearby. And when Clara's term expired next year, her plan was to head, with Mary, straight out of Haymaker. For good.

The people lining the street paid her no attention. They had no interest in small talk. Instead they stared west, waiting for the arrival, squinting like sentries toward the horizon. Clara approached the sign at Freshwater Community Church.

HEAVEN IS NO TRICK
HELL IS NO TREAT

She was an agnostic, and as she passed she stared at the art deco doors, squinting a little herself, trying to imagine Gary in the basement, sitting in a circle at Frontiers, confessing his sins to strange men.

Roosevelt unwrapped a cigarillo and fumbled a matchbox within his cold fingers. Josef stood on the opposite side of the street, glancing at his watch and hopping in place a little to stay warm. The two of them had shaken hands as they'd left the coffee shop and then amicably separated to their own corners, their own thoughts, as they waited for the arrival.

It occurred at two twelve in the afternoon and was not the roaring, frothing surge of last year. No music blared. No horns honked. Lee Mooneyham did not skip alongside in the Liberty Bear suit. The long line of vehicles snaked quietly onto Marquette Street, fifteen in all, most of them vans and SUVs and RVs, all swollen with possessions and towing U-Hauls—bound for the promised land.

A murmur seeped up from the band of onlookers. Small flags flew from every vehicle's window. Like a presidential motorcade, thought Roosevelt. Like a funeral.

Most were American flags, a few displayed the Black Bear image, and one—at the rear, on a silver minivan—bore the skull and crossbones of the Jolly Roger.

A silver Ram pickup with tinted windows led the way, and when it reached Parson Park—the midpoint of Marquette Street—something like an atmospheric shift occurred. In near unison, the windows of the silver pickup and several other vehicles slid down, and drivers and passengers alike extended their arms skyward—fists clenched in silent defiance. One of them was a little boy sitting in the back of an old Corolla. He looked right at Roosevelt as he passed.

The onlookers had remained strangely silent, but when those fists rose up out of the windows, a collective gasp seemed to follow—a sudden tug of air into lungs—that stretched all the way down the block. Later that night, Roosevelt would describe it to Rusty as the sound of a whole town's guts turning inside out at once.

Roosevelt tried to see Josef across the street, in the gaps between passing vehicles, but only caught a quick glimpse of him. Josef was shaking his head and motioning with both hands for people to lower their fists.

They wouldn't do as he said. Roosevelt knew before they'd arrived that this next group would be carved from hardier stuff than even the first. These were people who had known what was happening in Haymaker—the vandalism, the threats, the Shit-Kickin'—and who'd nodded and said, "Count me in."

The brake lights flashed on the lead pickup as it reached Parson Avenue. The entire procession came to a halt. Then the driver's-side door flew open to reveal Carl Farmer. He jogged to the back of the truck, reached over into the bed, and pulled out a long orange extension cord. While he jogged across the street to the park—the cord unraveling in his wake—the passenger door opened, and Gorman Tate emerged with his lips curled in a smile beneath his gray mustache. He wore tight black jeans and a black leather jacket, his ponytail swinging like a pendulum as he walked to the back bumper and hoisted himself into the bed of the truck. A few people on the curb began to boo, but the street was still quiet enough for everyone to hear Carl yell, "We're good!" and give the thumbs-up from beside the restrooms where there was an electrical outlet.

Gorman bent over and fiddled with something until a shriek of feedback cut through the air. Then he stood up straight and tall with a microphone in his hand, a large black amp at his feet. "Well, a happy Halloween to you, everybody." His voice boomed and then echoed off the downtown buildings. He smiled and surveyed the group. "I'm sorry I didn't dress in costume today. We come to you only as proud libertarians and Americans, and we do not disguise this truth."

Regina Grimm, a short and wiry woman who worked the register at Seney Hardware, stormed into the street, pointing up at him. "You're a wolf!"

Gorman smiled and gently touched the microphone to his lips. "And what's that make you? A little pig?"

People shouted and booed, but he merely smiled, relishing it, like the heel in a wrestling match.

"Are you all still afraid that I'm going to huff and puff and blow your little town down? Do you all persist in painting me as the villain and you all as the heroes, when I think history—the history of this past year—has proven otherwise?"

Most onlookers fell silent. A few supporters along the curb clapped their hands. Regina Grimm shouted once more. "You're a wolf!"

"Yes, I heard you." Gorman made a little growling sound. "Is that better? Does that suit you?" He paced ever so slightly in the bed of the truck. "I'm not a grifter come to town, despite what many of you think. I am not the duke nor the dauphin. Never touched snake oil in my life. What I am is the leader of a cause I believe in." He glanced at the string of cars behind him. "These people followed me here because of something they'd die for. We didn't come to pick a fight. You did that. Literally, in some cases. We came here because—oh sin of sins—we liked the place. Of all the towns in all the fifty states, we chose this one. And I hate to say it—and please, don't despise me more than you already do—but there are places more beautiful and comfortable than this. There are places with a more tropical air, places with a few less feet of snow every winter and a few more things like shopping malls and fine dining and maybe a place to see a movie. But you know what? Those places have their own problems. And so for the type of life we wanted to live—a life of liberty—this was the very best place."

Roosevelt didn't even turn his head but peeked from the corners of his eyes at those around him. They actually seemed to be listening.

"The very point of this migration was to live a life of individual freedom. To be *left alone*. And to be honest with you, we've encountered nothing but the opposite."

A voice came from above. "Take the hint!" People craned their necks and looked up into the gray sky, and there in the window of his apartment, with one leg dangling outside and a cigarette pinched between his lips, was Donnie.

"We have, Mr. Sarver," said Gorman, giving him a little wave. "Oh, we have. But it is, in our minds, just that. A hint. A suggestion. We've considered it and decided, no, we're here to stay. Part of it's the continued belief that this remains our Canaan. But more than that, our basic human nature is taking over. We're like the teenager who's told not to smoke weed or drink booze. And guess what? Now that's all we want to do. We're stubborn. We're ornery. Quite frankly, we're pissed off. You get shoved by anyone, and it's enough to make you want to shove right back."

Gorman dropped his head and rubbed the back of his neck. He was a preacher filled with the spirit. The temperature was in the thirties, but his brow shone with sweat. Roosevelt felt it, too. A sudden heat.

"I don't know," said Gorman, still looking down, shaking his head. "I just don't know anymore. I am a homeowner in this community. I pay my taxes, though I hate them. I follow the letter of the law, even when I dispute it. I am an American." He looked up and stared at his audience. "And yet I am made to feel like a criminal here." He turned and waved his hand. "These people—the ones already living here—they feel like criminals. These new folks who've just arrived, who will move into Freedom Springs—mark my words, they will soon feel like criminals in their own homes, in their own neighborhood, on their own streets."

The vehicles lined up behind Gorman had begun emptying out. Men, women, and children stood in the middle of the street, basking in his words.

He acknowledged them. "These fine people are certainly going to bolster our numbers. And, friends, those numbers are going to jump dramatically in just a couple of short months."

The people on the sidewalk stirred.

"This here's just the point of the spear." He paused and smiled. "On Christmas morning, I will make this drive again, and I'm going to roll into town with a slew of jolly old elves."

And with that he dropped the microphone, sending a boom through the amp, and climbed back down into the street. Carl unplugged the extension cord, gathered it up in his arms, and ran back to the truck. The others in the procession returned to their vehicles, too, and then all of them moved as one again, like the rattlesnake on the Gadsden flag, turning right and circling back toward Freedom Springs. To the Field of Blood. To the home of these new Haymakes.

Chapter 18

Friday, November 27

It was the day after Thanksgiving, and even in Haymaker it was the busiest shopping day of the year. The 12 Months of Christmas was holding its annual open house, and Ash had stopped by to visit.

Snow covered the lawns but not the sidewalks, so she'd been able to bundle Patrick John in his winter gear and push the stroller to the shop. He was two now, and the moment they arrived he struggled out of his snowsuit and began plodding through the aisles of fragile things.

A table near the entrance featured cookies and coffee and punch. Betty Mead's mother, Harriet, had reprised her role as Mrs. Claus and sat in her red-and-white costume in the corner, listening to the wishes of a little girl before handing her a small candy cane in cellophane. Ash called over to Patrick John, who was fingering the silver ornaments on a fake tree. "Come on, little man. Let's go talk to the missus."

"No," he said, rumbling now toward a mechanical, blinking Rudolph.

Ash shook her head and walked toward the counter, where Denise and Betty were talking with Marjorie Powell, an elder at Freshwater Church.

"It's slow for Black Friday," said Betty.

"Better than a Black Christmas," said Marjorie. "Did you see the article in the paper, about J.J.'s?" J.J.'s was the bait, tackle, and firearm shop on Schoolcraft. "Record gun sales. I hear a lot of the people moving in have criminal records."

Denise rolled her eyes. "That's hysteria. I heard they were all anarchists, atheists, and addicts. Don't take the bait."

Betty nodded. "I agree. But I don't think it's going to be a bunch of families looking for new homes this time around. It wouldn't shock me."

"If what?" asked Denise.

"I don't know." Betty shrugged. "If it was closer to an army."

Denise walked away, shaking her head, and approached Ash. "Don't listen to them," she whispered.

Marjorie zipped up her coat as if to leave, but her feet stayed planted. "It's not their politics that bother me. I don't vote and never have. You do and you automatically start hating half the people you know, and they start hating you. So I stay out of it. But what bothers me is that they're doing it on Christmas. So instead of the arrival of the Christ Child, we're all worked into a lather about these Bear people. It's all crazy. They're crazy, and now we're crazy." She stepped toward the exit. "All the same, have a merry Christmas."

Denise waved good-bye. "Every day's Christmas here. I can hardly tell when it's the real one."

"You will this year," said Marjorie, and she slipped out into the cold.

In the corner of the store, Patrick John approached Mrs. Claus, smiled, and then climbed onto her lap.

Ash looked at Denise. "I'm sorry. I know you don't like us showing up here, but we had to get out of the house."

Denise leaned forward and kissed her on the cheek. "It's the open house. I wanted you to bring him. There's cookies and punch."

Ash touched her own cheek. "Is there vodka in that punch? What's up with you?"

"Shush," said Denise, smiling.

Patrick John climbed down from the lap of Mrs. Claus, who handed him a candy cane. "I want more," he said.

Denise strode toward him. "One is just fine. Come on."

"More!"

"Patrick John, you calm yourself." Denise picked him up. "Look. There's cookies." She tickled his belly, and they both smiled.

"Why are you so happy today?" asked Ash. "Isn't this, like, the worst day of the year for you guys?"

Denise shrugged. "I don't know."

"You buttering me up for something?"

"No. But I do need a favor." Denise reached for a tree-shaped cookie and handed it to Patrick John. "I need you to watch him on Christmas Eve."

Ash cocked her head. "What?" She straightened out her posture and looked down on her mom. "You said the store would be closed Christmas Eve. You said—"

"I know what I said, Ash." She gritted her teeth and lowered her voice. Betty glanced at them from the counter. "And I'm telling you that we're now going to be open and I now have to work. I'm sorry."

Ash took Patrick John from her and began squeezing him into his winter clothes. He struggled and started to cry and threw his hat on the floor. Ash picked him up and marched toward the door. "This is bull."

Denise followed, speaking in an angry hush. "You think I can afford to turn down any hours these days? You want a bunch of empty boxes under the tree Christmas morning?" She picked Patrick John's hat up off the floor and handed it to Ash. "Help your brother."

Ash tossed it back at her. "Help your son."

Denise stared at her and then silently reached forward and stretched the hat over his round head.

"Let's go, P.J." Ash stared back at her mother before grabbing a handful of star-shaped cookies from the table, turning around, and shouldering her way out the door.

She lay in bed, the room dark except for a string of Christmas lights that she'd taped to the wall above her headboard and dresser. They revealed only pockets of sight, dimly washing over dirty laundry in blue and red. Reflecting off basketball posters in green and orange. Carols played from the clock radio on her nightstand. Ash wrapped herself in three blankets and lay still, eyes open, enjoying the weight of the covers and the calm of the early nightfall.

Headlights slipped through her curtains and disappeared as the car turned into the driveway. Moments later she heard the side door open and her mom's heavy footfalls as she crossed the kitchen floor in boots. A few seconds of silence followed, her mom right outside her bedroom door, and then the door cracked open enough for a blade of yellow hallway light to cut across the floor and over her bed.

"Are you asleep?"

"No," said Ash.

The door opened wider, making Ash squint.

Denise quietly stepped inside. "I was going to say," she whispered. "It's only eight thirty." She stepped again and reached out to touch the string of lights. "I see you've got the spirit."

"The colors make me happy when the rest of the room is dark. The music, too."

"Yeah," said Denise. "This is nice." She sat down on the floor amid crumpled jeans and underwear. "I'm sorry."

"Me, too."

Denise sighed. "But before I go on telling you how much I appreciate all you do for me and your little brother, I want to get all the bad news out of the way."

"You're pregnant."

"You're funny." She sighed again. "No. We're having Christmas at Aunt Joy's this year."

Ash kicked at the blankets covering her legs. "God, everything sucks!" She sat up. "I don't want to drive all the way to stupid Munising for Christmas. I thought Grandma Sarver was having it again this year."

"Her gallstones are giving her pain, and I don't want her fussing in her own kitchen."

"It'll be a blizzard and take us all day to get there."

"It will not."

"A few years ago when we had it at Aunt Joy's there was a blizzard and Dad could barely keep the car on the road."

"Because he was drunk and I let him drive and it was one of the many stupid things that I've done."

Ash shrugged. "I'm staying home on Christmas."

"No you're not."

"Yes I am."

"Listen." Denise stood up and then sat on the edge of the bed. "It's not just because of Grandma that we're heading out of town."

Ash studied her mom's face. "What do you mean?" she asked quietly.

Denise opened her mouth, shut it, and then shook her head and spoke. "It might get a little crazy here. You never know."

"Here at home?"

"Here in Haymaker."

"Oh yeah," said Ash. "Black Bear Fever."

"And I don't want any of us here. And I don't want your uncle Donnie here when it all goes down. I don't want him spending the next Christmas in a prison cell." Denise pinched her fingers together. "And I think he's *this* close to coming off the rails."

"He won't go to Aunt Joy's," said Ash.

"But he will. Because he's one of those tough, mean mama's boys and would never skip Christmas as long as Grandma's still alive."

Ash reclined and turned on her side with her back to Denise. "You know I'll be there," she said.

"I know," said Denise, rubbing Ash's back. "Because you're a good kid."

Ash stared at the wall, at a pocket of red light, her chest tightening, her breath quickening.

Chapter 19

Friday, December 25

Donnie pressed his palm against the frosty glass of the second-floor window and watched the snow slant earthward. Six inches had fallen since last night, atop the foot and a half already aground. He grabbed the remote and turned the TV to channel 29. The camera slowly panned along Marquette Street—the view, just one block away, was nearly the same as his. No cars or people. Only white.

The phone rang and Donnie lunged at it. "This is?" he asked.

"Is this what?"

"Damn it, Denise, I got to keep the line open."

"Just listen," she said. "I'm not driving to Joy's in this weather. My car's not up to it. We're going to hitch a ride with you, if that's all right."

He picked up a glass from the coffee table—a disk of mold floating atop an ounce or two of old beer—and walked it to the sink. "You better hitch a ride with someone else."

"They're *not* coming today, Donnie. Not in this weather."

"Well, I'll worry about that, and you can worry about slamming eggnog and finding someone to tongue under the mistletoe."

"You rather Mom drop dead from you skipping Christmas or from you landing in jail?"

"Long as she leaves me all her fine china, I'm good."

"Pick us up in an hour."

"Merry Xmas," he said and hung up the phone. Then Donnie returned to the window—the watchman at his post. He'd enlisted others. Some would make phone calls, each man calling ten other men—a communications pyramid. Some worked as scouts at various points south of town where Gorman Tate and his followers might pass.

A half hour later his phone rang again. "What's going on?"

"They're coming, Donnie."

"That you, Frank?" Frank Tibbs was an old high school friend and a bartender at the VFW. Donnie had stationed him in Trout Lake in case Tate decided to head north on 123.

"It's me. Oh Jesus, they're coming, Donnie. Probably fifty cars. I mean, they're passing me as we speak, and I've lost count."

"They're getting through the snow okay?"

"Well, goddamn, that's the thing. Salt trucks have been going by all morning, and not the orange MDOT ones. Must have been their own. And now they got two huge plows leading the way. They hired some private sons of bitches to blaze their trail."

"How fast they all going?"

"I mean, slow, but not slow enough. I'd say they'll reach you in under two hours."

"Here it comes," said Donnie. He snatched his hooded flannel jacket off the kitchen card table and jammed his left arm through the sleeve. "By Christ, here it comes! I gotta go."

He hung up and immediately dialed Ray. "They're in Trout Lake on 123. Call your guys and have them call their guys. I'm going to round up a few more troops."

Donnie shoved the phone in his jacket pocket and charged into the bedroom, finding a wool hunting cap in his closet that he tugged onto his head, earflaps dangling. He reached to the back of the top shelf and grabbed an air horn that he'd used in the woods to scare off bears. And seconds later he plunged out of his apartment, skidding down the ice-slick staircase to the snow below.

A plow roared down the road—one of the Snow Soldiers from town—tossing up a white and blinding fog. But as it receded, Haymaker fell as silent as Donnie had ever experienced in broad daylight. He ran down Parson Avenue, down the middle of the street, his feet sliding, earflaps swaying, lungs burning from the cold and from cigarettes. The houses slouched under the snow. Orange light glowed behind closed curtains. Christmas trees sparkled like constellations. But the open air of the neighborhood remained eerily still, the people cloistered because of the weather and the holiday, and maybe fear. But Donnie aimed to rouse them from the grip of all three. He raised his arm overhead to sound the alarm.

"They're coming! They're coming! One if by land, motherfuckers!" And he laid on the air horn.

Curtains were shoved aside. Heads poked out of front doors.

"Call your friends! Get in your cars!"

One person yelled, "Shut your mouth hole, you prick!" But a few other people cheered.

"Give 'em hell, Donnie!"

"Let's go, Huskies!"

"Go get those bastards!"

He turned down Cincinnati Street, sliding and shouting between fresh bursts of the air horn. His feet went out from under him then, and he sprawled out on his stomach with his arms and legs splayed, the air horn spinning away from him into a snowbank. He winced, coughed, and climbed back to his feet. When he reached the horn, he gave one final, extended blast. Then he stood, gasping, and watched as a handful of men and women, some in pajamas, emerged to scrape ice off their windshields amid clouds of frigid exhaust.

Josef sat in the passenger's seat of Carl's truck, which was parked along Cooper Avenue on the south end of town, and poured coffee from a thermos. "Deck the Halls" played from the speakers. Carl turned to him. "Jeanie upset you had to work Christmas morning?"

Josef handed him a steaming Styrofoam cup. "You don't want to know."

"Just tell me."

"She said, 'I thought only one prophet worked on Christmas.'"

Carl sipped his coffee and excitedly shifted in his seat, squinting through the snow. He turned off the radio and leaned forward a little. "He's not being Jesus. More like Washington crossing the Delaware."

Josef bent down and picked his notebook up off the floor. He'd be writing an article on today's events for *The Paw.* "You and Marissa have any plans this evening?"

"No. Not really. You?"

Josef, Jeanie, and the girls had been invited to a large dinner that afternoon at Roosevelt's, but they'd politely declined. "No. Just lying low and wrestling the girls' new toys out of their packaging."

His phone rang. It was Gorman.

"We're about one mile from you," said Gorman. "Ain't it beautiful?"

"For a blizzard."

"Come on, now," said Gorman. "There's glory and beauty in this glistening white. Especially today. 'Cleanse me with hyssop, and I will be clean; wash me, and I will be whiter than snow.'"

"All right. We'll be looking for you." Josef hung up and mumbled.

Carl turned to him. "What?"

"They're almost here."

"No," said Carl, "something's up with you."

"What?"

"I don't know. But you're not even hiding it anymore."

Josef looked straight ahead, at the horizon of road. "Let's drop this shit, Carl."

"All those years of planning, you were the hardest-working guy I knew. But lately you've been acting the sad sack. What's going on?"

"Jesus Christ, Carl. The girls got up at five o'clock to open presents. I'm fucking tired."

"Bullshit."

Josef turned toward him, struggling with the seat belt. "I'm fucking tired, Carl. I'm fucking tired of parades and pageants and 'rah-rah, look at me' stunts like this. It's bush league. We don't need it. It's working against us."

"You're wrong." Carl pointed an index finger in Josef's face. "This is why our numbers are going up all over the country. This is why all these people are showing up here today. They want to be part of a movement, and this feels like a movement. You're good with words and shit, but you ain't good with action and inspiration."

Josef closed his eyes, reclined, and took a deep breath. Then he heard the honking. He shot up and squinted through the glass. "That them?"

Carl twisted in his seat and looked over his shoulder. "What the hell?"

Behind them, headed from the north, dim yellow headlights approached through the snow like cats' eyes, pair after pair. It was a caravan—from the wrong direction—turning the snow red with brake lights. Then the eyes began to wink, their hazards turned on.

Josef looked out the front windshield again as two black snowplows approached from the opposite direction, leading Gorman's column. Then he exploded out of the truck, plunging knee-deep in snow but burrowing through it to the road. He faced the southbound vehicles, which straddled the yellow line, blocking off the road, and from the lead truck emerged Donnie Sarver.

A low groan shook the sky as the plows ground their brakes. Josef watched them and gasped, expecting an accordion of crashes from behind. Cars and trucks fishtailed, some sliding into the snow, but they all stopped without collision.

Donnie struggled to climb onto the slick hood of his truck, grabbing the windshield wipers for balance. Other men, and a couple of women, exited their own vehicles and tried to follow his lead, some slipping and rolling off onto the road, but many standing tall, looking down upon the stalemate.

Donnie raised his arm, removed his glove, and extended his middle finger toward the plows. And those standing behind him followed his lead.

"Welcome to Haymaker!" shouted Donnie. "Population: way too many!"

Gorman appeared from beyond the plows and approached Josef on the roadside. "Sarver made a blockade." He smiled a little. "A goddamned blockade."

"What are we going to do?"

"Turn around," said Gorman.

Josef peered south down the road. "With these huge trucks and all this snow? No way. It's too narrow."

Gorman stopped smiling. "Then tell everyone to put it in reverse."

Carl started to climb the massive blade of the lead plow, and from his perch he aimed two middle fingers of his own at Donnie. Shouting followed. People on both sides streamed out of their cars.

Gorman jogged down his line of vehicles. "Back up!" He motioned for people to get back inside and put it in reverse, but he stopped as tires began to spin, victims of an almost invisible hill.

Josef walked toward Donnie's truck. Someone from another car threw a snowball but missed. "Let's talk, Donnie." Cold wind and noxious exhaust surrounded everything.

Donnie crossed his arms, still standing atop his hood. "Why sure, my man. How about them Red Wings?"

Josef looked up at him and smirked. "Eventually we're going to turn all these vehicles around and head into town another way. You're not going to accomplish anything. And if you're not careful, something bad could break out."

Donnie smiled. "You can try and enter town on Schoolcraft. We got some friends waiting for you there, too."

"Jesus, Donnie, what's the point?"

"Oh, the sheer ecstasy of it all. The looks on your faces. I'd say Christmas has come early, but really, it's come right on time."

Josef shook his head. "You know someone's called the cops already."

"Now, why do you need public servants? Didn't you bring your own private mercenaries? Maybe some Blackwater goons?" Donnie sat down, reclined against his truck's windshield, and began to make a snow angel.

People on both sides had started shouting and laying on their horns.

"You're accomplishing nothing," said Josef. "You're postponing the inevitable."

Donnie sat up and admired his angel. "Unless your people get so fed up that, shit, they ain't mad at *us* no more—they're mad at *you*. And mad at themselves for being suckered into all of it. Damn, this was supposed to be easy and pleasant and fun! And now we've come along and made it ugly."

"My God, how you underestimate us," said Josef. All of the doubts he'd had just moments ago when talking with Carl were being replaced by other things.

"Like you've underestimated us?" asked Donnie. "You ready to change your mind about this town and its people?"

"We are its people."

Donnie swiveled his head, looking over both shoulders. "Does it look like the town's embraced you, Novak? Does it look like we're tossing out flowers and greeting you as liberators?"

Carl approached.

"Hey, fatty," said Donnie.

Carl ignored him. "Called the cops," he said to Josef. "And Gorman told them if they don't clear everyone out in fifteen minutes, he's telling the plows to just ram on through."

"That'll do it!" said Donnie. "That'll win their hearts and minds!" He hopped down onto the road. "I'm going to warm up a bit in the car. Smoke a cigarette. Enjoy the show."

"That's it!" Gorman appeared from the line of cars and yelled up at the drivers of the plows. "Go through these criminals!"

The lead plow driver leaned out the window and slowly shook his head. "No fucking way, man."

"You want to take us down?" A large, bearded man struggled through the snow, emerging from the blockade and approaching Gorman. "You want to fuck with us, you fuck with *me*!"

Josef recognized him in an instant. He'd first seen him last year, shouting from his seat at the city council meeting, much to the shock of his wife, the mayor. And in recent months, Josef had heard the rumors like everyone else. It was Gary Hollingshead.

Gary raised his fists up in front of his face. "You got to get through all of us to get to this town."

Donnie sauntered up behind him, smirking and setting a hand on his shoulder. "No need for violence, my man, though I always appreciate the sentiment."

Sirens approached from the north.

"And no need for the authorities or their handcuffs." He reached into his jacket pocket and removed the prop. "I brought my own."

With a sort of flourish, he locked one of the cuffs around his left wrist and the other through the grill of his truck. Then he waved the key in the air, like a magician, wanting everyone to see, before tossing it off the side of the road, into the white void. He looked so happy. So jolly.

This was Christmas in Haymaker.

YEAR THREE

Chapter 1

Monday, January 4

Brenda drove her powder-blue cruiser down Cooper Avenue, along the very spot where the wave of newcomers had met Donnie's breakwater. They'd had to call up Luce County sheriff's deputies from Newberry—men who'd resented leaving their Christmas dinners because of another squabble in Haymaker. Apparently the resentment had seeped throughout the U.P. The negative press. The extra traffic. The drain on resources. Haymaker was an embarrassment to the peninsula.

When she'd arrested Donnie on Christmas, Brenda had cinched the cuffs a bit tighter than usual. They'd taken in eight other men as well, all of whom had brought their own handcuffs and tossed their own keys into the snow. As for the cars of those arrested, a group of Gorman's men happily pushed them onto the side of the road. The next day, Sarver Towing and Repair hauled them away, free of charge.

Brenda glanced to her left, through a thinned-out stretch of pines, to where Big Deep Lake lay frozen and steely like a smooth sheet of scrap metal. She passed the junction with Blackberry Road, and two signs caught her eye. The first was the identity of the town. HAYMAKER: RISEN FROM SAWDUST AND SWEAT. The second was a stop sign facing the wrong direction. It should have faced west but was twisted and angled to face northbound Cooper traffic—to face people entering the town. She made a mental note of it, figuring it had been struck by a car that had hit a patch of ice. Then she noticed the spray paint.

STOP THEM.

Someone had started vandalizing the signs again. Brenda shook her head. The town was about to double in size in only two years' time. Hatred continued to mount. And yet there were still only three police officers, only three referees in this intricate game. A millage request would go before voters in November, to hire two or three more officers, but considering the new voting block, it didn't stand a chance.

She turned onto Marquette and stopped at the Parson intersection. There was another one.

STOP THEM.

"Fuck them," she said, and she drove on to the Civic Centre.

After plodding into her cubicle and sitting with a heavy sigh, Brenda gazed for a moment at a framed photograph on her desk, of Brian lugging a huge backpack during their trip last year to the Porcupine Mountains. She closed her eyes and rubbed the lids.

Keeping them closed, she reached for her phone and punched the key for voice mail. She had two messages.

"They did it again, Sergeant DeBoer."

Her eyes opened wide as she shot up in her chair. The voice was slightly distorted, as if filtered through something electronic.

"They've vandalized and threatened and wasted more tax dollars. And then they went and closed off a road. You arrested some, but not enough. And they're already out of jail. Fix this. Because you don't want to look like one of them, do you? You don't want us to think you're on their side. So stop playing dead. Even Black Bears go crazy sometimes and get a taste for human flesh and bone."

Brenda's heartbeat pounded in her ears. She saved the message and waited for the next one.

"Are you one of us or one of them?"

It was a woman's voice, and for some reason this shocked her more than it probably should have.

"If you're smart, you'll take care of the people who've always lived here. When the war starts and the north woods burn, you better look the other way. Don't look for clues. And don't follow trails."

Brenda saved it for evidence, hung up, and shoved the phone off her desk so that it clattered to the floor. Then she stood up, staring at the photo of Brian, and placed her palm against the cubicle wall for support.

Chapter 2

Saturday, January 9

Ash sat behind the wheel of her mom's Malibu, spinning the wheels up the Ross Road hill, approaching the multicolored mansion of Roosevelt Bly. She passed Gorman Tate's house but refused to look at it.

She parked in Roosevelt's driveway and marched toward the front door, but before she could knock, it opened and there stood the cowboy, beaming in his white suit. "Congrats, Youngblood! Sweet sixteen and hittin' the road!"

Ash stood tall before him momentarily but then lowered her eyes and her head. "I don't know what I'm doing here," she said softly. "I need to talk to someone."

Roosevelt nodded, his smile evaporating as he gravely led her inside. "I made some banana bread this morning," he said. "And I'll make some coffee for me and cocoa for you."

"I'll have coffee," she said.

"You don't want coffee at your age. It'll stunt your growth."

Ash waved her hands over her body. "Please. Stunt it."

Roosevelt filled the pot with water. "You're a basketball star, my dear. Don't fear your height."

Ash removed her coat and slumped down on a bar stool at the counter. She was varsity now and leading the team in points, rebounds, and blocks. "As long as it gets me a scholarship somewhere, fine. But if I'm six feet tall and stuck in Haymaker, I'll kill myself."

Roosevelt looked over his shoulder and frowned at her. "A scholarship like that boy Murphy?"

"He's gotten some playing time at State."

"Probably has to ride the pine quite a bit as a freshman."

Ash broke off a piece of the bread, popped it in her mouth, and licked her fingers. "Who cares? The bench in East Lansing's better than center court here."

Roosevelt sat down beside her. "I've heard you talking about leaving town for over a year now. Your broken record doesn't just repeat itself, my dear. It's worn thin. You're pretty down on this place."

She shrugged. "No shit."

"Ash."

"I'm sorry." She stood up, her back to him, and paced toward the far windows with their view of the frozen lake. "No I'm not." She kicked at something invisible on the floor. "These stupid parades of cars all the time." She turned back to face Roosevelt. "Uncle Donnie spent two nights in jail. *Christmas* night. We knew he would. And my mom's acting all scared about living here now and wants to move, but she can't because of money and her job. And it's all because of these stupid people who keep coming to our town. They're so *stupid*! I'll trade with them! They can move into my house, and I can move to wherever they're from."

"I know," said Roosevelt, sitting still, watching her closely. "It's affecting us all. It's a confusing time."

"I might go live with my dad in Sault Ste. Marie."

"Are you close to your father?"

Ash stuck out her jaw. "We're not talking about him," she said.

The coffeepot gurgled as the percolating stopped. Roosevelt stood up. "Let me get us some mugs." He walked across the kitchen and spoke with his back to her. "You're a smart kid, Ms. Capagrossa. You have a very keen sense of perception." He turned around and smiled. "And so I won't lie to you. All of this—what's been happening to the town—is unfair to those of us who were just minding our own business."

"Then why aren't you pissed off?"

"Who says I'm not?"

"Because you just stand there all the time. In your suit. You're always happy. You're always nice to everyone. Don't you ever want to just punch someone, like Uncle Donnie does? Or just say 'screw it' and leave?"

"I've done that before. In a past life."

Ash rolled her eyes, stood up, and strode across the room into the foyer, where she peered out a narrow rectangular window at Gorman Tate's house. "He made all the problems," she said in a low voice.

Roosevelt approached her, gently guiding her by one arm and the small of her back. "Come on," he said softly. "The coffee's ready."

“No!” She squirmed away from him “I’m tired of doing what everyone wants. Taking care of my brother. Doing shit for my mom. Carrying my whole team on my back.” She reached for the front door, opened it, and stood there at the threshold, her broad shoulders filling the space. She didn’t have her coat.

Roosevelt stayed back. Ash felt him watching her, but he never said anything. Not even when she started running—off the front porch and down the slope of the driveway. The sun broke through the gray ceiling of sky for a moment. She ran across the diamond surface of the sun-soaked snow, in the direction of Gorman Tate’s.

When Ash looked back over her shoulder, there stood Roosevelt—brilliant as the snow—with his hands in his pockets, staring at her. But then her focus settled again on Tate’s. She stopped in his front yard, plunged her bare hands into the snow, packed a hard snowball, and chucked it at his house. It exploded beside the front door. She packed another and hurled it at the windows on the second floor.

Tate’s face never appeared behind the glass. No curtains stirred. The place was silent. But after Ash threw a few more and slowly turned back toward Roosevelt, she felt certain that the mysterious man had seen her. And she was glad. Ash wanted to be seen.

Chapter 3

Monday, February 15

Josef ran his fingers through his hair and slowly shook his head. "I'm at that point where it's too late and I'm too tired to write anything remotely cogent."

With a final sip of another beer, Carl stood from the dining room table—stumbling a bit as he put weight on his bad right knee—and crossed the room to turn off the two a.m. *SportsCenter.* Marissa lay asleep in the next room. The condo was dark save for the hanging lamp above their table, which shone down on their laptops, a bag of pretzels, eight empty beer bottles, and an old football Carl sometimes tossed to himself while brainstorming. "So stop," he said through a yawn. "We got a good enough outline of ideas."

Josef smirked. "Good enough for *him*?"

Seemingly from nowhere Gorman had called them that morning, insisting on a range of ideas related to smoothing the transition for the next wave of what he'd called "pilgrims." And—as was always the case lately—opinions differed. Josef proposed something akin to organizational training. He referred to the newcomers as "cohorts." He outlined a mentor system where established members of the Community helped acclimate them to Haymaker and shepherd them to needed resources.

Carl wanted flash. Technology. He'd talked to Calvin about creating virtual tours for both Freedom Springs and the town as a whole. He wanted online, emotion-fueled testimonials. He wanted a goddamned smartphone app featuring databases of Haymaker information and a library of libertarian thought.

"That would take," Josef had said, "like, a shitload of money."

Pacing and tossing the football in the air, Carl had merely shrugged. "Gorman wants results. Gorman has money."

Now he grabbed the football again and spun it through his half-laced fingers. Neither he nor Josef spoke but merely stared at their computers.

A single crack sounded outside—distant thunder—followed by a long echo. Josef cocked his head, confused. At first he thought it was a rainstorm, but this was February and light snow still fell from the frozen sky.

Another sound shattered the night, closer and sharper now and nothing like thunder. He stood and took a few steps toward the dining room window.

Then Josef collapsed—the reflex like a lightning strike: a flash behind his eyes and the sounds—glassfall and gunshot—rushing over his crouched body.

Carl dropped to the floor, too, still instinctively clutching the football, as Marissa screamed from the other room. "Stay in there!" he shouted.

Josef pressed his back against the wall and curled into something like a ball, his hands covering his head as bits of the condo rained over him. Across the room, Carl squirmed toward the bedroom on all fours. Marissa crouched in the doorway, still screaming, a blue light cast over her hand and face. She had her phone. "Oh my God! Oh my God! Oh my God!"

Through splintered half thoughts, Josef imagined a tornado of lead. A hurricane of fire. But almost immediately came a quiet. The tinkling of tiny broken things. And then, another gunshot farther down the street. The storm moved on but still raged.

Clara shot up in bed, the phone slicing through her sleep. She slapped at her alarm clock before reaching for the phone and knocking it off the nightstand. It continued ringing until she stretched down to the dark floor and finally clutched it and cradled it against the side of her head with both hands.

"What! What?"

"Clara?"

"Who's this? What?"

"It's Shirley Tanner." Shirley used to wait tables at the Shipwreck. She lived on Schoolcraft, just down the road from Freedom Springs. "I'm so sorry to call you in the middle of the night. Garth told me not to. I know you've got your little one—"

Clara leapt to her feet on a current of adrenaline. Her parents were in town, sleeping in the guest room down the hall, but it took a moment for her to realize she hadn't dreamt that fact. "What's going on, Shirley!"

"There's sirens and lights over at those condominiums. Someone opened fire. I don't know who or what, but I could hear the shots from my place."

Red numbers glowed on the alarm clock. It was two forty in the morning. Clara's confusion was a physical—almost painful—thing as she pressed her palm against her closed eyes. She opened the dark closet and ran her hands over the floor to find her boots and slipped her bare feet into them.

"Are you there, Clara?"

"God yes, I'm here, Shirley. I'm putting on my boots."

"I'm sorry. I don't even know if this is something a mayor deals with in the middle of the night, but this just seems like such a big thing."

"I've got to go," Clara said and hung up. She tucked her sweatpants into the boots, threw on her ski jacket, and began searching another coat's pockets for her car keys. When she found them, she went down the hall to where her parents slept. They'd been visiting often—to see Mary, but also, she knew, to help in the wake of the divorce.

She leaned over her mother. "Mom?" she whispered. "Mom?"

"What? What is it?"

"Shh. It's okay. I just have to go out for a bit."

"What? What time is it?"

Her dad snored on the other side of the bed.

"It's after two. Shh. Look—everything's fine. I just got a call and I have to check on something. Just go to sleep. Mary's in her crib. I'll be home before you're awake."

And moments later she was outside with her scraper, chipping away little pockets from the snow and ice on the windshield. Then she got behind the wheel and gunned the engine in reverse to make it through the deep, tightly packed snow at the bottom of the drive, left there by the Snow Soldiers' plows. A late-night DJ played rock ballads for Valentine's Day, though the day had passed a few hours before. Clara turned off the radio and fishtailed down Hemlock Street, headed for the Field of Blood.

Huge white flakes fell through the night and came at her like stars—galaxies cascading at her through the headlights. She turned south and drove down LaRock, through a deeply wooded stretch of town, headed toward the Deep Lakes, where Gary sometimes fished. Red and blue lights wavered above the tree line. Clara turned onto Schoolcraft and approached the strobed chaos at the gates of Freedom Springs. Yellow police tape wrapped the place like bandages. She slowed to a stop among a small group of gawkers and emergency workers. Brenda DeBoer—her eyes ignited in a way that startled Clara—stepped in front of the truck with her arm extended. "Turn around right now!"

Clara lowered her window and stuck her head out into the cold. "It's me, Brenda!"

Brenda lowered her arm, leaned forward, and squinted. "My God, Clara, I didn't know. I'm sorry, but you shouldn't be here right now."

Clara stepped out into the snow. "What happened? Who did it?"

"We still don't know much. Lenny's talking to people. Someone scaled the fence and went down the street with a shotgun just firing into random windows. We think it was random. Nobody was hurt. Thank God, nobody was."

Clara peered toward the homes. People with coats and pajamas stood outside their front doors or wandered—dazed—in small, snowy circles.

Brenda looked back and saw them, too. "Jesus, where's Trevor? He's supposed to keep everyone inside." She turned again to Clara. "The gunman hasn't been found yet. Lenny got a tip that he's following and officers are heading up from Newberry, but these people should *not* be out here." She turned her gaze on Clara. "*You* should definitely not be out here."

Clara nodded. She was right. It was stupid and unsafe. Brenda marched toward the people in the pajamas, waving them toward their homes. Clara turned to leave.

Someone grabbed her by the sleeve and pulled her back. It was a thirty-something woman wearing a bathrobe, her black hair pressed against her face from a frozen wind. She nearly fell into Clara's arms. "You got to help us."

"What?" said Clara. "I will."

"Help my family."

Clara pulled away and held the woman at arm's length, examining her, looking for blood. "Are you okay? Are you hurt?"

The woman stared at Clara, tears mixed with snow on her face. She gritted her teeth. "I want to go back home."

Clara frowned and nodded. "That's where you should be. It's not safe out here. Go back inside your home with your family."

The woman creased her brow and held her mouth open for a moment. "Not there," she said, disgusted, pointing back over her shoulder. "I don't want to go back *there*. I want to go *home*."

Clara nodded slowly and said nothing.

"Why do they hate us?" asked the woman, her voice almost a whisper.

Clara had no idea if this woman knew she was mayor or thought she was another neighbor, someone with buckshot scattered over her own home. "Who?"

The woman tugged free from Clara's grip and shook her head. "All of them."

Red light to blue light to red light—they stood like women in a cathedral of falling stained glass.

Chapter 4

Sunday, March 7

Donnie sat on the windowsill of his second-story apartment, the screen plucked out and lying on the floor beneath his dangling left foot. Churchgoers parked along the curb, headed to Freshwater. A wind blew into his apartment and rustled the week's issues of the *Star-Picayune*, which draped his couch and coffee table. The air was cool but not frozen. Unseasonable warmth had settled on Haymaker, the mercury rising to the upper thirties and the snow already vanishing. They said the whole world was warming.

Donnie stood and slid the window shut and walked to the couch, stepping over a few car parts, a hunting knife, a book on libertarianism, and a half-eaten Pop-Tart. He sat and then reclined, newspapers crinkling beneath his body.

The faces and words of Haymaker's people lit up the dark spaces of his mind that he wanted kept dark. He thought about turning on the TV to make them go away, but everything on TV—news and sitcoms and even sports—made him angry, so he just lay still. This stuff outside would pass for a time—spring snow would return—but summer would eventually awaken and Gorman's people would pour into town, despite a condo sprayed with buckshot. And they would vote in the fall. Vote for a new mayor.

A few weeks back—when those first real shots were fired—a knock came to his door at the break of dawn. Sergeant DeBoer had seemed surprised when he'd casually opened it.

"I seen lights and heard sirens and been up all night," he'd said, "getting phone calls from guys around town. Figured you'd eventually show up and pull a gun on me."

"My gun's tight in its holster, Donnie."

He opened the door wide and made a sweeping motion with his arm for her to enter. "I know you don't have no warrant, but you're welcome in. I got nothing to hide."

She asked him what he knew, and he told her the truth: it was like when Gillickson beat up Jimmy Bruce. He had no idea Derek Kelly, who sometimes hung out with the Bearslayers, would pull a gun on those condos. These guys had plunged into the dark side.

"I want to intimidate and scare, and I definitely want to win. But the town won't mean shit to me if I'm sitting thirty years in the state prison. Fuck that. Them trolls ain't worth suicide."

She left and said she'd be back, but she never returned. Because he was clean, despite the fact that—Christ above—it had gotten away from him. Those fuckers around the table those nights at Rusty's couldn't keep it in their pants. Gillickson and Kelly. Mickey Jenks and Scott Speck and that half-wit, Bill Prefontaine. The dim room, big talk, and alcohol had gone straight to their heads. To their trigger fingers. The Bearslayers had disbanded. Every man for himself.

All of which led him to mornings like this—gray light diffusing throughout the room, coming from the window and the sky but seemingly no real source. It made him want to fold. He'd been like a cardplayer—trying to win it back, win it back—and now he just wanted to walk away with the few coins left jingling in his near-empty pocket. For the first time, Donnie had thought about moving.

He rubbed his eyes and shifted on the couch, the newspapers crinkling with the slightest movement. When he thought about staying, he thought about Ash—his only kin with any real fire. He'd seen it on the court. She was from the same lumberjack stock as him, with that same taste in her teeth: sand and pine and a little blood from a smack to the mouth. They were alike in this way. They smiled—a little more alive—when someone threw an elbow and they could run their tongues over the flavor in their gums.

He stood up and breathed deeply and slowly. Then he searched for his wallet among the mess. His refrigerator was empty, and he had a craving for red meat.

Josef stepped through slush. The thaw smelled like spring, but he'd heard the rumblings among the innkeepers, restaurant owners, and gas station managers that this wasn't good for snowmobiling—the winter cash crop.

He stood near the shore of Little Deep Lake and couldn't remember exactly how he'd gotten here. He'd gone for a morning walk and had moved unconsciously, like a highway truck driver. He smoked a cigarette and watched the ice fishermen.

Josef hadn't smoked since college but had taken it up again—at first just once in awhile with Denny, away from home—but habitually these days. Ever since the shootings at the condos. Before the move, he'd rarely sipped a drink. Now he and Jeanie lulled themselves to sleep each night with a fifth of vodka and late-night talk shows.

He exhaled and wondered how the hell the fishermen could walk onto the ice melt when it looked like they might plunge through the surface at any moment. But they knew things he didn't know. It was another mystery of the north. Another secret hidden from him and his.

Unseen birds chirped in the pine boughs above him, lured into a false spring. But the landscape had only gone from white to gray. It was there in the bark of the trees. On the half-frozen lake. There, above the land, in a sky pulled taut like a hospital blanket. The sky loomed both infinitely high and yet just out of reach of Josef's fingertips. Even if he could touch it, the sky would scrape the skin off his fingers. The lake was softening. The sky was not.

Like Gorman. Always close and always distant. Always available for a long talk but never betraying a single thought. The gunfire had spooked Gorman almost as much as it had spooked Josef himself. He'd installed a new security system in his mansion and at the Headquarters. And he now carried a handgun at all times.

"You need to arm yourself," Gorman had said last night.

"Jeanie would never go for it. Even after everything. She doesn't even like the one locked up in our house." Josef had shaken his head. "It's not going to happen."

"*Something's* going to happen, brother." Gorman untied his ponytail, his gray hair falling over his face as he stared at the floor. "If not Revelation, then Exodus."

A man emerged from a shanty on the center of the lake, stared up at the sky for a moment, and then disappeared inside again. Josef flicked his cigarette onto the rotten ice along shore and turned toward home. He had e-mails and articles to write—to prevent the exodus. One would describe the heightened security measures at Freedom Springs. Another would rally the troops, imagining a future where libertarian ideas—and libertarian men and women—had taken root in Haymaker soil. And the final would discuss the next step in achieving that.

It was an election year. The people needed a new leader.

Chapter 5

Saturday, April 10

The permafrost floor at Rusty's had thawed and reverted to mud. It was fair to call it spring in Haymaker, even though roadside puddles still froze at night. Roosevelt entered and stepped gingerly across the cardboard pathway that Bep had laid from the front door to the bar. He held a folded newspaper under his right arm and squinted as he approached his stool. Another light-bulb had burnt out, above the cash register at the center of the room.

"Evening, Bly," said Rusty. His toupee sat straight on his head tonight. He appeared well rested.

"We having ourselves an eclipse?" Roosevelt pointed at the dead light.

"Ambiance," said Rusty.

"You need some of those new curlicue bulbs that last for seven years."

"You buy 'em, I'll screw 'em."

"That sounds like something our friend, Mr. Sarver, would say." Roosevelt unfolded the newspaper and spread it over the bar. "He been in tonight?"

"He's here," said Rusty, setting Roosevelt's drink down on the newspaper. "In the john."

Roosevelt sipped and nodded. He scanned the room. It was quiet for a Saturday night. Amid the dimness and the antique lumber tools there were only a few other men, two of whom were heavyset guys wearing DNR jackets who rubbed their necks and chins a lot while they spoke.

Rusty glanced at the newspaper. "What's this shit? More politics?" He wiped the bar with a wet rag. "Left wings and right wings and all a bunch of ostriches that can't get off the goddamned ground. Place makes me sick."

"Why not leave? Retire to some tropical paradise?"

"I find my paradise like everyone else," he said, pointing a thumb at the shelf above him. "At the bottom of these bottles."

Roosevelt raised his drink. "Cheers to that."

The bathroom door swung open and Donnie emerged. "Cowboy," he said quietly. He walked to the opposite end of the bar, picked up the beer sitting there, and carried it over to the stool beside Roosevelt. "Cowboy's got news. I can see it in his eyes."

The two hadn't spoken much in the past year. Donnie's crew was gone. Their table sat vacant in the far, dark corner.

"You've probably already seen it," said Roosevelt. He tapped the paper with his finger.

"I ain't seen shit today except the business end of Willie Sutton's Toyota. Electrical pain up the ass. Checked every circuit ten times, and it turns out to be a bad ground." He squinted and leaned toward the paper. "It's dark as death in here. What am I looking at?" He pulled it closer to him and read the lead story.

LIBERTARIAN THROWS HAT INTO RACE

The first mayoral candidate has thrown his hat into the Haymaker mayoral race, and to the surprise of almost no one, it is a libertarian newcomer. Josef Novak, 40, announced this morning that he will run for the seat soon to be vacated by Clara Hollingshead, who has announced she will step down at the end of her term this year.

"We have always sought our goals through peaceful and democratic means," said Novak. "Yes, we have libertarian philosophies that we believe, if implemented, would benefit everyone . . . both longtime Haymaker residents and newcomers. This isn't about libertarian or non-libertarian governance. It's about improved governance. Reformed governance."

A major player in the creation of the Freedom Community and its move to Haymaker, Novak has managed to assuage the fears of critics, many of whom disagree with his politics but find him mild-mannered and likeable.

"He'll be a worthy adversary," said Councilman Ernest Mears.

The growing libertarian population in Haymaker makes the Novak candidacy even stronger. If he and the rest of the Freedom Community leadership (including chairman Gorman Tate) have their way, simple arithmetic may guarantee victory.

Susan Abram, a member of the leadership, explained it this way: "We're hoping that by the fall the registered voting population of the Freedom Community is such that—with our obviously expected high turnout—it should just be a numbers game."

City councilman Tyrus "Ty" Moroney agrees and states that a Novak victory—along with suspected challenges to council seats—could change the makeup of the town forever.

"People whose families have lived in Haymaker for generations will up and leave, some for nearby towns, others out of the peninsula entirely, just to wash their hands of it all. It would be a local and regional tragedy."

And so both sides plan on working hard to register voters.

"At the very least," said Novak, "the turnout will be extraordinary in November, and that can only be called a victory for democracy."

"If he wins," said Moroney, "that's no victory for 50 percent of this town."

If he wins, however, might well depend on his opponent. At this hour, no other townsperson has answered the call.

Roosevelt expected a rage, expected Donnie to break bottles or furniture. But he just sat quietly for a long stretch, sipping the beer and then staring off in the distance. "That Merv Grubb's a fucking poet, ain't he?"

"That all you're going to say?"

"What you want me to say, Cowboy? It's over? Because it is."

"Why?"

Donnie lowered his voice. "Because it's Novak."

"What's that mean?"

Donnie turned on his stool to face Roosevelt, speaking with both hands half-open in front of him, as if to grasp at something. "It means it ain't Gorman Tate or some other crazy. It ain't some libertarian version of *me*." He didn't smile. He meant no humor by this. "He's about as vanilla as you can get for somebody who blueprinted an invasion. Jesus Christ, Bly, even I have a hard time hating the guy."

"But you do."

"Of course I do. Especially now." Donnie squeezed the newspaper with his left hand. "It's talking here about people just up and leaving?" He tossed it, fluttering, over his shoulder. "That's already started, my man. Guy who worked for me—Darren Buzzard—took off a couple weeks ago with his girlfriend and their baby. Said, 'Fuck this, I can fix cars anywhere,' and got a good job in Mackinaw City. There ain't enough to keep most people rooted here. Especially when jobs are involved." He took several swallows of his beer.

Roosevelt said nothing and stared at vodka and gin and whiskey bottles on the shelf above Rusty.

"Fuck," said Donnie, "I need something stronger than this." He finished off his beer. "Place is dead tonight. Where is everybody?"

"Where's your crew?" asked Roosevelt.

Donnie shook his head and rubbed his eyes. "Dissolved, man. All went to smash. When you get too crazy for me, then you got too goddamned crazy." He turned and leaned toward Roosevelt. "Them guys went nuclear. I didn't have shit to do with that stuff. The shootings and the other violent shit. You know that, right?"

"So let's cut to the bone," said Roosevelt, leaning in himself. "Politics are politics, but they're still going to mean something this time around. Who are you going to get to run for your side?"

"Run for what?"

"Mayor."

"*My* side?"

Roosevelt nodded.

"Ain't it your side, too?"

"Is it?"

"You a libertarian?"

"Not really. I'm not a quote, unquote Black Bear."

"And you ain't a Husky," said Donnie. "But you're at least something in the same family." He paused and sipped again. "A Lab, maybe. Some kind of retriever."

Roosevelt smiled in a way different from how he usually smiled. "Well, I appreciate that, Mr. Sarver. That's kind in a way you might not realize."

"I'd still kick the shit out of you during Boomtown if you wasn't so goddamned old."

"I am that," said Roosevelt. "Old for most things. Not all, but most."

"Too old to fight. Too old to fuck. You're just killing time, old man."

"You warm my heart like springtime, Donnie. It's like the good old days. Keep it going."

Donnie shook his head and smiled. "Well shit, Bly, you're talking about *the good old days*? You're starting to sound like me. Like a Husky. You wishing things hadn't changed? You wishing you and I were still the two biggest nutjobs in this town?"

Roosevelt tipped his hat low on his brow, covering his eyes. "I really don't know, Donnie."

The two fell silent for a spell. Donnie finished his beer and ordered a whiskey. "And get Cowboy another one of his sarsaparillas. On me, goddamn it."

"My heart," said Roosevelt, placing his palm over his chest. "My heart can't endure such kindness."

Donnie ran his fingers through his black hair. He spoke quietly. "Hey, I hear my niece comes by and talks to you sometimes."

"She's a good kid."

"Hell of a ballplayer." Donnie nodded. "Been pretty down since her dad left."

"She respects you," said Roosevelt. "Defends you, even. Tooth and nail."

Donnie said nothing and stared down at the wood grain on the bar.

Rusty approached and set their drinks before them. Roosevelt raised his glass and smiled. "You know, it's good to converse with you again, Mr. Sarver. A toast!"

Donnie took a sip of his whiskey, never raising his glass, never even looking at The Man in White. "Go fuck yourself, Bly, you Miss Manners dinosaur."

Chapter 6

Tuesday, May 4

Donnie sat on the landing of his apartment smoking a cigarette, sipping a beer, and looking down on the flower shop parking lot and the offices of the *Star-Picayune.* Orange light splayed out over the evening sky. The days were getting longer. The tourist season approached. He wondered how many of those tourists would have their minivans and RVs repaired at Ron's Automotive, the new shop down the road. Ron Adams was a libertarian who met the demands of all the newcomers boycotting Sarver Towing and Repair.

The doors to the newspaper office opened and closed, and Merv Grubb stepped into the evening air, wandering below where Donnie sat. Donnie reached out over the railing to tap his cigarette. Merv brushed the ashes off his sleeves before looking up. "Well, look at old Wile E. Coyote up on his perch."

"You better step aside before I start dropping anvils instead of ashes."

"The coyote always fails." Merv walked slowly up the stairs, his eyes hidden within his squint. "All his scheming don't amount to shit." He stood before Donnie and smiled, resting his elbow on the handrail. "That you, Donnie? All your years of scheming and you can't stop these meep-meep fuckers from flooding our town. Come on, man. We need a hero."

Donnie tried to think of something to say but instead took a sip of his beer, letting his lips smile from behind the glass.

"Come on. Run for office. Mayor Donnie Sarver."

A handful of Haymakes had talked about running, including Rita Gumpert; Doc Brewer; "Slim" Jim Johnstone, whose football team had gone 8–1 last year; and that Judas, Bud Wilmington. But so far nobody had actually committed to being tangled up in a mess that looked like a lost cause.

"Them libs got this one beat," said Donnie. "No one wants to play when there's no shot of winning. It's like getting drafted by the Lions."

Merv smiled. "Give me a sip of that." He reached for Donnie's beer.

Donnie pulled away. "I don't share my fluids with men."

"Or women, either. You know how many high-heeled shoes I've seen waltzing up these steps to your apartment over the past couple years?" He made his hand into the shape of a zero.

"You think you take the pulse of this town, but you don't know shit about me," said Donnie, though in a way Merv was right. His passions had all been focused in one direction.

"That's right, Donnie," said Merv. "Nobody knows anything except you. You know all the theories and angles, all the plan As and plan Bs. But what about the story I'm breaking tomorrow? What about that big news?"

Donnie smoked casually, staring off at the orange sky. "You want me to beg? You want me to whimper and wag my tail?"

"Like you do with women?"

Donnie stood up and opened the door to his apartment.

"Hold up," said Merv. "I'll let you in on the secret. Extra, extra, read all about it. A new candidate is throwing his highly recognizable hat into the mayoral race."

Donnie stared at him now. There was another pause. "Quit dickin' around."

Merv smiled. "The Man in White. The Gold-Plated Cowboy. That wheelin-dealin', kiss-stealin' son of a gun, Roosevelt Bly."

"Oh, you're full of shit."

"No, man. I'm not. He called me up late last night. And on Friday he's going to announce it formally. At Parson Park. High noon. Like a new sheriff come to town."

"Why?"

"Because he wants to get the word out."

"No, asshole. Why's he running? Why the fuck's he care about it?"

"Save the town?"

Donnie flicked his cigarette past Merv's head and into the twilight. The orange had slowly vanished from above, the dusk swooping into its wake.

Chapter 7

Friday, May 7

About two dozen Haymakes gathered before the white band shell at Parson Park. Some leaned against budding maples with their arms crossed over their chests. Others slouched on picnic tables or on lawn chairs they'd brought from home. An elderly couple wearing fanny packs and licking ice-cream cones—clearly tourists—stood toward the back. A few kids squealed and played tag around a flowering dogwood. The scene reminded Roosevelt of Thursday evenings in the summertime, when a local jazz band played free concerts here. It was all a kind of performance.

He stood out back of the band shell, behind a blue spruce, peeking out at the audience and recognizing many of the folks. Ash was there, of course, sitting cross-legged in the grass with Patrick John nearby chasing seagulls. Earl Henneman sat up front, like a stoic. Merv Grubb and Cecil Grove—the press corps—waited with notebook and camera. And Sergeant DeBoer stood near the back, her eyes tracking Donnie, who'd just arrived and now moseyed on over to his niece.

Roosevelt reached into his white coat pocket for his speech and was about to head over to the band shell when he noticed Josef and Jeanie Novak and their girls approach through the trees. His heart jumped and sweat broke out on his back. He unfolded his speech and stared at it for a moment. The papers rustled in his newly trembling hands.

Ash leaned forward and ran her fingers through the grass the way she saw lovers do to each other's hair in the movies. A young redheaded woman walked through the crowd handing out rally signs. She gave one to Ash, who studied it for a moment. It was gold, and the only text on the entire sign was the word BLY in huge black letters. A white cowboy hat sat tilted atop the "B."

Gold and black. Not orange. Not red, white, and blue.

Roosevelt peeked out from behind the band shell. At first the sight of him and his white hat made Ash smile. But after a while, as he continued to sneak glances and then disappear again, she had to look away. The feeling was hard to describe. It was like the time she'd ridden her bike past Pines Place—the old folks' home—on a beautiful sunny day. A nurse had tossed a huge beach ball high into the air—underhand, the way Ash tossed a ball to Patrick John—and the men and women in wheelchairs had raised their rigid arms overhead, trying to catch it.

"I knew you'd be here." Donnie plopped down in the grass next to her. Patrick John scrambled by, and Donnie scooped him up and tickled him until the boy squealed with delight.

"Why are *you* here?" asked Ash.

"When the circus comes to town, you go. Especially when it's free." He pointed to Josef and his family. "Even the enemy likes a good freak show."

A different young woman—this one blonde—walked up the steps onto the stage. She wore a modern cut of jeans that Ash saw in magazines and on TV but never in Haymaker. Her face was pretty in a way Ash knew boys and men liked—large eyes that always sparkled as if they were teary, even while smiling.

"Shit," said Donnie, "that's Stephanie Noles. What's she still doing hanging around Bly?"

Ash had heard rumors that Roosevelt spent time with young women, but she'd never believed them. She wondered if people knew that she sometimes visited him to talk. That she considered him a friend, even though he was way older than Grandma Sarver.

"Good afternoon," said Stephanie. "I want to welcome you to this announcement, which I know so many of us were hoping would come. The announcement that will save this town!"

Hardly anyone clapped. Everyone stared at the stage.

"I won't waste too much of your time. We're here for the words of the future mayor of Haymaker himself, Roosevelt Bly!" Her voice screeched a bit with the final burst of energy, and now a few people, including Ash, politely applauded. Stephanie glanced at a small piece of paper cupped in her right hand and read from it. "The cowboy has always been a hero of Americana. He's a symbol of freedom and toughness and hard work. He takes on overwhelming problems amid a bleak landscape and meets those problems with a shrug. Then he goes to work and gets results. And that's exactly what this man—our cowboy—represents." She looked up from the paper, at the crowd again, and smiled with relief. "Ladies and gentlemen, I give you my good friend, Mr. Roosevelt Bly!"

Everyone except Donnie applauded now—even the Novaks, though it seemed they were just being polite.

Roosevelt appeared from his hiding area, all smiles and ease, embodying all of the confidence, grace, and charm that Ash expected of his face and form. He hugged Stephanie and kissed her on the cheek. Then, after waving to the crowd, he shaped his hands into pistols and fired away. Bang-bang.

"Thank you, thank you." There was no podium. Roosevelt stood behind a tall and narrow microphone stand that mirrored his own body. His normally brilliant white diffused into the white backdrop of the band shell so that his face seemed to float. "I want to thank you all," he said. Feedback screeched through the speakers. "I'm sorry. Whoa, ouch. Sorry about that." He tapped the microphone with his index finger. "I just wanted to thank you for coming today. I know this is short notice."

Even from where Ash sat she could make out a sheen on his face. It was the first time she'd ever seen him sweat.

"I'm not one for controversy. I like making friends, not enemies, so I guess this isn't the wisest of decisions or wisest of professions. Let me explain why I'm doing this."

"Whose side are you on?" someone shouted. It was Fever, the flag burner, wearing a sleeveless shirt and holding a sign above his head that read DRIVE THE OUTSIDERS OUT.

Roosevelt stared at him for a moment, his jaw slightly slack. "Well, I don't know. You tell me."

The crowd was silent.

"I love this town, so many would consider me a loyal Haymake. What some like to call a 'Husky.' But I'm not so naïve as to say my friend Josef Novak over there doesn't care about this town either." He politely nodded in the direction of the Novaks, and everyone turned, most seeming to notice Josef for the first time. Jeanie put an arm around her younger daughter.

"I guess," said Roosevelt, "I don't want Haymaker to change as much as it has. And I hold both sides responsible for those changes. But I also sympathize with both. This is my adopted home, and so I can speak for all those newcomers who've uprooted themselves and come to this small town by their own choice, who've made a hell of an investment in it, and who care for it very much."

There was a smattering of applause.

"That said, I've lived here now for thirty-one years. Any turnip truck I'd once fallen from is now thousands of miles down the road. But I will tell you this." He shook his finger toward the crowd. "I have never found this place I love as distasteful as I do now."

A few people applauded and then stopped. People exchanged glances with those beside them.

"I don't like what's happening to the people. I don't like the hate. The fights. The guns. And yet I love the people. I love the lake."

Donnie shifted where he sat.

"So I'm entering the race for mayor. I have no problem with my opponent and will say nothing negative about him except that I'm afraid that his being elected—by no fault of his own—would only further divide this town."

Roosevelt removed his hat and placed it over his chest. "I may not be loved by everyone, but I'm not hated by half. This town may well survive if I'm elected. I'll be sure to represent everyone."

A thin stratum of applause.

"Most of you know that I live on the dunes. I guess if you're foolish enough to build your house on a foundation of sand, you've got to expect change to come. But I'm like one of those beech trees you see clinging to the duneside. Its roots look like old bones, but by God it'll cling to that sand with all its might, just to keep its view of the lake."

More applause. Donnie stood up, his hands in his jeans pockets.

"They call it Superior because of its size, but we call it Superior because of the people living on its shores. Those who were born here. Those of us who've moved here. We all choose to stay, so I'll meet those changes with my eyes set to the horizon—where the sky meets the lake, where the present meets the future, and where newcomer and old-timer can wade out together through the purity of Superior waves. Thank you for your time."

Cheers bubbled up out of the park grounds and then burst overhead. The people clapped and whistled and raised their gold rally signs. Patrick John ran into Ash's arms, startled by the noise. Donnie slipped a cigarette between his lips, turned, and walked back toward the street. The Novaks quickly followed.

Rita Gumpert appeared, ascending the stage holding a large white box. She handed it to Roosevelt, who shook his head in confusion before opening it and removing its contents. He turned the thing in his hands: a white Stetson, similar to the hat he wore every day, but with a bright orange band wrapped around its crown and a large orange "H" embroidered on its side.

"Put it on!" a few people shouted.

Roosevelt smiled, shook Rita's hand, and then gave a short wave to the crowd before slipping out of sight behind the band shell, the new Stetson pressed against his hip.

In his wood-paneled library, overlooking the twilight lake, Roosevelt sat in a leather chair with a drink in one hand and Tocqueville's *Democracy in America* in the other. He tipped his head back and polished off the drink, until the ice clinked against his teeth. The setting sun reflected a long strip of orange across the lake, like a flaming sword. He set the dog-eared book on the end table and stood up to make another Presbyterian, his fourth of the night.

The doorbell rang. Roosevelt crinkled his brow and then glanced in the mirror above the bar, smoothing down his hair, smoothing down the wrinkles in his white shirt. He bent and picked up his jacket, which was neatly laid over the other leather chair, and slipped it on while rambling through the dim house to the front door.

When he opened it, that flash of fear struck his heart again. "Josef, my boy. Please come in."

"I'm sorry. I gave you no warning."

"None's needed for friends." He turned into the foyer and beckoned Josef with a wave. "Come on, I'll make you a drink."

Josef followed with his hands in the pockets of his khaki pants. "No, I'm good. I've got to head back home in a few minutes."

They entered the library. Roosevelt picked his hat up off the table, slipped it on, and went right back to making his drink. "Nothing? You sure?"

"Positive." Josef stood and watched him and then turned to stare at the lake.

"Well, take a load off." Roosevelt gestured to one chair before sitting in the other. He could feel the smile—huge and numb—on his face. "I'd ask what I can do for you, though I have a sense I know what's on your mind."

Josef sat. "I'm not happy, Roosevelt."

"You see, I'm a mind reader. I have the sixth sense."

"I don't understand why you're doing this. I have never in all of our talks—and I've enjoyed those talks immensely over the past couple of years—but I have never gotten the sense from you that you care one iota about politics."

Roosevelt crossed his right leg over his left and then switched them. "Oh, I care very much about politics. I don't like them, but I care about them. I don't like going to the doctor, but I care about what he has to say."

"That doesn't mean you want to become a doctor."

"Touché. But in a town full of quacks I'd probably start reading *Gray's Anatomy.*"

Josef leaned forward, just a touch. "So are you calling *me* a quack or Clara Hollingshead?"

"Oh Christ, boy—neither." Roosevelt winced and shook his head. "I've got a head full of spiders right now. Don't listen to anything I say."

"But that's exactly why I came here tonight. I want to know what you have to say."

"I've said it. At the park today."

Josef nodded at Roosevelt's drink. "And now you're celebrating."

Roosevelt's face went serious but quickly smiled in a new way. "You're a smart young man, but you don't know as much as you think you do. And I'm not talking about politics right now."

Josef leaned back into his chair again and spoke gently. "So what *is* going on with you, Roosevelt? And I'm saying this only half as an opponent. I do consider you a friend, even now."

"Well, first, don't confuse this with betrayal. If I weren't going to vote for myself, I'd vote for you."

Josef rolled his eyes and turned away.

"Now just calm down. Enough hijinks." Roosevelt took another long sip. "Hell, boy, this ain't a toast of celebration. It's Dutch courage. It was all I could do to keep my lunch down out there today."

"I doubt you've ever been nervous in your whole life."

Roosevelt sighed, shook his head, and looked out at the lake. "There are nights I wake up choking like I'm drowning. And there are mornings I can't get out of bed for all the muck inside my brains."

Josef smiled and bounced slightly in his chair. He followed Roosevelt's gaze toward the lake. "Come on, with that view? That's one hell of a view. I look out my back window, and all I see are a sandbox and toys and the girls' bikes lying in the brown grass."

"But that's *living.* That's a *life.* This view's only good on days like today, when the sky makes the water blue. In the winter there's nothing lonelier than that long sheet of white. It's a sight that makes me want to stop my heart and quick go join my wife." He looked up at the ceiling and took another sip.

Josef paused before continuing. "Well now, don't do that. Attempting suicide's illegal. Any libertarian could tell you that."

Roosevelt shot him a glance, but Josef was smiling. "I appreciate the humor," he said. "Though I myself would hope a community would keep people out of harm's way."

"Don't confuse community with government," said Josef, his smile evaporating. "Government's supposed to protect people from other people, not from themselves. They start protecting people for their own good and then you've got totalitarianism."

Roosevelt sipped his drink and shook his head. "Jesus Christ, it's too late in the day for such talk." Now he leaned forward, pointing a long, white finger at Josef. "Enough with the black helicopters and New World Orders and the bogeymen in Washington who'll take away your mind."

"Don't attack the straw man with me, Roosevelt. You've lived long enough to witness the constant growth of governmental power, the constant increase in laws and rules and restrictions. That's why we're doing this. That's why I'm running. All we're doing is digging in our heels and finally pushing back against the tide."

"All right. Can of worms." Roosevelt stood to make another drink. He lost his balance and slowly—almost gracefully—slanted toward the window until his shoulder rested against the glass.

Josef stood and guided him by the arms. "Why don't you have a seat and I'll make some coffee."

"No thank you." Roosevelt shrugged him off and stepped toward the bar. When he turned around, Josef was leafing through the pages of Tocqueville.

"So was this your inspiration, or are you doing some last-minute cramming?" Roosevelt frowned through the numbness in his face, but Josef quickly smiled. "I'm joking, man."

Roosevelt relaxed, took a deep breath, and then sat a little too quickly, spilling some of his drink. He took the book from Josef and flipped through the dog-eared pages. "Listen to this," he said. "I read this the other day. I've got all these books in here and I want to read each before I die, which means I've got to live to be three hundred." He continued to turn pages. "I thought now was as good a time as any to read this one. Wait, here it is. You listen to this. I read this just the other day. 'As the election draws near,' et cetera, 'the whole nation glows with a feverish pitch,' and so forth. Okay, here. 'It is true that as soon as the choice is determined this ardor is dispelled, calm returns, and the river, which had nearly broken its banks, sinks to its usual level; but who can refrain from astonishment that such a storm should have arisen?'" He slapped the book shut. "Now, how's that for relevance, my boy? How's that for prophecy?"

"You mean that no matter what, the storm will calm? No matter who's elected? Then why's it matter if you run or not? Why's it matter if I win and you lose?"

Roosevelt closed his eyes and waved him away. "I'm not in the mood now, Josef. There'll be plenty of time for debates."

Josef sighed. "Okay," he said, "I'm just going to say it, and I'm sorry if it offends. You're eighty-one years old, Roosevelt."

"Reginald McPhee was eighty-four when he fell through the ice. He'd have served another decade if it weren't for global warming."

"But why take it on at this point in your life if it's not your passion? Why go through all this?"

"You mean why care about preserving something I might not be around long enough to see?"

"No." Josef shook his head. "Listen. You just—you're not going to win. Okay? Too many people are going to think too many things. That you're too old. That you're too rich. That you're too strange. They might all be wrong, but I'm a PR guy, and you'd need three of me to pull this thing off."

The sun had set. The lake was dark. "Oh hell, people think I'm a homosexual," said Roosevelt. "Others think I've got a harem of dames. And yet I care about people in this town who don't even know it. I care so goddamned much for this place, and its people don't even like me. But who cares? I'll love them anyway. And maybe I'll get their votes, too." He took another sip. "I care about you and your family. I want you here. But this place is never going to be your utopia. Any group, no matter what their beliefs, can't flood into a town the way you have and not have conflict. You'd have to start a town from scratch to make this work. People here don't begrudge your politics. They begrudge your methods. By God, despite what you think, these forests ain't all government land. Go buy some and settle your own political frontier. Make your own town. People will leave you alone. Maybe even give you their blessing." He drank some more.

"You know the last time we sat here," said Josef, "I was the one who was drunk."

"I'm not drunk."

"No, not at all." Josef stood up.

Roosevelt cupped a frail hand over his eyes. His shoulders shook, and a few tears ran down his concave cheeks. "Ignore this." He wiped his nose with the side of his hand. "This is old-man crap. This is memories and self-pity and eventide crap. I'm not ashamed. Just don't use it against me in any negative campaigning." He winked a teary eye and pointed his pistol-shaped hand at Josef. Bang-bang.

Josef stared, his expression revealing his horror at the sight. "I promise." He took a step forward. "You want me to help you to bed?"

"No, hell no," said Roosevelt, waving him away. "I'll probably sleep right here tonight. Just let yourself out and lock the door behind you, if you could. I hate not walking you out, but I'm afraid I just don't have the sea legs for it." He closed his eyes. "Donnie Sarver would be happy to see this. I'm no Miss Manners dinosaur tonight." He chuckled as he leaned back and lowered his cowboy hat.

"Sweet dreams," said Josef.

Roosevelt sighed. "Merry nightmares."

Chapter 8

Monday, June 21

Brenda parked her cruiser along the curb on Marquette Street in front of Rita's Floral and Gift. She turned the engine off and rubbed her eyes. It was summer solstice—the longest day of the year. Though really, that had been yesterday. She and Brian had planned to hike at Pictured Rocks. But then the day had blown up, and the station had called her in.

It was now two o'clock in the morning but in no way the shortest of nights. Brenda stepped out of the car. The streetlights buzzed overhead. The town still shuddered beneath her feet.

It had begun around noon. A silver van had slowed down in front of the entrance of Freedom Springs, and a passenger had tossed a hand grenade in the direction of the guard shack. It turned out to be a dummy grenade—the kind sold at an army-navy surplus—which rattled down the concrete and bounced harmlessly into the grass. But the guard—a man named Zane Alexander—told Brenda that if she didn't arrest the criminal by the end of the day, he'd handle it himself with his Glock 17.

A couple of hours later a twenty-five-year-old libertarian named John Flowers attacked the statue of Frederick Parson with a hammer, taking the bayonet off the native son's rifle and denting a chunk of square bronze jaw.

Around four o'clock an anonymous woman called to report that someone was putting fish in mailboxes. All of the victims—including the Novaks—

were libertarians who lived not in Freedom Springs but amid the general populace, in the old Haymaker neighborhoods. Some of the fish were still alive. Brenda pulled them off of white envelopes, their mouths gaping, their gills pulsing like fresh lacerations.

Near eight o'clock—the sun still sharp and bright—three children playing in Blue Spruce Park screamed at the discovery of five huskies—or, at least, husky stuffed animals—hanging from evergreens by nooses, their fabric tongues hanging out, their eyes X'd out, and red paint splashed across their bodies like blood.

By ten o'clock the sun finally slept, and a group of local teenagers on the northern, forested edge of the development tossed about a hundred empty beer bottles over the fence of Freedom Springs, smashing them on the sides of condos before disappearing into the trees.

At approximately ten thirty someone shot a husky—a real husky, in one of the kennels at Marx Iditarod—with a .22 caliber rifle. Jeremy cradled the howling animal as he ran to his truck, expecting the whole time that more bullets would rain down on him out of the dark. He drove the dog to a clinic in Sault Ste. Marie, and Brenda had just received word that it had survived—was only grazed—but would forever walk with a limp and never again pull a sled.

And just before midnight, a wandering band of three middle-aged locals attacked a white-bearded man who was stumbling his way down the sidewalk after a night at Rusty's. The man was Clifford Kirby, a native Haymake who'd spent two decades in the state prison in Jackson for armed robbery. Now he lived at the end of Oshkosh Drive, in a cabin heated by a wood-burning stove and with no indoor plumbing. He'd become a bit of a hermit over the past ten years and ventured out only for a few groceries or the occasional drink. The men didn't recognize him, pegged him as an outsider, and they beat and kicked Clifford in the dark pockets between streetlights. The old man curled into a ball and covered his head, his breathing turning desperate from two broken ribs. The broken ring finger on his right hand was bent to the side at a sharp angle. Blood soaked the white hair at the back of his head.

His life was saved by Bep Leach, who'd been walking a bag of garbage to the Dumpster behind the tavern when she'd heard Clifford's screams of pain. She rushed back inside, grabbed the near-antique Winchester that Rusty kept behind the bar, and returned into the dark summer air, firing shots at the stars and screaming curses that shook the moon.

◆ ◆ ◆

Brenda trudged through the dark now, beneath the buzzing streetlights, to the wooden staircase that ran along the building's side. Next door, Merv, Cecil, and two other newspapermen appeared framed in yellow window light, slicing through the room like mad insects, no doubt scrambling to put all of these stories together into one very special edition. Brenda believed she was invisible, but when Merv looked up from his computer, his eyes went wide—he'd seen her beneath the lights—and seconds later he came plunging out of the door, crunching over the gravel toward her.

"You arresting Donnie?"

"Not now, Merv."

"You mean 'not now' you don't want to talk or that you're not arresting him now?"

"Both." Brenda ascended the rickety stairs.

"Was he the one that threw that grenade? Or was he one of the men who jumped Clifford Kirby?"

Brenda said nothing and reached the top of the stairs.

"Oh shit, we need pictures. I got to get Cecil." Merv turned and ran down the stairs and back to the office.

Brenda removed her flashlight from her belt and used it to pound the door three times. "Donnie!" She pounded again.

"Who is it?" he called from the other side.

"You know who it is."

"That you, DeBoer?"

"Open up."

"I didn't do *shit.*"

"Open up!"

Dim golden light broke—a thin rectangle running up the door frame with Donnie's shadow-sliced face hiding behind it. "I didn't do any of it," he said quietly.

"I'd like to come inside, Donnie."

"As long as you believe me when I say I had nothing to do with anything that happened today. I didn't plan it. I didn't carry it out. I didn't even hear about it until most of it was done." He turned his face away from her. "Fuck this fucked-up place."

"You know some of these people. That's why I want to talk."

Donnie shook his head, stared at the floor, and opened the door wide. "I'm done knowing people." He turned and walked back inside.

Brenda followed but stopped after only a few steps. "What—where are you going?"

The living room was filled with cardboard boxes of all sizes. Furniture and shelves were pushed along the far wall. Books and dishes were stacked in piles. A packaging tape dispenser lay in the middle of the floor, and yet, she saw now, the cardboard boxes in the room were torn open, the tape hanging limp.

"Are you packing?"

"Was." Donnie sat cross-legged in the middle of the room and lit a cigarette. "A week ago I made the decision to get the fuck out of Dodge. Once Bly and Novak started talking about the future of this town, I said fuck it, this place ain't mine anymore. I can take the shit behind door number one or the shit behind door number two, but I'm stuck with filth either way."

Brenda circled him slowly while scanning the room, looking for weapons, dirty boot prints, drops of blood.

"I mean, we tried. But these fuckers are like locusts." Donnie looked down and shook his head. His hair had grown longer, and the bangs fell over his eyes. "I ain't one to quit, but there—I'm quitting."

Brenda stopped and looked down at him. "Then why are you unpacking everything you already packed?"

"Because of those assholes."

"Who?"

"Whoever they are. The ones on my side. The side that *was* mine. Those sons of bitches who started the war just as I'm about to leave. So if I'm suddenly halfway across the peninsula, it looks like I'm running from Janey Law."

"You really weren't involved, were you?"

Donnie smoked and stared at the empty wall across from him. He shook his head, began to speak, and then just shrugged. Brenda realized he was drunk. The sight of him there reminded Brenda of her grandfather, years ago, when he was first succumbing to Alzheimer's and had started crying—mystified—while struggling to make a pot of coffee.

She sat on a folding chair that was up against the wall and removed her hat. "Where were you going to go?"

Donnie shook his head, smoke pouring from his nostrils. "If I tell you, people might find out. They might try to find me." He turned and looked at her. "Loose lips sink ships, Sergeant." With an imaginary key in his fingers, he locked his mouth, raised his hand over his head, and tossed the key into the imaginary abyss.

Chapter 9

Wednesday, June 30

One could almost mark time by what sprang from the earth. In April came the crocuses on the heels of the snowmelt. By May, volunteers had begun planting political signs on street sides. BET ON BLY. NOVAK: A NEW VISION. A few other names had appeared here and there—libertarians running for city council seats currently held by Waldo Buff and Ernest Mears.

And now, in late June, as Haymaker leaned closer to the sun than any northern town had a right, a batch of new signs took root in the soil, and all of them read the same.

FOR SALE.

The havoc of last week—the bleeding dog, the beaten hermit, the tossing of the dummy grenade—wasn't fully to blame. It was merely the tipping point. By last Friday, green-and-yellow North Country Realty markers had dotted the Haymaker landscape. Many of the houses on the market were owned by longtime residents who no longer recognized their town. But many of the signs stood in front of condos in Freedom Springs. For the first time, newcomers had begun to bail.

"It's all one and the same," Roosevelt said to Rusty at the bar on this night. "Disenchantment. People either figure it's not the town it once was or it's not the town it was supposed to be." He shrugged and removed a cigarillo from his breast pocket. "And there are a whole lot less tourists this year. News has spread, I'm afraid. They're buying their fudge and their T-shirts and their Christmas ornaments in other towns. Grand Marais or Paradise."

Rusty—his toupee askew—set both hands on the bar and leaned forward. "You can't smoke that in here."

"What?" Roosevelt spoke with the unlit cigarillo between his teeth. "Oh," he said removing it. He remembered the statewide public smoking ban that had gone into effect last month. "That's right."

Rusty returned to real estate. "None of them homes are going to sell, Bly. We're just an island broke free from the shore now." He turned his back to Roosevelt and began pouring a beer. "No one's coming in. And nobody can get the hell out."

One wall of the Freedom Community headquarters was now nothing but American flag—stars the size of fists and stripes as wide as a man. It was Gorman's idea, and now he paced back and forth before it with a long cardboard tube in his hand, a slight smile on his face. He looked like a presidential candidate. He looked like Patton as he convened the monthly meeting of the Freedom Congress.

Only it wasn't. Josef had convinced Gorman to change the name to the Freedom Community Board of Trustees since the group wasn't fully representative or chosen from members of the Community. It consisted of the same six-person core as before: Josef and Gorman, Susan and Denny, Calvin and Carl. But a few months back, after an anonymous libertarian had written an op-ed piece in the paper describing the group as a "cabal," concerned it had too many secrets, Josef convinced Gorman to allow two elected Freedom Community members to sit in on the meetings on an annual, rotating basis.

The two new members were Tina Holcomb—a former Montessori teacher from Kenosha who now taught ten kids in Freedom Springs—and Pete Canary, a retired ob-gyn with a long white goatee. Both anxiously sat with notepads and pens, ready to go. Their enthusiasm seemed to Josef almost exotic.

Carl was the only member absent. He and Marissa were in Costa Rica on their honeymoon. The wedding had been small but joyful, held at Grace Lutheran Church in town. And at the reception afterward, in the basement of the VFW, Gorman had slipped Carl an envelope full of hundred-dollar bills and told him to enjoy his well-earned vacation.

Gorman now stopped pacing before the giant flag and spoke to the group. "How are the nation's freedom-loving people on this day?"

People nodded and mumbled.

"Two big items on the agenda. First: Josef's race for mayor. Second: the fact that some of our folks want to get out of town."

The exodus, thought Josef. The start of it, at least. They'd always planned for some loss: people who would move and find the place too cold and lonely or the progress too slow-moving. But they'd never expected 20 percent of Freedom Springs to go up for sale at once.

Susan tried to officially convene the meeting and read the minutes of last month's gathering. But Gorman was already pulling a sheet of paper out of the cardboard tube. He unfurled it and began taping it to the board. "Remember this beauty?"

It was the PIZ map. Possible Immigration Zones. Josef had thought it had been lost in the move or intentionally discarded. But there it was—all that wide-open space, the once limitless opportunity.

"Manifest Destiny," said Gorman. He reached into his pocket, removing a handful of tacks, and began placing them in all of the places they'd once pierced the land—red tacks in all of those failed states, and then the green tack on Haymaker, which triggered an almost out-of-body experience for Josef as he remembered standing in the old War Room, staring at that tack, trying to imagine his future.

"I hope you're not instilling regret," said Denny.

Susan laughed. "We're not pulling up stakes and moving on, are we?"

"I wouldn't quite say that," said Gorman. He faced them with his hands on his hips, grinning and then stroking his gray mustache. "It's time to expand. Time to franchise. It's time—" he turned and stuck two more green tacks into the map, on opposite ends of the continent, "—to hone in on Montana and New Hampshire."

Calvin actually laughed out loud, thinking it was a joke. Pete Canary smiled a bit. But the rest knew he was serious.

"And the crowd goes wild," said Gorman.

Josef stood up, shaking his head. He walked slowly to the PIZ map and plucked the two new green tacks from it. "No we're not," he said. He looked at Gorman and shrugged. "We're just not. You don't expand until your home base is stable."

Susan spoke up. "Jesus, Gorman—" She composed herself and spoke in a low voice. "We're trying everything we can outside of locking the front gate to keep people from moving."

"There's that Velvet Hammer again," said Gorman. "Got me good. But let's not mistake focusing outside of Haymaker with abandoning our cause here."

"Wait." Calvin stood up. He rarely spoke at their meetings. "Are *you* going to leave?"

"At present, I have no plans."

"We're not even close here," said Susan. "Not even—" She shook her head, mouth agape, and tossed her hands in the air.

Josef sighed and ambled to his chair. Denny just stared at a spot on the floor. The two elected representatives now slouched in their seats.

Josef sat and gazed at the enormous American flag covering the far wall. The stripes were straight and wide, like the lanes of outstretched highways.

His doorbell rang at about ten o'clock that night. He was three beers into a six-pack he'd picked up at Gassy Charlie's, and as Jeanie put the girls to bed he half watched baseball highlights in the living room, the floor littered with sticker books, colored pencils, and naked Barbies. Any other night—after the shooting and the mailbox fish and all the rest—he'd have greeted a late-night visitor with a baseball bat resting on his shoulder. But ever since the meeting had adjourned around eight, he'd been expecting someone to stop by.

Josef opened the door to find Susan and Denny standing on the stoop. "Well, if it isn't the nation's freedom-loving people," he said. "Come on in."

Susan's heels clicked across the foyer's tile floor. Denny shuffled in after her holding a paper bag against his chest. He pulled out a fifth of Jack Daniel's and handed it to Josef. "We're going to need the big guns," he said.

A half hour later Jeanie was downstairs with them, and all four sat among the toys, staring at the ice in their highball glasses. They were like those wintertime fishermen who stared at their ice, waiting for some kind of movement.

"I hardly ever drank before I moved here," said Josef.

"And I'm still smoking," said Denny.

"And I've gained fifteen pounds," said Susan.

"We're in the right," said Josef. He took another long sip of bourbon. "Even when we've executed poorly, our foundation's always been solid. A private community. Less government." He shook his head and almost whispered. "We're in the right."

"*We* are," said Susan. "Those of us sitting here."

"What's that mean?" asked Jeanie.

"You know what it means." Susan glanced at Denny.

"Go ahead," he said. "My defenses are down. I'm too drunk to stop you."

"Gorman, right?" said Jeanie. "The problem is Gorman."

Susan swirled the ice in her drink and then looked up at Josef. "Denny and I've known something for a little while now, but we've been sitting on it because it hasn't been an issue. Until now, with people putting their places up for sale."

"What?" asked Josef. "What?"

Susan hesitated, her mouth open, and then continued. "You were mentioning earlier today that it doesn't matter too much that people are trying to move out now because they won't be able to sell the places anyway."

Josef nodded.

"But that's not the case," she said. "Most of the people who've moved in the past year haven't been signing mortgages with banks. In order to entice people to come, Gorman secretly offered most of them month-to-month leases, along with land contracts with no money down. He did the same for Carl."

"Holy shit," said Josef, standing up.

"And clearly he hid it from you because he knew you'd blow your top."

"They're not invested in the community," said Josef. He ran the fingers of both hands through his hair. "They have nothing at stake."

Denny cleared his throat. "And from what Gorman was hinting at today, it's obvious he's not going to continue investing in Freedom Springs. Which means pretty soon there will be no lawn care or snowplowing or security or anything else. Especially since not enough people will be paying an association fee."

Josef stormed across the living room and kicked a stuffed pink pony against the wall. "He's cutting his losses!" He walked into the kitchen and opened a drawer, looking for his car keys.

Jeanie stood up. "What are you doing?"

Josef found the keys and slammed the drawer shut. "I don't know yet."

Susan stood and followed them into the other room. "Put the keys down," she said, "and listen. He's long stopped thinking of Freedom Springs as part of a libertarian movement. It started that way, but now that it's tanking he just sees it as a failed real estate investment. And if you get in his face, he's going to get right back in yours and tell you that it was his right, his money, and his risks, and now that it's failed it's his problem." She glared at Josef. "And you know what he's going to say next. That he's paid you handsomely over the years, and that while you were writing *The Paw* and coming up with clever new names for the War Room, it was his money on the line the whole time."

"Bullshit," said Josef.

"These aren't my words," said Susan. "I'm just reading his mind. And you know it."

Josef set the keys down on the kitchen counter and followed her back to the living room couch.

Denny sat on the edge of his chair, leaning toward him. "Listen," he said. "All that Susan's said is only the first half of why we're here tonight. The second has to do with new leadership."

"I'm already running for mayor."

"Not just of the town," said Denny. "Of the movement. Gorman's not inspiring faith on our side, but he's inspiring hate on the other. And even though we in this room know it's not true, most people in town—on both sides of the issue—see you as his right-hand man. But if you speak out against him, suddenly our side has faith again and the other side can't use him against us anymore."

"And suddenly you're in a real position to be elected mayor," said Susan. "Even if we lose some of our numbers over the next few months."

Josef picked his empty drink up off the coffee table. He dipped his index and middle fingers into the glass and stirred the half-melted ice. "I can't do any of that yet," he said. "He pulls the plug on me and my salary, and he pulls the plug on my home and my family." He closed his eyes. "You're going to hate me," he said, "but I'm going to let it play out a little longer."

Jeanie leaned over and rested her forehead on his shoulder. Josef pressed his cold fingertips against each temple, then against his lips.

Chapter 10

Sunday, July 4

American flags hung from the streetlamps along Marquette Street, as they did every Fourth of July, though this year it had become—like so many things in Haymaker—a kind of competition. Flags bloomed forth from front porches throughout town, often accompanied by either an orange-and-black "H" flag or the Freedom Community bear flag, to clarify allegiances.

Miniature flags waved from cars. Townspeople wore flag-draped T-shirts. And then Rhonda O'Leary raised a thirty-foot flagpole in her front yard, which got people talking about ordinances, which riled up more than a few libertarians. Mel Madsen, who worked at Seney Hardware, painted red stripes on the hood of his white F-150 and tried to paint blue stars on the roof, though they looked like asterisks. And then a guy named Mark Poland painted his entire Freedom Springs condo, alternating red and white paint on the vinyl strips, with the garage serving as a field of blue.

But to the relief of most, the fervor never spilled over into anything violent or destructive. And the only other competition seemed to occur high on the dune at the west end of town, where parked cars lined the entire stretch of Ross Road as two parties sought to outdo the amount of beer and grilled meat each could consume.

Ash—her hair split into pigtails, one side red and the other blue—sat at a picnic table in Roosevelt's sprawling side lawn. Candidate Bly was hosting a rowdy barbeque, entertaining guests and working to make them all feel at ease on this lovely summer afternoon. A series of red Weber grills lined the wall outside of his barn, where Hal Jager—a fry cook from The Lucky

Lumberjack—kept watch over hot dogs, chicken breasts, brats, steaks, and venison burgers. In the center of the lawn stood a volleyball net, and surrounding that were several red picnic tables, all newly built and freshly painted. Closer to the house were two huge, shining aluminum trash cans filled with ice and overflowing with bottles of beer and Coke. Beside those was a keg of Haymaker Hefeweizen, donated by Tim Rogers, who'd just developed the new brew for sale at The Venison. There were lawn darts—the old, sharp ones that could kill and which people liked to play. Beneath a white tent, near the back edge of the lawn, played a jazz trio called A Love Superior—three college students from the music department at NMU—whom Roosevelt paid in both cash and beer. And among it all was a throng of townspeople—folks of all kind. Folks who might vote for Roosevelt this fall and folks who very well might not.

Next door, Gorman Tate hosted an extravaganza of a pig roast. His old Smith mansion stood draped in red, white, and blue bunting with a huge sign out front that read THE GREAT LIBERTY SHINDIG and a smaller one with the message PORK CHOPS: YES! PORK BARREL: NO! A few other signs scattered throughout the lawn promoted Josef Novak for mayor, though many were knocked over or trampled on by guests playing badminton in the front yard.

Out back, children at the Tate party somersaulted in an inflatable bounce house, while children at the Bly party cried and pointed and tried to pull free from their parents to run next door. Beyond the bounce house, in the tamarack shade, a bartender served drinks and a deejay cranked out country and old Southern rock hits.

Ash sat alone, poking at potato salad with a plastic fork and sipping a Diet Coke.

"What up, Kid Dynamite?"

She looked up at her uncle Donnie walking toward her in a tight gray T-shirt that read FEAR THE REAPER, sweat rings under his arms.

"What are you doing here?" she asked.

"What are *you* doing here?"

"I was invited."

"So was I," said Donnie. He sat next to her.

"Yeah, but you never come to stuff like this. I thought you hated Roosevelt."

"I don't hate the cowboy. Never have. I think he's a half a queer, but I don't hate him."

"You trying to make friends with the next mayor?"

Donnie slipped a cigarette in his mouth and lit it with cupped hands. "Hell, he won't win."

"Why not?"

He exhaled and returned the lighter to his jeans pocket. "Because too many people think he's a Black Bear in sheep's clothing. That he'll win and then just hand the whole thing over to the libertarian agenda."

"You think that?"

"I don't think that. But enough do." He took in the panorama and shook his head. "Look at all of these assholes."

"You shouldn't have come if you got a sparkler up your butt." Ash looked out over the lawn, through the limbs of beech trees. She could see the water, calm and flat and bluer than the sky. "Why don't you like them?"

"Like who?" asked Donnie.

"The libertarians. Aren't you really one of them? Kind of?" She looked at him. "I've always wondered this. Don't you hate being told what to do? Don't you love that you get to have your Shit-Kickin' because there's no law that tells you not to. Don't you—"

"Stop," said Donnie, almost in a whisper. "Don't you ever confuse me with them."

"But isn't all that true?"

"To be a libertarian I'd have to care one way or another about politics, and I don't care shit about any of it. I'm on my own. I'm head of the Donnie Sarver Party. My mascot ain't an elephant or a donkey. And it ain't a husky or a goddamned bear. It's a fist to the face." He extended a super-slow-motion punch to Ash's chin and smiled. "I'm loyal to my home and to my land. If they were Democrats or Republicans or Nazis or Commies or Martians, I'd fight to get them the fuck out of Haymaker. It's just the idea of all them moving in because they like what they see."

"Didn't we move in here?"

"Who move in where?"

"Didn't the Indians live here first? Didn't our ancestors kick them out because they liked what they saw?"

"Aw, shit," said Donnie, standing up. "Take your powwow somewhere else. And if you find an Indian who wants his land back, tell him to meet me at the edge of the fucking pier in a couple months. That's where I'm having the Shit-Kickin' this year." He looked over his shoulder, at the party next door. "Maybe I can get Novak to fight me. Maybe I can get the head hog, Gorman Tate."

"And then it'll be over?" said Ash. "Then you'll be the winner and they'll be the losers?"

Donnie leaned toward her, his palms on the table. "Listen," he said. He looked both ways and lowered his voice. "You want to know who's going to win and who's going to lose when all this shit is through?"

Ash nodded.

"Those of us who stay," said Donnie, "will be the winners. The people who leave?" He dragged his thumb across his neck, over the JANE tattoo, like he was slitting a throat. "The losers."

Roosevelt appeared, bright as a star, approaching them with a smile. "My Lord! Mr. Sarver! Thank you for coming!"

"Let freedom ring," said Donnie, straightening up. He turned his head and spat.

"Freedom to party," said Roosevelt. "Freedom to eat and drink and dance."

Ash nodded at Gorman's party. "Freedom to be fools."

Roosevelt smiled. "That's a right we're all exercising these days."

"Can't wait till I'm gone," said Ash. "Two more years. Less than that. And then I'm out of Idiotsville."

"Loser," said Donnie, pointing at her heart with his index finger.

"What?"

"Like I said. You leave? You're a loser. All these people trying to sell their houses? You'll be just like them. You got to stay if you want to win."

Roosevelt set a hand on Donnie's shoulder. "Whoa, there. Let's go easy on the youngblood. If a person like her wants to leave to chase a dream, she in no way has lost at anything."

Donnie ignored him. He kept staring at Ash. "I'm serious," he said. Then he turned and walked away in the direction of the beer. An errant volleyball rolled his way. Donnie trotted a few steps toward the ball and kicked it, launching it over the volleyball players, launching it over the jazz trio and into the trees.

Roosevelt sighed. The hand he'd set on Donnie's shoulder now hung limp by his side. "Don't listen to him, my dear. He'd never intentionally steer you wrong, but he's gravely mistaken this time around."

Ash nodded, watching her uncle disappear into the crowd of partiers.

Roosevelt tipped his hat. "I need to keep making the rounds. Why don't you track down the other young people in attendance. Have yourself some fun."

She said nothing. People continued to arrive at Gorman Tate's pig roast. They stared out across the grass at Roosevelt's party, but despite the town's tension, despite the alcohol, no one on either side did so much as aim a middle finger toward the other.

A man on Gorman's front lawn raised his hand. It was a moment before Ash realized it was Josef Novak and that he was waving at her. She waved back—her hand at her chest, slightly hidden—and then watched as he and one of his daughters began to play Frisbee.

◆ ◆ ◆

At about eight o'clock that evening, with the sun hovering above the tree line and the sky still too bright for fireworks, Josef got in his car and headed down the Ross Road hill to pick up a couple of bags of marshmallows for Gorman's bonfire. As the road dipped down into the trees and the car slipped into the shade, he removed his sunglasses and leaned forward in his seat. But as he approached Gray Wolf Drive, a large black dog ambled out of the woods, crossing his lane in the distance. Josef braked, but the animal noticed his approach and paused in the middle of the road, turning and watching the car.

It was a bear. Josef came to a complete stop, still fifty yards or so from it. And for a few seconds they stared at each other. The bear's slender, tapered muzzle pointed toward him, its rounded ears silhouetted against a distant strip of sky.

Josef breathed deeply and slowly, barely moving in his seat except to slacken his grip on the steering wheel and gradually drop his hands onto his lap. It all lasted three—maybe four—seconds, until the bear turned toward the opposite edge of the woods and plunged forward in a series of powerful but rhythmical strides. And then it was gone, slipping amid the trees like something ethereal.

Josef sat in the unmoving car for a few more seconds, staring at those trees, wanting the bear to return. Wanting one more glimpse of its blurred secret.

Chapter 11

Wednesday, August 11

Brenda opened the screen door, stepping out of her lightless house and onto the back porch. Jesse and Owen sprinted past her legs and leapt off the porch and into the dry grass. Jesse found a ragged tennis ball under the apple tree, clamped it in his jaws, and tore back to Brenda on the deck, where he dropped it at her feet. She picked up the ball and hurled it to the edge of the yard. In the distance, above the canopies of pines, rose the black plume of smoke.

A wildfire raging ten miles south of town had just topped eighteen thousand acres. The month-long drought was followed by a stiff breeze that—though usually welcomed in August, to keep the flies at bay—now stoked a summertime hell. The state police had closed off H-37 to Newberry for all traffic except emergency personnel. Yesterday afternoon the power company cut all electricity to Haymaker and announced it would be at least another day or two before it was back up and running. And this morning, two college students who'd been camping in the state forest were declared missing and presumed dead.

Two hundred men and women fought the blaze. They came from everywhere: Michigan and Wisconsin DNR, Fish and Wildlife, US Forest Service, National Guard, Nature Conservancy, state police, sheriff's department, Red Cross, and the regional fire departments. They also included Brian—Blond Boy—and the other public works employees who tackled whatever miscellaneous labor was needed in the off-season.

Brenda hadn't seen him for two days. Then he returned home last night to clean up and snag a few hours of sleep. She'd stood naked with him in the shower, the bathroom lit only by a few candles. He'd closed his eyes, rocking from exhaustion while she'd kissed his shoulders and neck and scrubbed his black-stained skin with a washcloth.

And then he returned to the fire, to the dozer line, which now bordered 70 percent of the fire perimeter. Brenda stared at the distant smoke plume, guilty of that one sin in their relationship that she'd always feared Brian would commit. She was terrified. She thought endlessly of his safety. The one man who had never failed her in this way now stood before an inferno.

When he'd returned home for those few hours, she'd had the urge—touched the edges of that weakness—and almost wrapped her arms around him in the shower, demanding that he quit the job or she'd quit him. But she'd stayed silent and let him go.

The deck began to shake. The greyhounds barked, and Brenda shielded her eyes from the sun and looked up. One of the Chinooks roared by overhead, its twin blades whirring to invisibility, its red bucket dangling beneath from a wire.

The sky had been alive for days. DNR detection aircraft. A heli-torch from Fort Frances, Ontario. And the big guns: four Black Hawks and two Chinooks from the base down in Grayling, which descended over Lake Superior to scoop up seven hundred gallons a pop in their huge water buckets before rising up again over the trees, back to the fire. They landed every two hours at the little airfield in Newberry to refuel.

Brenda tossed the ball a few more times before the Chinook returned from the lake, the massive bucket of water beneath it reminding her of the thurible her childhood priest would gently swing from a gold chain as he walked past the pews, dispensing incense.

The inside of the dark house still smelled like smoke—even after washing Brian's clothes. Even after washing his body. Tonight she would sleep on his pillow and breathe it all in. The smoke. His skin. Her fear.

Chapter 12

Saturday, September 11

Donnie stood at the end of the pier, looking for a fight. Dark clouds gathered overhead, and waves crashed over his boots. The wind and the water made his skin burn cold, but he stood in short sleeves anyway, smoking a cigarette, staring at the shore, and knowing exactly how he looked to those watching.

He had lied. After spreading word that this year's Shit-Kickin' would occur at a small abandoned cabin on Sawyer Drive, he sent the real message—the real challenge—to the Freedom Community leadership. At high noon on the Saturday of Boomtown Days they could find him at the end of the pier—on public land and thus in violation of the law—where there would be no Doc Brewer nor Sergeant DeBoer supervising the fight. In his challenge he had said this would end it all, though he hadn't said what or how.

The small crowd that lined the narrow pier to gather round the spectacle included Ray, Ash, Gary Hollingshead, and those others who'd discovered the true location. No doubt the rest—including Brewer and DeBoer—were milling about that old cabin right now, checking their watches, waiting for Donnie's arrival, which would never come.

Ash sat on a rock with an orange poncho flapping in the wind, the hood tied tight around her head. Donnie had no idea why she still came to these things. Roosevelt hadn't joined her this time. The Gold-Plated Cowboy knew the real details of this year's fight, but as a mayoral candidate he would in no way attend something this shady.

More waves crashed against the rocks, draping mist over Donnie's face. He'd always fantasized about fighting here on the pier, with the freshwater sea on three sides—a peninsula on a peninsula—and was thrilled that the water was behaving this way. He smiled at the crowd and flicked his cigarette butt into the lake. "Wolf teeth ain't as sharp as these waves!" he shouted.

Two men approached the pier. One of them was Doug Butcher, who'd defeated Donnie in the snowmobile race almost two years ago, a race Donnie was forever barred from participating in again. He wore a camouflage jacket like he'd lived here forever.

"Tate coming?" Donnie called.

Butcher shrugged. "I ain't his keeper."

A few minutes later a silver pickup approached.

"Our foes," said Donnie. He spat and began hopping in place.

The truck crept quietly up the drive to the Fitzgerald Beach lot and parked in the sand. Its engine stopped, its lights went out, and from its doors stepped Gorman and Carl.

"I can't believe he fucking showed," said Donnie with a smile. There was no one standing close to him. In the noise of this wind, he was speaking to himself.

Carl led the way, his hands stuffed in the pockets of his red fleece jacket. Gorman took small, deliberate steps onto the pier, squinting as the wind tossed his gray ponytail.

Donnie stopped hopping and stared at him. "You ready for this?"

Gorman cinched the band around his ponytail and shook his head. "I'm not fighting you, Sarver."

The small crowd of spectators—most of them fans of Donnie—chuckled and grinned and nodded at one another. In past years, Donnie would have riled them up further and taunted his opponent like a north woods Cassius Clay. But not today. "You showed up to tell me that?"

Gorman stepped past Carl. "Why do you want to fight me, anyway?"

"You drove out here to tell me that and ask me this?"

"Answer my question."

"Don't talk to me like I'm your dog, Tate. I ain't going to cower and whimper like your boy here."

Gorman smiled at Donnie and slowly shook his head. "I'm too old for you, brother. And I'm an ideas man. I'm no good with my hands. What do you hope to accomplish by splitting my lip and swelling my eye?"

"Chop the head off," said Donnie.

"Say again?"

"Chop the head off the snake. Then this town will tread on you, all right."

Gorman chuckled. "What, so if our people hear that you made me a bloody mess, they'll pack it up and move it out? They didn't follow me here because of my fists."

"They're wishing they ain't followed you, period. Whole town knows you're hanging on to power by a thread."

Gorman's smile receded but then resurfaced, like a buoy amid the waves. He composed himself. "I won't give the cops an excuse to throw me in jail. They're chomping at the bit. And I won't take your bait."

"But you came here to tell me that to my face. You think that makes you a man?"

Gorman shook his head. "No," he said. "I came here so I could leave you, just like this." He turned and began walking in the direction of his truck. "With your dick in your hand."

He called over his shoulder. "Come on, Carl."

Because of his size, it was hard to call a man like Carl Farmer "invisible," but the truth was that Donnie had barely noticed him during his talk with Gorman. Now, however, the big man remained still and continued staring at their challenger.

"Come on, Carl."

Carl shook his head. "Nah. I'm gonna stay."

Gorman had reached the sand. "What?"

"I'm not worried about jail," said Carl. "Not right now." He shrugged at Donnie. "I'm not the head of the snake, but I'll accept your challenge."

Donnie began hopping in place again, shaking his arms to loosen them. "You want to do this, fatty?"

Carl nodded, unzipped his fleece jacket, and dropped it at his feet. He grabbed his right elbow with his left hand and stretched his arm across his body. "I think I do."

The other men on the pier began to whoop and applaud. Ash perked up and pulled the orange hood off her head, revealing bright orange hair, braided into cornrows.

Gorman approached the pier. "All right. Hero time's over, brother. Let's go."

Carl didn't budge.

"You want me to call your bride?" asked Gorman. "See if she has anything to say about this?"

Carl took one step toward Donnie and raised his fists. "She'd understand."

Gorman stood on the water's edge with his hands behind his back. "Well, free country. I'll just watch from here. They can't arrest me for that."

Donnie shadowboxed and stretched his neck. "You ready, Ray?"

Ray trotted over between the two men. Droplets of mist clung to his beard. "I got it, Donnie." He turned to face the crowd—a quick indulgence of theater. "Lady and gentlemen, Black Bears and Huskies, you who are good, you who are bad, and you"—he pointed down at Gorman on the beach—"who are ugly, welcome to the tenth annual Welcome Wagon Shit-Kickin'. Mr. Donnie Sarver, self-proclaimed hippie hater and Yooper Darth Vader, will now perform infinite justice—a long overdue welcome to our out-of-town guests, who, I do believe, will soon be leaving."

Cheers overpowered the wind and the waves.

Donnie sized up his opponent. He'd heard Carl had once played football, and even now he looked huge and relatively young. But he had a broken feeling about him, like a grizzly with a gimp.

"You both know the rules," yelled Ray, the waves crashing around them. "Knock the guy out or make him quit. Only other rule on this special day: nobody throws the other guy off the pier. You do and this goes from a little scuffle to attempted murder. Stay on the fucking pier. Leave the water to the sturgeon."

He raised his right arm and looked each man in the eye. "You ready?" he asked Donnie, receiving a nod in reply. "You ready?" he asked Carl.

"Absolutely."

"Then you all know what's next." He dropped his arm. "Commence!"

Carl stood still, fists raised but sort of slackened, clearly waiting for Donnie to step inside and throw the first punch. Donnie hopped in place, hands circling—a frenetic bundle of anticipation—and then skipped in close to throw a left jab that Carl blocked with his meaty forearms. Donnie punched again, then again—quick bursts to Carl's body. Carl gave a little grunt and doubled over slightly. Donnie continued to punch, sharp shots at the eyes, nose, and jaw. But Carl covered his face and the blows glanced away.

Most any defensive lineman has strength. But a good one has quickness, too, in his hands and feet. Donnie had misjudged his opponent. He'd never guessed that broken-down, bad-kneed, soft-bellied Carl Farmer still had some athletic gifts simmering beneath his bulk. A good lineman won't beat you in a race, but he'll bury you in a blur.

Carl shoved Donnie's arms aside as if blowing past a tight end and threw a hook that smacked him in the ear. The waves went silent, then resonated like small bells. Donnie cried out in pain and cupped a hand over the left side of his head. Carl lunged forward and threw two more heavy right hands, the first hitting Donnie above his left eye, the second landing square in the nose. Donnie sprawled backward in a white shock, and for a moment he thought he'd fallen off the pier, into the lake. His mouth and chin felt sopping wet. He blinked a few times and turned his head to the side. Blood poured from his nose and over his shoulder like a running faucet.

Then the lake did find him—a huge wave cresting the pier and breaking over his body. The shock of the cold roused him a bit. From flat on his back, Donnie kicked his legs at nothing. The ringing in his ear softened. The only voice he could make out was someone shouting, "Bury him at sea!"

He rolled to his side, raised himself with his right hand, and rested for a few seconds on his left elbow. Carl approached, bending low and cocking his fist. Donnie, struggling for balance, rolled into a crouch. Then he lunged, delivering a chop block into Carl's right knee that dropped him like a tree in a lightning strike.

Carl screamed, clutched his leg, and rolled near the edge. White foam spilled over him. Donnie stood and wobbled—the front of his shirt red and wet from neck to belt—and stumbled toward him with his fists clenched.

Carl sat up and grasped Donnie's bloody shirt in his huge mitt before yanking him down on the concrete. The two men lay sprawled side by side for a moment—chalk outlines of themselves. And then Carl dragged himself closer, grabbed a handful of Donnie's hair, and locked his arms around Donnie's head. He sent a massive blow hammering down on Donnie's skull. Then another.

Carl hit him again—maybe seven or eight times before Ash started screaming. "He's gonna kill him! He's gonna kill him!"

Ray and a couple of others jumped into the fight and started pulling at Carl's clothes and arms and legs. Ash pushed forward, through other men, and joined them. She grabbed Carl's right ankle and pulled his leg, making him scream and release his grip. He rolled aside, allowing Ray to stoop with his ear to Donnie's lips, checking for breath, before gently slapping the side of his face. Another wave broke over the pier, the water sliding under Donnie's body like cold silk.

"I'm good." Donnie raised his head up from the cement. He clenched his right fist and held it against his chest.

"It's over, buddy," said Ray.

"Bullshit," said Donnie. A small red bubble formed over his mouth and popped as he spoke. "I ain't tapped."

"You were out for probably thirty seconds."

Ash knelt beside him and wiped her eyes. "Are you okay?"

Donnie stared at her for a moment. Then he winced and held it—creases fanning from the edges of his swollen eyes. He rolled over onto his side and then his belly. "Don't anybody fucking touch me!" Pebbles stuck to the flesh on his neck and arms. He began to drag himself forward on his elbows and shook his head. "That's some bullshit!" He continued to writhe, inching toward the edge of the pier.

Ash was the first to realize what he was doing. "No! Uncle Donnie!"

She leaned over him and looped her arms beneath one of his elbows. Ray grabbed his other arm, and the two pulled him back from the teeth of the lake.

"Let me the fuck go!" screamed Donnie. "Oh Christ, let me swim!"

Chapter 13

Monday, October 18

Brenda drove up H-37 to Haymaker, the road curving through the charcoal forest where the wildfire had once raged. Blackened skeletal pines leaned and sagged. The ground was gray and dotted with dark stumps. Acres and acres of charred earth surrounded her in all directions, a brittle husk of a world that was impossible to imagine as once—or ever again—green. Brian never spoke much about the war he'd fought here. And Brenda understood this. She spoke little about her daily battles and skirmishes, and even less about the larger conflict that had settled over the town like a permanent fog.

She'd spent the last three days back home in Grand Haven, where yesterday she'd cohosted a baby shower for her sister, Danielle. Her mother had been following Haymaker's story. She'd read articles online, seen the piece on CNN, and yesterday at the shower she'd approached while Brenda stood beside the punch bowl.

"You can't expect to keep watch over all those crazy people," she said. Then she held up a dessert napkin with its picture of a yellow stork. "And if you and Brian are ever planning on settling, you sure as heck can't raise a family up there."

The blackened trees fell away to become merely the normal gray of autumn after the leaves have fallen. The road climbed the hill at the edge of town, and near the top, the familiar orange-and-black sign welcomed Brenda back. She caught herself with a smile creeping over her cheeks. But as she crested the hill and began the gradual descent into town, the smile faded and she squeezed the steering wheel. Signs ran along both sides of the street, dozens of them in a stretch of less than a mile.

BET ON BLY
NOVAK: A NEW VISION

The sheer number of signs astounded her.

BLY: A CALMING PRESENCE
NOVAK: RATIONAL REFORM

They lined the roadside like rows of teeth.

RESTORE OUR HOME—VOTE ROOSEVELT
LIBERTY'S WITHIN REACH—VOTE NOVAK

She took a longer route home, driving up to Marquette and then cutting through the neighborhoods to better witness the change. She'd been gone only three days, but new signs had mushroomed over the landscape: hung on storefronts, taped to windows, nailed to trees. Some were for city council candidates: the incumbents, Waldo Buff and Ernest Mears, as well as their libertarian opponents, Jackie Underwood and Steven Bailey.

Neither Brenda nor Brian followed the politics too closely, but from what they'd heard and read it had become a numbers game, a matter of voter turnout. Nobody had exact figures, but—even after the growing exodus on both sides—estimates claimed that the libertarians held a slight advantage. Their voters were rabid, and their turnout was expected to top 90 percent.

Brenda circled back toward her home. She pulled into the driveway, parked in the garage, and turned off the ignition. The engine ticked in the new silence. The house, she knew, was dark. Brian would be working leaf cleanup at the park. Jesse and Owen would be inside, waiting to circle and thread between her legs as she walked through the door. She had to work tonight—security at the high school for the big debate between the candidates. But she stayed in the truck a few moments longer and wondered what those two men could say—what anyone could say—that would ease the sensation—the panic-laced weight—upon her chest.

Josef checked his reflection in the mirror of the high school bathroom. The fluorescent lights and surrounding green tile gave his navy suit a brownish hue and sapped some of the boldness from his wine-red tie. But his shoulders looked broad and sharp, and his square silver cuff links—an anniversary gift from Jeanie, engraved with the date of their move to Haymaker—gave a subtle weight to his wrists that made his arms feel strong.

With a deep breath and a quick, sharp exhale, he stepped out and strode toward the auditorium, the heels of his polished oxfords clacking against the floor and echoing down the empty hallways. The debate wouldn't start for nearly three hours, but Gorman, Susan, and Denny would arrive soon to assist with last-minute prep, and Josef felt more confident—even while rehearsing—when wearing a suit.

He stopped in the doorway of the small auditorium. A woman strung bunting along the front of the stage, and a man tapped the microphones at each podium, the rapid thuds startling Josef for a moment. He exhaled again and smoothed down the front of his coat. A teenager entered a back door carrying a video camera and tripod. They'd be filmed, he and Roosevelt, for the overflow audience that would watch from the gymnasium.

A shout came from down the hall. A woman Josef didn't recognize—someone from the school—appeared around the corner, approaching a set of double doors that led to the outside. She spotted Josef and waved at him to follow. "Someone said there's a bomb! We have to get out!" As she shoved the door open she reached for the small red-and-white box next to her on the wall. The fire alarm instantly blared. Josef turned to look back inside the auditorium, where the startled workers now stared at him in the doorway as if he'd triggered the sound.

He hesitated for a moment—the alarm rattling through his rib cage, through the floor beneath his feet. "Bomb!" he screamed. "There's a bomb in the building!"

As the workers fled to the back door of the auditorium, Josef turned and ran toward the set of double doors, his wine-red tie flapping over his shoulder.

Roosevelt crouched down on old knees, twisting newspaper and shoving it beneath the kindling to stoke a fire in the hearth. The paper caught, and the flames roared big and briefly before settling into a controlled burn. He stood and straightened, groaning a bit, and then walked over to the sofa and his mug of black tea. Though he'd often failed, he'd tried to stay away from bourbon since his crying jag in front of Josef nearly six months ago. It was to be a short-term prohibition—only a few weeks longer, until the voting was over. And when the polls finally closed on election night, he'd tie one on—to cope with the loss or cope with the win. Jubilation was just a breath away from dread.

The phone rang. Roosevelt sighed and stood and groaned again before walking to the kitchen and answering. It was Josef.

"Well, speak of the devil," said Roosevelt.

"Were you talking about me?"

"Something like that."

"I just got off the phone with Lenny Boston," said Josef. "The call to the school office was from some punk kid teenager. Stephen Roach."

"Never heard of him."

"Me neither. Neither had Lenny. The kid said it was just a joke. His friend turned him in."

"Did he actually have the pipe bombs?"

"No."

"You see now," said Roosevelt, leaning against the kitchen counter. "We're not just a punch line for the neighboring towns anymore. We've become a joke to schoolboys."

"I think the debate's off. Joke or not, it's spooked people. Lenny said they'd have to find a secure location, but he didn't sound like he was going to get right on that."

"You disappointed?" asked Roosevelt.

"Yeah, I am. I would have liked the forum. I always want to share our ideas."

"But you don't think you *need* the debate."

"No," said Josef. "You're a great guy, Roosevelt, but the numbers are on our side. So's the enthusiasm. We'll turn out in force."

Roosevelt sighed. "Yes, I think you're right. And I can't say I'm heartbroken. Though it would have been nice, in a way, having the debate."

"We could have shown them how men can disagree and still be civil."

"You got that right."

"And have different ideas but enjoy each other's company."

"Preach it, brother."

"Well, if our side does come out ahead," said Josef, "I'd really like to get you involved in some way. As a consultant. Or just someone to have a drink with. Bounce ideas off."

"That'd be fine." The kindling crumbled to ash in the fireplace. The larger logs struggled to catch fire.

"Otherwise, outside of bomb threats, you doing okay?"

"Oh sure," said Roosevelt. "And the bombs are no big deal. There are scarier things."

"Like what?"

"Stepping out of the bath. Catching a glimpse of my naked self in the mirror."

Josef laughed. "Now, that's a fright."

"But of course I don't have a family to worry about. If I still had a young wife and little ones under my roof, I'd probably walk the streets with a shotgun."

"See, Roosevelt. You're more of a libertarian than you'll ever know."

"Maybe so."

"Well, it's settled. You and me. Steaks and drinks a few weeks from now. Win, lose, or draw."

Roosevelt agreed, and they said good-bye and hung up. He walked back to the coffee table for his tea and took a sip. It had turned lukewarm. And the fire in the hearth had gone out. He crossed the dining area to the back sliding door, opened it, and stepped into the brisk twilight air, to his view of the lake. It wore the gray of winter in its waves, like a man with white in his beard.

Ash slowed her blue '97 Taurus to a stop, placed it in park, and idled on a quiet, wooded stretch of Schoolcraft Avenue near the outskirts of town. She'd awoken to the car in her driveway two weeks ago, the keys in the ignition and a note on the dash that read, *Fixed it up. All yours.—D*

And that was Uncle Donnie's good-bye. That day on the pier he'd lost two teeth, a great deal of blood, and a little bit of hearing in his left ear. He lay low for the first week, healing his face, and then returned to work as if nothing had changed. But a week later he disappeared—his apartment empty as if picked clean by crows—and the only message he'd left anyone was the one for Ash in the blue Taurus.

Ray Valentine—and only Ray Valentine—had known in advance of his departure. Donnie sold him the auto shop for an absolute steal. But even Ray had no idea where he was headed or what he had planned.

When Ash asked her mom about it, Denise only shook her head and smirked. "He'll be back. It's a stunt. He's probably raising an army somewhere. Or maybe he's gone for good. I don't know. Either way, I don't give a shit."

But Ash didn't believe it. She didn't believe he'd ever fight again. But she also didn't believe he could live anywhere else. He'd be an outsider there.

The thought of him bleeding and crawling toward the waves made her sick. So did the thought of Carl Farmer at the 3-F last week, hobbling around on crutches; and the thought of that wildfire creeping toward her home; and the thought of Stephen Roach calling a bomb threat into her school; and the election—

Along the road before her stretched two rows of signs. BET ON BLY. NOVAK: A NEW VISION. The sparkling gold of Roosevelt's. The deep blue of Josef's. The signs were the brightest colors in sight. The bare trees reached upward, spindly and twisted like Grandma Sarver's hands.

With no one in view behind or ahead, Ash put the car in drive and slowly pressed the accelerator. She eased off onto the gravel shoulder of the road, approaching the signs, and then hit the gas. They snapped beneath her tires. Bly. Novak. Bly. Novak. Mud flew from her tires as she braked and turned sharply in a U, across the yellow line to the other lane, aiming in the other direction, aiming at the other set of signs. Mangled wires and torn paper littered the road. Bly. Novak. Bly. Novak. A vote for our freedom. A vote for our ancestors.

Her front-right tire slipped farther off the edge of the road, pulling the car down into a ditch filled with autumn mud. She lurched forward and stopped dead. When she floored it, the tires merely spun.

She needed a tow truck. She'd have to call Ray, owner of the newly renamed Valentine Towing and Repair.

Chapter 14

Sunday, October 31

Gary Hollingshead knelt among the darkened hardwoods and brush near the edge of Ross Road, unseen by anything but opossums and nightjars, and yet himself able to see the smallest of details at the house across the street. He wore a camouflage fleece jacket—hood pulled over his head—along with a pair of camouflage cargo pants and camouflage gloves. He'd parked his truck a little west of here, at the dunes, and hiked through the forest, beneath a half-moon, to this spot among the maples, where he'd removed the rifle scope from his jacket pocket and now held it up to his left eye, aimed at Gorman Tate's.

It was eleven thirty. Gorman would be home soon. Gary knew this because he'd watched him all fall and had crouched in these woods on other nights. Gorman and some friends would be at The Venison watching Sunday night football, and he'd return home around midnight, pulling into the detached garage and then ambling toward and through the brightly lit front door, to the keypad for the security system.

Gary had watched Gorman from other parts of the dark forest, watched him through windows from a distance—the rifle scope to his eye—to see his fingers punching the keypad. On his third trip to these woods, he'd seen the numbers of the security code without Gorman's body blocking his view. The fourth time he'd come just for confirmation.

Gary would stay here—silent and hidden like any hunter in these woods—and would not ruin the attack by rushing it. He would wait for the illuminated windows to follow Gorman through the house, up to the second level.

Gorman would stand—silhouetted—in his bedroom window before closing the curtains. And then Gary would move in, swift for his size, looping south, crossing the road while out of view, and once more approaching, unseen, through the trees.

It was all about time: Gorman's time on the upper floor of his house. The time it would take Gary to cross the road. The time of day—late enough on this Halloween that the families would be asleep. And yet, because it was Halloween, a time to mark an anniversary. Two years since the town had gone mad. And if there was any time for Gary to change things, it had nearly passed. So he would be quick, but he would not rush. Like any hunter in these woods, his power would be his patience.

Brenda turned around and straddled Brian, her naked back facing him, and used his thighs as leverage as she pushed up and let herself slide down. Brian's hands moved with her, his fingers running down her back and then squeezing her hips, just below the purple bruise that was a day away from going yellow.

She'd gotten the bruise yesterday after handcuffing Sully Huff, who'd been so blitzed at the aerie of the Fraternal Order of Eagles that he'd urinated in the corner pocket of the pool table and shattered some liquor bottles with a cue. As she'd walked him to the cruiser, Sully fell to his knees and head-butted her in the hip. Brenda tightened the cuffs until he yelped and threw him in the back of the car.

She didn't want to think about these things now. Thoughts like these sprang up too often in her mind when they were in bed. So she concentrated on Brian and on the sensation, closing her eyes, biting her lower lip.

He began to guide her up and down with his hands. She knew when he did this—when he took control of her body and her motions—that he was about to come. She arched her back as he moved faster—as he moved *her* faster.

Brenda's phone rang. It came from deep within her purse, which was nearly under the bed and beneath their crumpled clothes, and was almost too quiet to hear above the squeaking of the box spring. Brian squeezed the flesh on her hips more tightly, kneading it like dough. The phone kept ringing.

He lifted her off. She lay on her side, her legs sore from the position and the flexing motion. The sheets clung to her sweat. "Just answer it," he said. "I was there and I lost it." He spun his legs over the edge of the bed and sat up.

Brenda stretched her naked body toward the floor and rummaged amid the clothes with her right hand. "I'm sorry." She slipped her index finger through her purse straps and pulled it onto the bed.

Brian stood up, walked over to her side of the bed, and reached down to pick up his underwear, which he slipped up his legs and stretched tight over his erection. He smiled. "There better be a riot if they're calling you in. The lake better be on fire."

It was the state police dispatcher out of Newberry. "We have a hostage situation in Haymaker at 837 Ross Road. Hostage taker is armed. SWAT members are assembling."

She got the remaining information and hung up. "I have to go." She bent down to find her bra and underwear.

Brian stood and approached her from behind, wrapping his arms around her, cupping her breasts in his palms, and pressing his erection against her bruised hip. She pulled away and began to dress. "I'm serious."

In a single swift motion Brian reclined on the bed, his head resting on an open hand. "So the lake *is* on fire."

On the other side of the shut bedroom door, Jesse and Owen whimpered and scratched at the wood. Brenda walked across the room, flipped on the lights, and let them in. They entered, sniffing her legs and then sniffing upward at the air. In her new, sharp alertness, she could detect it herself: the mixed scents of blackberry body lotion, spermicidal jelly, and the vinegar sex sweat of Brian's groin.

"Someone's taken a hostage on Ross Road," she said.

He sat up. "In Haymaker?"

It wasn't until he'd asked this that Brenda realized she'd never had to negotiate here in town. The incidents were usually in isolated cabins or ramshackle farmhouses on the edges of villages. "Yeah," she said. She slipped a gray sweatshirt over her head and reached for a pair of jeans. "At Gorman Tate's."

She watched his eyes as she said it, expecting to notice some shift in his expression—a dilation of his pupils or crease along his brow. But he only gave a quick nod. "Be safe," he said, and his voice was neither too low nor too soft for this to mean anything other than, *Do good work. See you in the morning.*

So why, she wondered minutes later—in her truck, speeding west toward Ross Road—did her chest feel hollow, the words *Be safe* rattling around the empty space inside her, teetering as if they would soon settle to a stop?

Gary stood in the upstairs bedroom of the old Victorian mansion, in a rotunda with windows that looked out in all directions and that felt to him now like the battlement of a castle. The room was dark except for a small halogen camping lantern he'd set on the dresser. In one hand he held his phone, which he'd used to call 911—the cops and press and everyone else, he figured, now on their way. In the other he gripped a compact Beretta, the barrel aimed at Gorman, who lay on his stomach with his face pressed against the carpet and fingers interlaced behind his head. His body rose and fell from hyperventilation. Blood dripped from his forehead, where Gary had pistol-whipped him in his sleep.

"Keep your hands behind your head," said Gary, "and slowly—slowly—get up on your knees. But keep your back to me."

Gorman struggled to sit up without using his hands. He rolled onto his side and grunted as he ascended. His gray hair—usually pulled back in its customary ponytail—flowed over his ashen face.

Gary opened the video option and aimed his phone at him. "All right, motherfucker, we only got a few minutes till this hill lights up like the Fourth of July. You sure as shit better get it right the first time."

This was the critical moment in the plan: the recorded orders and confession. The images that would make the news, go viral on the Internet, and infect every libertarian even thinking about voting on Tuesday. He extended each arm, aiming the camera phone and gun at Gorman's head as he slowly walked around to face him. "Say hello to America."

Gorman glanced at the camera but then stared at the gun.

"Say hello to America!"

"Hello, America," said Gorman, his voice tight and low, his eyes deeply shadowed in the dim light.

"What's your name?"

"Gorman Tate."

"Get your hair out of your face."

Gorman swept his bangs away from his eyes and tucked them behind his ears. He placed his hands, once more, behind his head.

"And what's your position within the Freedom Community?"

Gorman took a deep breath, his lungs trembling during exhalation. "I am the founder. And the head of the Freedom Committee."

"You're the leader of the libertarians in Haymaker. Just say that."

Gorman shook his head momentarily before closing his eyes and slowly nodding. "I'm the leader of the libertarians in Haymaker."

"That's right," said Gary. "And why do you think I'm here tonight? Why am I talking to you?"

"I don't know."

"Take a fucking guess!"

Gorman winced, his hands still behind his head but almost pulling apart for a second, as if to shield his face. "Because you're angry at us."

"Sure. And why might that be? Why might people who've lived here their whole lives be a tiny bit angry at a bunch of outsiders flooding into our fucking streets, calling this town their own, and trying to change all the laws? Why might that be?"

Gorman creased his brow in confusion. "I guess because of what you just said. I don't know what you want me to say."

"People don't like change forced down their fucking throats. Right? On their home turf. Maybe that's it, huh?"

"Maybe."

"That's right." Gary's arms began to shake from fatigue and adrenaline. "We probably only got a few minutes, so I want to make this quick. If your man Novak wins the election this Tuesday, you think people are going to be angry? Like I am?"

"Maybe."

"Definitely!" He shook the Beretta in Gorman's face and pushed the phone closer, still recording. "And you're not the only ones in this town with guns. So if your people want to be safe, what do you recommend they do on Election Day?"

Gorman looked Gary in the eye. "Stay home?"

Gary nodded. "You got it. You're a bright one. Just stay the fuck home." Gary found himself smiling. He wondered where the police were. He couldn't hear sirens. "And what are you going to do if I let you go?"

"I'll leave," said Gorman. "I'll leave town."

It shocked Gary—how quickly those words had come. "Why?"

Gorman's stare left Gary, and he peered into the camera. "Because I was leaving anyway."

Gary squinted and slowly shook his head. "What do you mean you were leaving?"

"I was planning on leaving anyway." Gorman winced from pain and licked at a trickle of blood that had crept toward the corner of his mouth. "Haymaker was the first place we set up shop, but it wasn't ever going to be the only place. I was heading back to Florida to get ready for the next town. In New Hampshire. So I was about to leave." His eyes went wide as he nodded at Gary. "You can ask my people in the Freedom Committee. It's in the official record. It's in the minutes. I swear to God."

Gary shook his head. He smiled again. "No shit. You were gone all the time." He turned the camera phone on himself, holding it just inches from his face. "You hear that, America? My man was so committed to his cause that he was going to leave on his own." He quickly returned his attention—and the attention of the camera—to Gorman. "Your people must be proud."

Gorman lowered and shook his head slightly. His hair fell over his eyes. "Come on, brother. What do you want me to say?"

"Say bye-bye."

"I'm leaving town. I swear to God. You can let me go."

Gary leaned forward, causing Gorman to flinch from the approaching gun barrel. Gritting his teeth, Gary asked, "What about the others?"

"What about them, man?"

"Tell them to leave."

"Jesus, it don't work like that. They're here because they want to be here. I got them here, but they're staying for their own reasons. There's nothing I can do. And I want to save my life and I know you're in control, but I'm telling you the truth and hoping you respect it. I can't make them go. Just myself. And I'm going."

Gary swung the gun, cracking Gorman above the left ear and sending him down to the floor with a long moan. Then he turned off the video, stepped toward the window, and used the gun to push the curtain aside, just enough to stare down at the street. The police had arrived, and he was ready for the next step. For the punishment and the redemption.

A few teenagers slouched along sidewalks or slipped in between the dark houses, but for the most part the rituals of the night had ended: the orange lights strung along house eaves, the plastic skeletons in front yards, the cotton cobwebs over porches—already a part of something passed.

Her green dashboard clock read one fifteen. Above the numbers, above the rising speedometer as Brenda charged up the hill, the landscape materialized amid flashing reds and blues. Travis, who'd had road duty tonight, was the first on the scene. She passed Gorman's dark house. Hostage events were so often nocturnal and, like bats and rats, made from the same fabric of human fears.

Travis's cruiser was parked in front of Roosevelt's lawn, protected by a few trees in case the hostage taker took any potshots through a window. Travis was walking from the front door of the house, guiding Roosevelt toward The Man in White's Town Car. Roosevelt wore slippers and a dark red robe. His short silver hair stuck up in all directions.

In a way they were lucky; he was the only neighbor on the street, making for a quick evacuation of the area. After he drove off, Brenda parked her truck alongside the cruiser at the dead end of the road. This would be their command center.

She rolled her window down as Travis approached. "Where we at?" she asked.

He stared through the dark trees toward Gorman's house. "Chief's on his way with the equipment. Haven't seen activity next door."

Brenda nodded and turned off the engine. She picked up her phone. The dispatcher had passed along the number of the man who'd made the call. He'd wanted an audience. He'd invited them to come. "Any word on the SWAT team?"

The sparse population of the region meant that SWAT members came from various state police posts in the U.P. "They're rendezvousing in Newberry, but it could be an hour before they get here."

Brenda nodded. "I'll keep him talking till then."

Sirens sounded in the distance and were then cut off as Lenny's cruiser ascended the hill. His lights mixed with those of the other patrol car so that the surrounding trees turned kaleidoscopic. After parking beside them and stepping out, he glared at the dark house down the road. "This is a new one," he said. "Right in our own backyard."

Brenda got out as well, and she and Travis gathered around Lenny as he unlocked his trunk. Inside lay a blue-and-silver case containing the throw phone and all of its equipment: the system controls, headsets, microphones, and the steel remote speaker. Beside it sat a heavy-duty reel containing five hundred feet of plastic-coated cable, which Lenny pulled out with a grunt and dropped on the ground. He turned to Travis. "Head down the hill and tape off the end of the road. And make an area for the media. It'll just be Grubb at first, but you wait. If this thing drags on, we'll have camera crews from out of town."

As he got in his cruiser and drove off, Brenda grabbed an extra Kevlar vest that Lenny had brought and slipped it over her sweatshirt. Then she removed a whiteboard and an easel, which they'd use for notes. Things to say during the call. Things not to say.

"You ready to establish contact?" asked Lenny.

She nodded.

"You even get service out here?"

She checked her phone. "Yeah, but I'll feel a whole lot better when the SWAT guys show and we can use that." She nodded toward the case in the trunk containing the throw phone.

Lenny unsnapped a pouch on his belt, checking his extra magazine clips. "I'll feel better when they show for a hell of a lot of reasons."

Brenda dialed, set the cell phone to her ear, and stared through the trees to the house while she waited. Names, faces, and possibilities streamed through her mind. Her first thought was Donnie Sarver, back from the dead, out to assassinate a leader like old Leon Czolgosz did with McKinley. She wondered if Carl Farmer was lying on the other side of town with a bullet in his head.

And then, in these flashes of thoughts—these synaptic calculations—it seemed most obvious that the man was a disgruntled Black Bear, someone who thought their dream was dying from a failure of leadership.

A man answered the phone. "Who's this?" he asked.

She slipped back into her CNT training. Training and instincts. "Hello, sir. This is Sergeant Brenda DeBoer of the Haymaker Police Department. I was wondering if you could tell me who I'm speaking with and what's going on where you are right now?"

The man chuckled. "I know who you are. And you know who I am."

Lenny had set up the whiteboard. Brenda walked over, took the marker out of his hand, and wrote KNOWS ME. "Well, that's good that you know me. It'll make it easier for us to talk. Now, why don't you tell me your name so we're all evened up."

"Why's it matter?" said the man. "I'm the bogeyman. That what you want to hear?"

The invisible thread between her and the house, between her phone and this other, grew taut and strained like the muscles in her chest. Brenda stared hard through the branches at the dark windows, looking for any movement. And all the while she tried to place the voice, which she distantly recognized, like the residue of memory.

"Well, why don't you tell me what's going on in the house," she said.

"My name's Gary," he said.

She wrote the name on the board.

"Hollingshead," he added.

Brenda started to write and then stopped. Her training fought to suppress the adrenaline. She'd met him a few times, seen him around the Civic Centre. "Hello, Gary." She wrote HOLLINGSHEAD on the board followed by three exclamation points. Lenny shook his head and mouthed the words, "Sweet Jesus."

She'd heard they'd divorced. She'd heard the rumors of an affair—a woman new to the town. And she'd heard of some erratic behavior over the years but couldn't recall the details. "Thank you, Gary. I appreciate you telling me your name. Now could you tell me what's happening where you are?"

He chuckled again. "What's happening is I got a gun aimed at Gorman Tate. And I also got video of him saying some things that I want everyone out there to watch."

Lenny grabbed another marker and wrote the word ARMED with a question mark behind it. Brenda nodded and erased the punctuation. "Tell me more about this message," she said.

"It's all about how they need to leave."

"Who needs to leave, Gary?"

"Jesus Christ! The libertarians! The Black Bears! Whatever the fuck you want to call them!"

She had to pull back—rely once more on her training. Build rapport. Listen actively. "Yeah, this town's been crazy since they arrived, hasn't it?"

"My life's been fucked." There was a long pause. "Two years ago today. And you ain't solving this problem with a goddamned election. Others have said the same thing. You got to cut the head off the snake. Cut the head off that rattlesnake on all their yellow flags."

Brenda nodded to herself. On the whiteboard she wrote WANTS LIBS TO LEAVE. "Okay," she said, "all right. So you're telling me you want them all to get out of town. Make Haymaker the way it was before they arrived."

"I want it all changed back. All of it."

Lenny wrote on the board: CLARA?

Brenda nodded again. "It's been a crazy couple of years. You're right. Lots of changes." She paused before asking, "You had a daughter last year. She must be getting pretty big by now. How old is she?"

"She's over a year and a half, and my ex-wife won't let me see her."

Brenda quickly crossed out Clara's name on the board. "Tell me more about your little girl, Gary. You said she's a year and a half? She must be talking and running around like crazy. What's her name again?"

"Mary."

"Mary. That's right. Rhymes with Gary. What a sweetheart she is, I bet."

"She's everything," he said, his voice calmer.

Brenda took a deep breath and began nodding. She had to develop this theme. Connect through justification. "And a person could understand why you're so upset. All of these new people in the town are putting your back against the wall. And then your wife puts you in a bad place so that you can't see Mary as much as you'd like. That'd make anyone angry. I get that."

There was a long pause.

"Are you there, Gary?"

"I put myself in a bad place."

"What do you mean, Gary?"

"I fucked up. That's why I don't see my daughter that much. I fucking fucked up."

Brenda's pulse increased. On the board she wrote: DEPRESSED? "We all make mistakes, Gary. We're human. We all do it."

"I want to talk to Clara," he said, his voice strong and stable.

"You want to talk to Clara," she said. It was his first demand. She stared at Lenny and began the stalling procedures. "I'll tell you what I'm going to do,

Gary. That's not a request I can approve. I'm just a sergeant. I have to relay that to my supervisor. But I will pass that request along."

"Do it fast," he said, "because this is all going to end real soon."

Brenda squinted as she peered through the night at the house. "Tell me what you mean by that, Gary. Because when you say something like that, I get concerned that you want to hurt yourself or someone else."

"I need pain. I deserve it." There was a beeping sound on his end of the call. "My phone's about to die," he said.

Brenda wrote down PHONE/SWAT and underlined it three times. Beneath it Lenny wrote THERE'S NO LANDLINE.

"Okay, Gary. Look. Listen. We've got a special phone here. It's like a big box at the end of a cable. It'll let you and me talk back and forth to each other, okay? But here's the thing. It means someone has to come up close and bring it by the house. They have to throw it through the window, and you have to go downstairs to talk through it. It's a speaker. You just need to get in the room and we can talk through it."

"Fuck that, man."

"No, it's okay. Listen. They'll bring the phone and then they'll back off. There won't be any tricks. They'll bring the phone, they'll send it through the window, and they'll back off. That's it."

She waited for him to answer.

"Gary?" She shook her head and turned to Lenny. "His phone died. We lost him."

A breeze shook the naked tree branches. The SWAT team was likely on its way. Brenda slumped against her car, watched the house, and settled in for the terrible waiting.

Over the next forty-five minutes she strategized with Lenny, and both of them agreed that the key was to keep him talking about his daughter, give him something to be hopeful about.

"It's not about politics," said Brenda. "It's not about Gorman at all. Maybe since he had an affair with one of them, he's making that connection in some weird way, but it's all about his wife and his daughter."

"Why you think he wants to talk to Clara?" asked Lenny.

"Prove something," she said. "I don't know. Show her he's some kind of town hero." She shrugged. "It's tough to follow the train of logic once a person's come unhinged. But there's no way we let him. She could say something to set him off, or he might have some idea about saying his last words before dying."

Periodically, Brenda spoke into a bullhorn, telling him that the phone would arrive shortly and to stay as calm as possible. But she had no idea if he heard.

The nine-man SWAT team arrived, with the four snipers rapidly positioning themselves to cover all four corners of the house. The others gathered around the control center and prepared the throw phone.

"All right," said Lenny, "we need to get him that damned thing."

The team approached Gorman's house. With four members at his side, protecting him with their ballistic shields, a fifth pitched the heavy remote speaker through the front picture window in a shatter of glass.

Brenda raised the bullhorn as the SWAT team swiftly moved away. "All right, Gary. That was the phone. It's in the living room. Everyone has backed away. No one is on the property. Now we need you to come downstairs so we can talk."

She set the horn down, slipped on her headset, and then plugged it into the base unit to oversee the controls. It had a built-in microphone and was activated when she pressed the PUSH TO TALK button. A light indicated when she could be heard on the other end. Lenny slipped on a second headset without a microphone that was used for monitoring purposes.

"Gary? This is Sergeant Brenda DeBoer again. Can you hear me?"

"I can hear you."

"Good, good. I can hear you, too. I'm glad we're talking again."

"I want to talk to Clara."

"I'm still working on it."

"Bullshit!"

Brenda released the TALK button.

"The girl," said Lenny. "You got to get him talking about his little girl."

She nodded and pressed the button again. "Gary, when was the last time you saw your daughter?"

"Last weekend."

"And what's she doing nowadays? At her age? Talking a lot, I bet. Maybe starting to scribble with crayons."

"Do you have kids, Sergeant?"

Lenny shook his head, reminding her to keep the focus on him.

"We're here to work with you, Gary. We're here to solve this situation that we're all in right now."

His voice sounded far away. Brenda pressed the padded earmuffs tighter against her head. "I'm so fucked," he said. "I am so fucked."

"Minimize," said Lenny. "You got to minimize this problem for him."

She nodded and pressed the TALK button once more. "Listen, Gary. It's not that bad. You haven't shot anyone, have you? You haven't killed anyone, right?"

It sounded as if he were sniffling, as if he'd started to cry. "Right."

"You probably just hit Tate and shoved him around a bit, right?"

"Yeah."

Brenda took a deep breath. "There you go, then. Everyone's alive. Everyone's healthy. You let Tate go, and this becomes a much, much smaller incident. Something we can work with."

He didn't respond, but she felt sure he was listening closely. A frigid breeze blew through, rattling the high branches.

"Marriage problems are terrible, Gary. Custody problems are terrible. And men usually get the raw deal in that, don't they?"

"Yes."

"You're a good father. And this town knows you're a good man. All of this is just a terrible situation. All these changes in your family and in the town. They've put you in a tough position. But you can rise above this, Gary. Do you hear what I'm saying? You can make the right decisions now so that nobody gets badly hurt and we can all go about the business of making life better."

She released the button and let out another deep breath, which plumed in the cold air like wildfire smoke. The snipers watched the windows through their scopes. Lenny glanced at her and then leaned forward as if straining to hear some kind of response.

"These fuckers," said Gary softly, "these fuckers are always saying, 'Give me liberty or give me death.' They sound so damn tough when they give speeches and chant in parades." His voice rose. "But I'll actually fix it. Tell Clara and everyone else in town talking shit about me that *I'm* the one who's fixing it. I'll go to jail. Probably for the rest of my life. But you know they'll all leave."

Someone whimpered in the darkened house. "Please. Please. Please." It was Gorman Tate.

"But you'll never get to see Mary," said Brenda. "You'll never see her grow up. Right now, no one's seriously hurt. Right now we're probably talking an assault charge. I can't promise anything. I can't make promises. But you'll likely be out of jail in a few years. Mary will still be a little girl, and you'll have your whole life ahead of you as her father."

"Shut up!" yelled Gary, but he seemed to be speaking to Gorman. Then his voice sounded absent, speaking to nobody. "I'm going to paint these walls red. I swear to God, I'm going to paint these walls red."

"Talk to me some more, Gary. Why? Why do you want to do that?"

A gunshot cracked through the house and echoed throughout the cold autumn air of the dead-end street. Three—maybe four—seconds passed before the scream followed. By then the SWAT team was swarming the house, splintering wood with the battering ram and breaching the door. And although it completely went against protocol, Brenda ripped off her headset and sprinted behind them. SWAT members were shouting instructions as she reached the entrance. Those shouts were overwhelmed by an awful scream of pain and desperation. Brenda squeezed into the room, where three officers restrained Gary's huge, writhing body on the floor. Blood and bits of flesh spattered the wall and a sofa. An officer pinned down Gary's left arm with his knee. On the end of the arm hung red ribbons of flesh. He'd blown his hand off at point-blank range.

"I deserve this pain! I deserve this hell!"

Gorman was also pinned down, the SWAT team uncertain of who was the victim. "Let him go!" yelled Brenda, pointing at him. "He's the hostage! Let him go!"

Facedown on the floor, Gorman stared at Gary with huge, glassy eyes, immersed in the last moments of their shared horror.

Chapter 15

Tuesday, November 2

At dawn on this Election Day—with her daughter still sleeping in the room down the hall—Clara, who was still mayor of this town, stared at the Doppler radar on the TV news. She'd watched it last night, as the storm had approached, with something akin to wonderment. And now, as the day began, the digital blob rolled over the map of the U.P. and settled over Haymaker. The snow was rendered as shades of gray, the darker hues for flurries, the lighter for heavy precipitation. This thing above Haymaker was a pure, perfect white, like the world outside her windows.

Storms like this were not unknown to the town. Not in January, at least. But this was a mid-autumn blizzard, and it bore down on the shoreline like an angry bull moose. Nearly twenty-two inches had fallen in twenty-four hours, breaking the old November record set in '88, and it continued now into day two—the Snow Soldiers unprepared and overwhelmed.

Still in her nightgown and stocking feet, Clara stepped into the foyer to the front door, where Gary had once slumped and spilled to the outside. She unlocked the storm door and pushed, but it gave only a couple of inches. A hip-deep drift of snow blocked the front porch.

A quick panic rose in her chest and throat, connected—she thought at first—to claustrophobia, to being trapped inside. But the sensation came, she knew, from what it reminded her of: a cell, like the one in which Gary would languish once the hospital released him. The panic also came from thinking about the endgame just nights ago. Her ex-husband had broken into a man's house, held a gun to the man's head, made demands of hundreds of people, and then blown off three of his own fingers. She had loved this man, shared a life with this man, and made a beautiful little girl with him. To think that somewhere beneath his skin, for all of those years, had dwelt such darkness now made anything—anything human and horrible—seem possible.

The wind blew the door shut. Immediately Clara opened it again, shoving it at first only those few inches but then leaning with all of her weight, grunting and wincing and then—in a wild way beneath a wild blizzard wind—screaming with the force of her muscles. She opened the foyer closet to the right, grabbed her boots, and slipped her feet into their cold insides. She returned to the storm door again. The snow on the other side resisted but then gave way. The bottom of the door cut and smoothed over a fan-shaped swath of white. The rest of it collapsed, like a person sick of fighting.

With one final shove, Clara made the gap wide enough that she could squeeze through, her left boot disappearing into powder. The snow bit her bare legs and tumbled inside the shaft of the boot. And then she fell, her left knee buckling and sending her stumbling into the door. The frozen wind tore at her face and hair. The air was like a fog, the snow obscuring the road, the other houses. With bare hands, Clara scooped up a large handful of it and pressed it against her face. She patted it on her cheeks, smeared it over her forehead, and ran it through her hair on frozen fingers. Then she breathed deeply through her nose and returned inside.

Power lines had collapsed. Pipes had burst. Schools and most businesses were closed. She'd make sure the polls were open, but most voters would likely look out their windows, struggle to distinguish the white earth from the white sky, remove their hats and gloves, and say, "Screw this," before returning to *Good Morning America.* The rest would attempt the expedition, sink to their groins, and claw their way back to their doorsteps like victims of quicksand.

Clara picked her phone up off the kitchen counter and called Roosevelt. "Can you be mayor of a town that no longer exists?"

"This is why Freshwater Church does so well," he said. "Days like this."

"Are you okay?"

"More than okay," he said. "I'm not in charge of cleaning up this mess. Not yet."

Clara grabbed the coffeepot with her free hand and began filling it with water. "You might never get the chance. I don't know how we can have an election."

"What do you mean?"

She poured the water into the coffeemaker and flipped the orange switch. "Well, last I heard, by the grace of God, they managed to clear the roads right in front of the church and Willow Street School, where the polls are, but there's no power on Marquette Street. Hardly any volunteers have shown up. The only one who's shown at Freshwater is Bernadette Wagman. She's eighty-five years old. I swear, she's a superhero. She brought candles and blankets and Fig Newtons and says she's fine. The ballots are all punch card, so I guess the power's not a problem."

"Sure," he said, "we'll be fine. It's cold. It's snowy. But we'll live."

"Roosevelt, if we don't do something, nobody's going to vote."

"We're of hardy stock. You know that, Clara. Especially those of us who've lived through more than one or two of these storms."

"You obviously haven't stepped outside."

"It's a small town. People will walk."

"A few maybe. But not most. Especially the elderly. No way."

Roosevelt paused. "I guess it's just as impossible for the other side. If only ten votes are cast, let's just make sure we get six of them."

"Let's make sure we get more than that," said Clara. "That's why I'm calling."

The coffeemaker gurgled, and down the hall, Mary had awoken and called for Mommy. Clara removed a mug from the cupboard and braced herself. She'd let Mary jabber for a few minutes. There were more phone calls to make.

The next was to Chet Newhof, owner of Fitzgerald Outfitters, which sold and rented things like kayaks, camping supplies, and mountain bikes. But she was calling about snowshoes.

"I need a favor, Chet. I need you to take your snowmobile to your store and find a way to get ten pairs of snowshoes to Freshwater Church. Roosevelt's campaign staff needs to go door-to-door, and they can't walk in this white stuff."

"You want a backcountry style or day-hiking? Or I got a model that's more for trail walking."

"They all going to let them walk on snow?"

"Like Jesus on Juneau Street."

"Well then, Chet, I really don't give a great damn."

A few minutes later she started calling nearly a dozen friends in town who owned snowmobiles, asking them to go throughout the neighborhoods, offering voters a lift to the polls. "And tell anyone else you know to do the same."

Finally, she called Jeremy Marx, though she'd dreaded it. "Hi, Jeremy. It's Clara."

"Clara," he said softly. She could hear the sad sigh that followed. They hadn't spoken since Gary's arrest.

"I know this is a strange request, Jeremy, but it's all hands on deck. I need a huge favor."

He didn't respond right away, but she pictured him nodding slowly on the other end. "Anything," he said before releasing another long, mournful sigh.

Ash sat cross-legged on the couch, eating a Pop-Tart, watching ESPN, and reveling in the snow day. Patrick John played with Weebles on the floor beside her. Their mom paced through the house, glancing outside at the storm, though Ash didn't know why. "You need to chill," she said.

"This is probably a good thing," said Denise. "The crazies won't be able to go out and do anything stupid." The high-pitched whine of snowmobiles approached. Denise went to the window again to watch them speed by. "What are all these people doing out so early? They're like little kids. Day off from work, so let's go for a joyride."

Ash only half listened. She was thinking over her mom's comment about the crazies. She wondered where Uncle Donnie was in this storm. Her team's first game of the season was just a few weeks away. She wondered if she'd ever see him again in the stands.

The snowmobiles continued to skate up and down the street over the next half hour, followed occasionally by the rumble and violent scrape of the plows. And then one of the snowmobiles grew louder. Ash rose and approached the window where Denise stood. A man in a bright green snowsuit and green helmet had parked in their driveway and now trudged toward their door. He knocked, and the Capagrossas—including Patrick John—shuffled to meet him.

"Good morning," the man said, his visor lifted to expose his bearded face and the plumes of steam rising from his mouth. "I'm sorry to bother you on such a morning, but a bunch of us is asking folks if they'd like a ride to the voting booths. Figured it might be awhile till it's good enough for cars. We'll take you there and take you back. Makes for a pretty short trip."

Denise shook her head. "No thank you. We're fine." She began to close the door. "I think we'll stay in today."

"Well okay," said the man, his brow creased. And then he was gone behind the door, and Denise turned to walk away.

"What the hell!" said Ash.

Denise whirled around with her index finger pointed. "Don't you dare raise your voice to me, and don't you dare swear at me."

"Why aren't you going to vote?"

"And don't you judge me neither." She walked into the other room and changed the TV to The Weather Channel.

Patrick John wandered back to his toys, but Ash remained standing by the front door, her jaw clenched and her chin jutting outward. "If I was eighteen, I'd be out there voting."

Denise spoke from the other room. "When you're eighteen, you can do a lot of things."

Ash nodded. "Like move out of here." And she marched to the closet, to her coat and boots and scarf.

Denise must have recognized the sound of the hangers jangling in the hallway closet, or at least the tonal shift in the air. She appeared in the hall and crossed her arms. "You going to be cool now? You going to be tough and go outside and act stupid like everyone else?"

Ash said nothing. She'd dropped a glove onto the floor among the family's shoes and now searched for it amid the closet's dimness.

"If you go out that door and into that snow, I'm not giving you gas money ever again. And there's no way in hell I'm buying you those new high-tops. No way in hell."

With her coat half-zipped and no hat atop her head, Ash turned toward the door that led to the garage. She never glanced at Denise. "See ya," she said, waving behind her back. And as she entered the dark garage, attached Uncle Donnie's old pine-and-caribou snowshoes to her feet, and clumsily passed through another door to the great storming world itself, she wasn't thinking about whether or not the exhilaration coursing through her was from the fight with her mom or the whiteout before her. She only knew that she felt it and loved it, and she began to plod forward.

The plan was to head to Freshwater Church. She didn't know why she had to be there, but she thought maybe—even though she wasn't old enough to vote—she could help Roosevelt's cause in some other way. It was the first time in months that she'd felt this urge. Like the storm, the need had arrived unexpectedly and violently. Something intangible crackled in the air. It was fear and danger, but it was also excitement. Something was happening.

Ash walked along the road's edge, squinting as ice collected on her eyelashes. The sky churned in ways she'd seen only during thunderstorms, clouds like gray waves curling and crashing over one another. In the snow-fog, the snowmobiles became visible only seconds before they passed, and she worried that one would crash into her. She climbed off the barely plowed road and onto the softer snow of the lawns. The snowshoes allowed her to stay afloat, but she moved so slowly that the regret—from the fight with her mom and her thin layer of clothes—would probably cut her down long before she made it to the church.

From behind, the low roar of a plow approached. Ash veered farther from the edge of the road, but as the truck passed, its blade still managed to pummel her with an arc of heavy snow. Fit as she was, she wiped the snow from her red, raw cheeks and then bent forward, panting, with her hands resting on her knees.

Another vehicle approached. She started to move farther away, anticipating another plow. A tow truck appeared with an orange strobe flashing from its roof and, just after passing her, stained the road red with its brake lights. It began to slowly move in reverse, curving toward her. Ash straightened up and approached. The driver opened his door and stood up, squinting at her from over the roof. "That you, Ash?" he called. It was Ray Valentine.

"Yeah," she said, gasping. "It's me."

He never asked her to get in, and she never asked permission. All was understood. She opened the passenger's-side door, removed the snowshoes, and climbed up into the rubber-smelling warmth of the truck. "Thanks," she said.

Ray put the truck in drive and moved forward again. "Don't ask me how I knew it was you. Guess I noticed a tall girl with orange hair and just used all my powers of deductive reasoning."

Ash stared out the windshield at the white road. She nodded.

"Where you headed? I got to drag someone out on Pulpwood, but I can drop you off first."

"The church," she said. "Where everyone's voting."

Ray shook his head and stroked his beard. "Everyone is right. I figured I'd be the only one on this road. But I've seen more people on snow machines and dogsleds and cross-country skis than I've ever seen in my life. It's Election Day, boy. If I ever get a break in my day, I'll cast a vote myself."

Ash turned to him. "For Roosevelt?"

He smirked. "Maybe I'll write in Donnie Sarver." He glanced at her, but she turned away, looking forward again. His smile faded. "Yeah," he said. "Bly. Who else?" He shifted in his seat. "And don't worry. I ain't pulling anyone out of the snow that's going to vote for Novak. Any calls to Freedom Springs will be ignored." He smirked again. "Not that I'm expecting any from there."

They turned onto Marquette and approached the church, but Ray had to stop a half block from its front doors. Parked snowmobiles littered the middle of the street, clogging it like a logjam. "I'll get out here," said Ash. She grabbed the snowshoes, thanked him again, and then hopped down into the knee-deep snow.

Men and women congregated out front of the church and passed in and out through its doors and beneath its marquee.

COUNT YOUR BLESSINGS. RECOUNTS ARE OKAY.

They were bloated in their clothing, dressed for the extreme environment like astronauts or Inuit. People arrived on skis with grins on their faces. From the west came the shush and padded footfalls of a dogsled driven by Bra Dardon. On the front of the sled sat an old woman whose gray, curly hair was nearly the only thing exposed to the frigid air. Ski goggles covered most of her face. The dogs came to a stop, pink tongues hanging over their fangs, and Bra came around to assist the woman to her feet. "I hope you enjoyed riding the Roosevelt Rickshaw," he said.

The woman raised the goggles to her forehead, a smile beaming on her pale face. "Ooh, that was thrilling."

Ash trudged toward the entrance and pushed through the art deco doors. And then she stood inside, surrounded by what could only be called a jamboree. The actual business of voting was taking place through the next set of doors, on the stage. But here, in the old theater lobby, flush-faced voters milled about, drinking coffee and cocoa and laughing off the weather. Men had hauled over and hooked up generators, and so the room was lit; and the old popcorn machine overflowed with yellow kernels; and volunteers—including Pastor Zuber—emerged from the church kitchen with bowls of chicken soup and trays full of pasties; and children wove through their parents, playing tag and eating Jujyfruits; and an old man with a white beard and banjo stood under red, white, and blue bunting singing "This Land Is Your Land."

She wandered, dazed and smiling, through the crowd, listening in on the conversations and learning all the events of the day, though it was barely even noon. The delicate effort to bring elderly voters from Pines Place Retirement Village over on Jeremy Marx's larger freight sleds. The get-out-the-vote campaign among those trapped in the backcountry, in the shacks south of Big Deep Lake and the dune country around Oslo Creek. People mentioned Clara Hollingshead's name with tones approaching reverence. More than one person, when referring to the storm, used the word "miracle." Benny Kane, who worked as a custodian at St. Peter's, said they were considering changing the parish's name to Our Lady of Perpetual Snowfall.

And then a buzz flowed through the crowd. Someone shouted from the doorway. "Roosevelt's coming!" And a mass of people, Ash among them, pushed its way outside into the cold.

Even if someone hadn't said who was arriving, any longtime resident of Haymaker would have known. Sitting low, with legs bent, in the front of a sled driven by Jeremy Marx and pulled by eight honest-to-God huskies, was Roosevelt. His white oilskin duster had been replaced with a yellow snowmobile suit and his Stetson replaced with a bright red ski cap, but he made himself known through the disguise, both hands shaped like six-shooters and raised above his head, firing into the white sky—the new sheriff in town.

Ash approached. A smell rising off the fur of the dogs was faintly electric. When Roosevelt noticed her, he smiled more broadly. She rushed forward and they embraced.

That evening Roosevelt stood in his kitchen, leaning over a pot of chili boiling on the stove top. He raised the wooden spoon to his lips, blew lightly, and then tasted. It was hotly spiced, with the right mix of beef and venison and vegetables. It was good, and it was originally meant for a small gathering of friends he'd arranged to host on election night, so that he could share the results with them, good or bad.

But the storm had ruled the day, and it had also ruled that nobody should make it up the hill to join him. So he tasted the chili, content to be alone, and then picked up the Presbyterian beside him.

The phone rang. Roosevelt glanced at the time—eight thirty—and was surprised by the adrenaline that surged through his body. He exhaled deeply and walked across the room to answer it.

Clara Hollingshead spoke from the other end. She was breathless while telling him the results. A victory by four points. Remarkable turnout considering the conditions. A historic day, for all the right reasons.

He thanked her repeatedly, smiling as he spoke. And he continued to smile after hanging up—smiling as he shaped his right hand into a pistol and fired an imaginary, celebratory shot into the sky. Smiling even as he shook his head slightly, putting the barrel of his index finger against his temple and firing again.

Chapter 16

Saturday, November 20

Clara set two mugs of coffee in front of Carl and Marissa Farmer. She did this all day at the Shipwreck. But she did this now at her own dining room table, in her own house, though she hoped that, very soon, it would no longer be hers. She'd put it on the market the day after the election—piercing the deep snow of her front lawn with a black-and-white FOR SALE BY OWNER sign.

"Can I get you two anything else?" she asked. "I've got some blueberry muffins that are pretty good if you pop them in the microwave."

"Maybe later," said Marissa, smiling and dropping her eyes. "Where's your little one?"

"Napping down the hall." Clara sat across from them with her hands resting on the table, her fingers interlaced. "I'm asking ninety-five," she said. "I like you two. And quite frankly I'm in awe of the fact that you're staying, considering what you've gone through. But I'm done negotiating with people, you know? Nothing personal to you guys. The café's been doing well and an employee has agreed to buy it, so I'm doing okay. I'm not looking to get rich, and I'm not looking to get ripped off. But I *am* looking to get out. I know the market here's gone to hell, but I just want everyone to be fair and not play games and not have to deal with some landshark like Bud Wilmington. It's ninety-five, it's ninety-five, it's ninety-five. You know?"

"I know," said Carl. He looked over at Marissa and set his large hand on her knee.

"We'll take it for ninety-five," she said.

Clara smiled. "Forget coffee—I feel like we should uncork some champagne." She reached across the table and shook their hands. "That was a little too easy. Considering everything."

Carl sipped from his mug. "Considering everything," he said. Then he smiled a little, too, as he surveyed the kitchen. "I think we'll be happy here." He locked eyes with Clara. "And I don't just mean *here* in the house."

Clara nodded. "I know what you mean. And I really respect it."

"Considering everything," said Marissa.

Carl ran his fingers through his short hair. "Yeah. If someone had told me a week and a half ago that I'd be doing business with you today, I'd have called them crazy. Not after the Great Northern Vote Drive. It was genius. I hate it, but it was genius."

Clara sipped her coffee and nodded. "Home-field advantage." She stood up. "But look." She motioned toward the window. The sun shone on wet November grass. Only a few slushy mounds remained of the snowdrifts. "The world's still turning. The sun's still rising. And the next election's only a few years away."

"God, let's not think about it," said Marissa.

Carl coughed softly. "Where you moving to, Clara? If you don't mind me asking."

"I don't mind." She could feel the wetness in her eyes and strode into the kitchen to get the muffins and keep her back to the Farmers. "I'm moving way down near my parents' place. To Hillsdale, near the Indiana border."

"I know Hillsdale," said Carl. "That's close to our old neck of the woods."

The three dipped into an awkward silence. Clara warmed the muffins briefly in the microwave and then set them on a glass dish and carried them to the table. "So are you planning on starting a family? If you don't mind *me* asking."

"We'll get to that soon," said Carl, half grinning. "I'm sure we will. I'm not exactly a young man."

"It feels right now," said Marissa. "We know we're staying, no matter what. And this place feels like a real house. A real place to raise kids. It's not so brand-new and bright white like the condo. It's lived-in."

Clara's mouth curled into something like a smile. "Lived-in. That's a sweet way of saying it." The room dimmed slightly, a cloud slipping in front of the sun. "And you don't have a problem moving into the old mayor's house? Not even after we've all been to hell and back and then off to purgatory?"

Carl shrugged. "Really?" He frowned and shook his head. "Not really. No."

"I see one of your boys moved in just down the street."

"Lee?" Carl's eyebrows rose in surprise. "I wouldn't call him one of my boys, but he ain't the worst. Yeah, he's settling in down there on the corner, from what I understand."

The sun returned, but so did the silence.

"We should get going," said Marissa.

Carl nodded, braced himself on the table, and winced as he stood. "Call us about the paperwork."

"How's your knee?" asked Clara.

Marissa shook her head. "Don't ask."

"My knee's my knee." He took a few limping steps. "Probably be better off with an elbow connecting my shin to my thigh, but," he sniffed and shrugged and looked at Clara, "it got me here today."

Clara walked to the closet and returned with their coats. As he took his, Carl—as if trying to hide his size—bent down toward her. "I just want you to know I've never had a problem with you personally. You always seemed pretty fair and did what I'd expect the mayor to do. Couldn't have been easy." They both held on to the coat momentarily. He lowered his voice. "I know things have turned upside down for you over the past couple years. I guess I just hope you do all right once you leave."

Clara released his coat, gave a slight smile, and patted his forearm. "Thank you. I hope you do all right once I leave, too."

They said good-bye, and she closed the door behind them. And as she cleaned up the dishes, Clara allowed herself to glimpse the unmade future. She would leave like so many others, dissolved into memory like last week's snow. Like Gorman Tate himself, who had disappeared just after the election, his house for sale and still full, she'd heard, of all his possessions.

She would strap Mary into her car seat, and they would head south for the bridge. She would not linger with the good-byes. In fact, she would tell everyone the wrong date of departure and leave—in the middle of the night—a few days prior. She would not feel bad about lying. It seemed like such a harmless sin these days.

Brenda opened the sliding glass door, and Jesse and Owen plunged into the darkened backyard. She started to close it but then looked skyward and changed her mind. She slipped outside, into the night, with the dogs.

Overhead, a bright moon cast a cool blue light. It was a rare enough sight on most days, let alone this time of year, when the stratus clouds rarely broke their grip. The dogs ran along the far fence line, visible as if the sun were dimly shining. Brenda wrapped her arms around herself for warmth, breathed a plume of steam into the night, and stepped over the frosty grass.

Her shadow bent before her. She couldn't remember ever seeing her shadow cast from moonlight.

"Come here, boys," she said, though not loudly. She crouched and softly snapped her fingers, and the dogs rushed toward her voice. They licked her hands and then slid their muzzles underneath so that she'd pet the tops of their heads.

The door slid open behind her, and Brian's shadow angled across the lawn. "You okay, babe?"

Brenda nodded and hoped he noticed it under the dim blue light. She didn't feel like speaking. The moment was beautiful and fragile, as if the moon might shatter if the earth didn't whisper. They'd spent the evening talking, weighing their options, poring over their finances, pondering potential jobs. And though she'd been nearly certain just moments before, she was now ready to say the words for sure.

We're staying.

But she didn't want to crack the moon with her voice.

Chapter 17

Tuesday, November 30

Roosevelt walked through the nighttime air, entered Rusty's Tavern, and immediately squinted.

"What in the world?" He shielded his eyes. The bar blazed in electric light. Despite the recent rain and the mud-puddled floor, Roosevelt forgot to step carefully along the cardboard squares. His white boots turned a moist brown as he approached Rusty. He hesitantly swung his left leg over his usual bar stool, as if settling into the saddle of an unknown horse, and then eyed the ceiling suspiciously. "What have you done?"

Rusty leaned against the bar across from him. "Bep changed all the bulbs this weekend. Place was turning into a cave."

"She might have eased into it. Replace one at a time, every week or so. It's a shock to the system."

Rusty shrugged. "So far, more compliments than complaints."

Roosevelt stared at him. "Is that what you actually look like? Good God."

"Let me make you a drink," said Rusty. "Booze makes me look more handsome."

"Make it two. Just for me. At the same time."

Rusty chuckled but made the two drinks. "Just 'cause you're the mayor," he said, setting them down, "doesn't mean the first one's on the house."

Roosevelt nodded but didn't smile. He drank the first cocktail quickly and then pushed it a few inches away.

The door opened and Josef appeared. He squinted slightly himself before noticing Roosevelt and giving a little wave. They shook hands, and Josef patted him on the shoulder before taking a seat alongside. "I'm glad we're finally doing this." He gazed around the room, at the walls with the cant hooks and peaveys and saws, at the black-and-white photos of old Haymaker. "I've never been here before," he said.

Roosevelt nodded slightly. "I feel the same way."

They settled into small talk, of Josef's family and of the coming winter and, finally, of the election.

"It was something we never planned on," said Josef. "Something we never could have foreseen. We let nature make the case against us that we were outsiders."

Roosevelt lowered his Stetson over his eyes. "I think you're overanalyzing it a tad."

"I don't think so. It's okay, though. I'm at peace with the results. We picked up two city council seats, at least. And I'm not sure, in the short term, anything would have been that different had I won. The condos couldn't last. We were going to lose people anyway." He took a long sip of his beer. "But I'll probably run again in four years. Just so you know."

Roosevelt nodded slowly, staring ahead at the line of liquor bottles. "Just so *you* know, I've got something along those lines to get off my chest as well."

Josef made his hand into the shape of a pistol and aimed it at Roosevelt. "Shoot."

"A great nexus of events has occurred in my life these past few months." Roosevelt continued to stare ahead. "Few know about them."

Josef gave a single, soft laugh and grinned. "That's a dramatic statement, even for you."

Roosevelt nodded but still didn't smile. "My boy—" He turned to make eye contact and paused further before saying, "I'm leaving Haymaker."

Josef grinned again, moving the beer to his lips but then stopping short. He cocked his head. "You're serious?"

"As a heart attack, the saying goes. And it applies. Early last month I went in for some tests."

"Okay," said Josef, setting down his beer. "That sucks. That's scary. But what does that have to do with leaving town?"

"I'm going to need someone to care for me. My daughter, Elizabeth, out in Denver. She wants me to move in with her and my grandson."

Josef raised his right hand, palm toward Roosevelt. "Wait a minute. This is insane. You hire a nurse or someone here to take care of you in your home. I think you can afford it."

Roosevelt looked down at his drink and continued to shake his head. "As I said, there are other events at play. Elizabeth is recently divorced. It was a terrible marriage she was in, but she's devastated, and the boy could use me around. I'll be taking care of her as well."

"I don't believe this," said Josef, though he said it softly, almost under his breath. He straightened up on his stool and gazed into the mirror across from the bar. "Okay, so, serious heart condition. Daughter goes through nasty divorce." He ran both hands through his hair, causing it to feather and stick up on top. "But none of this happened in the past few weeks, right? You knew, ahead of the election, that these things were happening, that you'd likely be moving. I'm getting these facts straight, correct? We're talking about the same timeline, the two of us?"

Roosevelt sighed. "Yes." He finally glanced at Josef, his eyes moving though the rest remained still. "You have to realize, son. I never thought I had a prayer of winning. *You* never thought I had a prayer of winning. The series of occurrences that led to my becoming mayor was beyond improbable. People kept calling it a miracle." He shook his head again. "Not me."

"Bullshit," said Josef. "I saw you. I saw pictures of you the next day in the paper, sitting in a goddamned dogsled, your hands raised in the air, a big tooth-filled grin covering your face. Don't tell me you didn't know what was happening at that moment. You were already basking in the victory."

"I'll admit it. By Christ, I got caught up in the spectacle. I did. I'm too fond of theater. You know what I'm like sometimes."

"Yeah, you're an actor all right. You had us all fooled."

"It wasn't worth mentioning any of this if there were no chance of me winning. I'd have had to drop out, and who knows who would have taken my place at the last minute. They wouldn't have won, but it might have been some wild card. Someone dangerous. It would have been bad for the town."

"But this," said Josef, "this is *great* for the town. Who knows what happens now."

"I do." Roosevelt leaned toward him and gently set his hand on Josef's forearm. "I had to talk to a lawyer. That's why I've waited these past few weeks since the election. I wanted to make sure. And the way it will work is that the city council will name an interim mayor. That'll be followed by a special election next fall."

"You're going to put the town through all this again?"

"Come on, my boy. That town's already gone. Those people left. Or they're leaving. But the rest who've stayed are ready to get on with the business of normal living. And the council will name the right person to lead them."

"Who?"

"You."

Josef grimaced and lurched backward. "You're insane. No they won't."

"They will."

"You guys still have a majority. They're not going to pick me or anyone on my side."

"Don't you get it?" said Roosevelt. "That garbage is over. There isn't *my side* and *your side*. Tate's gone. Donnie's gone. The people left are just the town now. They're all Haymakes now. You," he patted Josef's arm, "you're a Haymake."

"And now you're not."

"They'll name you mayor because they see you as a moderate."

Josef stood up and started to put on his coat.

Roosevelt laid a hand on his shoulder. "Sit down," he said gently.

"This isn't democracy. If I'm going to be mayor, I'm going to be voted in as mayor."

"And you will be. Next year, in the special election. And in the meantime you'll have ten months to prove that you're smart and capable and that you want reforms but you're not going to burn the place down in the process."

"I don't want it this way."

Roosevelt removed his hat and smoothed his hand over his silver hair. "But you'll take it and lead and be great."

Rusty approached to see if either of them wanted another drink, but Roosevelt gave him a quick, serious look and shook his head.

Josef finally sat again, though his eyes avoided Roosevelt. "I remember in the spring when you told me you were running. And at that time I couldn't figure out what on earth you were trying to achieve. And then you win, and you walk away from it." He shook his head, mouth slightly agape. "I have no idea what you want."

"It's not about what I want. It's about my heart."

"It's about your heart, all right." Josef stood again, more forcefully this time. He put on his coat. "Years of this shit. Years of struggle and anger and violence. Actual bloodshed. And it ends like this."

Roosevelt spoke softly. "Not with a bang but a whimper."

"Whatever," said Josef. "You can buy my drink." And he turned and left, disappearing in an instant as he passed from the brightly lit tavern into the dark rectangle of the night.

Chapter 18

Wednesday, December 1

A light snow fell, though a fierce wind from the north continually lifted and tossed the flakes, suspending them in an arctic current. Roosevelt had lit a fire, and the warm light inside met the cool light from the windows in a visible border of gray illumination that ran from the hearth to the study, where he now stood. He ran a finger along the dusty bindings of books, looking for any he might give away to lighten the load of the move. So far he'd chosen none.

The doorbell rang, and he walked with a surprising bounce, excited by the prospect of a visitor—someone with whom to share the fire. He opened the front door and smiled at the sight. "Well, so good to see you, my dear."

The basketball struck him in the sternum—a perfectly quick and crisp two-handed thrust that sent him stumbling backward, into the foyer wall. Roosevelt clutched the front of his white coat and slowly slid down the wall until seated on the hardwood floor.

Ash stepped over the threshold but said nothing. She wore a huge red ski jacket with the hood tight around her head. She untied the hood and pulled it back. Her hair—naturally black—spilled out over her shoulders. "Why are you doing this?" she asked.

He looked up at her, his hand still pressed against his chest. "What?"

Ash kicked the basketball. It ricocheted off the wall behind Roosevelt and bounced six or seven times between the two walls, through the narrow space between them. "Why are you moving away!"

"Oh, Ash."

"Shut up," she said. Tears formed in her eyes. The corners of her mouth turned down. "You're going to punk out, huh?"

"No."

"Run away."

Roosevelt rolled onto his knees and slowly stood. When erect, he methodically smoothed his hands over his clothes. "I'm not running."

"Because you can't run. Because you're old as dirt," she said, the tears breaking down her face like lightning strikes. But her voice never cracked, never changed. "Suddenly you don't have any strength and your heart's all bad and shit." She stepped forward and pointed her index finger at his face. "You're as crazy as everyone's always said you were."

"Let's go in the other room and talk."

"And I was the one always defending you and saying how nice you were to me. Telling my mom and Uncle Donnie and people on my team. And then you go through this election and change the town, and then you're gone."

"I know it must seem hard to understand." He looked at her sadly, wanting to comfort her with the look.

"No!" Ash picked up the ball and hurled it into the kitchen, where it crashed against the copper pots suspended from the ceiling rack. She panted, her shoulders rising and falling, and finally she spoke quietly. "Where are you going?"

"To Denver. To be with my daughter."

She looked around her. "What about your home?"

"My home will be with my family. Out West."

"Just because you're sick. You've made it this long up here."

He nodded sheepishly. "It's other things. Her divorce. And more. Silly sentimental things. About my wife. Being back in that part of the country after all these years."

"What do you mean?"

He paused. "I need to confront the mountains again."

"Oh shut up," she said. "What a fucking canned line. Your wife is dead. She was probably a good lady, but she'd want you here. If your daughter loved you, she'd know you should be here. She'd move into this place."

Roosevelt didn't say anything for a long time. He just looked at her and nodded slowly. "You remind me of her right now." He smiled. "That's meant as a compliment."

He expected another explosion, but Ash just stared at him, seemingly baffled, and then said quietly, "I want to come."

"Oh, Ash." He approached her with a hug.

She shrugged him off like he was a feeble point guard. "Don't touch me." She clenched her jaw and looked into the other room. "I want to see mountains. I've never seen mountains."

"You will."

"Shut up." She kept staring into the other room. "I hate it here. I hate living in my house, and I hate school." Ash wiped her eyes with the sleeves of her ski jacket. "But I don't really want to go." She calmed again and looked at Roosevelt. "Uncle Donnie was right."

"About what?" asked Roosevelt. He put his hands in his pockets, comfortable with the tone of her voice now.

"What he said back on the Fourth of July."

"I don't remember what he said."

"He said the people who stayed would be the winners and the ones who left were the losers." She jabbed a thumb toward her chest. "*I'm* staying. *I'm* one of the winners." She shook her head. "But good old Uncle Donnie left. He's a loser. Mayor Hollingshead's leaving. She's a loser. Gorman Tate's a loser." Then Ash spat on the floor, right beside Roosevelt's shiny white boots. She stared at him. "And now, so are you."

With that she turned and walked out of the house, leaving the door wide open so that the cold air poured inside. Roosevelt watched her until she got into her car. She never looked back in his direction. Then he slowly closed the door, turned, and looked down at the wad of spit. While gingerly bending at the knees, he removed a white handkerchief from his front pocket and wiped it away in one short, swift motion.

Epilogue

As you leave town, headed south, and climb that rise of land, take a final peek over your shoulder. The place has never needed winter more than this year. The cold and snow will slow its pulse till it slips into something like an induced coma. There's been trauma: transplants, hemorrhaging, and a long stretch of life support. And now it simply needs rest.

From this view above the canopies of jack pines and naked birches—above the roofs of the people's houses, the steeples of their churches—you can make out the lake. It is the forever boundary, ebbing and flowing but remaining a border that the people cannot cross or settle.

It's colder here than wherever you're headed. The old-timers know cold and the newcomers are learning. Spring is an uncertain dream every year. Don't mark it on your calendar. It will come when you think it has failed you.

From this distance, the snowy flesh of the town seems to rise and fall, slowly and gently, as if taking the softest of breaths. Perhaps it is not a coma at all but something else. Like the bear, it will shift its weight and groan. In time it will lift its head and stiffly rise. It will awaken with a great hunger.

Acknowledgments

Haymaker was over ten years in the making, and its publication would not have been possible without the talents and empathy of a great many people in my life.

Even beyond the unsung spousal support—the patience, the understanding, the sympathetic ear, the mantra-like affirmation that it would all work out eventually—Jennifer Schuitema played a critical editorial role in the shaping of this novel, helping me to delete vast sections of it when it had grown unwieldy, rearrange scenes, refine language, and to cut anything that even remotely caused her to roll her eyes.

My daughter Elizabeth always kept it cool and kept me grounded.

Others in my family provided constant moral support: Bruce and Diane Schuitema, Larry and Sally Prusinowski, and Amy and Adam Hanson.

Thanks to my great friend, Dan Mancilla, for serving as my brother-in-arms in this writing racket—for reading various drafts of the work, for inspiring me with his own fiction, and for sharing our successes, failures, and bad jokes over e-mail and over drinks.

Donna Bagdasarian believed in this book as passionately as anyone—believed in it when I'd nearly stopped myself—and never hesitated to champion it at any opportunity.

Note: Some of the libertarian ideas expressed through character dialogue stem from *Libertarianism: A Primer* by David Boaz.

Amy Bailey played an invaluable role as one of the manuscript's final readers.

Several others kindly offered help in their various areas of expertise, including Matt Brown, Dustin M. Hoffman, and Katie Zychowski. Special thanks to my cousin, Sergeant Lisa Bancuk of the Holland Department of Public Safety in Holland, Michigan.

Thanks to Tim Chilcote and Roberta King for their enthusiastic support of my work.

Thanks to Matt Hansen for the spectacular illustrated map of Haymaker at the front of the book.

Thanks to Linda Manning at Switchgrass for embracing the novel and supporting its publication.

And thanks to Donnie Sarver, wherever you are.